Praise for ~~Bujold~~

'A tour de force of topnotch characterization and thrilling adventure' *–Rave Reviews*

'A marvellous mixture of grace and cunning . . . this is SF fully equipped with brains, humour and heart' *–Locus*

'All the virtues we have come to expect from Bujold, including more and more prose that sings' *–Chicago Sun-Times*

'It's the swashbuckling that makes this story fun' *–Philadephia Enquirer*

Praise for LOIS McMASTER BUJOLD

'A fun romp through the spaceways – not so much space opera as space ballet . . . has all the right stuff. A lot of thought and thoughtfulness stand behind the all-too-human characters. Enjoy this one' *– SF Reviews*

'Another winner with all kinds of unexpected adventures . . . A sprightly conducted romance with twists and turns that could only happen in a Vorkosigan-inspired novel . . . Boy, can she write!' *–Anne McCaffrey*

'Bujold successfully mixes quirky humour with just enough action, a dab of feminist social commentary and her usual superb character development . . . enormously satisfying' *–Publishers Weekly*

'One of SF's oustanding talents' *–Booklist*

'Bujold is as audacious as her favourite hero, and as brilliantly (if sneakily) successful' *–Locus*

Also by Lois McMaster Bujold from EARTHLIGHT

The Vorkosigan Saga:
The Warrior's Apprentice
Shards of Honour
Memory
Komarr
A Civil Campaign
Diplomatic Immunity

BARRAYAR

LOIS McMASTER BUJOLD

EARTHLIGHT

SIMON & SCHUSTER

London • New York • Sydney • Tokyo • Singapore • Toronto • Dublin

A VIACOM COMPANY

First published in United States of America by Baen Books, 1991
This edition published in Great Britain by Earthlight, 2003
An imprint of Simon & Schuster UK Ltd
A Viacom Company

1 3 5 7 9 10 8 6 4 2

Simon & Schuster UK Ltd
Africa House
64–78 Kingsway
London WC2B 6AH

www.simonsays.co.uk

Simon & Schuster Australia
Sydney

A CIP catalogue record for this book is available from the
British Library

ISBN 0 7434 6841 4

This book is a work of fiction. Names, characters, places and
incidents are either a product of the author's imagination or are
used fictiously. Any resemblance to actual people living or dead,
events or locales is entirely coincidental.

Printed and bound in Great Britain by
Cox & Wyman Ltd, Reading, Berkshire

BARRAYAR

For Anne and Paul

CHAPTER ONE

I am afraid. Cordelia's hand pushed aside the drape in the third-floor parlor window of Vorkosigan House. She stared down into the sunlit street below. A long silver groundcar was pulling into the half-circular drive that serviced the front portico, braking past the spiked iron fence and the Earth-imported shrubbery. A government car. The door of the rear passenger compartment swung up, and a man in a green uniform emerged. Despite her foreshortened view Cordelia recognized Commander Illyan, brown-haired and hatless as usual. He strode out of sight under the portico. *Guess I don't really need to worry till Imperial Security comes for us in the middle of the night.* But a residue of dread remained, burrowed in her belly. *Why did I ever come here to Barrayar? What have I done to myself, to my life?*

Booted footsteps sounded in the corridor, and the door of the parlor creaked inward. Sergeant Bothari stuck his head in, and grunted with satisfaction at finding her. "Milady. Time to go."

"Thank you, Sergeant." She let the drape fall, and turned to inspect herself one last time in a wall-mounted

3

mirror above the archaic fireplace. Hard to believe people here still burned vegetable matter just for the release of its chemically-bound heat.

She lifted her chin, above the stiff white lace collar of her blouse, adjusted the sleeves of her tan jacket, and kicked her knee absently against the long swirling skirt of a Vor-class woman, tan to match the jacket. The color comforted her, almost the same tan as her old Betan Astronomical Survey fatigues. She ran her hands over her red hair, parted in the middle and held away from her face by two enameled combs, and flopped it over her shoulders to curl loosely halfway down her back. Her grey eyes stared back at her from the pale face in the mirror. Nose a little too bony, chin a shade too long, but certainly a servicable face, good for all practical purposes.

Well, if she wanted to look dainty, all she had to do was stand next to Sergeant Bothari. He loomed mournfully beside her, all two meters of him. Cordelia considered herself a tall woman, but the top of her head was only level with his shoulder. He had a gargoyle's face, closed, wary, beak-nosed, its lumpiness exaggerated to criminality by his military-burr haircut. Even Count Vorkosigan's elegant livery, dark brown with the symbols of the house embroidered in silver, failed to save Bothari from his astonishing ugliness. *But a very good face indeed, for practical purposes.*

A liveried retainer. What a concept. What did he retain? *Our lives, our fortunes, and our sacred honors, for starters.* She nodded cordially to him, in the mirror, and about-faced to follow him through the warren of Vorkosigan House.

She must learn her way around this great pile of a residence as soon as possible. Embarrassing, to be lost in one's own home, and have to ask some passing guard or servant to de-tangle one. In the middle of the night, wearing only a towel. *I used to be a jumpship navigator. Really.* If she could handle five dimensions upside, surely she ought to be able to manage a mere three downside.

They came to the head of a large circular staircase, curving gracefully down three flights to a black-and-white stone-paved foyer. Her light steps followed Bothari's measured tread. Her skirts made her feel she was floating, parachuting inexorably down the spiral.

A tall young man, leaning on a cane at the foot of the stairs, looked up at the echo of their feet. Lieutenant Koudelka's face was as regular and pleasant as Bothari's was narrow and strange, and he smiled openly at Cordelia. Even the pain lines at the corners of his eyes and mouth failed to age that face. He wore Imperial undress greens, identical but for the insignia to Security Commander Illyan's. The long sleeves and high neck of his jacket concealed the tracery of thin red scars that netted half his body, but Cordelia mapped them in her mind's eye. Nude, Koudelka could pose as a visual aid for a lecture on the structure of the human nervous system, each scar representing a dead nerve excised and replaced with artificial silver threads. Lieutenant Koudelka was not quite used to his new nervous system yet. *Speak truth. The surgeons here are ignorant clumsy butchers.* The work was certainly not up to Betan standards. Cordelia permitted no hint of this private judgment to escape onto her face.

Koudelka turned jerkily, and nodded to Bothari. "Hello, Sergeant. Good morning, Lady Vorkosigan."

Her new name still seemed strange in her ear, ill-fitting. She smiled back. "Good morning, Kou. Where's Aral?"

"He and Commander Illyan went into the library, to check out where the new secured comconsole will be installed. They should be right along. Ah." He nodded, as footsteps sounded through an archway. Cordelia followed his gaze. Illyan, slight and bland and polite, flanked—was eclipsed by—a man in his mid-forties resplendent in Imperial dress greens. The reason she'd come to Barrayar.

Admiral Lord Aral Vorkosigan, retired. Formerly retired, till yesterday. Their lives had surely been turned upside down, yesterday. *We'll land on our feet somehow, you bet*. Vorkosigan's body was stocky and powerful, his dark hair salted with grey. His heavy jaw was marred by an old L-shaped scar. He moved with compressed energy, his grey eyes intense and inward, until they lighted on Cordelia.

"I give you good morrow, my lady," he sang out to her, reaching for her hand. The syntax was self-conscious but the sentiment naked-sincere in his mirror-bright eyes. *In those mirrors, I am altogether beautiful*, Cordelia realized warmly. *Much more flattering than that one on the wall upstairs. I shall use them to see myself from now on*. His thick hand was dry and hot, welcome heat, live heat, closing around her cool tapering fingers. *My husband*. That fit, as smoothly and tightly as her hand fit in his, even though her new name, *Lady Vorkosigan*, still seemed to slither off her shoulders.

She watched Bothari, Koudelka, and Vorkosigan standing together for that brief moment. *The walking wounded, one, two, three. And me, the lady auxiliary*. The survivors. Kou in body, Bothari in mind, Vorkosigan in spirit, all had taken near-mortal wounds in the late war at Escobar. *Life goes on. March or die. Do we all begin to recover at last?* She hoped so.

"Ready to go, dear Captain?" Vorkosigan asked her. His voice was a baritone, his Barrayaran accent guttural-warm.

"Ready as I'll ever be, I guess."

Illyan and Lieutenant Koudelka led the way out. Koudelka's walk was a loose-kneed shamble beside Illyan's brisk march, and Cordelia frowned doubtfully. She took Vorkosigan's arm, and they followed, leaving Bothari to his Household duties.

"What's the timetable for the next few days?" she asked.

"Well, this audience first, of course," Vorkosigan replied. "After which I see men. Count Vortala will be choreographing that. In a few days comes the vote of consent from the full Councils Assembled, and my swearing-in. We haven't had a Regent in a hundred and twenty years, God knows what protocol they'll dig out and dust off."

Koudelka sat in the front compartment of the

groundcar with the uniformed driver. Commander Illyan slid in opposite Cordelia and Vorkosigan, facing rearward, in the back compartment. *This car is armored,* Cordelia realized from the thickness of the transparent canopy as it closed over them. At a signal from Illyan to the driver, they pulled away smoothly into the street. Almost no sound penetrated from the outside.

"Regent-consort," Cordelia tasted the phrase. "Is that my official title?"

"Yes, Milady," said Illyan.

"Does it have any official duties to go with it?"

Illyan looked to Vorkosigan, who said, "Hm. Yes and no. There will be a lot of ceremonies to attend—grace, in your case. Beginning with the emperor's funeral, which will be grueling for all concerned—except, perhaps, for Emperor Ezar. All that waits on his last breath. I don't know if he has a timetable for that, but I wouldn't put it past him.

"The social side of your duties can be as much as you wish. Speeches and ceremonies, important weddings and name-days and funerals, greeting deputations from the Districts—public relations, in short. The sort of thing Princess-dowager Kareen does with such flair." Vorkosigan paused, taking in her appalled look, and added hastily, "Or, if you choose, you can live a completely private life. You have the perfect excuse to do so right now—" his hand, around her waist, secretly caressed her still-flat belly, "—and in fact I'd rather you didn't spend yourself too freely.

"More importantly, on the political side . . . I'd like it very much if you could be my liaison with the Princess-dowager, and the . . . child emperor. Make friends with her, if you can; she's an extremely reserved woman. The boy's upbringing is vital. We must not repeat Ezar Vorbarra's mistakes."

"I can give it a try," she sighed. "I can see it's going to be quite a job, passing for a Barrayaran Vor."

"Don't bend yourself painfully. I shouldn't like to see you so constricted. Besides, there's another angle."

"Why doesn't that surprise me? Go ahead."

He paused, choosing his words. "When the late Crown Prince Serg called Count Vortala a phoney progressive, it wasn't altogether nonsense. Insults that sting always have some truth in them. Count Vortala has been trying to form his progressive party in the upper classes only. Among the people who matter, as he would say. You see the little discontinuity in his thinking?"

"About the size of Hogarth Canyon back home? Yes."

"You are a Betan, a woman of galactic-wide reputation."

"Oh, come on now."

"You are seen so here. I don't think you quite realize how you are perceived. Very flattering for me, as it happens."

"I hoped I was invisible. But I shouldn't think I'd be too popular, after what we did to your side at Escobar."

"It's our culture. My people will forgive a brave soldier almost anything. And you, in your person, unite two of the opposing factions—the aristocratic military, and the pro-galactic plebians. I really think I could pull the whole middle out of the People's Defense League through you, if you're willing to play my cards for me."

"Good heavens. How long have you been thinking about this?"

"The problem, long. You as part of the solution, just today."

"What, casting me as figurehead for some sort of constitutional party?"

"No, no. That is just the sort of thing I will be sworn, on my honor, to prevent. It would not fulfill the spirit of my oath to hand over to Prince Gregor an emperorship gutted of power. What I want . . . what I want is to find some way of pulling the best men, from every class and language group and party, into the Emperor's service. The Vor have simply too small a pool of talent. Make the government more like the military at its best, with ability promoted regardless of background. Emperor Ezar tried to do something like that, by strengthening the Ministries at the expense of the Counts, but it swung too far.

The Counts are eviscerated and the Ministries are corrupt. There must be some way to strike a balance."

Cordelia sighed. "I guess we'll just have to agree to disagree, about constitutions. Nobody appointed me Regent of Barrayar. I warn you, though—I'll keep trying to change your mind."

Illyan raised his brow at this. Cordelia sat back wanly, and watched the Barrayaran capital city of Vorbarr Sultana pass by through the thick canopy. She hadn't married the Regent of Barrayar, four months back. She'd married a simple retired soldier. Yes, men were supposed to change after marriage, usually for the worse, but—this much? This fast? *This isn't the duty I signed up for, sir*.

"That's quite a gesture of trust Emperor Ezar placed in you yesterday, appointing you Regent. I don't think he's such a ruthless pragmatist as you'd have me believe," she remarked.

"Well, it is a gesture of trust, but driven by necessity. You didn't catch the significance of Captain Negri's assignment to the Princess's household, then."

"No. Was there one?"

"Oh, yes, a very clear message. Negri is to continue right on in his old job as Chief of Imperial Security. He will not, of course, be making his reports to a four-year-old boy, but to me. Commander Illyan will in fact merely be his assistant." Vorkosigan and Illyan exchanged mildly ironic nods. "But there is no question where Negri's loyalties will lie, in case I should, um, run mad and make a bid for Imperial power in name as well as fact. He unquestionably has secret orders to dispose of me, in that event."

"Oh. Well, I guarantee I have no desire whatsoever to be Empress of Barrayar. Just in case you were wondering."

"I didn't think so."

The groundcar paused at a gate in a stone wall. Four guards inspected them thoroughly, checked Illyan's passes, and waved them through. All those guards, here, at Vorkosigan House—what did they guard against? Other

Barrayarans, presumably, in the faction-fractured political landscape. A very Barrayaran phrase the old Count had used that tickled her humor now ran, disquieting, through her memory. *With all this manure around, there's got to be a pony someplace.* Horses were practically unknown on Beta Colony, except for a few specimens in zoos. *With all these guards around . . . But if I'm not anyone's enemy, how can anyone be my enemy?*

Illyan, who had been shifting in his seat, now spoke up. "I would suggest, sir," he said tentatively to Vorkosigan, "even beg, that you re-consider and take up quarters here at the Imperial Residence. Security problems—my problems," he smiled slightly, bad for his image, with his snub features it made him look puppyish, "will be very much easier to control here."

"What suite did you have in mind?" asked Vorkosigan.

"Well, when . . . Gregor succeeds, he and his mother will be moving into the Emperor's suite. Kareen's rooms will then be vacant."

"Prince Serg's, you mean." Vorkosigan looked grim. "I . . . think I would prefer to take official residence at Vorkosigan House. My father spends more and more time in the country at Vorkosigan Surleau these days, I don't think he'll mind being shifted."

"I can't really endorse that idea, sir. Strictly from a security standpoint. It's in the old part of town. The streets are warrens. There are at least three sets of old tunnels under the area, from old sewage and transport systems, and there are too many new tall buildings overlooking that have, er, commanding views. It will take at least six full-time patrols for the most cursory protection."

"Do you have the men?"

"Well, yes."

"Vorkosigan House, then." Vorkosigan consoled Illyan's disappointed look. "It may be bad security, but it's very good public relations. It will give an excellent air of, ah, soldierly humility to the new Regency. Should help reduce palace coup paranoia."

And here they were at the very palace in question. As

an architectural pile, the Imperial Residence made Vorkosigan House look small. Sprawling wings rose two to four stories high, accented with sporadic towers. Additions of different ages crisscrossed each other to create both vast and intimate courts, some justly proportioned, some rather accidental-looking. The east façade was of the most uniform style, heavy with stone carving. The north side was more cut-up, interlocking with elaborate formal gardens. The west was the oldest, the south the newest construction.

The groundcar pulled up to a two-story porch on the south side, and Illyan led them past more guards and up wide stone stairs to an extensive second-floor suite. They climbed slowly, matching steps to Lieutenant Koudelka's awkward pace. Koudelka glanced up with a self-conscious apologetic frown, then bent his head again in concentration—or shame? *Doesn't this place have a lift tube?* Cordelia wondered irritably. On the other side of this stone labyrinth, in a room with a northern view of the gardens, a white old man lay drained and dying on his enormous ancestral bed. . . .

In the spacious upper corridor, softly carpeted and decorated with paintings and side tables cluttered with knickknacks—objets d'art, Cordelia supposed—they found Captain Negri talking in low tones with a woman who stood with her arms folded. Cordelia had met the famous, or infamous, Chief of Barrayaran Imperial Security for the first time yesterday, after Vorkosigan's historic job interview in the northern wing with the soon-to-be-late Ezar Vorbarra. Negri was a hard-faced, hard-bodied, bullet-headed man who had served his emperor, body and blood, for the better part of forty years, a sinister legend with unreadable eyes.

Now he bowed over her hand and called her "Milady" as if he meant it, or at least no more tinged with irony than any of his other statements. The alert blonde woman—girl?—wore an ordinary civilian dress. She was tall and heavily muscled, and she looked back at Cordelia with even greater interest.

Vorkosigan and Negri exchanged curt greetings in the telegraphic style of two men who had been communicating for so long all of the amenities had been compressed into some kind of tight-burst code. "And this is Miss Droushnakovi." Negri did not so much introduce as label the woman for Cordelia's benefit, with a wave of his hand.

"And what's a Droushnakovi?" asked Cordelia lightly and somewhat desperately. Everybody always seemed to get briefed around here but her, though Negri had also failed to introduce Lieutenant Koudelka; Koudelka and Droushnakovi glanced covertly at each other.

"I'm a Servant of the Inner Chamber, Milady." Droushnakovi gave her a ducking nod, half a curtsey.

"And what do you serve? Besides the chamber."

"Princess Kareen, Milady. That's just my official title. I'm listed on Captain Negri's staff budget as Bodyguard, Class One." It was hard to tell which title gave her the more pride and pleasure, but Cordelia suspected it was the latter.

"I'm sure you must be good, to be so ranked by him."

This won a smile, and a "Thank you, Milady. I try."

They all followed Negri through a nearby door to a long, sunny yellow room with lots of south-facing windows. Cordelia wondered if the eclectic mix of furnishings were priceless antiques, or merely shabby seconds. She couldn't tell. A woman waited on a yellow silk settee at the far end, watching them gravely as they trooped toward her en masse.

Princess-dowager Kareen was a thin, strained-looking woman of thirty with elaborately dressed, beautiful dark hair, though her grey gown was of a simple cut. Simple but perfect. A dark-haired boy of four or so was sprawled on the floor on his stomach muttering to his cat-sized toy stegosaurus, which muttered back. She made him get up and turn off the robot toy, and sit beside her, though his hands still clutched the leathery stuffed beast in his lap. Cordelia was relieved to see the boy prince was sensibly dressed for his age in comfortable-looking play clothes.

In formal phrases, Negri introduced Cordelia to the princess and Prince Gregor. Cordelia wasn't sure whether to bow, curtsey, or salute, and ended up ducking her head rather like Droushnakovi. Gregor, solemn, stared at her most doubtfully, and she tried to smile back in what she hoped was a reassuring way.

Vorkosigan went down on one knee in front of the boy—only Cordelia saw Aral swallow—and said, "Do you know who I am, Prince Gregor?"

Gregor shrank a little against his mother's side, and glanced up at her. She nodded encouragement. "Lord Aral Vorkosigan," Gregor said in a thin voice.

Vorkosigan gentled his tone, relaxed his hands, self-consciously trying to dampen his usual intensity. "Your grandfather has asked me to be your Regent. Has anybody explained to you what that means?"

Gregor shook his head mutely; Vorkosigan quirked a brow at Negri, a whiff of censure. Negri did not change expression.

"That means I will do your grandfather's job until you are old enough to do it yourself, when you turn twenty. The next sixteen years. I will look after you and your mother in your grandfather's place, and see that you get the education and training to do a good job, like your grandfather did. Good government."

Did the kid even know yet what a government was? Vorkosigan had been careful not to say, *in your father's place,* Cordelia noted dryly. Careful not to mention Crown Prince Serg at all. Serg was well on his way to being disappeared from Barrayaran history, it seemed, as thoroughly as he had been vaporized in orbital battle.

"For now," Vorkosigan continued, "your job is to study hard with your tutors and do what your mother tells you. Can you do that?"

Gregor swallowed, nodded.

"I think you can do well." Vorkosigan gave him a firm nod, identical to the ones he gave his staff officers, and rose.

I think you can do well too, Aral, Cordelia thought.

"While you are here, sir," Negri began after a short wait to be certain he wasn't stepping on some further word, "I wish you would come down to Ops. There are two or three reports I'd like to present. The latest from Darkoi seems to indicate that Count Vorlakail was dead before his Residence was burned, which throws a new light—or shadow—on that matter. And then there is the problem of revamping the Ministry of Political Education—"

"Dismantling, surely," Vorkosigan muttered.

"As may be. And, as ever, the latest sabotage from Komarr . . ."

"I get the picture. Let's go. Cordelia, ah . . ."

"Perhaps Lady Vorkosigan would care to stay and visit a while," Princess Kareen murmured on cue, with only a faint trace of irony.

Vorkosigan shot her a look of gratitude. "Thank you, Milady."

She absently stroked her fine lips with one finger, as all the men trooped out, relaxing slightly as they exited. "Good. I'd hoped to have you all to myself." Her expression grew more animated, as she regarded Cordelia. At a wordless touch, the boy slid off the bench and returned, with backward glances, to his play.

Droushnakovi frowned down the room. "What was the matter with that lieutenant?" she asked Cordelia.

"Lieutenant Koudelka was hit by nerve disruptor fire," Cordelia said stiffly, uncertain if the girl's odd tone concealed some kind of disapproval. "A year ago, when he was serving Aral aboard the *General Vorkraft*. The neural repairs do not seem to be quite up to galactic standard." She shut her mouth, afraid of seeming to criticize her hostess. Not that Princess Kareen was responsible for Barrayar's dubious standards of medical practice.

"Oh. Not during the Escobar war?" said Droushnakovi.

"Actually, in a weird sense, it was the opening shot of the Escobar war. Though I suppose you would call it friendly fire." Mind-boggling oxymoron, that phrase.

"Lady Vorkosigan—or should I say, Captain

Naismith—was there," remarked Princess Kareen. "She should know."

Cordelia found her expression hard to read. How many of Negri's famous reports was the princess privy to?

"How terrible for him! He looks as though he had been very athletic," said the bodyguard.

"He was." Cordelia smiled more favorably at the girl, relaxing her defensive hackles. "Nerve disruptors are filthy weapons, in my opinion." She scrubbed absently at the sense-dead spot on her thigh, disruptor-burned by no more than the nimbus of a blast that had fortunately not penetrated subcutaneous fat to damage muscle function. Clearly, she should have had it fixed before she'd left home.

"Sit, Lady Vorkosigan." Princess Kareen patted the settee beside her, just vacated by the emperor-to-be. "Drou, will you please take Gregor to his lunch?"

Droushnakovi nodded understandingly, as if she had received some coded underlayer to this simple request, gathered up the boy, and walked out hand in hand with him. His child-voice drifted back, "Droushie, can I have a cream cake? And one for Steggie?"

Cordelia sat gingerly, thinking about Negri's reports, and Barrayaran disinformation about their recent aborted campaign to invade the planet Escobar. Escobar, Beta Colony's good neighbor and ally . . . the weapons that had disintegrated Crown Prince Serg and his ship high above Escobar had been bravely convoyed through the Barrayaran blockade by one Captain Cordelia Naismith, Betan Expeditionary Force. That much truth was plain and public and not to be apologized for. It was the secret history, behind the scenes in the Barrayaran high command, that was so . . . treacherous, Cordelia decided, was the precise word. Dangerous, like ill-stored toxic waste.

To Cordelia's astonishment, Princess Kareen leaned over, took her right hand, lifted it to her lips, and kissed it hard.

"I swore," said Kareen thickly, "that I would kiss the hand that slew Ges Vorrutyer. Thank you. Thank you." Her voice was breathy, earnest, tear-caught, grateful

emotion naked in her face. She sat up, her face growing reserved again, and nodded. "Thank you. Bless you."

"Uh . . ." Cordelia rubbed at the kissed spot. "Um . . .
I . . . this honor belongs to another, Milady. I was present,
when Admiral Vorrutyer's throat was cut, but it was not by
my hand."

Kareen's hands clenched in her lap, and her eyes
glowed. "Then it *was* Lord Vorkosigan!"

"No!" Cordelia's lips compressed in exasperation. "Negri
should have given you the true report. It was Sergeant
Bothari. Saved my life, at the time."

"Bothari?" Kareen sat bolt upright in astonishment.
"Bothari the monster, Bothari, Vorrutyer's mad batman?"

"I don't mind getting blamed in his place, ma'am,
because if it had become public they'd have been forced
to execute him for murder and mutiny, and this gets him
off and out. But I . . . but I should not steal his praise.
I'll pass it on to him if you wish, but I'm not sure he
remembers the incident. He went through some draco-
nian mind-therapy after the war, before they discharged
him—what you Barrayarans call therapy"—on a par with
their neurosurgery, Cordelia feared, "and I gather he
wasn't exactly, uh, normal before that, either."

"No," said Kareen. "He was not. I thought he was
Vorrutyer's creature."

"He chose . . . he chose to be otherwise. I think it was
the most heroic act I've ever witnessed. Out of the middle
of that swamp of evil and insanity, to reach for . . ." Cordelia
trailed off, embarrassed to say, *reach for redemption.* After
a pause she asked, "Do you blame Admiral Vorrutyer for
Prince Serg's, uh, corruption?" As long as they were clearing the air . . . *Nobody mentions Prince Serg. He thought
to take a bloody shortcut to the Imperium, and now he's
just . . . disappeared.*

"Ges Vorrutyer . . ." Kareen's hands twisted, "found a like-
minded friend in Serg. A fertile follower, in his vile amuse-
ments. Maybe not . . . all Vorrutyer's fault. I don't know."

An honest answer, Cordelia sensed. Kareen added lowly,
"Ezar protected me from Serg, after I became pregnant.

I had not even seen my husband for over a year, when he was killed at Escobar."

Perhaps I will not mention Prince Serg again either. "Ezar was a powerful protector. I hope Aral may do as well," Cordelia offered. Ought she to refer to Emperor Ezar in the past tense already? Everybody else seemed to.

Kareen came back from some absence, and shook herself to focus. "Tea, Lady Vorkosigan?" She smiled. She touched a comm link, concealed in a jeweled pin on her shoulder, and gave domestic orders. Apparently the private interview was over. Captain Naismith must now try to figure out how Lady Vorkosigan should take tea with a princess.

Gregor and the bodyguard reappeared about the time the cream cakes were being served, and Gregor set about successfully charming the ladies for a second helping. Kareen drew the line firmly at thirds. Prince Serg's son seemed an utterly normal boy, if quiet around strangers. Cordelia watched him with Kareen with deep personal interest. Motherhood. Everybody did it. How hard could it be?

"How do you like your new home so far, Lady Vorkosigan?" the princess inquired, making polite conversation. Tea-table stuff; no naked faces now. Not in front of the children.

Cordelia thought it over. "The country place, south at Vorkosigan Surleau, is just beautiful. That wonderful lake—it's bigger than any open body of water on the whole of Beta Colony, yet Aral just takes it for granted. Your planet is beautiful beyond measure." *Your planet. Not my planet?* In a free-association test, "home" still triggered "Beta Colony" in Cordelia's mind. Yet she could have rested in Vorkosigan's arms by the lake forever.

"The capital here—well, it's certainly more varied than anything we have at ho—on Beta Colony. Although," she laughed self-consciously, "there seem to be so many soldiers. Last time I was surrounded by that many green uniforms, I was in a POW camp."

"Do we still look like the enemy to you?" asked the princess curiously.

"Oh—you all stopped looking like the enemy to me even before the war was over. Just assorted victims, variously blind."

"You have penetrating eyes, Lady Vorkosigan." The princess sipped tea, smiling into her cup. Cordelia blinked.

"Vorkosigan House does tend to a barracks atmosphere, when Count Piotr is in residence," Cordelia commented. "All his liveried men. I think I've seen a couple of women servants so far, whisking around corners, but I haven't caught one yet. A Barrayaran barracks, that is. My Betan service was a different sort of thing."

"Mixed," said Droushnakovi. Was that the light of envy in her eyes? "Women and men both serving."

"Assignment by aptitude test," Cordelia agreed. "Strictly. Of course the more physical jobs are skewed to the men, but there doesn't seem to be that strange obsessive status-thing attached to them."

"Respect," sighed Droushnakovi.

"Well, if people are laying their lives on the line for their community, they ought certainly to get its respect," Cordelia said equably. "I do miss my—my sister-officers, I guess. The bright women, the techs, like my pool of friends at home." There was that tricky word again, home. "There have to be bright women around here somewhere, with all these bright men. Where are they hiding?" Cordelia shut her mouth, as it suddenly occurred to her that Kareen might mistakenly construe this remark as a slur on herself. Adding *present company excepted* would put her foot in it for sure, though.

But if Kareen so construed, she kept it to herself, and Cordelia was rescued from further potential social embarrassment by the return of Aral and Illyan. They all made polite farewells, and returned to Vorkosigan House.

That evening Commander Illyan popped in to Vorkosigan House with Droushnakovi in tow. She clutched a large valise, and gazed about her with starry-eyed interest.

"Captain Negri is assigning Miss Droushnakovi to the Regent-consort for her personal security," Illyan explained briefly. Aral nodded approval.

Later, Droushnakovi handed Cordelia a sealed note, on thick cream paper. Brows rising, Cordelia broke it open. The handwriting was small and neat, the signature legible and without flourishes.

With my compliments, it read. *She will suit you well. Kareen.*

CHAPTER TWO

The next morning Cordelia awoke to find Vorkosigan already gone, and herself facing her first day on Barrayar without his supportive company. She decided to devote it to the shopping project that had occurred to her while watching Koudelka negotiate the spiral staircase last night. She suspected Droushnakovi would be the ideal native guide for what she had in mind.

She dressed and went hunting for her bodyguard. Finding her was not difficult; Droushnakovi was seated in the hall, just outside the bedroom door, and popped to attention at Cordelia's appearance. The girl really ought to be wearing a uniform, Cordelia reflected. The dress she wore made her near-six-foot frame and excellent musculature look heavy. Cordelia wondered if, as Regent-consort, she might be permitted her own livery, and bemused herself through breakfast mentally designing one that would set off the girl's Valkyrie good looks.

"Do you know, you're the first female Barrayaran guard I've met," Cordelia commented to her over her egg and coffee, and a kind of steamed native groats with butter, evidently a morning staple here. "How did you get into this line of work?"

"Well, I'm not a real guard, like the liveried men—"

Ah, the magic of uniforms again.

"—but my father and all three of my brothers are in the Service. It's as close as I can come to being a real soldier, like you."

Army-mad, like the rest of Barrayar. "Yes?"

"I used to study judo, for sport, when I was younger. But I was too big for the women's classes. Nobody could give me any real practice, and besides, doing all katas was so dull. My brothers used to sneak me into the men's classes with them. One thing led to another. I was all-Barrayar women's champion two years running, when I was in school. Then three years ago a man from Captain Negri's staff approached my father with a job offer for me. That's when I had weapons training. It seemed the Princess had been asking for female guards for years, but they had a lot of trouble getting anyone who could pass all the tests. Although," she smiled self-depreciatingly, "the lady who assassinated Admiral Vorrutyer could scarcely be supposed to need my poor services."

Cordelia bit her tongue. "Um. I was lucky. Besides, I'd rather stay out of the physical end of things just now. Pregnant, you know."

"Yes, Milady. It was in one of Captain—"

"Negri's reports," Cordelia finished in unison with her. "I'm sure it was. He probably knew before I did."

"Yes, Milady."

"Were you much encouraged in your interests, as a child?"

"Not . . . really. Everyone thought I was just odd." She frowned deeply, and Cordelia had the sense of stirring up a painful memory.

She regarded the girl thoughtfully. "Older brothers?"

Droushnakovi returned a wide blue gaze. "Why, yes."

"Figured." *And I feared Barrayar for what it did to its sons. No wonder they have trouble getting anyone to pass the tests.* "So, you've had weapons training. Excellent. You can guide me on my shopping trip today."

A slightly glazed look crept over Droushnakovi's face.

"Yes, Milady. What sort of clothing do you wish to look at?" she asked politely, not quite concealing a glum disappointment with the interests of her "real" lady soldier.

"Where in this town would you go to buy a really good swordstick?"

The glazed look vanished. "Oh, I know just the place, where the Vor officers go, and the counts, to supply their liveried men. That is—I've never been inside. My family's not Vor, so of course we're not permitted to own personal weapons. Just Service issue. But it's supposed to be the best."

One of Count Vorkosigan's liveried guards chauffeured them to the shop. Cordelia relaxed and enjoyed the view of the passing city. Droushnakovi, on duty, kept alert, eyes constantly checking the crowds all around. Cordelia had the feeling she didn't miss much. From time to time her hand wandered to check the stunner worn concealed on the inside of her embroidered bolero.

They turned into a clean narrow street of older buildings with cut stone fronts. The weapons shop was marked only by its name, *Siegling's*, in discreet gold letters. Evidently if you didn't know where you were you shouldn't be there. The liveried man waited outside when Cordelia and Droushnakovi entered the shop, a thick-carpeted, wood-grained place with a little of the aroma of the armory Cordelia remembered from her Survey ship, an odd whiff of home in an alien place. She stared covertly at the wood paneling, and mentally translated its value into Betan dollars. A great many Betan dollars. Yet wood seemed almost as common as plastic, here, and as little regarded. Those personal weapons which were legal for the upper classes to own were elegantly displayed in cases and on the walls. Besides stunners and hunting weapons, there was an impressive array of swords and knives; evidently the Emperor's ferocious edicts against dueling only forbade their use, not their possession.

The clerk, a narrow-eyed, soft-treading older man,

came up to them. "What may I do for you ladies?" He
was cordial enough. Cordelia supposed Vor-class women
must sometimes enter here, to buy presents for their mas-
culine relations. But he might have said, *What may I do
for you children?* in the same tone of voice.
Diminutization by body language? Let it go.

"I'm looking for a swordstick, for a man about six-foot-
four. Should be about, oh, yea long," she estimated, calling
up Koudelka's arm and leg length in her mind's eye, and
gesturing to the height of her hip. "Spring-sheathed,
probably."

"Yes, madam." The clerk disappeared, and returned
with a sample, in an elaborately carved light wood.

"Looks a bit . . . I don't know." *Flashy*. "How does it
work?"

The clerk demonstrated the spring mechanism. The
wooden sheathing dropped off, revealing a long thin blade.
Cordelia held out her hand, and the clerk, rather reluctantly, handed it over for inspection.

She wriggled it a little, sighted down the blade, and
handed it to her bodyguard. "What do you think?"

Droushnakovi smiled first, then frowned doubtfully. "It's
not very well balanced." She glanced uncertainly at the
clerk.

"Remember, you're working for me, not him," said
Cordelia, correctly identifying class-consciousness in action.

"I don't think it's a very good blade."

"That's excellent Darkoi workmanship, madam," the
clerk defended coolly.

Smiling, Cordelia took it back. "Let us test your
hypothesis."

She raised the blade suddenly to the salute, and lunged
at the wall in a neat extension. The tip penetrated and
caught in the wood, and Cordelia leaned on it. The blade
snapped. Blandly, she handed the pieces back to the clerk.
"How do you stay in business if your customers don't survive long enough for repeat sales? Siegling's certainly didn't
acquire its reputation selling toys like that. Bring me something a decent soldier can carry, not a pimp's plaything."

"Madam," said the clerk stiffly, "I must insist the damaged merchandise be paid for."

Cordelia, thoroughly irritated, said, "Very well. Send the bill to my husband. Admiral Aral Vorkosigan, Vorkosigan House. While you're about it you can explain why you tried to pass off sleaze on his wife—Yeoman." This last was a guess, based on his age and walk, but she could tell from his eyes she'd struck home.

The clerk bowed profoundly. "I beg pardon, Milady. I believe I have something more suitable, if Milady will be pleased to wait."

He vanished again, and Cordelia sighed. "Buying from machines is so much easier. But at least the Appeal to the Irrelevant Authorities at Headquarters works just as well here as at home."

The next sample was a plain dark wood, with a finish like satin. The clerk handed it to her unopened, with another little bow. "You press the handle there, Milady."

It was much heavier than the first swordstick. The sheathing sprang away at velocity, landing against the wall on the other side of the room with a satisfying thunk, almost a weapon in itself. Cordelia sighted down the blade again. A strange watermark pattern down its length shifted in the light. She saluted the wall once more, and caught the clerk's eye. "Do these come out of your salary?"

"Go ahead, Milady." There was a little gleam of satisfaction in his eye. "You can't break that one."

She gave it the same test as she had the other. The tip went much further into the wood, and leaning against it with all her strength, she could barely bend it. Even so, there was more bend left in it; she could feel she was nowhere near the limit of its tensile strength. She handed it to Droushnakovi, who examined it lovingly.

"That's *fine*, Milady. That's worthy."

"I'm sure it will be used more as a stick than as a sword. Nevertheless . . . it should indeed be worthy. We'll take this one."

As the clerk wrapped it, Cordelia lingered over a case of enamel-decorated stunners.

"Thinking of buying one for yourself, Milady?" asked Droushnakovi.

"I . . . don't think so. Barrayar has enough soldiers, without importing them from Beta Colony. Whatever I'm here for, it isn't soldiering. See anything you want?"

Droushnakovi looked wistful, but shook her head, her hand going to her bolero. "Captain Negri's equipment is the best. Even Siegling's doesn't have anything better, just prettier."

They sat down three to dinner that night, late, Vorkosigan, Cordelia, and Lieutenant Koudelka. Vorkosigan's new personal secretary looked a little tired.

"What did you two do all day?" asked Cordelia.

"Herded men, mostly," answered Vorkosigan. "Prime Minister Vortala had a few votes that weren't as much in the bag as he claimed, and we worked them over, one or two at a time, behind closed doors. What you'll see tomorrow in the Council chambers isn't Barrayaran politics at work, just their result. Were you all right today?"

"Fine. Went shopping. Wait'll you see." She produced the swordstick, and stripped off the wrapping. "Just to help keep you from running Kou completely into the ground."

Koudelka looked politely grateful, over a more fundamental irritation. His look changed to one of surprise as he took the stick and nearly dropped it from the unexpected weight. "Hey! This isn't—"

"You press the handle there. Don't point it—!"

Thwack!

"—at the window." Fortunately, the sheath struck the frame, and bounced back with a clatter. Kou and Aral both jumped.

Koudelka's eyes lit up as he examined the blade, while Cordelia retrieved the sheath. "Oh, Milady!" Then his face fell. He carefully resheathed it, and handed it back sadly. "I guess you didn't realize. I'm not Vor. It's not legal for me to own a private sword."

"Oh." Cordelia was crestfallen.

Vorkosigan raised an eyebrow. "May I see that,

Cordelia?" He looked it over, unsheathing it more cautiously. "Hm. Am I right in guessing I paid for this?"

"Well, you will, I suppose, when the bill arrives. Although I don't think you should pay for the one I broke. I might as well take it back, though."

"I see." He smiled a little. "Lieutenant Koudelka, as your commanding officer and a vassal secundus to Ezar Vorbarra, I am officially issuing you this weapon of mine, to carry in the service of the Emperor, long may he rule." The unavoidable irony of the formal phrase tightened his mouth, but he shook off the blackness, and handed the stick back to Koudelka, who bloomed again.

"Thank you, sir!"

Cordelia just shook her head. "I don't believe I'll ever understand this place."

"I'll have Kou find you some legal histories. Not tonight, though. He has barely time to put his notes from today in order before Vortala's due here with a couple more of his strays. You can take over part of the Count my father's library, Kou; we'll meet in there."

Dinner broke up. Koudelka retreated to the library to work, while Vorkosigan and Cordelia retired to the drawing room next to it to read, before Vorkosigan's evening meeting. He had yet more reports, which he ran rapidly through a hand viewer. Cordelia divided her time between a Barrayaran Russian phrase earbug, and an even more intimidating disk on child care. The silence was broken by an occasional mutter from Vorkosigan, more to himself than her, of phrases like, "Ah ha! So that's what the bastard was really up to," or "Damn, those figures are strange. Got to check it out. . . ." Or from Cordelia, "Oh, my, I wonder if all babies do that," and a periodic *thwack!* penetrating the wall from the library, which caused them to look up at each other and burst out laughing.

"Oh, dear," said Cordelia, after the third or fourth of these. "I hope I haven't distracted him unduly from his duties."

"He'll do all right, when he settles down. Vorbarra's personal secretary has taken him in hand, and is showing him how to organize himself. After Kou follows him through the funeral protocol, he should be able to tackle anything. That swordstick was a stroke of genius, by the way; thank you."

"Yes, I noticed he was pretty touchy about his handicaps. I thought it might unruffle his feathers a little."

"It's our society. It tends to be . . . rather hard on anyone who can't keep up."

"I see. Strange . . . now that you mention it, I don't recall seeing any but healthy-looking people, on the streets and so on, except at the hospital. No float chairs, none of those vacuous faces in the tow of their parents . . ."

"Nor will you." Vorkosigan looked grim. "Any problems that are detectable are eliminated before birth."

"Well, we do that, too. Though usually before conception."

"Also at birth. And after, in the backcountry."

"Oh."

"As for the maimed adults . . ."

"Good heavens, you don't practice euthanasia on them, do you?"

"Your Ensign Dubauer would not have lived, here."

Dubauer had taken disruptor fire to the head, and survived. Sort of.

"As for injuries like Koudelka's, or worse . . . the social stigma is very great. Watch him in a larger group sometime, not his close friends. It's no accident that the suicide rate among medically discharged soldiers is high."

"That's horrible."

"I took it for granted, once. Now . . . not anymore. But many people still do."

"What about problems like Bothari's?"

"It depends. He was a usable madman. For the unusable . . ." he trailed off, staring at his boots.

Cordelia felt cold. "I keep thinking I'm beginning to adjust to this place. Then I go around another corner and run headlong into something like that."

"It's only been eighty years since Barrayar made contact with the wider galactic civilization again. It wasn't just technology we lost, in the Time of Isolation. That we put back on again quickly, like a borrowed coat. But underneath it . . . we're still pretty damned naked in places. In forty-four years, I've only begun to see how naked."

Count Vortala and his "strays" came in soon after, and Vorkosigan vanished into the library. The old Count Piotr Vorkosigan, Aral's father, arrived from his District later that evening, come up to attend the full Council vote.

"Well, that's one vote he's assured of tomorrow," Cordelia joked to her father-in-law, helping him get stiffly out of his jacket in the stone-paved foyer.

"Ha. He's lucky to get it. He's picked up some damned peculiar radical notions in the last few years. If he wasn't my son, he could whistle for it." But Piotr's seamed face looked proud.

Cordelia blinked at this description of Aral Vorkosigan's political views. "I confess, I've never thought of him as a revolutionary. Radical must be a more elastic term than I thought."

"Oh, he doesn't see himself that way. He thinks he can go halfway, and then stop. I think he'll find himself riding a tiger, a few years down the road." The count shook his head grimly. "But come, my girl, and sit down and tell me that you're well. You look well—is everything all right?"

The old count was passionately interested in the development of his grandson-to-be. Cordelia sensed her pregnancy had raised her status with him enormously, from a tolerated caprice of Aral's to something bordering perilously on the semi-divine. He fairly blasted her with approval. It was nearly irresistible, and she never laughed at him, although she had no illusions about it.

Cordelia had found Aral's earlier sketch of his father's reaction to her pregnancy, the day she'd brought home the confirming news, to be right on target. She'd returned to the estate at Vorkosigan Surleau that summer day to search Aral out down by the boat dock. He was puttering around with his sailboat, and had the sails laid out,

drying in the sun, as he squished around them in wet
shoes.

He looked up to meet her smile, unsuccessful at concealing the eagerness in his eyes. "Well?" He bounced
a little, on his heels.

"Well." She attempted a sad and disappointed look, to
tease him, but the grin escaped and took over her whole
face. "Your doctor says it's a boy."

"Ah." A long and eloquent sigh escaped him, and he
scooped her up and twirled her around.

"Aral! Awk! Don't drop me." He was no taller than
herself, if, um, thicker.

"Never." He let her slide down against him, and they
shared a long kiss, ending in laughter.

"My father will be ecstatic."

"You look pretty ecstatic yourself."

"Yes, but you haven't seen anything until you've seen
an old-fashioned Barrayaran paterfamilias in a trance over
the growth of his family tree. I've had the poor old man
convinced for years that his line was ending with me."

"Will he forgive me for being an offworlder plebe?"

"No insult intended, but by this time I don't think he'd
have cared what *species* of wife I dragged home, as long
as she was fertile. You think I'm exaggerating?" he added
at her trill of laughter. "You'll see."

"Is it too early to think of names?" she asked, slightly
wistful.

"No thinking to it. Firstborn son. It's a strict custom
here. He gets named after his two grandfathers. Pater-
nal for the first, maternal for the second."

"Ah, that's why your history is so confusing to read. I
was always having to put dates next to those duplicate
names, to try and keep track. Piotr Miles. Hm. Well, I guess
I can get used to it. I'd been thinking of . . . something else."

"Another time, perhaps."

"Ooh, ambitious."

A short wrestling match ensued, Cordelia having pre-
viously made the useful discovery that in certain moods
he was more ticklish than she. She extracted a reasonable

amount of revenge, and they ended laughing on the grass in the sun.

"This is very undignified," Aral complained as she let him up.

"Afraid I'll shock Negri's fisher of men out there?"

"They're beyond shock, I guarantee."

Cordelia waved at the distant hoverboat, whose occupant steadfastly ignored the gesture. She had been at first angered, then resigned to learn that Aral was being kept under continuous observation by Imperial Security. The price, she'd supposed, of his involvement in the secret and lethal politics of the Escobar War, and the penalty for some of his less welcome outspoken opinions.

"I can see why you took up baiting them for a hobby. Maybe we ought to unbend and invite them to lunch or something. I feel they must know me so well by now, I'd like to know them." Had Negri's man recorded the domestic conversation she'd just had? Were there bugs in their bedroom? Their bathroom?

Aral grinned, but replied, "They wouldn't be permitted to accept. They don't eat or drink anything but what they bring themselves."

"Heavens, how paranoid. Is that really necessary?"

"Sometimes. Theirs is a dangerous trade. I don't envy them."

"I'd think sitting around down here watching you would constitute a nice little vacation. He's got to have a great suntan."

"The sitting around is the hardest part. They may sit for a year, and then be called to five minutes of all-out action of deadly importance. But they have to be instantly ready for that five minutes the whole year. Quite a strain. I much prefer attack to defense."

"I still don't understand why anybody would want to bother you. I mean, you're just a retired officer, living in obscurity. There must be hundreds like you, even of high Vor blood."

"Hm." He'd rested his gaze on the distant boat, avoiding answer, then jumped to his feet. "Come on. Let's go spring the good news on Father."

Well, she understood it now. Count Piotr drew her
hand through his arm, and carried her off to the dining
room, where he ate a late supper between demands for
the latest obstetrical report, and pressed fresh garden
dainties upon her that he'd brought with him from the
country. She ate grapes obediently.

After the Count's supper, walking arm in arm with him
into the foyer, Cordelia's ear was caught by the sound of
raised voices coming from the library. The words were
muffled but the tones were sharp, chop-cadenced.
Cordelia paused, disturbed.

After a moment the—argument?—stopped, the library
door swung open, and a man stalked out. Cordelia could
see Aral and Count Vortala through the aperture. Aral's
face was set, his eyes burning. Vortala, an age-shrunken
man with a balding liver-spotted head fringed with white,
was brick-pink to the top of his naked scalp. With a curt
gesture the man collected his waiting liveried retainer, who
followed smartly, blank-faced.

The curt man was about forty years old, Cordelia
guessed, dressed expensively in the upper-class style, dark-
haired. He was rendered a bit dish-faced by a prominent
forehead and jaw that his nose and·moustache had trouble
overpowering. Neither handsome nor ugly, in another
mood one might call him strong-featured. Now he just
looked sour. He paused, coming upon Count Piotr in the
foyer, and managed—just barely—a polite nod of greeting. "Vorkosigan," he said thickly. A reluctant *good evening*
was encoded in his jerky half-bow.

The old count tilted his head in return, eyebrows up.
"Vordarian." His tone made the name an inquiry.

Vordarian's lips were tight, his hands clenching in
unconscious rhythm with his jaw. "Mark my words," he
ground out, "you, and I, and every other man of worth
on Barrayar will live to regret tomorrow."

Piotr pursed his lips, wariness in the crow's-feet corners of his eyes. "My son will not betray his class,
Vordarian."

"You blind yourself." His stare cut across Cordelia, not

lingering long enough to be construed as insult, but cold, very cold, repelling introduction. With effort, he made the minimum courtesy of a farewell nod, turned, and exited the front door with his retainer-shadow.

Aral and Vortala emerged from the library. Aral drifted to the foyer to stare moodily into the darkness through the etched glass panels flanking the door. Vortala placed a placating hand on his sleeve.

"Let him go," said Vortala. "We can live without his vote tomorrow."

"I don't plan to go running down the street after him," Aral snapped. "Nevertheless . . . next time, save your wit for those with the brains to appreciate it, eh?"

"Who was that irate fellow?" asked Cordelia lightly, trying to lift the black mood.

"Count Vidal Vordarian." Aral turned from the glass panel back to her, and managed a smile for her benefit. "Commodore Count Vordarian. I used to work with him from time to time when I was on the General Staff. He is now a leader in what you might call the next-to-most conservative party on Barrayar; not the back-to-the-Time-of-Isolation loonies, but, shall we say, those honestly fearing all change is change for the worse." He glanced covertly at Count Piotr.

"His name was mentioned frequently, in speculation about the upcoming Regency," Vortala commented. "I rather fear he may have been counting on it for himself. He's made great efforts to cultivate Kareen."

"He should have been cultivating Ezar," said Aral dryly. "Well . . . maybe he'll come down out of the air overnight. Try him again in the morning, Vortala—a little more humbly this time, eh?"

"Coddling Vordarian's ego could be a full-time task," grumbled Vortala. "He spends too damn much time studying his family tree."

Aral grimaced agreement. "He's not the only one."

"He is to hear him tell it," growled Vortala.

CHAPTER THREE

The next day Cordelia had an official escort to the full Joint Council session in the person of Captain Lord Padma Xav Vorpatril. He turned out to be not only a member of her husband's new staff, but also his first cousin, son of Aral's long-dead mother's younger sister. Lord Vorpatril was the first close relative of Aral's Cordelia had encountered besides Count Piotr. It wasn't that Aral's relatives were avoiding her, as she might have feared; he had a real dearth of them. He and Vorpatril were the only surviving children of the previous generation, of whom Count Piotr was himself the last living representative. Vorpatril was a big cheerful man of about thirty-five, clean-cut in his dress greens. He had also, she discovered shortly, been one of her husband's junior officers during his first captaincy, before Vorkosigan's military successes of the Komarr campaign and its politically ruinous aftermath.

She sat with Vorpatril on one side and Droushnakovi on the other, in an ornate-railed gallery overlooking the Council chamber. The chamber itself was a surprisingly plain room, though heavy with what still seemed to Cordelia's Betan eye to be incredibly luxurious wood paneling. Wooden benches and desks ringed the room. Morning light poured through stained-glass windows high in the east wall. The colorful ceremonies were played out below with great punctilio.

The ministers wore archaic-looking black and purple robes set off by gold chains of office. They were outnumbered by the nearly sixty District counts, even more splendid in scarlet and silver. A sprinkling of men young enough to be on active service in the military wore the red and blue parade uniform. Vorkosigan had been right in describing the parade uniform as gaudy, Cordelia reflected, but in the wonderful setting of this ancient room the gaud seemed most appropriate. Vorkosigan looked quite good in his set, she thought.

Prince Gregor and his mother were seated on a dais to one side of the chamber. The princess wore a black gown shot with silver decoration, high-necked and long-sleeved. Her dark-haired son looked rather like an elf in his red and blue uniform. Cordelia thought he fidgeted remarkably little, under the circumstances.

The Emperor too had a ghostly presence, over closed circuit commlink from the Imperial Residence. Ezar was shown in the holovid seated, in full uniform, at what physical cost Cordelia could not guess, the tubes and monitor leads piercing his body concealed at least from the vid pickup. His face was paper-white, his skin almost transparent, as if he were literally fading from the stage he had dominated for so long.

The gallery was crammed with wives, staff, and guards. The women were elegantly dressed and decorated with jewelry, and Cordelia studied them with interest, then turned her attention back to pumping Vorpatril for information.

"Was Aral's appointment as Regent a surprise to you?" she asked.

"Not really. A few people took that resignation-and-retirement business after the Escobar mess seriously, but I never did."

"He meant it seriously, I thought."

"Oh, I don't doubt it. The first person Aral fools with that prosey-stone-soldier routine is himself. It's the sort of man he always wanted to be, I think. Like his father."

"Hm. Yes, I had noticed a certain political bent to his conversations. In the middle of the most extraordinary circumstances, too. Marriage proposals, for instance."

Vorpatril laughed. "I can just picture it. When he was young he was a real conservative—if you wanted to know what Aral thought about anything, all you had to do was ask Count Piotr, and multiply by two. But by the time we served together, he was getting . . . um . . . strange. If you could get him going . . ." There was a certain wicked reminiscence in his eye, which Cordelia promptly encouraged.

"How did you get him going? I thought political discussion was forbidden to officers."

He snorted. "I suppose they could forbid breathing with about as much chance of success. The dictum is, shall we say, sporadically enforced. Aral stuck to it, though, unless Rulf Vorhalas and I took him out and got him really relaxed."

"Aral? Relaxed?"

"Oh, yes. Now, Aral's drinking was notable—"

"I thought he was a terrible drinker. No stomach for it."

"Oh, that's what was notable. He seldom drank. Although he went through a bad period after his first wife died, when he used to run around with Ges Vorrutyer a lot . . . um . . ." He glanced sideways, and took another tack. "Anyway, it was dangerous to get him too relaxed, because then he'd go all depressed and serious, and then it didn't take a thing to get him on to whatever current injustice or incompetence or insanity was rousing his ire. God, the man could talk. By the time he'd had his fifth drink—just before he slid under the table for the night—he'd be declaiming revolution in iambic pentameter. I always thought he'd end up on the political side someday." He chuckled, and looked rather lovingly at the stocky red-and-blue-clad figure seated with the Counts on the far side of the chamber.

The Joint Council vote of confirmation for Vorkosigan's

Imperial appointment was a curious affair, to Cordelia's mind. She hadn't imagined it possible to get seventy-five Barrayarans to agree on which direction their sun rose in the morning, but the tally was nearly unanimous in favor of Emperor Ezar's choice. The exceptions were five set-jawed men who abstained, four loudly, one so weakly the Lord Guardian of the Speaker's Circle had to ask him to repeat himself. Even Count Vordarian voted yea, Cordelia noticed—perhaps Vortala had managed to repair last night's breach in some early-morning meeting after all. It all seemed a very auspicious and encouraging start to Vorkosigan's new job, anyway, and she said as much to Lord Vorpatril.

"Uh . . . yes, Milady," said Lord Vorpatril after a sideways smile at her. "Emperor Ezar made it clear he wanted united approval."

His tone made it clear she was missing cues, again. "Are you trying to tell me some of those men would rather have voted no?"

"That would be imprudent of them, at this juncture."

"Then the men who abstained . . . must have some courage of conscience." She studied the little group with new interest.

"Oh, *they're* all right," said Vorpatril.

"What do you mean? They are the opposition, surely."

"Yes, but they're the open opposition. No one plotting serious treason would mark himself so publicly. The fellows Aral will need to guard his back from are in the other mob, among the yes-men."

"Which ones?" Cordelia's brow wrinkled in worry.

"Who knows?" Lord Vorpatril shrugged, then answered his own question. "Negri, probably."

They were surrounded by a ring of empty seats. Cordelia hadn't been sure if it was for security or courtesy. Evidently the second, for two latecomers, a man in commander's dress greens and a younger one in rich-looking civilian clothes, arrived and apologetically sat in front of them. Cordelia thought they looked like brothers, and had the guess confirmed when the younger said,

"Look, there's Father, three seats behind old Vortala. Which one's the new Regent?"

"The bandy-legged character in the red-and-blues, just sitting down to Vortala's right."

Cordelia and Vorpatril exchanged a look behind their backs, and Cordelia put a finger to her lips. Vorpatril grinned and shrugged.

"What's the word on him in the Service?"

"Depends on who you ask," said the commander. "Sardi thinks he's a strategic genius, and dotes on his communiques. He's been all over the place. Every brushfire in the last twenty-five years seems to have his name in it someplace. Uncle Rulf used to think the world of him. On the other hand, Niels, who was at Escobar, said he was the most cold-blooded bastard he'd ever met."

"I hear he has a reputation as a secret progressive."

"There's nothing secret about it. Some of the senior Vor officers are scared to death of him. He's been trying to get Father with him and Vortala on that new tax ruling."

"Oh, yawn."

"It's the direct Imperial tax on inheritances."

"Ouch! Well, that wouldn't hit *him*, would it? The Vorkosigans are so damn poor. Let Komarr pay. That's why we conquered it, isn't it?"

"Not exactly, my fraternal ignoramus. Have any of you town clowns met his Betan frill yet?"

"Men of fashion, sirrah," corrected his brother. "Not to be confused with you Service grubs."

"No danger of that. No, really. There are the damnedest rumors circulating about her, Vorkosigan, and Vorrutyer at Escobar, most of which contradict each other. I thought Mother might have a line on it."

"She keeps a low profile, for somebody who's supposed to be three meters tall and eat battle cruisers for breakfast. Scarcely anybody's seen her. Maybe she's ugly."

"They'll make a pair, then. Vorkosigan's no beauty either."

Cordelia, vastly amused, hid a grin behind her hand,

until the commander said, "I don't know who that three-legged spastic is he has trailing him, though. Staff, do you suppose?"

"You'd think he could do better than that. What a mutant. Surely Vorkosigan has the pick of the Service, as Regent."

She felt she'd received a body blow, so great was the unexpected pain of the careless remark. Captain Lord Vorpatril scarcely seemed to notice it. He had heard it, but his attention was on the floor below, where oaths were being made. Droushnakovi, surprisingly, blushed, and turned her head away.

Cordelia leaned forward. Words boiled up within her, but she chose only a few, and fired them off in her coldest Captain's voice.

"Commander. And you, whoever you are." They looked back at her, surprised at the interruption. "For your information, the gentleman in question is Lieutenant Koudelka. And there are no better officers. Not in anybody's service."

They stared at her, irritated and baffled, unable to place her in their scheme of things. "I believe this was a private conversation, madam," said the commander stiffly.

"Quite so," she returned, equally stiffly, still boiling. "For eavesdropping, unavoidable as it was, I beg your pardon. But for that shameful remark upon Admiral Vorkosigan's secretary, *you* must apologize. It was a disgrace to the uniform you both wear and the service to your Emperor you both share." She kept her voice very low, almost hissing. She was trembling. *An overdose of Barrayar. Get hold of yourself.*

Vorpatril's wandering attention was drawn, startled, back to her by this speech. "Here, here," he remonstrated. "What is this—"

The commander turned around further. "Oh, Captain Vorpatril, sir. I didn't recognize you at first. Um . . ." He gestured helplessly at his red-haired attacker, as if to say, Is this lady with you? And if so, can't you keep her under control? He added coldly, "We have not met, madam."

"No, but I don't go 'round flipping over rocks to see what's living underneath." She was instantly conscious of having been lured into going too far. With difficulty, she put a lid on her temper. It wouldn't do to be making new enemies for Vorkosigan at the very moment he was taking up his duties.

Vorpatril, waking up to his responsibilities as escort, began, "Commander, you don't know who—"

"*Don't* . . . introduce us, Lord Vorpatril," Cordelia interrupted him. "We should only embarrass each other further." She pressed thumb and forefinger to the bridge of her nose, closing her eyes and gathering more conciliating words. *And I used to pride myself on keeping my temper.* She looked up at their furious faces.

"Commander. My lord." She correctly deduced the young man's title from his reference to his father, sitting among the counts. "My words were hasty and rude, and I take them back. I had no right to comment on a private conversation. I apologize. Most humbly."

"As well you should," snapped the young lord.

His brother had more self-control, and replied reluctantly, "I accept your apology, madam. I presume the lieutenant is some relative of yours. I apologize for whatever insult you felt was implied."

"And I accept your apology, Commander. Although Lieutenant Koudelka is not a relation, but only my second-dearest . . . enemy." She paused, and they exchanged frowns, hers of irony, his of puzzlement. "I would ask a favor of you, however, sir. Don't let a comment like that fall in Admiral Vorkosigan's hearing. Koudelka was one of his officers aboard the *General Vorkraft*, and was wounded in his defense during that political mutiny last year. He loves him as a son."

The commander was calming down, although Droushnakovi still looked as if she had a bad taste in her mouth. He smiled a little. "Are you implying I'd find myself doing guard duty on Kyril Island?"

What was Kyril Island? Some distant and unpleasant outpost, apparently. "I . . . doubt it. He wouldn't use his office to carry out a personal grudge. But it would cause him unnecessary pain."

"Madam." She had puzzled him thoroughly now, this plain-looking woman, so out-of-place in the glittering gallery. He turned back with his brother to watch the show below, and all maintained a sticky silence for another twenty minutes, until the ceremonies stopped for lunch. The crowds in both gallery and floor broke away to meet in the corridors of power.

She found Vorkosigan, Koudelka at his side, speaking with his father Count Piotr and another older man in count's robes. Vorpatril delivered her and vanished, and Aral greeted her with a tired smile.

"Dear Captain, are you holding up all right? I want you to meet Count Vorhalas. Admiral Rulf Vorhalas was his younger brother. We must go shortly, we're scheduled for a private lunch with the Princess and Prince Gregor."

Count Vorhalas bowed profoundly over her hand. "Milady. I'm honored."

"Count. I . . . only saw your brother briefly. But Admiral Vorhalas struck me as a man of outstanding worth." *And my side blew him away.* She felt queasy, with her hand in his, but he seemed to hold no personal animosity.

"Thank you, Milady. We all thought so. Ah, there are the boys. I promised them an introduction. Evon is itching for a place on the Staff, but I told him he'd have to earn it. I wish Carl had as much interest in the Service. My daughter will be mad with jealousy. You've stirred up all the girls, you know, Milady."

The count darted away to round up his sons. *Oh, God,* thought Cordelia. *It would have to be them.* The two men who had sat before her in the gallery were presented to her. They both blanched, and bowed nervously over her hand.

"But you've met," said Vorkosigan. "I saw you talking in the gallery. What did you find to discuss so animatedly, Cordelia?"

"Oh . . . geology. Zoology. Courtesy. Much on courtesy. We had quite a wide-ranging discussion. We each of us taught the other something, I think." She smiled, and did not flick an eyelid.

Commander Evon Vorhalas, looking rather ill, said, "Yes. I've . . . had a lesson I'll never forget, Milady."

Vorkosigan was continuing the introductions. "Commander Vorhalas, Lord Carl; Lieutenant Koudelka."

Koudelka, loaded with plastic flimsys, disks, the baton of the commander-in-chief of the armed forces that had just been presented to Vorkosigan as Regent-elect, and his own stick, and uncertain whether to shake hands or salute, managed to drop them all and do neither. There was a general scramble to retrieve the load, and Koudelka went red, bending awkwardly after it. Droushnakovi and he put a hand on his stick at the same time.

"I don't need your help, miss," Koudelka snarled at her in a low voice, and she recoiled to go stand rigidly behind Cordelia.

Commander Vorhalas handed him back some disks. "Pardon me, sir," said Koudelka. "Thank you."

"Not at all, Lieutenant. I was almost hit by disruptor fire myself once. Scared the hell out of me. You are an example to us all."

"It . . . didn't hurt, sir."

Cordelia, who knew from personal experience that this was a lie, held her peace, satisfied. The group broke up for its separate destinations. Cordelia paused before Evon Vorhalas.

"Nice to meet you, Commander. I predict you will go far, in your future career—and *not* in the direction of Kyril Island."

Vorhalas smiled tightly. "I believe you will, too, Milady." They exchanged wary and respectful nods, and Cordelia turned to take Vorkosigan's arm, and follow him to his next task, trailed by Koudelka and Droushnakovi.

The Barrayaran Emperor slipped into his final coma a week later, but lingered on another week beyond that. Aral and Cordelia were routed out of bed at Vorkosigan House in the early hours of the morning by a special messenger from the Imperial Residence, with the simple words, "The doctor thinks it's time, sir." They dressed hastily, and accompanied the messenger back to the beautiful chamber Ezar had chosen for the last month of his life, its priceless antiques cluttered over with off-worlder medical equipment.

The room was crowded, with the old man's personal physicians, Vortala, Count Piotr and themselves, the Princess and Prince Gregor, several ministers, and some men from the General Staff. They kept a quiet, standing death-watch for almost an hour before the still, decayed figure on the bed took on, almost imperceptibly, an added still-ness. Cordelia thought it a gruesome scene to which to subject the boy, but his presence seemed ceremonially necessary. Very quietly, beginning with Vorkosigan, they turned to kneel and place their hands between Gregor's, to renew their oaths of fealty.

Cordelia too was guided by Vorkosigan to kneel before the boy. The prince—Emperor—had his mother's hair, but hazel eyes like Ezar and Serg, and Cordelia found her-self wondering how much of his father, or his grandfather, was latent in him, its expression waiting on the power that would come with age. *Do you bear curses in your chro-mosomes, child?* she wondered as her hands were placed between his. Cursed or blessed, regardless, she gave him her oath. The words seemed to cut her last tie to Beta Colony; it parted with a *ping!* audible only to her.

I am a Barrayaran now. It had been a long strange journey, that began with a view of a pair of boots in the mud, and ended in these clean child's hands. *Do you know I helped kill your father, boy? Will you ever know? Pray not.* She wondered if it was delicacy or oversight, that she had never been required to give oath to Ezar Vorbarra.

Of all present, only Captain Negri wept. Cordelia only knew this because she was standing next to him, in the darkest corner of the room, and saw him twice brush his face with the back of his hand. His face grew suffused, and more lined, for a time; when he stepped forward to take his oath, it had returned to its normal blank hardness.

The five days of funeral ceremonies that followed were grueling for Cordelia, but not, she was led to understand, so grueling as the ones had been for Crown Prince Serg, which had run for two weeks, despite the absence of a body for a centerpiece. The public view was that Prince Serg had died the death of a heroic soldier. By Cordelia's count, only five human beings knew the whole truth of that subtle assassination. No, four, now that Ezar was no more. Perhaps the grave was the safest repository of Ezar's secrets. Well, the old man's torment was over now, his time done, his era passing.

There was no coronation as such for the boy Emperor, but instead a surprisingly business-like, if elegantly garbed, several days spent back in the Council chambers collecting personal oaths from ministers, counts, a host of their relatives, and anybody else who had not already made their vows in Ezar's death chamber. Vorkosigan too received oaths, seeming to grow burdened with their accumulation as if each had a physical weight.

The boy, closely supported by his mother, held up well. Kareen made sure Gregor's hourly breaks to rest were respected by the busy, impatient men who had thronged to the capital to discharge their obligation. The strangeness of the Barrayaran government system, with all its unwritten customs, pressed on Cordelia not so much at first glance, but gradually. And yet it seemed to work for them, somehow. They made it work. Pretending a government into existence. Perhaps all governments were such consensus fictions, at their hearts.

After the spate of ceremonies had died down, Cordelia began at last to establish her domestic routine at Vorkosigan House. Not that there was that much to do. Most days Vorkosigan left at dawn, Koudelka in tow, and returned after dark, to snatch a cold supper and lock himself in the library, or see men there, until bedtime. His long hours were a start-up cost, Cordelia told herself. He would settle in, become more efficient, when everything wasn't all for the first time. She remembered her first ship command in the Betan Astronomical Survey—not so very long ago—and her first few months of nervous hyper-preparedness. Later, the painfully studied tasks had become automatic, then nearly unconscious, and her personal life had re-emerged. Aral's would, too. She waited patiently, and smiled when she did see him.

Besides, she had a job. Gestating. It was a task of no little status, judging from the cosseting she received from everyone from Count Piotr down to the kitchen maid who brought her nutritious little snacks at odd hours. She hadn't received this much approval even when she'd returned from a yearlong survey mission with a zero-accident record. Reproduction seemed far more enthusiastically encouraged here than on Beta Colony.

After lunch one afternoon she lay with her feet up on a sofa in a shaded patio between the house and its back garden—gestating assiduously—and reflected upon the assorted reproductive customs of Barrayar versus Beta Colony. Gestation in uterine replicators, artifical wombs, seemed unknown here. On Beta Colony replicators were the most popular choice by three to one, but a large minority stood by claimed psycho-social advantages to the old-fashioned natural method. Cordelia had never been able to detect any difference between vitro and vivo babies, certainly not by the time they reached adulthood at twenty-two. Her brother had been vivo, herself vitro; her brother's co-parent had chosen vivo for both her children, and bragged about it rather a lot.

Cordelia had always assumed that when her turn came, she'd have her own kid cooked up in a replicator bank at the start of a Survey mission, to be ready and waiting for her arms upon her return. If she returned—there was always that possible catch, exploring the blind unknown. And assuming, also, that she could nail down an interested co-parent with whom to pool, willing and able to pass the physical, psychological, and economic tests and take the course to qualify for a parent's license.

Aral was going to be a suberb co-parent, she was certain. If he ever touched down again, from his new high

place. Surely the first rush must be over soon. It was a
long fall from that high place, with nowhere to land. Aral
was her safe haven, if he fell first . . . she wrenched her
meditations firmly into more positive channels.

Now, family *size;* that was the real, secret, wicked
fascination of Barrayar. There were no legal limits here,
no certificates to be earned, no third-child variances to
be scrimped for; no rules, in fact, at all. She'd seen a
woman on the street with not three but four children in
tow, and no one had even stared. Cordelia had upped her
own imagined brood from two to three, and felt deliciously
sinful, till she'd met a woman with ten. Four, maybe? Six?
Vorkosigan could afford it. Cordelia wriggled her toes and
cuddled into the cushions, afloat on an atavistic cloud of
genetic greed.

Barrayar's economy was wide open now, Aral said,
despite the losses of the recent war. No wounds had
touched the surface of the planet this time. The
terraforming of the second continent opened new fron-
tiers every day, and when the new planet Sergyar was
cleared for colonization, the effect would triple. Labor was
short everywhere, wages rising. Barrayar perceived itself
to be severely underpopulated. Vorkosigan called the
economic situation his gift from the gods, politically. So
did Cordelia, for more personal, secret reasons; *herds* of
little Vorkosigans. . . .

She could have a daughter. Not just one, but two—
sisters! Cordelia had never had a sister. Captain Vorpatril's
wife had two, she'd said.

Cordelia had meet Lady Vorpatril at one of the rare
evening political-social events at Vorkosigan House. The
affair was managed smoothly by the Vorkosigan House
staff. All Cordelia had to do was show up appropriately
dressed (she had acquired more clothes), smile a lot, and
keep her mouth shut. She listened with fascination, trying to puzzle out yet more about How Things Were Done
Here.

Alys Vorpatril too was pregnant. Lord Vorpatril had sort
of stuck them together and ducked out. Naturally, they

talked shop. Lady Vorpatril mourned much at her personal discomforts. Cordelia decided she herself must be fortunate; the anti-nausea med, the same chemical formulation that they used at home, worked, and she was only naturally tired, not from the weight of the still-tiny baby but from the surprising metabolic load. *Peeing for two* was how Cordelia thought of it. Well, after five-space navigational math, how hard could motherhood be?

Leaving aside Alys's whispered obstetrical horror stories, of course. Hemorrhages, strokes, kidney failure, birth injuries, oxygen interruption to fetal brains, infant heads grown larger than pelvic diameters and a spasming uterus laboring both mother and child to death . . . Medical complications were only a problem if one was somehow caught alone and isolated at term, and with these mobs of guards about that wasn't likely to happen to her. Bothari as a midwife? Bemusing thought. She shuddered.

She rolled over again on the lawn sofa, her brow creasing. Ah, Barrayar's primitive medicine. True, moms had popped kids for hundreds of thousands of years, pre-spaceflight, with less help than what was available here. Yet the niggling worry gnawed still, *Maybe I ought to go home for the birth*.

No. She was Barrayaran now, oath-sworn like the rest of the lunatics. It was a two-month journey. And besides, as far as she knew there was still an arrest warrant outstanding for her, charging military desertion, suspicion of espionage, fraud, anti-social violence—she probably shouldn't have tried to drown that idiot army psychiatrist in her aquarium, Cordelia supposed, sighing in memory of her harried and disordered departure from Beta Colony. Would her name ever be cleared? Not while Ezar's secrets stayed chambered in four skulls, surely.

No. Beta Colony was closed to her, had driven her out. Barrayar held no monopoly on political idiocy, that much was certain.

I can handle Barrayar. Aral and I. You bet.

It was time to go in. The sun was giving her a slight headache.

CHAPTER FOUR

One aspect of her new life as Regent-consort that Cordelia found easier to deal with than she'd anticipated was the influx of personal guards into their home. Her experience in the Betan Survey, and Vorkosigan's in the Barrayaran military service, had given them both practice with life in close quarters. It didn't take Cordelia long to start to know the persons in the uniforms, and take them on their own terms. The guards were a lively young group, hand-picked for their service and proud of it. Although when Piotr was also in residence, with all his liveried men including Bothari, the sense it gave Cordelia of living in a barracks became acute.

It was the Count who first suggested the informal hand-to-hand combat tournament between Illyan's men and his own. In spite of a vague mutter from the security commander about free training at the Emperor's expense, a ring was set up in the back garden, and the contest quickly became a weekly tradition. Even Koudelka was roped in, as referee and expert judge, with Piotr and Cordelia as cheering sections. Vorkosigan attended whenever time permitted, to Cordelia's gratification; she felt he needed the break in the grinding routine of government business to which he subjected himself daily.

Cordelia was settling down on the upholstered lawn sofa to watch the show one sunny autumn morning, attended by her handmaiden, when she suddenly remarked, "Why aren't you playing, Drou? Surely you need the practice as much as any of them. The excuse for this thing in the first place—not that you Barrayarans seem to need an excuse to practice mayhem—was that it was supposed to keep everybody on their toes."

Droushnakovi looked longingly at the ring, but said, "I wasn't invited, Milady."

"A rude oversight on somebody's part. Hm. Tell you what—go change your clothes. You can be my team. Aral can root for his own today. A proper Barrayaran contest should have at least three sides anyway, it's traditional."

"Do you think it will be all right?" she said doubtfully. "They might not like it."

The *they* in question were what Droushnakovi called the "real" guards, the liveried men.

"Aral won't mind. Anyone else who objects can argue with him. If they dare." Cordelia grinned, and Droushnakovi grinned back, then dashed off.

Aral arrived to settle comfortably beside her, and she told him of her plan. He raised an eyebrow. "Betan innovations? Well, why not? Brace yourself for chaff, though."

"I'm braced. They won't be as inclined to make jokes if she can pound a few of them. I think she can—on Beta Colony that girl would be a commando officer by now. All that natural talent is wasted toddling around after me all day. If she can't—well, then she shouldn't be guarding me anyway, eh?" She met his eyes.

"Point taken . . . I'll make sure Koudelka puts her in the first round against someone of her own height and weight class. In absolute terms she's a bit on the small side."

"She's bigger than you are."

"In height. I imagine I have a few kilos on her in weight. Nevertheless, your wish is my command. Oof." He climbed back to his feet, and went to enter Droushnakovi on Koudelka's list for the lists. Cordelia could not hear what they said to each other, across the garden, but supplied her own dialogue from gesture and expression, murmuring, "Aral: Cordelia wants Drou to play. Kou: Aw! Who wants *gurls?* Aral: Tough. Kou: They mess everything up, and besides, they cry a lot. Sergeant Bothari will squash her— hm, I do hope that's what that gesture means, otherwise you're getting obscene, Kou—wipe that smirk off your face, Vorkosigan—Aral: The little woman insists. You know how henpecked I am. Kou: Oh, all right. Phooey. Transaction complete: the rest is up to you, Drou."

Vorkosigan rejoined her. "All set. She'll start against one of father's men."

Droushnakovi returned, attired in loose slacks and a knit shirt, as close to the men's workout suits as her wardrobe could provide. The Count came out to consult with Sergeant Bothari, his team leader, and find a place to warm his bones in the sun beside them.

"What's this?" Piotr asked, as Koudelka called Droushnakovi's name for the second pair up. "Are we importing Betan customs now?"

"The girl has a lot of natural talent," Vorkosigan explained. "Besides, she needs the practice as much as any of them—more; she has the most important job of any of them."

"You'll be wanting women in the Service, next," complained Piotr. "Where will it end? That's what I'd like to know."

"What's wrong with women in the Service?" Cordelia asked, baiting him a little.

"It's unmilitary," snapped the old man.

" 'Military' is whatever wins the war, I should think." She smiled blandly. A small friendly warning pinch from Vorkosigan restrained her from rubbing in the point any harder.

In any case it wasn't necessary. Piotr turned to watch his player, saying only, "Humph."

The Count's player carelessly underestimated his

opponent, and took the first fall for his error. It woke him up considerably. The onlookers shouted raucous comments. He pinned her on the next fall.

"Koudelka counted a bit fast there, didn't he?" asked Cordelia, as the Count's player let Droushnakovi up after the decision.

"Mm. Maybe," said Vorkosigan in a non-committal tone.

"She pulls her punches a bit, too, I notice. She'll never make it to the next round if she keeps doing that in this company."

On the next encounter, the deciding one for the two-out-of-three, Droushnakovi applied a successful arm-bar, but let it slip away from her.

"Oh, too bad," murmured the Count cheerfully.

"You should have let him break it!" cried Cordelia, getting more and more involved. The Count's player took a soft and sloppy fall. "Call it, Kou!" But the referee, leaning on his stick, let it pass. In any case, Droushnakovi spotted an opportunity for a choke, and grabbed it.

"Why doesn't he tap out?" asked Cordelia.

"He'd rather pass out," replied Aral. "That way he won't have to listen to his friends."

Droushnakovi was beginning to look doubtful, as the face clamped under her arm turned a dusky purple. Cordelia could see release coming, and leaped up to shout, "Hang on, Drou! Don't let him fake you out!" Droushnakovi took a firmer hold, and the figure stopped struggling.

"Go ahead and call it, Koudelka," called Piotr, shaking his head ruefully. "He has to be on duty tonight." And so the round went to Droushnakovi.

"Good work, Drou!" said Cordelia as Droushnakovi returned to them. "But you've got to be more aggressive. Release your killer instincts."

"I agree," said Vorkosigan unexpectedly. "That little hesitation you display could be deadly—and not just for yourself." He held her eye. "You're practicing for the real thing here, although we all pray that no such situation occurs. The kind of all-out effort it takes should be absolutely automatic."

"Yes, sir. I'll try, sir."

The next round featured Sergeant Bothari, who flattened his opponent twice in rapid succession. The defeated crawled out of the ring. Several more rounds went by, and it was Droushnakovi's turn again, this time with one of Illyan's men.

They connected, and in the struggle he goosed her effectively, loosing catcalls from the audience. In her angry distraction, he pulled her off-balance for a fairly clean fall.

"Did you see that!" cried Cordelia to Aral. "That was a dirty trick!"

"Mm. It wasn't one of the eight forbidden blows, though. You couldn't disqualify him on it. Nevertheless . . ." he motioned Koudelka for a time-out, and called Droushnakovi over for a quiet word.

"We saw the blow," he murmured. Her lips were tight and her face red. "Now, as Milady's champion, an insult to you is in some measure an insult to her. Also a very bad precedent. It is my desire that your opponent not leave the ring conscious. How, is your problem. You may take that as an order, if you like. And don't worry needlessly about breaking bones, either," he added blandly.

Droushnakovi returned to the ring with a slight smile on her face, eyes narrowed and glittering. She followed a feint with a lightning kick to her opponent's jaw, a punch to his belly, and a low body blow to his knees that brought him down with a boom on the matting. He did not get up. There was a slightly shocked silence.

"You're right," said Vorkosigan. "She was pulling her punches."

Cordelia smiled smugly, and settled herself more comfortably. "Thought so."

The next round to come up for Droushnakovi was the semi-final, and it was the luck of the draw that her opponent was Sergeant Bothari.

"Hm," murmured Cordelia to Vorkosigan. "I'm not sure about the psychodynamics of this. Is it safe? I mean for both of them, not just for her. And not just physically."

"I think so," he replied, equally quietly. "Life in the

Count's service has been a nice, quiet routine for Bothari. He's been taking his medication. I think he's in pretty good shape at the moment. And the atmosphere of the practice ring is a safe, familiar one for him. It would take more tension than Drou can provide to unhinge him."

Cordelia nodded, satisfied, and settled back to watch the slaughter. Droushnakovi looked nervous.

The start was slow, with Droushnakovi mainly concentrating on staying out of reach. Swinging around to watch, Lieutenant Koudelka accidently pressed the release of his swordstick, and the cover shot off into the bushes. Bothari was distracted for an instant, and Drou struck, low and fast. Bothari landed clean with a firm impact, although he rolled immediately to his feet with scarcely a pause.

"Oh, good throw!" cried Cordelia ecstatically. Drou looked quite as amazed as everyone else. "Call it, Kou!"

Lieutenant Koudelka frowned. "It wasn't a fair throw, Milady." One of the Count's men retrieved the cover, and Koudelka resheathed the weapon. "It was my fault. Unfair distraction."

"You didn't call it unfair distraction a while ago," Cordelia objected.

"Let it go, Cordelia," said Vorkosigan quietly.

"But he's cheating her out of her point!" she whispered back furiously. "And what a point! Bothari's been tops in every round to date."

"Yes. It took six months practice on the old *General Vorkraft* before Koudelka ever threw him."

"Oh. Hm." That gave her pause. "Jealousy?"

"Haven't you seen it? She has everything he lost."

"I have seen he's been blasted rude to her on occasion. It's a shame. She's obviously—"

Vorkosigan held up a restraining finger. "Talk about it later. Not here."

She paused, then nodded in agreement. "Right."

The round went on, with Sergeant Bothari putting Droushnakovi practically through the mat, twice, quickly, and then dispatching his final challenger with almost equal ease.

A conference of players on the other side of the garden sent Koudelka limping over as an emissary.

"Sir? We were wondering if you would go a demonstration round. With Sergeant Bothari. None of the fellows here have ever seen that."

Vorkosigan waved down the idea, not very convincingly. "I'm not in shape for it, Lieutenant. Besides, how did they ever find out about that? Been telling tales?"

Koudelka grinned. "A few. I think it would enlighten them. About what kind of game this can really be."

"A bad example, I'm afraid."

"I've never seen this," murmured Cordelia. "Is it really that good a show?"

"I don't know. Have I offended you lately? Would watching Bothari pound me be a catharsis?"

"I think it would be for you," said Cordelia, falling in with his obvious desire to be persuaded. "I think you've missed that sort of thing, in this headquarters life you've been leading lately."

"Yes. . . ." He rose, to a bit of clapping, and removed uniform jacket, shoes, rings, and the contents of his pockets, and stepped to the ring to do some stretching and warm-up exercises.

"You'd better referee, Kou," he called back. "Just to prevent undue alarm."

"Yes, sir." Koudelka turned to Cordelia before limping back to the arena. "Um. Just remember, Milady. They never killed each other in four years of this."

"Why do I find that more ominous than reassuring? Still, Bothari's done six rounds this morning. Maybe he's getting tired."

The two men faced off in the arena and bowed formally. Koudelka backed hastily out of the way. The raucous good humor died away among the watchers, as the icy cold and concentrated stillness of the two players drew all eyes. They began to circle, lightly, then met in a blur. Cordelia did not quite see what happened, but when they parted Vorkosigan was spitting blood from a lacerated mouth, and Bothari was hunched over his belly.

In the next contact Bothari landed a kick to Vorkosigan's back that echoed off the garden walls and propelled him completely out of the arena, to land rolling and running back in spite of disrupted breathing. The men in whose protection the Regent's life was supposed to lie began to look worriedly at one another. At the next grappling Vorkosigan underwent a vicious fall, with Bothari landing atop him instantly for a follow-up choke. Cordelia thought she could see his ribs bend from the knees on his chest. A couple of the guards started forward, but Koudelka waved them back, and Vorkosigan, face dark and suffused, tapped out.

"First point to Sergeant Bothari," called Koudelka. "Best two out of three, sir?"

Sergeant Bothari stood, smiling a little, and Vorkosigan sat on the mat a minute, regaining his wind. "One more, anyway. Got to get my revenge. Out of shape."

"Told you so," murmured Bothari.

They circled again. They met, parted, met again, and suddenly Bothari was doing a spectacular cartwheel, while Vorkosigan rolled beneath to grab an arm-bar that nearly dislocated his shoulder in his twisting fall. Bothari struggled briefly against the lock, then tapped out. This time it was Bothari who sat on the mat a minute before getting up.

"That's amazing," Droushnakovi commented, eyes avid. "Especially considering how much smaller he is."

"Small but vicious," agreed Cordelia, fascinated. "Keep that in mind."

The third round was brief. A blur of grappling and blows and messy joint fall resolved suddenly in an armlock, with Bothari in charge. Vorkosigan unwisely attempted a break, and Bothari, quite expressionlessly, dislocated his elbow with an audible pop. Vorkosigan yelled and tapped out. Once again Koudelka suppressed a rush of uninvited aid.

"Put it back, Sergeant," Vorkosigan groaned from his seat on the ground, and Bothari braced one foot on his former captain and gave the arm an accurately aligned yank.

"Must remember," gasped Vorkosigan, "not to do that."

"At least he didn't break it this time," said Koudelka encouragingly, and helped him up, with Bothari's assistance. Vorkosigan limped back to the lawn chair, and seated himself, very cautiously, at Cordelia's feet. Bothari, too, was moving a lot more slowly and stiffly.

"And that," said Vorkosigan, still catching his breath, "is how . . . we used to play the game . . . aboard the old *General Vorkraft*."

"All that effort," remarked Cordelia. "And how often did you ever get into a real hand-to-hand combat situation?"

"Very, very seldom. But when we did, we won."

The party broke up, with a murmuring undercurrent of comment from the other players. Cordelia accompanied Aral off to help with first-aid to his elbow and mouth, a hot soak and rubdown, and a change of clothes.

During the rubdown she brought up the personnel problem that had been growing in her notice.

"Do you suppose you could say something to Kou about the way he treats Drou? It's not like his usual self at all. She about does flips trying to be nice to him. And he doesn't even treat her with the courtesy he'd give one of his men. She's practically a fellow officer. And, unless I'm totally wide of the mark, madly in love with him. Why doesn't he see it?"

"What makes you think he doesn't?" asked Aral slowly.

"His behavior, of course. A shame. They'd make quite a pair. Don't you think she's attractive?"

"Marvelously. But then, I like tall amazons," he grinned over his shoulder at her, "as everyone knows. It's not every man's taste. But if that's a matchmaking gleam I detect in your eye—do you suppose it could be maternal hormones, by the way?"

"Shall I dislocate your other elbow?"

"Ugh. No thanks. I'd forgotten how painful a workout with Bothari could be. Ah, that's better. Down a bit . . ."

"You're going to have some astonishing bruises there tomorrow."

"Don't I know it. But before you get carried away over Drou's love life . . . have you thought carefully about Koudelka's injuries?"

"Oh." Cordelia was struck silent. "I'd assumed . . . that his sexual functions were as well repaired as the rest of him."

"Or as poorly. It's a very delicate bit of surgery."

Cordelia pursed her lips. "Do you know this for a fact?"

"No, I don't. I do know that in all our conversations the subject was never once brought up. Ever."

"Hm. Wish I knew how to interpret that. It sounds a little ominous. Do you think you could ask . . . ?"

"Good God, Cordelia, of course not! What a question to ask the man. Particularly if the answer is no. I've got to work with him, remember."

"Well, I've got to work with Drou. She's no use to me if she pines away and dies of a broken heart. He has reduced her to tears, more than once. She goes off where she thinks nobody's looking."

"Really? That's hard to imagine."

"You can hardly expect me to tell her he's not worth it, all things considered. But does he really dislike her? Or is it just self-defense?"

"Good question . . . For what it's worth, my driver made a joke about her the other day—not even a very offensive one—and Kou got rather frosty with him. I don't think he dislikes her. But I do think he envies her."

Cordelia left the subject on that ambiguous note. She longed to help the pair, but had no answer to offer for their dilemma. Her own mind had no trouble generating creative solutions to the practical problems of physical intimacy posed by the lieutenant's injuries, but shrank from the violation of their shy reserve that offering them would entail. She suspected wryly that she would merely shock them. Sex therapy appeared to be unheard of, here.

True Betan, she had always considered a double standard of sexual behavior to be a logical impossibility. Dabbling now on the fringes of Barrayaran high society in Vorkosigan's wake, she began to finally see how it could be done. It all seemed to come down to impeding the free flow of information to certain persons, preselected by an unspoken code somehow known to and agreed upon by all present but her. One could not mention sex to or in front of unmarried women or children. Young men, it appeared, were exempt from all rules when talking to each other, but not if a woman of any age or degree were present. The rules also changed bewilderingly with variations of the social status of those present. And married women, in groups free of male eavesdroppers, sometimes underwent the most astonishing transformations in apparent databases. Some subjects could be joked about but not discussed seriously. And some variations could not be mentioned at all. She had blighted more than one conversation beyond hope of recovery by what seemed to her a perfectly obvious and casual remark, and been taken aside by Aral for a quick debriefing.

She tried writing out a list of the rules she thought she had deduced, but found them so illogical and conflicting, especially in the area of what certain people were supposed to pretend not to know in front of certain other people, she gave up the effort. She did show the list to Aral, who read it in bed one night and nearly doubled over laughing.

"Is that what we really look like to you? I like your Rule Seven. Must keep it in mind . . . I wish I'd known it in my youth. I could have skipped all those godawful Service training vids."

"If you snicker any harder, you're going to get a nosebleed," she said tartly. "These are your rules, not mine. You people play by them. I just try to figure them out."

"My sweet scientist. Hm. You certainly call things by their correct names. We've never tried . . . would you like to violate Rule Eleven with me, dear Captain?"

"Let me, see, which one—oh, yes! Certainly. Now? And while we're about it, let's knock off Thirteen. My hormones are up. I remember my brother's co-parent told me about this effect, but I didn't really believe her at the time. She says you make up for it later, post-partum."

"Thirteen? I'd never have guessed. . . ."

"That's because, being Barrayaran, you spend so much time following Rule Two."

Anthropology was forgotten, for a time. But she found she could crack him up, later, with a properly timed mutter of "Rule Nine, sir."

The season was turning. There had been a hint of winter in the air that morning, a frost that had wilted some of the plants in Count Piotr's back garden. Cordelia anticipated her first real winter with fascination. Vorkosigan promised her snow, frozen water, something she'd experienced on only two Survey missions. *Before spring, I shall bear a son. Huh.*

But the afternoon had basked in the autumn light, warming again. The flat roof of Vorkosigan House above the front wing now breathed back that heat around Cordelia's ankles as she picked her way across it, though the air on her cheeks was cooling to crispness as the sun slanted to the city's horizon.

"Good evening, boys." Cordelia nodded to the two guards posted to this rooftop duty station.

They nodded back, the senior touching his forehead in a hesitant semi-salute. "Milady."

Cordelia had taken to regular sunset-watching up here. The view of the cityscape from this four-floors-up vantage was very fine. She could catch a gleam of the river that divided the town, beyond trees and buildings. Although the excavation of a large hole a few blocks away along the line of sight suggested that the riverine scene would be occluded soon by new architecture. The tallest turret of Vorhartung Castle, where she'd attended all those ceremonies in the Council of Counts' chamber, peaked from a bluff overlooking the water.

Beyond Vorhartung Castle lay the oldest parts of the capital. She'd not yet seen that area, its kinked one-horse-wide streets impassable to groundcars, though she'd flown over the strange, low, dark blots in the heart of the city. The newer parts, glittering out toward the horizon, were more like galactic standard, patterned around the modern transportation systems.

None of it was like Beta Colony. Vorbarr Sultana was all spread out on the surface, or climbed skyward, strangely two-dimensional and exposed. Beta Colony's cities plunged down into shafts and tunnels, many-layered and complex, cozy and safe. Indeed, Beta Colony did not have architecture so much as it had interior design. It was amazing, the variety of schemes people came up with to vary dwellings that had *outsides*.

The guards twitched and sighed, as she leaned on the stonework, gazing out. They really didn't like it when she strayed nearer than three meters to the edge, though the space was only six meters wide. But she should be able to spot Vorkosigan's groundcar turning into the street soon. Sunsets were all very well, but her eyes turned downward.

She inhaled the complex odors, from vegetation, water vapor, industrial waste gases. Barrayar permitted an amazing amount of air dumping, as if . . . well, air *was* free, here. Nobody measured it, there were no air processing and filtration fees. . . . Did these people even realize how rich they were? All the air they could breathe, just by stepping outdoors, taken for granted as casually as they took frozen water falling from the sky. She took an extra breath, as if she could somehow greedily hoard it, and smiled—

A distant, crackling, hard-edged *boom* shattered her thoughts and stopped her breath. Both guards jumped. *So, you heard a bang. It doesn't necessarily have anything to do with Aral.* And, icily, *It sounded like a sonic grenade. Not a little one. Dear God.* There was a column of smoke and dust rising from a street-canyon several blocks over, she couldn't see the source—she craned outward—

"Milady." The younger guard grasped her upper arm. "Please go inside." His face was tense, eyes wide. The senior man had his hand clamped to his ear, sucking info off his comm channel—*she* had no comm link.

"What's coming on?" she asked.

"Milady, please go below!" He hustled her toward the trapdoor to the attic, from which stairs led down to the fourth floor. "I'm sure it was nothing," he soothed as he pushed.

"It was a Class Four sonic grenade, probably air-tube launched," she informed his appalling ignorance. "Unless the thrower was suicidal. Haven't you ever heard one go off?"

Droushnakovi shot out the trapdoor, a buttered roll squashed in one hand and her stunner clutched in the other. "Milady?" The guard, looking relieved, shoved Cordelia at her and returned to his senior. Cordelia, screaming inside, grinned through clenched teeth and allowed herself to be guarded, climbing dutifully down the trap.

"What happened?" she hissed to Droushnakovi.

"Don't know yet. The red alert went off in the basement refectory, and everybody ran for their posts," panted Drou. She must have practically teleported up the six flights.

"*Ngh.*" Cordelia galloped down the stairs, wishing for a drop tube. The comconsole in the library would surely be manned—somebody must have a comm link—she spun down the circular staircase and pelted across the black and white stones.

The house guard commander was indeed at the post, channeling orders. Count Piotr's senior liveried man jittered at his shoulder. "They're coming straight here," the ImpSec man said over his shoulder. "You fetch that doctor." The brown-uniformed man dashed out.

"What happened?" Cordelia demanded. Her heart was hammering now, and not just from the dash downstairs.

He glanced up at her, started to say something calming and meaningless, and changed his mind in mid-breath. "Somebody took a potshot at the Regent's groundcar. They missed. They're continuing on here."

"How near a miss?"

"I don't know, Milady."

He probably didn't. But if the groundcar still functioned . . . Helplessly, she gestured him back to his work, and wheeled to return to the foyer, now manned by a couple of Count Piotr's men, who discouraged her from standing too near the door. She hung on the stair railing three steps up and bit her lip.

"Was Lieutenant Koudelka with him, do you think?" asked Droushnakovi faintly.

"Probably. He usually is," Cordelia answered absently, her eyes on the door, waiting, waiting. . . .

She heard the car pull up. One of Count Piotr's men opened the house door. Security men swarmed over the silver shape of the vehicle in the portico—God, where did they all *come* from? The car's shiny finish was scored and smoked, but not deeply dented; the rear canopy was not cracked, though the front was scarred. The rear doors swung up, and Cordelia stretched for a view of Vorkosigan, maddeningly obstructed by the green backs of the ImpSec men. They parted. Lieutenant Koudelka sat in the aperture, blinking dizzily, blood dripping down his chin, then was levered to his feet by a guard. Vorkosigan emerged at last, refusing to be hustled, waving back help. Even the most worried guards did not dare to touch him without an invitation. Vorkosigan strode inside, grim-faced and pale. Koudelka, propped by his stick and an ImpSec corporal, followed, looking wilder. The blood issued from his nose. Piotr's man swung closed the front door of Vorkosigan House, shutting out three-fourths of the chaos.

Aral met her eyes, above the heads of the men, and the saturnine look fixed on his face slipped just a little. He offered her a fractional nod, *I'm all right.* Her lips tightened in return, *You'd by-God better be. . . .*

Kou was saying in a shaken voice, "—bloody great hole in the street! Could've swallowed a freight shuttle. That driver has amazing reflexes—what?" He shook his head at a questioner. "Sorry, my ears are ringing—come again?" He stood openmouthed, as if he could drink in sound orally, touched his face and stared in surprise at his crimson-smeared hand.

"Your ears are only stunned, Kou," said Vorkosigan. His voice was calm, but much too loud. "They'll be back to normal by tomorrow morning." Only Cordelia realized the raised tone wasn't for Koudelka's benefit—Vorkosigan couldn't hear himself, either. His eyes shifted too quickly, the only hint that he was trying to read lips.

Simon Illyan and a physician arrived at almost the same moment. Vorkosigan and Koudelka were taken to a quiet back parlor, shedding all the—to Cordelia's mind—rather useless guards. Cordelia and Droushnakovi followed. The physician began an immediate examination, starting, at Vorkosigan's command, with the gory Koudelka.

"One shot?" asked Illyan.

"Only one," confirmed Vorkosigan, watching his face. "If they'd lingered for a second try, they could have bracketed me."

"If he'd lingered, we could have bracketed *him*. A forensic team's on the firing site now. The assassin's long gone, of course. A clever spot, he had a dozen escape routes."

"We vary our route daily," Lieutenant Koudelka, following this with difficulty, said around the cloth he pressed to his face. "How did he know where to set up his ambush?"

"Inside information?" Illyan shrugged, his teeth clenching at the thought.

"Not necessarily," said Vorkosigan. "There are only so many routes, this close to home. He could have been set up waiting for days."

"Precisely at the limit of our close-search perimeter?" said Illyan. "I don't like it."

"It bothers me more that he missed," said Vorkosigan. "Why? Could it have been some sort of warning shot? An attempt, not on my life, but on my balance of mind?"

"It was old ordnance," said Illyan. "There could have been something wrong with its tracker—nobody detected a laser rangefinder pulse." He paused, taking in Cordelia's white face. "I'm sure it was a lone lunatic, Milady. At least, it was certainly only one man."

"How does a lone maniac get hold of military-grade weaponry?" she inquired tartly.

Illyan looked uncomfortable. "We will be investigating that. It was definitely old issue."

"Don't you destroy obsolete stockpiles?"

"There's so much of it. . . ."

Cordelia glared at this wit-scattered utterance. "He only needed one shot. If he'd managed a direct hit on that sealed car, Aral'd have been emulsified. Your forensic team would be trying right now to sort out which molecules were his and which were Kou's."

Droushnakovi turned faintly green; Vorkosigan's saturnine look was now firmly back in place.

"You want me to give you a precise resonance reflection amplitude calculation for that sealed passenger cabin, Simon?" Cordelia went on hotly. "Whoever chose that weapon was a competent military tech—if, fortunately, a poorish shot." She bit back further words, recognizing, even if no one else did, the suppressed hysteria driving the speed of her speech.

"My apologies. Captain Naismith." Illyan's tone grew more clipped. "You are quite correct." His nod was a shade more respectful.

Aral tracked this interplay, his face lightening, for the first time, with some hidden amusement.

Illyan took himself off, conspiracy theories no doubt dancing in his head. The doctor confirmed Aral's combat-experienced diagnosis of aural stun, issued powerful anti-headache pills—Aral hung on to his firmly—and made an appointment to re-check both men in the morning.

When Illyan stopped back by Vorkosigan House in the late evening to confer with his guard commander, it was all Cordelia could do not to grab him by the jacket and pin him to the nearest wall to shake out his information. She confined herself to simply asking, "Who tried to kill Aral? Who *wants* to kill Aral? Whatever benefit do they imagine they'll gain?"

Illyan sighed. "Do you want the short list, or the long one, Milady?"

"How long is the short list?" she asked in morbid fascination.

"Too long. But I can name you the top layer, if you like." He ticked them off on his fingers. "The Cetagandans, always. They had counted on political chaos here, following Ezar's death. They're not above prodding it along. An assassination is cheap interference, compared to an invasion fleet. The Komarrans, for old revenge or new revolt. Some there still call the Admiral the Butcher of Komarr—"

Cordelia, knowing the whole story behind that loathed sobriquet, winced.

"The anti-Vor, because my lord Regent is too conservative for their tastes. The military right, who fear he is too progressive for theirs. Leftover members of Prince Serg and Vorrutyer's old war party. Former operatives of the now-suppressed Ministry of Political Education, though I doubt one of them would have missed. Negri's department used to train them. Some disgruntled Vor who thinks he came out short in the recent power-shift. Any lunatic with access to weapons and a desire for instant fame as a big-game hunter—shall I go on?"

"Please don't. But what about today? If motive yields too broad a field of suspects, what about method and opportunity?"

"We have a little to work with there, though too much of it is negative. As I noted, it was a very clean attempt. Whoever set it up had to have access to certain kinds of knowledge. We'll work those angles first."

It was the anonymity of the assassination attempt that bothered her most, Cordelia decided. When the killer could be anyone, the impulse to suspect everyone became overwhelming. Paranoia was a contagious disease here, it seemed; Barrayarans gave it to each other. Well, Negri and Illyan's combined forces must winkle out some concrete facts soon. She packed all her fears down hard into a little tiny compartment in the pit of her stomach, and locked them there. Next to her child.

Vorkosigan held her tight that night, curled into the

curve of his stocky body, though he made no sexual advances. He just held her. He didn't fall asleep for hours, despite the painkillers that glazed his eyes. She didn't fall asleep till he did. His snores lulled her at last. There wasn't that much to say. *They missed; we go on.*

Till the next try.

CHAPTER FIVE

The Emperor's Birthday was a traditional Barrayaran holiday, celebrated with feasting, dancing, drinking, veterans' parades, and an incredible amount of apparently totally unregulated fireworks. It would make a great day for a surprise attack on the capital, Cordelia decided; an artillery barrage could be well under way before anybody noticed it in the general din. The uproar began at dawn.

The duty guards, who had a natural tendency to jump at sudden noises anyway, were twitchy and miserable, except for a couple more youthful types who attempted to celebrate with a few crackers let off inside the walls. They were taken aside by the guard commander, and emerged much later, pale and shrunken, to slink off. Cordelia later saw them hauling rubbish under the command of a sardonic housemaid, while a scullery girl and the second cook galloped happily out of the house for a surprise day off. The Emperor's Birthday was a moveable feast. The Barrayarans' enthusiasm for the holiday seemed undaunted by the fact that, due to Ezar's death and Gregor's ascension, this was the second time they would celebrate it this year.

Cordelia passed up an invitation to attend a major

military review that gobbled Aral's morning in favor of staying fresh for the event of the evening—the event of the year, she was given to understand—personal attendence upon the Emperor's birthday dinner at the Imperial Residence. She looked forward to seeing Kareen and Gregor again, however briefly. At least she was certain that her clothing was all right. Lady Vorpatril, who had both excellent taste and an advance line on Barrayaran-style maternity wear, had taken pity on Cordelia's cultural bafflement and offered herself as an expert native guide.

As a result, Cordelia confidently wore an impeccably cut forest green silk dress that swirled from shoulder to floor, with an open overvest of thick ivory velvet. Live flowers in matching colors were arranged in her copper hair by the live human hairdresser Alys also sent on. Like their public events, the Barrayarans made of their clothes a sort of folk-art, as elaborate as Betan body paint. Cordelia couldn't be sure from Aral—his face always lit when he saw her—but judging from the delighted "Oohs" of Count Piotr's female staff, Cordelia's sartorial art team had outdone themselves.

Waiting at the foot of the spiral stairs in the front hall, she smoothed the panel of green silk surreptitiously down over her belly. A little over three months of metabolic overdrive, and all she had to show for it was this grape-fruit-sized lump—so much had happened since midsummer, it seemed like her pregnancy ought to be progressing faster to keep up. She purred an encouraging mental mantra bellywards, *Grow, grow, grow. . . .* At least she was actually beginning to look pregnant, instead of just feel exhausted. Aral shared her nightly fascination with their progress, gently feeling with spread fingers, so far without success, for the butterfly-wing flutters of movement through her skin.

Aral himself now appeared, with Lieutenant Koudelka. They were both thoroughly scrubbed, shaved, cut, combed, and chromatically blinding in their formal red-and-blue Imperial parade uniforms. Count Piotr joined them wearing the uniform Cordelia had seen him in at the Joint Council sessions, brown and silver, a more glittery version of his armsmen's livery. All twenty of Piotr's armsmen had some sort of formal function tonight, and had been driven to meticulous preparation all week by their frenzied commander. Droushnakovi, accompanying Cordelia, wore a simplified garment in Cordelia's colors, carefully cut to facilitate rapid movement and conceal weaponry and comm links.

After a moment for everyone to admire each other, they herded through the front doors to the waiting groundcars. Aral handed Cordelia into her vehicle personally, then stepped back. "See you there, love."

"What?" Her head swiveled. "Oh. Then that second car . . . isn't just for the size of the group?"

Aral's mouth tightened fractionally. "No. It seems . . . prudent, to me, that we should travel in separate vehicles from now on."

"Yes," she said faintly. "Quite."

He nodded, and turned away. *Damn* this place. Taking yet another bite out of their lives, out of her heart. They had so little time together anymore, losing even a little more hurt.

Count Piotr, apparently, was to be Aral's stand-in, at least for tonight; he slid in beside her. Droushnakovi sat across from them, and the canopy was sealed. The car turned smoothly into the street. Cordelia craned over her shoulder, trying to see Aral's car, but it followed too far back for her even to catch a glimpse. She straightened, sighing.

The sun was sinking yellowly in a grey bank of clouds, and lights were beginning to glow in the cool damp autumn evening, giving the city a somber, melancholy atmosphere. Maybe a raucous street party—they drove around several—wasn't such a bad idea. The celebrators reminded Cordelia of primitive Earth men banging pots and firing guns to drive off the dragon that was eating the eclipsing moon. This strange autumn sadness could consume an unwary soul. Gregor's birthday was well timed.

Piotr's knobby hands fiddled with a brown silk bag embroidered with the Vorkosigan crest in silver. Cordelia eyed it with interest. "What's that?"

Piotr smiled slightly, and handed it to her. "Gold coins."

More folk-art; the bag and its contents were a tactile treat. She caressed the silk, admired the needlework, and shook a few gleaming sculptured disks out into her hand. "Pretty." Prior to the end of the Time of Isolation, gold had had great value on Barrayar, Cordelia recalled reading. *Gold* to her Betan mind called up something like, *Sometimes-useful metal to the electronics industry,* but ancient peoples had waxed mystical about it. "Does this mean something?"

"Ha! Indeed. It's the Emperor's birthday present."

Cordelia pictured five-year-old Gregor playing with a bag of gold. Besides building towers and maybe practicing counting, it was hard to figure what the boy could do with it. She hoped he was past the age of putting everything in his mouth; those disks were just the right size for a child to swallow or choke on. "I'm sure he'll like it," she said a little doubtfully.

Piotr chuckled. "You don't know what's going on, do you?"

Cordelia sighed. "I almost never do. Cue me." She settled back, smiling. Piotr had gradually become an enthusiast in explaining Barrayar to her, always seeming pleased to discover some new pocket of her ignorance and fill it with information and opinion. She had the feeling he could be lecturing her for the next twenty years and not run out of baffling topics.

"The Emperor's birthday is the traditional end of the fiscal year, for each count's district in relation to the Imperial government. In other words, it's tax day, except— the Vor are not taxed. That would imply too subordinate a relationship to the Imperium. Instead, we give the Emperor a present."

"Ah . . ." said Cordelia. "You don't run this place for a year on sixty little bags of gold, sir."

"Of course not. The real funds went from Hassadar to Vorbarr Sultana by comm link transfer earlier today. The gold is merely symbolic."

Cordelia frowned. "Wait. Haven't you done this once this year?"

"In the spring for Ezar, yes. So we've just changed the date of our fiscal year."

"Isn't that disruptive to your banking system?"

He shrugged. "We manage." He grinned suddenly. "Where do you think the term 'Count' came from, anyway?"

"Earth, I thought. A pre-atomic—late Roman, actually—term for a nobleman who ran a county. Or maybe the district was named after the rank."

"On Barrayar, it is in fact a contraction of the term 'accountant.' The first 'counts were Varadar Tau's—an amazing bandit, you should read up on him sometime—Varadar Tau's tax collectors."

"All this time I thought it was a military rank! Aping medieval history."

"Oh, the military part came immediately thereafter, the first time the old goons tried to shake down somebody who didn't want to contribute. The rank acquired more glamour later."

"I never knew." She regarded him with sudden suspicion. "You're not pulling my leg, sir, are you?"

He spread his hands in denial.

Check your assumptions, Cordelia thought to herself in amusement. *In fact, check your assumptions at the door*.

They arrived at the Imperial Residence's great gate. The ambiance was much changed tonight from some of Cordelia's earlier, more morbid visits to the dying Ezar and to the funeral ceremonies. Colored lights picked out architectural details on the stone pile. The gardens glowed, fountains glittered. Beautifully dressed people warmed the landscape, spilling out from the formal rooms of the north wing onto the terraces. The guard checks, however, were no less meticulous, and the guards' numbers were vastly multiplied. Cordelia had the feeling this was going to be a much less rowdy party than some they'd passed in the city streets.

Aral's car pulled up behind theirs as they disembarked at a western portico, and Cordelia reattached herself gratefully to his arm. He smiled proudly at her, and in a relatively unobserved moment sneaked a kiss onto the back of her neck while stealing a whiff of the flowers perfuming her hair. She squeezed his hand secretly in return. They passed through the doors, and a corridor. A majordomo in Vorbarra House livery loudly announced them, and then they were pinned by the gaze of what to Cordelia for a moment seemed several thousand pairs of critical Barrayaran Vor-class eyes. Actually there were only a couple hundred people in the room. Better than, say, looking down the throat of a fully charged nerve disruptor any day. Really.

They circulated, exchanging greetings, making courtesies. *Why can't these people wear nametags?* Cordelia thought hopelessly. As usual, everyone but her seemed to know everyone else. She pictured herself opening a conversation, *Hey you, Vor-guy*—. She clutched Aral more firmly, and tried to look mysterious and exotic rather than tongue-tied and mislaid.

They found the little ceremony with the bags of coins going on in another chamber, the counts or their representatives lining up to discharge their obligation with a few formal words each. Emperor Gregor, whom Cordelia suspected was up past his bedtime, sat on a raised bench with his mother, looking small and trapped, manfully trying to suppress his yawns. It occurred to Cordelia to wonder if he even got to keep the bags of coins, or if they were simply re-circulated to present again next year. Hell of a birthday party. There wasn't another child in sight. But they were running the counts through pretty efficiently, maybe the kid could escape soon.

An offerer in red-and-blues knelt before Gregor and Kareen, and presented his bag of maroon and gold silk. Cordelia recognized Count Vidal Vordarian, the dish-faced man whom Aral had politely described as of the "next-most-conservative party," i.e., of roughly the same political views as Count Piotr, in a tone of voice that had made

Cordelia wonder if it was a code-phrase for "Isolationist fanatic." He did not look a fanatic. Freed of its distorting anger, his face was much more attractive; he turned it now to Princess Kareen, and said something which made her lift her chin and laugh. His hand rested a moment familiarly upon her robed knee, and her hand briefly covered his, before he clambered back to his feet and bowed, and made way for the next man. Kareen's smile faded as Vordarian turned his back.

Gregor's sad glance crossed Aral, Cordelia, and Droushnakovi; he spoke earnestly up to his mother. Kareen motioned a guard over, and a few minutes later a guard commander approached them, for permission to carry off Drou. She was replaced by an unobtrusive young man who trailed them out of earshot, a mere flicker at the corner of the eye, a neat trick for a fellow that large.

Happily, Cordelia and Aral soon ran across Lord and Lady Vorpatril, someone Cordelia dared talk to without a politico-social pre-briefing. Captain Lord Vorpatril's parade red-and-blues set off his dark-haired good looks to perfection. Lady Vorpatril barely outshone him in a carnelian dress with matching roses woven into her cloud of black hair, stunning against her velvety white skin. They made, Cordelia thought, an archetypal Vor couple, sophisticated and serene, the effect only slightly spoiled by the gradual awareness from his disjointed conversation that Captain Vorpatril was drunk. He was a cheerful drunk, though, his personality merely stretched a bit, not unpleasantly transformed.

Vorkosigan, drawn away by some men who bore down on him with Purpose in their eyes, handed Cordelia off to Lady Vorpatril. The two women cruised the elegant hors d'oeuvre trays being offered around by yet more human servants, and compared obstetrical reports. Lord Vorpatril hastily excused himself to pursue a tray bearing wine. Alys plotted the colors and cut of Cordelia's next gown. "Black and white, for you, for Winterfair," she asserted with authority. Cordelia nodded meekly, wondering if they were actually going to sit down for a meal soon, or if they were expected to keep grazing off the passing trays.

Alys guided her to the ladies' lavatory, an object of hourly interest to their pregnancy-crowded bladders, and introduced her on the return journey to several more women of her rarified social circle. Alys then fell into an animated discussion with a longstanding crony regarding an upcoming party for the woman's daughter, and Cordelia drifted to the edge of the group.

She stepped back quietly, separating herself (she tried not to think, *from the herd*) for a moment of quiet contemplation. What a strange mix Barrayar was, at one moment homey and familiar, in the next terrifying and alien . . . they put on a good show, though . . . ah! That's what was missing from the scene, Cordelia realized. On Beta Colony a ceremony of this magnitude would be fully covered by holovid, to be shared real-time planet-wide. Every move would be a carefully choreographed dance around the vid angles and commentators' timing, almost to the point of annihilating the event being recorded. Here, there wasn't a holovid in sight. The only recordings were made by ImpSec, for their own purposes, which did not include choreography. The people in this room danced only for each other, all their glittering show tossed blithely away in time, which carried it off forever; the event would exist tomorrow only in their memories.

"Lady Vorkosigan?"

Cordelia started from her meditations at the urbane voice at her elbow. She turned to find Commodore Count Vordarian. His wearing of red-and-blues, rather than his personal House livery colors, marked him as being on active service, ornamenting Imperial Headquarters no doubt—in what department? Yes, Ops, Aral had said. He had a drink in his hand, and smiled cordially.

"Count Vordarian," she offered in return, smiling, too. They'd seen each other in passing often enough, Cordelia decided to take him as introduced. This Regency business wasn't going to go away, however much she might wish it to; it was time and past time for her to start making connections of her own, and quit pestering Aral for guidance at every new step.

"Are you enjoying the party?" he inquired.

"Oh, yes." She tried to think of something more to say. "It's extremely beautiful."

"As are you, Milady." He raised his glass to her in a gesture of toast, and sipped.

Her heart lurched, but she identified the reason why before her eyes did more than widen slightly. The last Barrayaran officer to toast her had been the late Admiral Vorrutyer, under rather different social circumstances. Vordarian had accidently mimicked his precise gesture. This was no time for torture-flashbacks. Cordelia blinked. "Lady Vorpatril helped me a lot. She's very generous."

Vordarian nodded delicately toward her torso. "I understand you also are to be congratulated. Is it a boy or a girl?"

"Uh? Oh. Yes, a boy, thank you. He's to be named Piotr Miles, I'm told."

"I'm surprised. I should have thought the Lord Regent would have sought a daughter first."

Cordelia cocked her head, puzzled by his ironic tone. "We started this before Aral became Regent."

"But you knew he was to receive the appointment, surely."

"I didn't. But I thought all you Barrayaran militarists were mad after sons. Why did you think a daughter?" *I want a daughter. . . .*

"I assumed Lord Vorkosigan would be thinking ahead to his long-term, ah, employment, of course. What better way to maintain the continuity of his power after the Regency is over than to slip neatly into position as the Emperor's father-in-law?"

Cordelia boggled. "You think he'd bet the continuity of a planetary government on the chance of a couple of teenagers falling in love, a decade and a half from now?"

"Love?" Now he looked baffled.

"You Barrayarans are—" she bit her tongue on the *crazy.* Impolite. "Aral is certainly more . . . practical." Though she could hardly call him unromantic.

"That's extremely interesting," he breathed. His eyes flicked to and away from her abdomen. "Do you fancy he contemplates something more direct?"

Her mind was running tangential to this twisting conversation, somehow. "Beg pardon?"

He smiled and shrugged.

Cordelia frowned. "Do you mean to say, if we were having a girl, that's what everyone would be thinking?"

"Certainly."

She blew out her breath. "God. That's . . . I can't imagine anyone in their right mind wanting to get near the Barrayaran Imperium. It just makes you a target for every maniac with a grievance, as far as I can see." An image of Lieutenant Koudelka, bloody-faced and deafened, flashed in her mind. "Also hard on the poor fellow who's unlucky enough to be standing next to you."

His attention sharpened. "Ah, yes, that unfortunate incident the other day. Has anything come of the investigation, do you know?"

"Nothing that I've heard. Negri and Illyan are talking Cetagandans, mostly. But the guy who launched the grenade got away clean."

"Too bad." He drained his glass, and exchanged it for a freshly charged one presented immediately by a passing Vorbarra-liveried servant. Cordelia eyed the wineglasses wistfully. But she was off metabolic poisons for the duration. Yet another advantage of Betan-style gestation in uterine replicators, none of this blasted enforced clean living. At home she could have poisoned and endangered herself freely, while her child grew, fully monitored round-the-clock by sober techs, safe and protected in the replicator banks. Suppose *she* had been under that sonic grenade . . . She longed for a drink.

Well, she did not need the mind-numbing buzz of ethanol; conversation with Barrayarans was mind-numbing enough. Her eyes sought Aral in the crowd—there he was, Kou at his shoulder, talking with Piotr and two other grizzled old men in counts' liveries. As Aral had predicted, his hearing had returned to normal within a couple of days. Yet still his eyes shifted from face to face, drinking in cues of gesture and inflection, his glass a mere untasted ornament in his hand. On duty, no question. Was he ever off-duty, anymore?

"Was he much disturbed by the attack?" Vordarian inquired, following her gaze to Aral.

"Wouldn't you be?" said Cordelia. "I don't know . . . he's seen so much violence in his life, almost more than I can imagine. It may be almost like . . . white noise. Tuned out." *I wish I could tune it out.*

"You have not known him that long, though. Just since Escobar."

"We met once before the war. Briefly."

"Oh?" His brows rose. "I didn't know that. How little one truly knows of people." He paused, watching Aral, watching her watch Aral. One corner of his mouth crooked up, then the quirk vanished in a thoughtful pursing of his lips. "He's bisexual, you know." He took a delicate sip of his wine.

"Was bisexual," she corrected absently, looking fondly across the room. "Now he's monogamous."

Vordarian choked, sputtering. Cordelia watched him with concern, wondering if she ought to pat him on the back or something, but he regained his breath and balance. "He *told* you that?" he wheezed in astonishment.

"No, Vorrutyer did. Just before he met his, um, fatal accident." Vordarian was standing frozen; she felt a certain malicious glee at having at last baffled a Barrayaran as much as they sometimes baffled her. Now, if she could just figure out what she'd said that had thrown him . . . She went on seriously, "The more I look back on Vorrutyer, the more he seems a tragic figure. Still obsessed with a love affair that was over eighteen years ago. Yet I sometimes wonder, if he could have had what he wanted then—kept Aral—if Aral might have kept that sadistic streak that ultimately consumed Vorrutyer's sanity under control. It's as if the two of them were on some kind of weird see-saw, each one's survival entailing the other's destruction."

"A Betan." His stunned look was gradually fading to one Cordelia mentally dubbed as Awful Realization. "I should have guessed. You are, after all, the people who bioengineered hermaphrodites. . . ." He paused. "How long did you know Vorrutyer?"

"About twenty minutes. But it was a very *intense* twenty minutes." She decided to let him wonder what the hell *that* meant.

"Their, ah, affair, as you call it, was a great secret scandal, at the time."

She wrinkled her nose. "Great secret scandal? Isn't that an oxymoron? Like 'military intelligence,' or 'friendly fire.' Also typical Barrayaranisms, now that I think on it."

Vordarian had the strangest look on his face. He looked, she realized, exactly like a man who had thrown a bomb, had it go *fizz* instead of *BOOM!* and was now trying to decide whether to stick his hand in and tap the firing mechanism to test it.

Then it was her turn for Awful Realization. *This man just tried to blow up my marriage.* No—*Aral's* marriage. She fixed a bright, sunny, innocent smile on her face, her brain kicking—at last!—into overdrive. Vordarian couldn't be of Vorrutyer's old war party; their leaders had all met with their fatal accidents before Ezar had bowed out, and the rest were scattered and lying low. What did he want? She fiddled with a flower from her hair, and considered simpering. "I didn't imagine I was marrying a forty-four-year-old virgin, Count Vordarian."

"So it seems." He knocked back another gulp of wine. "You galactics are all degenerate . . . what perversions does he tolerate in return, I wonder?" His eyes glinted in sudden open malice. "Do you know how Lord Vorkosigan's first wife died?"

"Suicide. Plasma arc to the head," she replied promptly.

"It was rumored he'd murdered her. For adultery. Betan, beware." His smile had turned wholly acid.

"Yes, I knew that, too. In this case, an untrue rumor." All pretense of cordiality had evaporated from their exchange. Cordelia had a bad sense of all control escaping with it. She leaned forward, and lowered her voice. "Do you know why Vorrutyer died?"

He couldn't help it; he tilted toward her, drawn in. "No . . ."

"He tried to hurt Aral through me. I found that . . . annoying. I wish you would cease trying to annoy me, Count Vordarian, I'm afraid you might succeed." Her voice fell further, almost to a whisper. "You should fear it, too."

His initial patronizing tone had certainly given way to wariness. He made a smooth, openhanded gesture that seemed to symbolize a bow of farewell, and backed away. "Milady." The glance over his shoulder as he moved off was thoroughly spooked.

She frowned after him. _Whew_. What an _odd_ exchange. What had the man expected, dropping that obsolete datum on her as if it were some shocking surprise? Did Vordarian actually imagine she would go off and tax her husband with his poor taste in companions two decades ago? Would a naive young Barrayaran bride have gone into hysterics? Not Lady Vorpatril, whose social enthusiasms concealed an acid judgment; not Princess Kareen, whose naivete had surely been burned out long ago by that expert sadist Serg. _He fired, but he missed._

And, more coldly, _Has he fired and missed once before?_ That had not been a normal social interaction, not even by Barrayaran standards of one-upsmanship. _Or maybe he was just drunk._ She suddenly wanted to talk to Illyan. She closed her eyes, trying to clear her fogged head.

"Are you well, love?" Aral's concerned voice murmured in her ear. "Do you need your nausea medication?"

Her eyes flew open. There he was, safe and sound beside her. "Oh, I'm fine." She attached herself to his arm, lightly, not a panicked limpet-like clamp. "Just thinking."

"They're seating us for dinner."

"Good. It will be nice to sit down, my feet are swelling."

He looked as if he wanted to pick her up and carry her, but they paraded in normally, joining the other formal pairs. They sat at a raised table set a little apart from the others, with Gregor, Kareen, Piotr, the Lord Guardian of the

Speaker's Circle and his wife, and Prime Minister Vortala. At Gregor's insistence, Droushnakovi was seated with them; the boy seemed painfully glad to see his old bodyguard. *Did I take away your playmate, child?* Cordelia wondered apologetically. It seemed so; Gregor engaged in a negotiation with Kareen for Drou's weekly return "for judo lessons." Drou, used to the Residence atmosphere, was not so overawed as Koudelka, who was stiff with exaggerated care against betrayal by his own clumsiness.

Cordelia found herself seated between Vortala and the Speaker, and carried on conversations with reasonable ease; Vortala was charming, in his blunt way. Cordelia managed nibbles of all the elegantly served food except a slice off the carcass of a roast bovine, carried in whole. Usually she was able to put out of her mind the fact that Barrayaran protein was not grown in vats, but taken from the bodies of real dead animals. She'd known about their primitive culinary practices before she'd chosen to come here, after all, and had tasted animal muscle before on Survey missions, in the interests of science, survival, or potential new product development for the homeworld. The Barrayarans applauded the fruit- and flower-decked beast, seeming to actually find it attractive and not horrific, and the cook, who'd followed it anxiously out, took a bow. The primitive olfactory circuits of her brain had to agree, it smelled great. Vorkosigan had his portion bloody-rare. Cordelia sipped water.

After dessert, and some brief formal toasts offered by Vortala and Vorkosigan, the boy Gregor was at last taken off to bed by his mother. Kareen motioned Cordelia and Droushnakovi to join her. The tension eased in Cordelia's shoulders as they left the big public assembly and climbed to the Emperor's quiet, private quarters.

Gregor was peeled out of his little uniform and dove into pajamas, becoming boy and not icon once again. Drou supervised his teeth-brushing, and was inveigled into "just one round" of some game they'd used to play with a board and pieces, as a bedtime treat. This Kareen indulgently permitted, and after a kiss for and from her son, she and

Cordelia withdrew to a softly lit sitting room nearby. A night breeze from the open windows cooled the upper chamber. Both women sat with a sigh, unwinding; Cordelia kicked off her shoes immediately after Kareen did so. Distance-muffled voices and laughter drifted through the windows from the gardens below.

"How long does this party go on?" Cordelia asked.

"Dawn, for those with more endurance than myself. I shall retire at midnight, after which the serious drinkers will take over."

"Some of them looked pretty serious already."

"Unfortunately." Kareen smiled. "You will be able to see the Vor class at both its best and its worst, before the night is over."

"I can imagine. I'm surprised you don't import less lethal mood-altering drugs."

Kareen's smile sharpened. "But drunken brawls are *traditional*." She allowed the cutting edge of her voice to soften. "In fact, such things are coming in, at least in the shuttleport cities. As usual, we seem to be adding to rather than replacing our own customs."

"Perhaps that's the best way." Cordelia frowned. How best to probe delicately . . . ? "Is Count Vidal Vordarian one of those in the habit of getting publicly potted?"

"No." Kareen glanced up, narrowing her eyes. "Why do you ask?"

"I had a peculiar conversation with him. I thought an overdose of ethanol might account for it." She remembered Vordarian's hand resting lightly upon the Princess's knee, just short of an intimate caress. "Do you know him well? How would you estimate him?"

Kareen said judiciously, "He's rich . . . proud . . . He was loyal to Ezar during Serg's late machinations against his father. Loyal to the Imperium, to the Vor class. There are four major manufacturing cities in Vordarian's District, plus military bases, supply depots, the biggest military shuttleport. . . . Vidal's is certainly the most economically important area on Barrayar today. The war barely touched the Vordarians' District; it's one of the few the

Cetagandans pulled out of by treaty. We sited our first space bases there because we took over facilities the Cetagandans had built and abandoned, and a good deal of economic development followed from that."

"That's . . . interesting," said Cordelia, "but I was wondering about the man personally. His, ah, likes and dislikes, for example. Do you like him?"

"At one time," said Kareen slowly, "I wondered if Vidal might be powerful enough to protect me from Serg. After Ezar died. As Ezar grew more ill, I was thinking, I had better look to my own defense. Nothing appeared to be happening, and no one told me anything."

"If Serg had become emperor, how could a mere count have protected you?" asked Cordelia.

"He would have had to become . . . more. Vidal had ambition, if it were properly encouraged—and patriotism, God knows if Serg had lived he might have destroyed Barrayar—Vidal might have saved us all. But Ezar promised I'd have nothing to fear, and Ezar delivered. Serg died before Ezar and . . . and I have been trying to let things cool, with Vidal, since."

Cordelia abstractedly rubbed her lower lip. "Oh. But do you, personally—I mean, do you like him? Would becoming Countess Vordarian be a nice retirement from the dowager-princess business, someday?"

"Oh! Not now. The Emperor's stepfather would be too powerful a man, to set up opposite the Regent. A dangerous polarity, if they were not allied or exactly balanced. Or were not combined in one person."

"Like being the Emperor's father-in-law?"

"Yes, exactly."

"I'm having trouble understanding this . . . venereal transmission of power. Do you have some claim to the Imperium in your own right, or not?"

"That would be for the military to decide," she shrugged. Her voice lowered. "It is like a disease, isn't it? I'm too close, I'm touched, infected. . . . Gregor is my hope of survival. And my prison."

"Don't you want a life of your own?"

"No. I just want to live."

Cordelia sat back, disturbed. *Did Serg teach you not to give offense?* "Does Vordarian see it that way? I mean, power isn't the only thing you have to offer. I think you underestimate your personal attractiveness."

"On Barrayar . . . power is the only thing." Her expression grew distant. "I admit . . . I did once ask Captain Negri to get me a report on Vidal. He uses his courtesans normally."

This wistful approval was not exactly Cordelia's idea of a declaration of boundless love. Yet that hadn't been just desire for power she'd seen in Vordarian's eyes at the ceremony, she would swear. Had Aral's appointment as Regent accidentally messed up the man's courtship? Might that very well account for the sex-tinged animosity in his speech to her . . . ?

Droushnakovi returned on tiptoe. "He fell asleep," she whispered fondly. Kareen nodded, and tilted her head back in an unguarded moment of rest, until a Vorbarra-liveried messenger arrived and addressed her: "Will you open the dancing with my lord Regent, Milady? They're waiting."

Request, or order? It sounded more sinister-mandatory than fun, in the servant's flat voice.

"Last duty for the night," Kareen assured Cordelia, as they both shoved their shoes back on. Cordelia's footgear seemed to have shrunk two sizes since the start of the evening. She hobbled after Kareen, Drou trailing.

A large downstairs room was floored in multi-toned wood marquetry in patterns of flowers, vines, and animals. The polished surface would have been put on a museum wall on Beta Colony; these incredible people danced across it. A live orchestra—selected by cutthroat competition from the Imperial Service Band, Cordelia was informed—provided music, in the Barrayaran style. Even the waltzes sounded faintly like marches. Aral and the princess were presented to each other, and he led her off for a couple of good-natured turns around the room, a formal dance that involved each mirroring the other's steps and slides, hands raised but never quite touching. Cordelia was fascinated. She'd never guessed that Aral could dance. This seemed to complete the social requirements, and other couples filtered out onto the floor. Aral returned to her side, looking stimulated. "Dance, Milady?"

After that dinner, more like a nap. How did he keep up that alarming hyperactivity? Secret terror, probably. She shook her head, smiling. "I don't know how."

"Ah." They strolled, instead. "I could show you how," he offered as they exited the room onto a bank of terraces that wound off into the gardens, pleasantly cool and dark but for a few colored lights to prevent stumbles on the pathways.

"Mm," she said doubtfully. "If you can find a private spot." If they could find a private spot, she could think of better things to do than dance, though.

"Well, here we—shh." His scimitar grin winked in the dark, and his grip tightened warningly on her hand. They both stood still, at the entrance to a little open space screened from eyes above by yews and some pink feathery non-Earth plant. The music floated clearly down.

"Try, Kou," urged Droushnakovi's voice. Drou and Kou stood facing each other on the far side of the terrace-nook. Doubtfully, Koudelka set his stick down on the stone balustrade, and held up his hands to hers. They began to step, slide, and dip, Drou counting earnestly, "*One*-two-three, one-two-three . . ."

Koudelka tripped, and she caught him; his grip found her waist. "It's no damned good, Drou." He shook his head in frustration.

"Sh . . ." Her hand touched his lips. "Try again. I'm for it. You said you had to practice that hand-coordination thing, how long, before you got it? More than once, I bet."

"The old man wouldn't let me give up."

"Well, maybe I won't let you give up either."

"I'm tired," complained Koudelka.

So, switch to kissing, Cordelia urged silently, muffling a laugh. *That you can do sitting down.* Droushnakovi was determined, however, and they began again. "*One*-two-three, one-two-three . . ." Once again the effort ended in what seemed to Cordelia a very good start on a clinch, if only one party or the other would gather the wit and nerve to follow through.

Aral shook his head, and they backed silently away around the shrubbery. Apparently a little inspired, his lips found hers to muffle his own chuckle. Alas, their delicacy was futile; an anonymous Vor lord wandered blindly past them, stumbled across the terrace nook, freezing Kou and Drou in mid-step, and hung over the stone balustrade to be very traditionally sick into the defenseless bushes below. Sudden swearing, in new voices, one male, one female, rose up from the dark and shaded target zone. Koudelka retrieved his stick, and the two would-be dancers hastily retreated. The Vor lord was sick again, and his male victim started climbing up after him, slipping on the beslimed stonework and promising violent retribution. Vorkosigan guided Cordelia prudently away.

Later, while waiting by one of the Residence's entrances for the groundcars to be brought round, Cordelia found herself standing next to the lieutenant. Koudelka gazed pensively back over his shoulder at the Residence, from which music and party-noises wafted almost unabated.

"Good party, Kou?" she inquired genially.

"What? Oh, yes, astonishing. When I joined the Service, I never dreamed I'd end up here." He blinked. "Time was, I never thought I'd end up anywhere." And then he added, giving Cordelia a slight case of mental whiplash, "I sure wish women came with operating manuals."

Cordelia laughed aloud. "I could say the same for men."

"But you and Admiral Vorkosigan—you're different."

"Not . . . really. We've learned from experience, maybe. A lot of people fail to."

"Do you think I have a chance at a normal life?" He gazed, not at her, but into the dark.

"You make your own chances, Kou. And your own dances."

"You sound just like the Admiral."

Cordelia cornered Illyan the next morning, when he stopped in to Vorkosigan House for the daily report from his guard commander.

"Tell me, Simon. Is Vidal Vordarian on your short list, or your long list?"

"Everybody's on my long list," Illyan sighed.

"I want you to move him to your short list."

His head cocked. "Why?"

She hesitated. She wasn't about to reply, *Intuition*, though that was exactly what those subliminal cues added up to. "He seems to me to have an assassin's mind. The sort that fires from cover into the back of his enemy."

Illyan smiled quizzically. "Beg pardon, Milady, but that doesn't sound like the Vordarian I know. I've always found him more the openly bullheaded type."

How badly must he hurt, how ardently desire, for a bullheaded man to turn subtle? She was unsure. Perhaps, not knowing how deeply Aral's happiness with her ran, Vordarian did not recognize how vicious his attack upon it was? And did personal and political animosity necessarily run together? *No.* The man's hatred had been profound, his blow precisely, if mistakenly, aimed.

"Move him to your short list," she said.

Illyan opened his hand; not mere placation, by his expression some chain of thought was engaged. "Very well, Milady."

CHAPTER SIX

Cordelia watched the shadow of the lightflyer flow over the ground below, a slim blot arrowing south. The arrow wavered across farm fields, creeks, rivers, and dusty roads—the road net was rudimentary, stunted, its development leapfrogged by the personal air transport that had arrived in the blast of galactic technology at the end of the Time of Isolation. Coils of tension unwound in her neck with each kilometer they put between themselves and the hectic hothouse atmosphere of the capital. A day in the country was an excellent idea, overdue. She only wished Aral could have shared it with her.

Sergeant Bothari, cued by some landmark below, banked the lightflyer gently to its new course. Droushnakovi, sharing the back seat with Cordelia, stiffened, trying not to lean into her. Dr. Henri, in front with the Sergeant, stared out the canopy with an interest almost equal to Cordelia's.

Dr. Henri turned half around, to speak over his shoulder to Cordelia. "I do thank you for the luncheon invitation, Lady Vorkosigan. It's a rare privilege to visit the Vorkosigans' private estate."

"Is it?" said Cordelia. "I know they don't have crowds, but Count Piotr's horse friends drop in fairly often.

Fascinating animals." Cordelia thought that over a second, then decided Dr. Henri would realize without being told that the "fascinating animals" applied to the horses, and not Count Piotr's friends. "Drop the least little hint that you're interested, and Count Piotr will probably show you personally around the stable."

"I've never met the General." Dr. Henri looked daunted by the prospect, and fingered the collar of his undress greens. A research scientist from the Imperial Military Hospital, Henri dealt with high rankers often enough not to be awed; it had to be all that Barrayaran history clinging to Piotr that made the difference.

Piotr had acquired his present rank at the age of twenty-two, fighting the Cetagandans in the fierce guerilla war that had raged through the Dendarii Mountains, just now showing blue on the southern horizon. Rank was all then-emperor Dorca Vorbarra could give him at the time; more tangible assets such as reinforcements, supplies, and pay were out of the question in that desperate hour. Twenty years later Piotr had changed Barrayaran history again, playing kingmaker to Ezar Vorbarra in the civil war that had brought down Mad Emperor Yuri. Not your average HQ staffer, General Piotr Vorkosigan, not by anybody's standards.

"He's easy to get along with," Cordelia assured Dr. Henri. "Just admire the horses, and ask a few leading questions about the wars, and you can relax and spend the rest of your time listening."

Henri's brows went up, as he searched her face for irony. Henri was a sharp man. Cordelia smiled cheerfully.

Bothari was silently watching her in the mirror set over his control interface, Cordelia noticed. Again. The sergeant seemed tense today. It was the position of his hands, the cording of the muscles in his neck, that gave him away. Bothari's flat yellow eyes were always unreadable; set deep, too close together, and not quite on the same level, above his sharp cheekbones and long narrow jaw. Anxiety over the doctor's visit? Understandable.

The land below was rolling, but soon rucked up into the rugged ridges that channeled the lake district. The mountains rose beyond, and Cordelia thought she caught a distant glint of early snow on the highest peaks. Bothari hopped the flyer over three running ridges, and banked again, zooming up a narrow valley. A few more minutes, a swoop over another ridge, and the long lake was in sight. An enormous maze of burnt-out fortifications made a black crown on a headland, and a village nestled below it. Bothari brought the flyer down neatly on a circle painted on the pavement of the village's widest street.

Dr. Henri gathered up his bag of medical equipment. "The examination will only take a few minutes," he assured Cordelia, "then we can go on."

Don't tell me, tell Bothari. Cordelia sensed Dr. Henri was a little unnerved by Bothari. He kept addressing her instead of the Sergeant, as if she were some translator who would put it all into terms that Bothari would understand. Bothari was formidable, true, but talking past him wouldn't make him magically disappear.

Bothari led them to a little house set in a narrow side street that went down to the glimmering water. At his knock, a heavyset woman with greying hair opened the door and smiled. "Good morning, Sergeant. Come in, everything's all ready. Milady." She favored Cordelia with an awkward curtsey.

Cordelia returned a nod, gazing around with interest. "Good morning, Mistress Hysopi. How nice your house looks today." The place was painfully scrubbed and straightened—as a military widow, Mistress Hysopi understood all about inspections. Cordelia trusted the everyday atmosphere in the hired fosterer's house was a trifle more relaxed.

"Your little girl's been very good this morning," Mistress Hysopi assured the Sergeant. "Took her bottle right down—she's just had her bath. Right this way, Doctor. I hope you'll find everything's all right. . . ."

She guided the way up narrow stairs. One bedroom was clearly her own; the other, with a bright window

looking down over rooftops to the lake, had recently been
made over into a nursery. A dark-haired infant with big
brown eyes cooed to herself in a crib. "There's a girl,"
Mistress Hysopi smiled, picking her up. "Say hi to your
daddy, eh, Elena? Pretty-pretty."

Bothari entered no further than the door, watching the
infant warily. "Her head has grown a lot," he offered after
a moment.

"They usually do, between three and four months,"
Mistress Hysopi agreed.

Dr. Henri laid out his instruments on the crib sheet,
and Mistress Hysopi carried the baby back over and began
undressing her. The two began a technical discussion about
formulae and feces, and Bothari walked around the little
room, looking but not touching. He did look terribly huge
and out-of-place among the colorful, delicate infant furnishings, dark and dangerous in his brown and silver
uniform. His head brushed the slanting ceiling, and he
backed cautiously to the door.

Cordelia hung curiously over Henri and Hysopi's shoulders, watching the little girl wriggle and attempt to roll.
Infants. Soon enough she would have one of those. As
if in response her belly fluttered. Piotr Miles was not, fortunately, strong enough to fight his way out of a paper
bag yet, but if his development continued at this rate, the
last couple of months were going to be sleepless. She
wished she'd taken the parents' training course back on
Beta Colony even if she hadn't been ready to apply for
a license. Yet Barrayaran parents seemed to manage to
ad lib. Mistress Hysopi had learned on the job, and she
had three grown children now.

"Amazing," said Dr. Henri, shaking his head and
recording his data. "Absolutely normal development, as
far as I can tell. Nothing to even show she came out of
a uterine replicator."

"*I* came out of a uterine replicator," Cordelia noted
with amusement. Henri glanced involuntarily up and down
at her, as if suddenly expecting to find antennae sprout-
ing from her head. "Betan experience suggests it doesn't

matter so much how you got here, as what you do after you arrive."

"Really." He frowned thoughtfully. "And you are free of genetic defects?"

"Certified," Cordelia agreed.

"We *need* this technology." He sighed, and began packing his things back up. "She's fine, you can dress her again," he added to Mistress Hysopi.

Bothari loomed over the crib at last, to stare down, the lines creased deep between his eyes. He touched the infant only once, a finger to her cheek, then rubbed thumb and finger together as if checking his neural function. Mistress Hysopi studied him sideways, but said nothing.

While Bothari lingered to settle up the month's expenses with Mistress Hysopi, Cordelia and Dr. Henri strolled down to the lake, Droushnakovi following.

"When those seventeen Escobaran uterine replicators first arrived at Imp Mil," said Henri, "sent from the war zone, I was frankly appalled. Why save those unwanted fetuses, and at such a cost? Why land them on *my* department? Since then I've become a believer, Milady. I've even thought of an application, spin-off technology, for burn patients. I'm working on it now, the project approval came down just a week ago." His eyes were eager, as he detailed his theory, which was sound as far as Cordelia understood the principles.

"My mother is a medical equipment and maintenance engineer at Silica Hospital," she explained to Henri, when he paused for breath and approval. "She works on these sorts of applications all the time." Henri redoubled his technical exposition.

Cordelia greeted two women in the street by name, and politely introduced them to Dr. Henri.

"They're wives of some of Count Piotr's sworn armsmen," she explained as they passed on.

"I should have thought they'd choose to live in the capital."

"Some do, some stay here. It seems to depend on taste.

The cost of living is much lower out here, and these fellows aren't paid as much as I'd imagined. Some of the backcountry men are suspicious of city life, they seem to think it's purer here." She grinned briefly. "One fellow has a wife in each location. None of his brother-armsmen have ratted on him yet. A solid bunch."

Henri's brows rose. "How jolly for him."

"Not really. He's chronically short of cash, and always looks worried. But he can't decide which wife to give up. Apparently, he actually loves them both."

When Dr. Henri stepped aside to talk to an old man they saw pottering around the docks about possible boat rentals, Droushnakovi came up to Cordelia, and lowered her voice. She looked disturbed.

"Milady . . . how in the world did Sergeant Bothari come by a baby? He's not married, is he?"

"Would you believe the stork brought her?" said Cordelia lightly.

"No."

From her frown, Drou did not approve this levity. Cordelia hardly blamed her. She sighed. *How do I wriggle out of this one?* "Very nearly. Her uterine replicator was sent on a fast courier from Escobar, after the war. She finished her gestation in a laboratory in Imp Mil, under Dr. Henri's supervision."

"Is she really Bothari's?"

"Oh, yes. Genetically certified. That's how they identified—" Cordelia snapped that last sentence off midway. Carefully, now . . .

"But what was all that about seventeen replicators? And how did the baby get in the replicator? Was—was she an experiment?"

"Placental transfer. A delicate operation, even by galactic standards, but hardly experimental. Look." Cordelia paused, thinking fast. "I'll tell you the truth." *Just not all of it.* "Little Elena is the daughter of Bothari and a young Escobaran officer named Elena Visconti. Bothari . . . loved her . . . very much. But after the war, she would not return with him to Barrayar. The child was conceived, er . . .

Barrayaran-style, then transferred to the replicator when
they parted. There were some similar cases. The replicators
were all sent to Imp Mil, which was interested in learning more about the technology. Bothari was in . . . medical therapy, for quite a long time, after the war. But when
he got out, and she got out, he took custody of her."

"Did the others take their babies, too?"

"Most of the other fathers were dead by then. The
children went to the Imperial Service orphanage." There.
The official version, all right and tight.

"Oh." Drou frowned at her feet. "That's not at all . . .
it's hard to picture Bothari . . . To tell the truth," she said
in a burst of candor, "I'm not sure I'd want to give custody of a pet cat to Bothari. Doesn't he strike you as a bit
strange?"

"Aral and I are keeping an eye on things. Bothari's
doing very well so far, I think. He found Mistress
Hysopi on his own, and is making sure she gets everything she needs. Has Bothari—that is, does Bothari
bother you?"

Droushnakovi gave Cordelia an are-you-kidding? look.
"He's so big. And ugly. And he . . . mutters to himself,
some days. And he's sick so much, days in a row when
he won't get out of bed, but he doesn't have a fever or
anything. Count Piotr's Armsman-commander thinks he's
malingering."

"He's not malingering. But I'm glad you mentioned it, I'll
have Aral talk to the commander and straighten him out."

"But aren't you at all afraid of him? On the bad days,
at least?"

"I could weep for Bothari," said Cordelia slowly, "but
I don't fear him. On the bad days or any days. You
shouldn't either. It's . . . it's a profound insult."

"Sorry." Droushnakovi scuffed her shoe across the
gravel. "It's a sad story. No wonder he doesn't talk about
the Escobar war."

"Yes, I'd . . . appreciate it if you'd refrain from bringing
it up. It's very painful for him."

❖   ❖   ❖

A short hop in the lightflyer from the village across a tongue of the lake brought them to the Vorkosigans' country estate. A century ago the house had been an outlying guard post to the headland's fort. Modern weaponry had rendered aboveground fortifications obsolete, and the old stone barracks had been converted to more peaceful uses. Dr. Henri had evidently been expecting more grandeur, for he said, "It's smaller than I expected."

Piotr's housekeeper had a pleasant luncheon set up for them on a flower-decked terrace off the south end of the house by the kitchen. While she was escorting the party out, Cordelia fell back beside Count Piotr.

"Thank you, sir, for letting us invade you."

"Invade me indeed! This is your house, dear. You are free to entertain any friends you choose in it. This is the first time you've done so, do you realize?" He stopped, standing with her in the doorway. "You know, when my mother married my father, she completely re-decorated Vorkosigan House. My wife did the same in her day. Aral married so late, I'm afraid an updating is sadly overdue. Wouldn't you . . . like to?"

But it's *your* house, thought Cordelia helplessly. Not even Aral's, really . . .

"You've touched down so lightly on us, one almost fears you'll fly away again." Piotr chuckled, but his eyes were concerned.

Cordelia patted her rounding belly. "Oh, I'm thoroughly weighted down now, sir." She hesitated. "To tell the truth, I have thought it would be nice to have a lift tube in Vorkosigan House. Counting the basement, sub-basement, attic, and roof, there are eight floors in the main section. It can make quite a hike."

"A lift tube? We've never—" He bit his tongue. "Where?"

"You could put it in the back hallway next to the plumbing stack, without disrupting the internal architecture."

"So you could. Very well. Find a builder. Do it."

"I'll look into it tomorrow, then. Thank you, sir." Her brows rose, behind his back.

Count Piotr, evidently with the same idea in mind of encouraging her, was studiously cordial to Dr. Henri over lunch, New Man though Henri clearly was. Henri, following Cordelia's advice, hit it off well with Piotr in turn. Piotr told Henri all about the new foal, born in his stables over the back ridge. The creature was a genetically certified pureblood that Piotr called a *quarter horse*, though it looked like an entire horse to Cordelia. The stud-colt had been imported at great cost as a frozen embryo from Earth, and implanted in a grade mare, the gestation supervised anxiously by Piotr. The biologically trained Henri expressed technical interest, and after lunch was done Piotr carried him off for a personal inspection of the big beasts.

Cordelia begged off. "I think I'd like to rest a bit. You can go, Drou. Sergeant Bothari will stay with me." In fact, Cordelia was worried about Bothari. He hadn't eaten a single bite of lunch, nor said a word for over an hour.

Doubtful, but madly interested in the horses, Drou allowed herself to be persuaded. The three trudged off up the hill. Cordelia watched them away, then turned her face back to catch Bothari watching her again. He gave her a strange approving nod.

"Thank you, Milady."

"Ahem. Yes. I wondered if you felt ill."

"No . . . yes. I don't know. I wanted . . . I've wanted to talk to you, Milady. For—for some weeks. But there never seemed to be a good time. Lately it's been getting worse. I can't wait anymore. I'd hoped today . . ."

"Seize the moment." The housekeeper was rattling about in Piotr's kitchen. "Would you care to take a walk, or something?"

"Please, Milady."

They walked together, around the old stone house. The pavilion on the crest of the hill, overlooking the lake, would be a great place to sit and talk, but Cordelia felt too full and pregnant to make the climb. She led left,

instead, on the path parallel to the slope, till they came
to what appeared to be a little walled garden.

The Vorkosigan family plot was crowded with an odd
assortment of graves, of core family, distant relatives,
retainers of special merit. The cemetery had originally
been part of the ruined fort complex, the oldest graves
of guards and officers going back centuries. The
Vorkosigan intrusion dated only from the atomic destruction of the old district capital of Vorkosigan Vashnoi during
the Cetagandan invasion. The dead had been melted down
with the living there, then eight generations of family history obliterated. It was interesting to note the clusters of
more recent dates, and key them to their current events:
the Cetagandan invasion, Mad Yuri's War. Aral's mother's
grave dated exactly to the start of Yuri's War. A space was
reserved beside her for Piotr, and had been for thirty-
three years. She waited patiently for her husband. *And
men accuse us women of being slow.* Her eldest son, Aral's
brother, lay buried at her other hand.

"Let's sit over there." She nodded toward a stone bench
set round with small orange flowers, and shaded by an
Earth-import oak at least a century old. "These people are
all good listeners, now. And they don't pass on gossip."

Cordelia sat on the warm stone, and studied Bothari.
He sat as far from her as the bench permitted. The lines
on his face were deep-cut today, harsh despite the mut-
ing of the afternoon light by the warm autumn haze. One
hand, wrapped around the rough stone edge of the bench,
flexed arrhythmically. His breathing was too careful.

Cordelia softened her voice. "So, what's the trouble,
Sergeant? You seem a little . . . stretched, today. Is it
something about Elena?"

He breathed a humorless laugh. "*Stretched.* Yes. I guess
so. It's not about the baby . . . it's . . . well, not directly."
His eyes met hers squarely for almost the first time today.
"You remember Escobar, milady. You were there. Right?"

"Right." *This man is in pain,* Cordelia realized. What
sort of pain?

"I can't remember Escobar."

"So I understand. I believe your military therapists went to a great deal of trouble to make sure you did not remember Escobar."

"Oh yes."

"I don't approve of Barrayaran notions of therapy. Particularly when colored by political expediency."

"I've come to realize that, Milady." Cautious hope flickered in his eyes.

"How did they work it? Burn out selected neurons? Chemical erasure?"

"No . . . they used drugs, but nothing was destroyed. They tell me. The doctors called it suppression-therapy. We just called it hell. Every day we went to hell, till we didn't want to go there anymore." Bothari shifted in his seat, his brow wrinkling. "Trying to remember—to talk about Escobar at all—gives me these headaches. Sounds stupid, doesn't it? Big man like me whining about headaches like some old woman. Certain special parts, memories, they give me these really bad headaches that make red rings around everything I see, and I start vomiting. When I stop trying to think about it, the pain goes away. Simple."

Cordelia swallowed. "I see. I'm sorry. I knew it was bad, but I didn't know it was . . . that bad."

"The worst part is the dreams. I dream of . . . it . . . and if I wake up too slowly, I remember the dream. I remember too much, all at once, and my head—all I can do is roll over and cry, until I can start thinking about something else. Count Piotr's other armsmen—they think I'm crazy, they think I'm stupid, they don't know what I'm doing in there with them. *I* don't know what I'm doing in there with them." He rubbed his big hands over his burr-scalp in a harried swipe. "To be a count's sworn Armsman—it's an honor. Only twenty places to fill. They take the best, they take the bloody heroes, the men with medals, the twenty-year men with perfect records. If what I did—at Escobar—was so bad, why did the Admiral make Count Piotr make a place for me? And if I was such a bloody hero, why did they take away my memory of it?" His breath was coming faster, whistling through his long yellow teeth.

"How much pain are you in now? Trying to talk about this?"

"Some. More to come." He stared at her, frowning deeply. "I've got to talk about this. To you. It's driving me . . ."

She took a calming breath, trying to listen with her whole mind, body, and soul. And carefully. So carefully. "Go on."

"I have . . . four pictures . . . in my head, from Escobar. Four pictures, and I cannot explain them. To myself. A few minutes, out of—three months? Four? They all of them bother me, but one bothers me the most. You're in it," he added abruptly, and stared at the ground. Both hands clenched the bench now, white-knuckled.

"I see. Go on."

"One—the least-bad one—it was an argument. Prince Serg was there, and Admiral Vorrutyer, Lord Vorkosigan, and Admiral Rulf Vorhalas. And I was there. Except I didn't have any clothes on."

"Are you sure this isn't a dream?"

"No. I'm not sure. Admiral Vorrutyer said . . . something very insulting, to Lord Vorkosigan. He had Lord Vorkosigan backed up against the wall. Prince Serg laughed. Then Vorrutyer kissed him, full on the mouth, and Vorhalas tried to knock Vorrutyer's head off, but Lord Vorkosigan wouldn't let him. And I don't remember after that."

"Um . . . yeah," said Cordelia. "I wasn't there for that part, but I know there was some really weird stuff going on in the high command at that point, as Vorrutyer and Serg pushed their limits. So it's probably a true memory. I could ask Aral, if you wish."

"No! No. That one doesn't feel as important, anyway. As the others."

"Tell me about the others, then."

His voice fell to a whisper. "I remember Elena. So pretty. I only have two pictures in my head, of Elena. One, I remember Vorrutyer making me . . . no, I don't want to talk about that one." He stopped for a full minute, rocking gently, forward and back. "The other . . . we were in my cabin. She and I. She was my wife. . . ." His voice faltered. "She wasn't my wife, was she." It wasn't even a question.

"No. But you know that."

"But I remember *believing* she was." His hands pressed his forehead, and rubbed his neck, hard and futilely.

"She was a prisoner of war," said Cordelia. "Her beauty drew Vorrutyer's and Serg's attention, and they made a project of tormenting her, for no reason—not for her military intelligence, not even for political terrorism—just for their gratification. She was raped. But you know that, too. On some level."

"Yes," he whispered.

"Taking away her contraceptive implant and allowing—or compelling—you to impregnate her was part of their idea of sadism. The first part. They did not, thank God, live long enough to get to the second part."

His legs had drawn up, his long arms wrapped around them in a tight, tight ball. His breathing was fast and shallow, panting. His face was freezer-burn white, sheened with cold sweat.

"Do I have red rings around me now?" Cordelia asked curiously.

"It's all . . . kind of pink."

"And the last picture?"

"Oh, Milady." He swallowed. "Whatever it was . . . I know it must be very close to whatever it is they most don't want me to remember." He swallowed again. Cordelia began to understand why he hadn't touched his lunch.

"Do you want to go on? *Can* you go on?"

"I must go on. Milady. Captain Naismith. Because I remember you. Remember seeing you. Stretched out on Vorrutyer's bed, all your clothes cut away, naked. You were bleeding. I was looking up your . . . What I want to know. Must know." His arms were wrapped around his head, now, tilted toward her on his knees, his face hollow, haunted, hungry.

His blood pressure must be fantastically high, to drive

that monstrous migraine. If they went too far, pressed this through to the last truth, might he be in danger of a stroke? An incredible piece of psychoengineering, to program his own body to punish him for his forbidden thoughts . . .

"Did I rape *you,* Milady?"

"Huh? *No!*" She sat bolt upright, fiercely indignant. They had taken *that* knowledge away from him? They'd *dared* take that away from him?

He began to cry, if that's what that ragged breathing, tight-screwed face, and tears leaking from his eyes meant. Equal parts agony and joy. "Oh. Thank God." And, "Are you *sure* . . . ?"

"Vorrutyer ordered you to. You refused. Out of your own will, without hope of rescue or reward. It got you in a hell of a lot of trouble, for a little while." She longed to tell him the rest, but the state he was in now was so terrifying, it was impossible to guess the consequences. "How long have you been remembering this? Wondering this?"

"Since I first saw you again. This summer. When you came to marry Lord Vorkosigan."

"You've been walking around for over *six months,* with this in your head, not daring to ask—?"

"Yes, Milady."

She sat back, horrified, her breath trickling out between pursed lips. "Next time, don't wait so long."

Swallowing hard, he stumbled to his feet, a big hand waving in a desperate wait-for-me gesture. He swung his legs over the low stone wall, and found some bushes. Anxiously, she listened to him dry-vomiting his empty stomach for several minutes. An extremely bad attack, she judged, but finally the violent paroxysms slowed, then stopped. He returned, wiping his lips, looking very white and not much better, except for his eyes. A little life flickered in those eyes now, a half-suppressed light of overwhelming relief.

The light faded, as he sat in thought. He rubbed his palms on his trouser knees, and stared at his boots. "But

I'm not less a rapist, just because *you* were not my victim."

"That is correct."

"I can't . . . trust myself. How can you trust me? . . . Do you know what's better than sex?"

She wondered if she could take one more sharp turn in this conversation without running off screaming. *You encouraged him to uncork, now you're stuck with it.* "Go on."

"Killing. It feels even better, afterwards. It shouldn't be . . . such a pleasure. Lord Vorkosigan doesn't kill like that." His eyes were narrowed, brows creased, but he was uncurled from his ball of agony; he must be speaking generally, Vorrutyer no longer on his mind.

"It's a release of rage, I'd guess," said Cordelia cautiously. "How did you get so much rage, balled up inside of you? The density is palpable. People can sense it."

His hand curled, in front of his solar plexus. "It goes back a long way. But I don't feel angry, most of the time. It snaps out suddenly."

"Even Bothari fears Bothari," she murmured in wonder.

"Yet you don't. You're less afraid even than Lord Vorkosigan."

"I see you as bound up with him, somehow. And he's my own heart. How can I fear my own heart?"

"Milady. A bargain."

"Hm?"

"You tell me . . . when it's all right. To kill. And then I'll know."

"I can't—look, suppose I'm not there? When that sort of thing lands on you, there's not usually time to stop and analyze. You have to be allowed self-defense, but you also have to be able to discern when you're really being attacked." She sat up, eyes widening in sudden insight. "That's why your uniform is so important to you, isn't it? It tells you when it's all right. When you can't tell yourself. All those rigid routines you keep to, they're to tell you you're all right, on track."

"Yes. I'm sworn to the defense of House Vorkosigan,

now. So *that's* all right." He nodded, apparently reassured. By what, for God's sake?

"You're asking me to be your conscience. Make your judgments for you. But you are a whole man. I've seen you make right choices, under the most absolute stress."

His hands pressed to his skull again, his narrow jaw clenching, and he grated out, "But I can't *remember* them. Can't remember how I did it."

"Oh." She felt very small. "Well . . . whatever you think I can do for you, you've got a blood-right to it. We owe you, Aral and I. We remember why, even if you can't."

"Remember it for me, then, Milady," he said lowly, "and I'll be all right."

"Believe it."

CHAPTER SEVEN

Cordelia shared breakfast one morning the following week with Aral and Piotr in a private parlor overlooking the back garden. Aral motioned to the Count's footman, who was serving.

"Would you please rout out Lieutenant Koudelka for me? Tell him to bring that agenda for this morning that we were discussing."

"Uh, I guess you hadn't heard, my lord?" murmured the man. Cordelia had the impression that his eyes were searching the room for an escape route.

"Heard what? We just came down."

"Lieutenant Koudelka is in hospital this morning."

"Hospital! Good God, why wasn't I told at once? What happened?"

"We were told Commander Illyan would be bringing a full report, my lord. The guard commander . . . thought he'd wait for him."

Alarm struggled with annoyance on Vorkosigan's face. "How bad is he? It's not some . . . delayed aftereffect of the sonic grenade, is it? What happened to him?"

"He was beaten up, my lord," said the footman woodenly.

Vorkosigan sat back with a little hiss. A muscle jumped in his jaw. "You get that guard commander in here," he growled.

The footman evaporated instantly, leaving Vorkosigan tapping a spoon nervously and impatiently on the table. He met Cordelia's horrified eyes and produced a small false smile of reassurance for her. Even Piotr looked startled.

"Who could possibly want to beat up Kou?" asked Cordelia wonderingly. "That's sickening. He couldn't fight back worth a damn."

Vorkosigan shook his head. "Someone looking for a safe target, I suppose. We'll find out. Oh, we will find out."

The green-uniformed ImpSec guard commander appeared, to stand at attention. "Sir."

"For your future information, and you may pass it on, should any accident occur to any of my key staff members, I wish to be informed at once. Understood?"

"Yes, sir. It was quite late when word got back here, sir. And since we knew by then that they were both going to live, Commander Illyan said I might let you sleep. Sir."

"I see." Vorkosigan rubbed his face. "Both?"

"Lieutenant Koudelka and Sergeant Bothari, sir."

"They didn't get into a fight, did they?" asked Cordelia, now thoroughly alarmed.

"Yes. Oh—not with each other, Milady. They were set upon."

Vorkosigan's face was darkening. "You had better begin at the beginning."

"Yes, sir. Um. Lieutenant Koudelka and Sergeant Bothari went out last night. Not in uniform. Down to that area in back of the old caravanserai."

"My God, what for?"

"Um." The guard commander glanced uncertainly at Cordelia. "Entertainment, I believe, sir."

"Entertainment?"

"Yes, sir. Sergeant Bothari goes down there about once a month, on his duty-free day, when my lord Count is in town. It's apparently some place he's been going to for years."

"In the caravanserai?" said Count Piotr in an unbelieving tone.

"Um." The guard commander eyed the footman in appeal.

"Sergeant Bothari isn't very particular about his entertainment, sir," the footman volunteered uneasily.

"Evidently not!" said Piotr.

Cordelia questioned Vorkosigan with her eyebrows.

"It's a very rough area," he explained. "I wouldn't go down there myself without a patrol at my back. Two patrols, at night. And I'd definitely wear my uniform, though not my rank insignia . . . but I believe Bothari grew up there. I imagine it looks different to his eyes."

"Why so rough?"

"It's very poor. It was the town center during the Time of Isolation, and it hasn't been touched by renovation yet. Minimal water, no electricity, choked with refuse . . ."

"Mostly human," added Piotr tartly.

"Poor?" said Cordelia, bewildered. "No electricity? How can it be on the comm network?"

"It's not, of course," answered Vorkosigan.

"Then how can anybody get their schooling?"

"They don't."

Cordelia stared. "I don't understand. How do they get their jobs?"

"A few escape to the Service. The rest prey on each other, mostly." Vorkosigan regarded her face uneasily. "Have you no poverty on Beta Colony?"

"Poverty? Well, some people have more money than others, of course, but . . . no comconsoles?"

Vorkosigan was diverted from his interrogation. "Is not owning a comconsole the lowest standard of living you can imagine?" he said in wonder.

"It's the first article in the constitution. 'Access to information shall not be abridged.' "

"Cordelia . . . these people barely have access to food, clothing, and shelter. They have a few rags and cooking pots, and squat in buildings that aren't economical to repair or tear down yet, with the wind whistling through the cracks in the walls."

"No air-conditioning?"

"No heat in the winter is a bigger problem, here."

"I suppose so. You people don't really have summer. . . . How do they call for help when they're sick or hurt?"

"What help?" Vorkosigan was growing grim. "If they're sick, they either get well or die."

"Die, if we're lucky," muttered Piotr. "Vermin."

"You're not joking." She stared back and forth between the pair of them. "That's horrible . . . why, think of all the geniuses you must be missing!"

"I doubt we're missing very many, from the caravan-serai," said Piotr dryly.

"Why not? They have the same genetic complement as you," Cordelia pointed out the, to her, obvious.

The Count went rigid. "My dear girl! They most certainly do not! My family have been Vor for nine generations."

Cordelia raised her eyebrows. "How do you know, if you didn't have gene typing till eighty years ago?"

Both the guard commander and the footman were acquiring peculiar stuffed expressions. The footman bit his lip.

"Besides," she went on reasonably, "if you Vor got around half as much as those histories I've been reading imply, ninety percent of the people on this planet must have Vor blood by now. Who knows who your relatives are on your father's side?"

Vorkosigan bit his linen napkin absently, his eyes gone crinkly with much the same expression as the footman, and murmured, "Cordelia, you can't . . . you really *can't* sit at the breakfast table and imply my ancestors were bastards. It's a mortal insult here."

Where should I sit? "Oh. I'll never understand that, I guess. Oh, never mind. Koudelka, and Bothari."

"Quite. Go on, duty officer."

"Yes, sir. Well, sir, they were coming back, I was told,

about an hour after midnight, when they were set on by a gang of area toughs. Evidently Lieutenant Koudelka was too well dressed, and besides there's that walk of his, and the stick . . . anyway, he attracted attention. I don't know the details, sir, but there were four deaths and three in the hospital this morning, in addition to the ones that got away."

Vorkosigan whistled, very faintly, through his teeth. "What was the extent of Bothari's and Koudelka's injuries?"

"They . . . I don't have an official report, sir. Just hearsay."

"Say, then."

The duty officer swallowed a little. "Sergeant Bothari has a broken arm, some broken ribs, internal injuries, and a concussion. Lieutenant Koudelka, both legs broken, and a lot of, uh . . . shock burns." His voice trailed off.

"What?"

"Evidently—I heard—their assailants had a couple of high-voltage shock sticks, and they discovered they could get some . . . peculiar effects on his prosthetic nerves with them. After they'd broken his legs they spent . . . quite a long time working him over. That's how it was Commander Illyan's men caught up with them. They didn't clear off in time."

Cordelia pushed her plate away and sat trembling.

"Hearsay, eh? Very well. Dismissed. See that Commander Illyan is sent to me immediately he arrives." Vorkosigan's expression was introspective and grim.

Piotr's was sourly triumphant. "Vermin," he asserted. "You ought to burn them all out."

Vorkosigan sighed. "Easier to start a war than finish it. Not this week, sir."

Illyan attended on Vorkosigan within the hour, in the library, with his informal verbal report. Cordelia trailed in after them, to sit and listen.

"Sure you want to hear this?" Vorkosigan asked her quietly.

She shook her head. "Next to you, they are my best friends here. I'd rather know than wonder."

The duty officer's synopsis proved tolerably accurate, but Illyan, who had talked to both Bothari and Koudelka at the Imperial Military Hospital where they had been taken, had a number of details to add, in blunt terms. His puppy-dog face looked unusually old this morning.

"Your secretary was apparently seized with a desire to get laid," he began. "Why he picked Bothari as a native guide, I can't imagine."

"We three are the sole survivors of the *General Vorkraft*," Vorkosigan replied. "It's a bond, I suppose. Kou and Bothari always got on well, though. He appeals to Bothari's latent fatherly instincts, maybe. And Kou's a clean-minded boy—don't tell him I said that, he'd take it as an insult. It's good to be reminded such people still exist. Wish he'd come to me, though."

"Well, Bothari did his best," said Illyan. "Took him to this dismal dive, which I gather has a number of points in its favor from Bothari's point of view. It's cheap, it's quick, and nobody talks to him. It's also far removed from Admiral Vorrutyer's old circles. No unpleasant associations. He has a strict routine. According to Kou, Bothari's regular woman is almost as ugly as he is. Bothari likes her, it appears, because she never makes any noise. I don't think I want to think about that.

"Be that as it may, Kou got mismatched with one of the other employees, who terrified him. Bothari says he asked for the best girl for him—hardly a girl, woman, whatever—and apparently Kou's needs were misinterpreted. Anyway, Bothari was done and kicking his heels waiting while Kou was still trying to make polite conversation and being offered an assortment of delights for jaded appetites he'd never heard of before. He gave up and fled back downstairs at last, where Bothari was by this time pretty thoroughly tanked. He usually has one drink and leaves, it seems.

"Kou, Bothari, and this whore then got into an argument over payment, on the grounds that he'd burned up

enough time for four customers versus—most of this won't
be in the official report, all right?—she couldn't get his
circuits working. Kou forked over a partial payment—
Bothari's still grumbling over how much, insofar as he can
talk at all through that mouth of his this morning—and
they retreated in disorder, a lousy time having been had
by all."

"The first obvious question that arises," said Vorkosigan,
"is, was the attack ordered by anyone from that estab-
lishment?"

"To the best of my knowledge, no. I threw a cordon
around the place, once we'd found it, and questioned
everyone inside under fast-penta. Scared the shit out of
them all, I'm glad to say. They're used to Count Vorbohn's
municipal guards, whom they bribe, or who blackmail
them, and vice versa. We turned up a lot of information
on petty crimes, none of which was of the least interest
to us—do you want me to pass it on to the municipals,
by the way?"

"Hm. If they're innocent of the attack, just file it.
Bothari may want to go back there someday. Do they
know why they were questioned?"

"Certainly not! I insist my men work clean. We're here
to gather information, not pass it out."

"My apologies, Commander. I should have known.
Carry on."

"Well, they left the place about an hour after midnight,
on foot, and took a wrong turn somewhere. Bothari's
pretty upset about that. Thinks it's his fault, for getting
so drunk. Bothari and Koudelka both say they saw move-
ments in the shadows for about ten minutes before the
attack. So they were stalked, apparently, until they were
manuevered into a high walled alley, and found themselves
with six in front and six behind.

"Bothari pulled his stunner and fired—got three, before
he was jumped. Someone down there is richer by a good
service stunner this morning. Kou had his swordstick, but
nothing else.

"They ganged up on Bothari first. He took out two

more, after he'd lost the stunner. They stunned him, then tried to beat him to death after he was down. Kou had been using his stick as a quarterstaff up till then, but at that point he popped the cover off. He says now he wished he hadn't, because this murmur of 'Vor!' went up all around, and things got really ugly.

"He stabbed two, until somebody struck the sword with a shock stick, and his hand went into spasms. The five that were left sat on him and broke both his legs backwards at the knees. He asked me to tell you it wasn't as painful as it sounds. He says they broke so many circuits he had hardly any sensation. I don't know if that's true."

"It's hard to tell with Kou," said Vorkosigan. "He's been concealing pain for so long, it's almost second nature. Go on."

"I have to jump back a bit now. My man who was assigned to Kou followed them down into that warren by himself. He wasn't one of the men who are familiar with the place, supposedly, and he wasn't dressed for it—Kou had two reservations for some live musical performance last night, and until three hours before midnight that's where we thought he was going. My man went in there and vanished, between the first and second hourly checks. That's what has me going this morning. Was he murdered? Or kidnapped? Rolled and raped? Or was he a plant, a setup, a double agent? We won't know till we find the body, or whatever.

"Thirty minutes after the missed check my people sent in another tail. But he was looking for the first man. Kou was uncovered for three solid bloody hours last night before my night shift supervisor came on duty and woke to the fact. Fortunately, Kou'd spent most of that time in Bothari's old whore's retirement home.

"My night shift man, whom I commend, redirected the field agent, and put a patrol in the air to boot. So when the field agent finally got to that revolting scene, he was able to call a flyer down on top of it almost immediately, and drop half a dozen of my uniformed bruisers in to break up the party. That business with the shock sticks—it was bad, but not as bad as it might have been. Kou's assailants evidently lacked the sort of, hm, imaginative approach that, say, the late Admiral Vorrutyer might have had in the same situation. Or maybe they just didn't have time to get really refined."

"Thank God," murmured Vorkosigan. "And the deaths?"

"Two were Bothari's work, clean blows, one was Kou's— cut him across the neck—and one, I'm afraid, was mine. The kid went into anaphylactic shock in an allergic reaction to fast-penta. We zipped him over to ImpMil, but they couldn't get him going again. I don't like it. They're autopsying him now, trying to find out if it was natural or a planted defense against questioning."

"And the gang?"

"Appears to be a perfectly legitimate—if that's the word—caravanserai mutual benefit society. According to the survivors we captured, they decided to pick on Kou because he 'walked funny.' Charming. Although Bothari wasn't exactly walking in a straight line, either. None of the ones we captured is an agent for anybody but themselves. I cannot speak for the dead. I supervised the questioning personally, and will swear to it. They were quite shocked to find themselves of interest to Imperial Security."

"Anything else?" said Vorkosigan.

Illyan yawned behind his hand, and apologized. "It's been a long night. My night shift man got me out of bed after midnight. Good man, good judgment. No, that about wraps it up, except for Kou's motivation for going down there in the first place. He went all vague, and started asking for pain medication, when we came to that subject. I was hoping you might have a suggestion, to ease my paranoias. Being suspicious of Kou gives me a crick in the neck." He yawned again.

"I do," said Cordelia, "but for your paranoia, not for your report, all right?"

He nodded.

"I think he's in love with someone. After all, you don't test something unless you're planning to use it. Unfortunately his test was a major disaster. I expect he'll be pretty depressed and touchy for quite some time."

Vorkosigan nodded understanding.

"Any idea who?" asked Illyan automatically.

"Yes, but I don't think it's your business. Especially if it's not going to happen."

Illyan shrugged acceptance, and left to pursue his lost sheep, the missing man who'd first been assigned to follow Koudelka.

Sergeant Bothari was back at Vorkosigan House, though not yet back on duty, within five days, a plastic casing on the broken arm. He volunteered no information on the brutal affair, and discouraged curious questioners with a sour glower and noncommittal grunts.

Droushnakovi asked no questions and offered no comments. But Cordelia saw her occasionally cast a haunted look at the empty comconsole in the library, with its double-scrambled links to the Imperial Residence and the General Staff Headquarters, where Koudelka usually sat to work while at Vorkosigan House. Cordelia wondered just how much detail of that night's events had been poured, searing as lead, into her ears.

Lieutenant Koudelka returned to curtailed light duties the following month, apparently quite cheerful and unaffected by his ordeal. But in his own way he was as uninformative as Bothari. Questioning Bothari had been like questioning a wall. Questioning Koudelka was like talking to a stream; one got back babble, or little eddies of jokes, or anecdotes that pulled the current of the discussion inexorably away from the original subject. Cordelia responded to his sunniness with automatic good grace, playing along with his obvious desire to slide over the affair as lightly as possible. Inwardly she was far more doubtful.

Her own mood was not the best. Her imagination returned again and again to the assassination scare of six weeks ago, dwelling uncomfortably on the chances that had almost taken Vorkosigan from her. Only when he was with her was she completely at ease, and he was gone more and more now. Something was brewing at Imperial

HQ; he had been gone four times to all-night sessions, and had taken a trip without her, some flying inspection of military affairs, of which he gave her no details and from which he returned white-tired around the eyes. He came in and out at odd hours. The flow of military and political gossip and chitchat with which he was wont to entertain her at meals, or undressing for bed, dried up to an uncommunicative silence, though he seemed to need her presence no less.

Where would she be without him? A pregnant widow, without family or friends, bearing a child already a focal point of dynastic paranoias, inheritor of a legacy of violence. Could she get off-planet? And where would she go if she could? Would Beta Colony ever let her come back?

Even the autumn rain, and the fat lingering greenness of the city parks, began to fail to please her. Oh, for a breath of really dry desert air, the familiar alkali tang, the endless flat distances. Would her son ever know what a real desert was? The horizons here, crowded close with buildings and vegetation, seemed almost to rise around her like a huge wall at times. On really bad days the wall seemed to topple inward.

She was holed up in the library one rainy afternoon, curled on an old high-backed sofa, reading, for the third time, a page in an old volume from the Count's shelves. The book was a relic of the printer's art from the Time of Isolation. The English in which it was written was printed in a mutant variation of the cyrillic alphabet, all forty-six characters of it, once used for all tongues on Barrayar. Her mind seemed unusually mushy and unresponsive to it today. She turned out the light and rested her eyes a few minutes. With relief, she observed Lieutenant Koudelka enter the library and seat himself, stiffly and carefully, at the comconsole. *I shan't interrupt him; he at least has real work to do,* she thought, not yet returning to her page, but still comforted by his unconscious company.

He worked only for a moment or two, then shut down the machine with a sigh, staring abstractedly into the empty carved fireplace that was the room's original centerpiece, still not noticing her. *So, I'm not the only one who can't concentrate. Maybe it's this strange grey weather. It does seem to have a depressing effect on people. . . .*

Picking up his swordstick, he ran a hand down the smooth length of its casing. He clicked it open, holding it firmly and releasing the spring silently and slowly. He sighted along the length of the gleaming blade, which almost seemed to glow with a light of its own in the shadowed room, and angled it, as if meditating on its pattern and fine workmanship. He then turned it end for end, point over his left shoulder and hilt away from him. He wrapped a handkerchief around the blade for a hold, and pressed it, very lightly, against the side of his neck over the area of the carotid artery. The expression on his face was distant and thoughtful, his grip on the blade as light as a lover's. His hand tightened suddenly.

Her indrawn breath, the first half of a sob, startled him from his reverie. He looked up to see her for the first time; his lips thinned and his face turned a dusky red. He swung the sword down. It left a white line on his neck, like part of a necklace, with a few ruby drops of blood welling along it.

"I . . . didn't see you, Milady," he said hoarsely. "I . . . don't mind me. Just fooling around, you know."

They stared at each other in silence. Her own words broke from her lips against her will. "I hate this place! I'm afraid all the time, now."

She turned her face into the high side of the sofa, and, to her own horror, began to cry. *Stop it! Not in front of Kou of all people! The man has enough real troubles without you dumping your imaginary ones on him.* But she couldn't stop.

He levered himself up and limped over to her couch, looking worried. Tentatively, he seated himself beside her.

"Um . . ." he began. "Don't cry, Milady. I was just fooling around, really." He patted her clumsily on the shoulder.

"Garbage," she choked back at him. "You scare the hell

out of me." On impulse she transferred her tear-smeared face from the cold silken fabric of the sofa to the warm roughness of the shoulder of his green uniform. It tore a like honesty from him.

"You can't imagine what it's like," he whispered fiercely. "They pity me, you know? Even *he* does." A jerk of his head in no particular direction indicated Vorkosigan. "It's a hundred times worse than the scorn. And it's going to go on *forever*."

She shook her head, devoid of answer in the face of this undoubted truth.

"I hate this place, too," he continued. "Just as much as it hates me. More, some days. So you see, you're not alone."

"So many people trying to kill him," she whispered back, despising herself for her weakness. "Total strangers . . . one of them is bound to succeed in the end. I think about it all the time, now." Would it be a bomb? Some poison? Plasma arc, burning away Aral's face, leaving no lips even to kiss goodbye?

Koudelka's attention was drawn achingly from his pain to hers, brows drawing quizzically together.

"Oh, Kou," she went on, looking down blindly into his lap and stroking his sleeve. "No matter how much it hurts, don't do it to him. He loves you . . . you're like a son to him, just the sort of son he always wanted. That," she nodded toward the sword laid on the couch, shinier than silk, "would cut out his heart. This place pours craziness on him every day, and demands he give back justice. He can't do it except with a whole heart. Or he must eventually start giving back the craziness, like every one of his predecessors. And," she added in a burst of uncontrollable illogic, "it's so damn *wet* here! It won't be my fault if my son is born with *gills*!"

His arms encircled her in a kindly hug. "Are you . . . afraid of the childbirth?" he inquired, with a gentle and unexpected perceptiveness.

Cordelia went still, suddenly face-to-face with her

tightly suppressed fears. "I don't trust your doctors," she admitted shakily.

He smiled in deep irony. "I can't blame you."

A laugh puffed from her, and she hugged him back, around the chest, and raised her hand to wipe away the tiny drops of blood from the side of his neck. "When you love someone, it's like your skin covers theirs. Every hurt is doubled. And I do love you so, Kou. I wish you'd let me help you."

"Therapy, Cordelia?" Vorkosigan's voice was cold, and cut like a stinging spray of rattling hail. She looked up, surprised, to see him standing before them, his face frozen as his voice. "I realize you have a great deal of Betan . . . expertise, in such matters, but I beg you will leave the project to someone else."

Koudelka turned red, and recoiled from her. "Sir," he began, and trailed off, as startled as Cordelia by the icy anger in Vorkosigan's eyes. Vorkosigan's gaze flicked over him, and they both clamped their jaws shut.

Cordelia drew in a very deep breath for a retort, but released it only as a furious "Oh!" at Vorkosigan's back as he wheeled and stalked out, spine stiff as Kou's swordblade.

Koudelka, still red, folded into himself, and using his sword as a prop levered himself to his feet, his breath too rapid. "Milady. I beg your pardon." The words seemed quite without meaning.

"Kou," said Cordelia, "you know he didn't mean that hateful thing. He spoke without thinking. I'm sure he doesn't, doesn't . . ."

"Yes, I realize," returned Koudelka, his eyes blank and hard. "I am universally known to be quite harmless to any man's marriage, I believe. But if you will excuse me— Milady—I do have some work to do. Of a sort."

"Oh!" Cordelia didn't know if she was more furious with Vorkosigan, Koudelka, or herself. She steamed to her feet and left the room, throwing her words back over her shoulder. "Damn all Barrayarans to hell anyway!"

Droushnakovi appeared in her path, with a timid, "Milady?"

"And you, you useless . . . frill," snarled Cordelia, her rage escaping helplessly in all directions now. "Why can't you manage your own affairs? You Barrayaran women seem to expect your lives to be handed to you on a platter. It doesn't work that way!"

The girl stepped back a pace, bewildered. Cordelia contained her seething outrage, and asked more sensibly, "Which way did Aral go?"

"Why . . . upstairs, I believe, Milady."

A little of her old and battered humor came to her rescue then. "Two steps at a time, by chance?"

"Um . . . three, actually," Drou replied faintly.

"I suppose I'd better go talk to him," said Cordelia, running her hands through her hair and wondering if tearing it out would have any practical benefit. "Son of a bitch." She did not know herself if that was expletive or description. *And to think I never used to swear.*

She trudged after him, her anger draining with her energy as she climbed the stairs. *This pregnancy business sure slows you down.* She passed a duty guard in the corridor. "Lord Vorkosigan go this way?" she asked him.

"To his rooms, Milady," he replied, and stared curiously after her. *Great. Love it,* she thought savagely. *The old newlyweds' first real fight will have plenty of built-in audience. These old walls are not soundproof. I wonder if I can keep my voice down? Aral's no problem; when he gets mad he whispers.*

She entered their bedroom, to find him seated on the side of the bed, removing uniform jacket and boots with violent, jerky gestures. He looked up, and they glared at each other. Cordelia opened fire first, thinking, *Let's get this over with.*

"That remark you made in front of Kou was totally out of line."

"What, I walk in to find my wife . . . cuddling, with one of my officers, and you expect me to make polite conversation about the weather?" he bit back.

"You know it was nothing of the sort."

"Fine. Suppose it hadn't been me? Suppose it had been

one of the duty guards, or my father. How would you have explained it then? You know what they think of Betans. They'd jump on it, and the rumors would never be stopped. Next thing I knew, it would be coming back at me as political chaff. Every enemy I have out there is just waiting for a weak spot to pounce on. They'd love one like that."

"How the devil did we get onto your damned politics? I'm talking about a friend. I doubt you could have come up with a more wounding remark if you'd funded a study project. That was foul, Aral! What's the matter with you, anyway?"

"I don't know." He slowed, and rubbed his face tiredly. "It's the damn job, I expect. I don't mean to spill it on you."

Cordelia suspected that was as near as she could expect of an admission of his being in the wrong, and accepted it with a little nod, letting her own rage evaporate. She then remembered why the rage had felt so good, for the vacuum it left filled back up with fear.

"Yes, well . . . just how much do you fancy having to break down his door one of these mornings?"

Vorkosigan frowned at her, going still. "Do you . . . have some reason to believe's he's thinking along suicidal lines? He seemed quite content to me."

"He would—to you." Cordelia let the words hang in the air a moment, for emphasis. "I think he's about that close." She held up thumb and forefinger a bare millimeter apart. The finger still had a smear of blood on it, and it caught her eye in unhappy fascination. "He was playing around with that blasted swordstick. I wish I'd never given it to him. I don't think I could bear it if he used it to cut his own throat. That—seemed to be what he had in mind."

"Oh." Vorkosigan looked smaller, somehow, without his glittering military jacket, without his anger. He held out his hand to her, and she took it and sat beside him.

"So if you're having visions of, of playing King Arthur to our Lancelot and Guinevere in that—pig-head of yours, forget it. It won't wash."

He laughed a little at that. "My visions were closer to home, I'm afraid, and considerably more sordid. Just an old bad dream."

"Yeah, I . . . guess it would hit a nerve, at that." She wondered if the ghost of his first wife ever hovered by him, breathing cold death in his ear, as Vorrutyer's ghost sometimes did by her. He looked deathly enough. "But I'm Cordelia, remember? Not . . . anybody else."

He leaned his forehead against hers. "Forgive me, dear Captain. I'm just an ugly scared old man, and growing older and uglier and more paranoid every day."

"You, too?" She rested in his arms. "I take exception to the old and ugly part, though. Pigheaded did *not* refer to your exterior appearance."

"Thank you—I think."

It pleased her to amuse him even that little. "It is the job, isn't it?" she said. "Can you talk about it at all?"

His lips compressed. "In confidence—although that seems to be your natural state, I don't know why I bother to emphasize it—it looks like we could have another war on our hands before the end of the year. And we're not nearly well enough recovered for it, after Escobar."

"What! I thought the war party was half-paralyzed."

"Ours is. The Cetagandans' is still in good working order, however. Intelligence indicates they were planning to use the political chaos here following Ezar Vorbarra's death to cover a move on those disputed wormhole jump points. Instead they got me, and—well, I can hardly call it stability. Dynamic equilibrium, at best. Anyway, not the kind of disruption they were counting on. Hence that little incident with the sonic grenade. Negri and Illyan are now seventy percent sure it was Cetagandan work."

"Will they . . . try again?"

"Almost certainly. But with or without me, consensus in the Staff is that they'll be probing in force before the end of the year. And if we're weak—they'll just keep right on moving until they're stopped."

"No wonder you've been . . . abstracted."

"Is that the polite term for it? But no. I've known about

the Cetagandans for some time. Something else came up today, after the Council session. A private audience. Count Vorhalas came to see me, to beg a favor."

"I'd think it would be your pleasure, to do a favor for Rulf Vorhalas's brother. I gather not?"

He shook his head unhappily. "The Count's youngest son, who is a hotheaded young idiot of eighteen who should have been sent to military school—you met him at the Council confirmation, as I recall—"

"Lord Carl?"

"Yes. He got into a drunken fight at a party last night."

"A universal tradition. Such things happen even on Beta Colony."

"Quite. But they stepped outside to settle their affair armed, each one, with a pair of dull swords that had been part of a wall decoration, and a couple of kitchen knives. That made it, technically, a duel with the two swords."

"Uh-oh. Was anyone hurt?"

"Unfortunately, yes. More or less by accident, I gather, in a scrambling fall, the Count's son managed to put his sword through his friend's stomach and sever his abdominal aorta. He bled to death almost immediately. By the time the bystanders had gathered their wits sufficiently to get a medical team up there, it was much too late."

"Dear God."

"It was a duel, Cordelia. It began as a mockery, but it ended as the real thing. And the penalties for dueling apply." He rose, and paced the room, stopping by the window and staring out into the rain. "His father came to ask me for an Imperial pardon. Or, if I could not grant that, to see if I could get the charges changed to simple murder. If it were tried as a simple murder, the boy could plead self-defense, and possibly end up with a mere prison term."

"That seems . . . fair enough, I suppose."

"Yes." He paced again. "A favor for a friend. Or . . . the first crack in the door to let that hell-bred custom back into our society. What happens when the next case is brought before me, and the next, and the next? Where do I begin drawing the line? What if the next case involves some political enemy of mine, and not a member of my own party? Shall all the deaths that went into stamping this thing out be made void? I remember dueling, and what things were like back then. And worse—an entry point for government by friends, then cliques. Say what you will about Ezar Vorbarra, in thirty years of ruthless labor he transformed the government from a Vor-class club into some semblance, however shaky, of a rule of law, one law for everyone."

"I begin to see the problem."

"And me—me, of all men, to have to make that decision! Who should have been publicly executed twenty-two years ago for the selfsame crime!" He paused before her. "The story about last night is all over town, in various forms, this morning. It will be all over everywhere in a few days. I had the news service kill it, temporarily, but that was mere spitting in the wind. It's too late for a coverup, even if I wanted to do one. So what shall I betray this day? A friend? Or Ezar Vorbarra's trust? There is no doubt which decision *he* would have made."

He sat back beside her, and took her in his arms. "And this is only the beginning. Every month, every week, there will be some other impossible thing. What's going to be left of me after fifteen years of this? A husk, like that thing we buried three months ago, praying with his last breath that there may be no God? Or a power-corrupted monstrosity, like his son, so infected it could only be sterilized by plasma arc? Or something even worse?"

His naked agony terrified her. She held him tightly in return. "I don't know. I don't know. But somebody . . . somebody has been making these kinds of decisions right along, while we went along blissfully unconscious, taking the world as given. And they were only human, too. No better, no worse than you."

"Frightening thought."

She sighed. "You can't choose between evil and evil, in the dark, by logic. You can only cling to some safety line of principle. I can't make your decision. But whatever principles you choose now are going to be your safety lines, to carry you forward. And for the sake of your people, they're going to have to be consistent ones."

He rested in her arms. "I know. There wasn't really a question, about the decision. I was just . . . kicking a bit, going down." He disengaged himself, and stood again. "Dear Captain. If I'm still sane, fifteen years from now, I believe it will be your doing."

She looked up at him. "So what decision is it?"

The pain in his eyes gave her the answer. "Oh, no," she said involuntarily, then bit off further words. *And I was trying to speak so wisely. I didn't mean this.*

"Don't you know?" he said gently, resigned. "Ezar's way is the only way that can work, here. It's true after all. He does rule from his grave." He headed for their bathroom, to wash and change clothes.

"But you're not him," she whispered to the empty room. "Can't you find a way of your own?"

CHAPTER EIGHT

Vorkosigan attended Carl Vorhalas's public execution three weeks later.

"Are you required to go?" Cordelia asked him that morning, as he dressed, cold and withdrawn. "I don't have to go, do I?"

"God, no, of course not. I don't have to go, officially, except . . . I have to go. You can see why, surely."

"Not . . . really, except as a form of self-punishment. I'm not sure that's a luxury you can afford, in your line of work."

"I must go. A dog returns to its vomit, doesn't it? His parents will be there, do you know? And his brother."

"What a barbaric custom."

"Well, we could treat crime as a disease, like you Betans. You know what that's like. At least we kill a man cleanly, all at once, instead of in bits over years. . . . I don't know."

"How will they . . . do it?"

"Beheading. It's supposed to be almost painless."

"How do they know?"

His laugh was totally without humor. "A very cogent question."

He did not embrace her when he left. He returned

a bare two hours later, silent, to shake his head at a
tentative offer of lunch, cancel an afternoon appointment,
and withdraw to Count Piotr's library and sit, not-reading
a book-viewer. Cordelia joined him there after a while,
resting on the couch, and waited patiently for him to come
back to her from whatever distant country of the mind
he dwelt in.

"The boy was going to be brave," he said after an hour's
silence. "You could see that he had every gesture planned
out in advance. But nobody else followed the script. His
mother broke him down. . . . And to top it the damned
executioner missed his stroke. Had to take three cuts, to
get the head off."

"Sounds like Sergeant Bothari did better with a pock-
etknife." Vorrutyer had been haunting her more than usual
that morning, scarletly.

"It lacked nothing for perfect hideousness. His mother
cursed me, too. Until Evon and Count Vorhalas took her
away." The dead-expressioned voice escaped him then.
"Oh, Cordelia! It can't have been the right decision! And
yet . . . and yet . . . no other one was possible. Was
it?"

He came to her then, and held her in silence. He
seemed very close to weeping, and it almost frightened
her more that he did not. The tension eventually drained
out of him.

"I suppose I'd better pull myself together and go
change. Vortala has a meeting scheduled with the Minister of Agriculture that's too important to miss, and after
that there's the general staff. . . ." By the time he left
his usual self-possession had returned.

That night he lay long awake beside her. His eyes were
closed, but she could tell from his breathing it was pretense. She could not dredge up one word of comfort that
did not seem inane to her, so kept silence with him
through the watches of the night. Rain began outside, a
steady drizzle. He spoke once.

"I've watched men die before. Ordered executions,
ordered men into battle, chosen this one over that one,

committed three sheer murders and but for the grace of God
and Sergeant Bothari would have committed a fourth . . . I
don't know why this one should hit like a wall. It's stopped
me, Cordelia. And I dare not stop, or we'll all fall together.
Got to keep it in the air somehow."

She awoke in the dark to a tinkling crash and a soft
report, and drew in her breath with a start. Acridity seared
her lungs, mouth, nostrils, eyes. A gut-wrenching
undertaste pumped her stomach into her throat. Beside
her, Vorkosigan snapped from sleep with an oath.

"Soltoxin gas grenade! Don't breathe, Cordelia!"
Emphasizing his shout, he shoved a pillow over her face,
his hot strong arms encircling her and dragging her from
the bed. She found her feet and lost her stomach at the
same moment, stumbling into the hall, and he slammed
the bedroom door shut behind them.

Running footsteps shook the floor. Vorkosigan cried,
"Get back! Soltoxin gas! Clear the floor! Call Illyan!"
before he too doubled over, coughing and retching. Other
hands bundled them both toward the stairs. She could
scarcely see through her madly watering eyes.

Between spasms Vorkosigan gasped, "They'll have the
antidote . . . Imperial Residence . . . closer than ImpMil
. . . get Illyan at once. He'll know. Into the shower—
where's Milady's woman? Get a maid. . . ."

Within moments she was dumped into a downstairs
shower, Vorkosigan with her. He was shaking and barely
able to stand, but still trying to help her. "Start washing
it off your skin, and keep washing. Don't stop. Keep the
water cool."

"You, too, then. What was that crap?" She coughed
again, in the spray of the water, and they exchanged help
with the soap.

"Wash out your mouth, too. . . . Soltoxin. It's been
fifteen, sixteen years since I last smelled that stink, but
you never forget it. It's a poison gas. Military. Should
be strictly controlled. How the hell anyone got hold of
some . . . Damn Security! They'll be flapping around

like headless chickens tomorrow . . . too late." His face was greenish-white beneath the night's beard stubble.

"I don't feel too bad now," said Cordelia. "Nausea's passing off. I take it we missed the full dose?"

"No. It just acts slowly. Doesn't take much at all to do you. It mostly affects soft tissue—lungs will be jelly in an hour, if the antidote doesn't get here soon."

The growing fear that pounded in her gut, heart, and mind half-clotted her words. "Does it cross the placental barrier?"

He was silent for too long before he said, "I'm not sure. Have to ask the doctor. I've only seen the effects on young men." Another spasm of deep coughing seized him, that went on and on.

One of Count Piotr's serving women arrived, disheveled and frightened, to help Cordelia and the terrified young guard who had been assisting them. Another guard came in to report, raising his voice over the running water. "We reached the Residence, sir. They have some people on the way."

Cordelia's own throat, bronchia, and lungs were beginning to secrete foul-tasting phlegm, and she coughed and spat. "Anyone see Drou?"

"I think she took out after the assassins, Milady."

"Not her job. When an alarm goes up, she's supposed to run to Cordelia," growled Vorkosigan. The talking triggered more coughing.

"She was downstairs, sir, at the time the attack took place, with Lieutenant Koudelka. They both went out the back door."

"Dammit," Vorkosigan muttered, "not his job either." His effort was punished by another coughing jag. "They catch anybody?"

"I think so, sir. There was some kind of uproar at the back of the garden, by the wall."

They stood under the water for a few more minutes, until the guard reported back. "The doctor from the Residence is here, sir."

The maid wrapped Cordelia in a robe, and Vorkosigan

put on a towel, growling to the guard, "Go find me some clothes, boy." His voice rattled like gravel.

A middle-aged man, his hair standing up stiffly, wearing trousers, pajama tops, and bedroom slippers, was off-loading equipment in the guest bedroom when they came out. He took a pressurized canister from his bag and fitted a breathing mask to it, glancing at Cordelia's rounding abdomen and then at Vorkosigan.

"My lord. Are you certain of the identification of the poison?"

"Unfortunately, yes. It was soltoxin."

The doctor bowed his head. "I am sorry, Milady."

"Is it going to hurt my . . ." She choked on the mucus.

"Just shut up and give it to her," snarled Vorkosigan.

The doctor fitted the mask over her nose and mouth. "Breathe deeply. Inhale . . . exhale. Keep exhaling. Now draw in. Hold it. . . ."

The antidote gas had a greenish taste, cooler, but nearly as nauseating as the original poison. Her stomach heaved, but had nothing left in it to reject. She watched Vorkosigan over the mask, watching her, and tried to smile reassuringly. It must be reaction catching up with him; he seemed greyer, more distressed, with each breath she took. She was certain he had taken in a larger dose than she, and pushed the mask away to say, "Isn't it about your turn?"

The doctor pressed it back, saying, "One more breath, Milady, to be sure." She inhaled deeply, and the doctor transferred the mask to Vorkosigan. He seemed to need no instruction in the procedure.

"How many minutes since the exposure?" asked the doctor anxiously.

"I'm not sure. Did anyone note the time? You, uh . . ." She had forgotten the young guard's name.

"About fifteen or twenty minutes, Milady, I think."

The doctor relaxed measurably. "It should be all right, then. You'll both be in hospital for a few days. I'll arrange for medical transport. Was anyone else exposed?" he asked the guard.

"Doctor, wait." He had repossessed canister and mask,

and was making for the door. "What will that . . . soltoxin do to my baby?"

He did not meet her eyes. "No one knows. No one has ever survived exposure without an immediate antidote treatment."

Cordelia could feel her heart beating. "But given the treatment . . ." She did not like his look of pity, and turned to Vorkosigan. "Is that—" but was stopped cold by his expression, a leaden greyness lit from beneath by pain and growing anger, a stranger's face with a lover's eyes, meeting her eyes at last.

"Tell her about it," he whispered to the doctor. "I can't."

"Need we distress—"

"*Now*. Get it over with." His voice cracked and croaked.

"The problem is the antidote, Milady," said the doctor reluctantly. "It's a violent teratogen. Destroys bone development in the growing fetus. Your bones are grown, so it won't affect you, except for an increased tendency to arthritic-type breakdowns, which can be treated . . . if and when they arise. . . ." He trailed off as she closed her eyes, shutting him out.

"I must see that hall guard," he added.

"Go, go," replied Vorkosigan, releasing him. He maneuvered out the door past the guard arriving with Vorkosigan's clothes.

She opened her eyes to Vorkosigan, and they stared at each other.

"The look on your face . . ." he whispered. "It's not . . . Weep. Rage! Do something!" His voice rose to hoarseness. "Hate me at least!"

"I can't," she whispered back, "feel anything yet. Tomorrow, maybe." Every breath was fire.

With a muttered curse, he flung on the clothes, a set of undress greens. "I can do something."

It was the stranger's face, possessing his. Words echoed hollowly in her memory, *If Death wore a dress uniform He would look just like that.*

"Where are you going?"

"Going to see what Koudelka caught." She followed him through the door. "You stay here," he ordered.

"No."

He glared back at her, and she brushed the glare away with an equally savage gesture, as if striking down a sword thrust. "I'm going with you."

"Come on, then." He turned jerkily, and made for the stairs to the first floor, rage rigid in his backbone.

"You will not," she murmured fiercely, for his ear alone, "murder anyone in front of me."

"Will I not?" he whispered back. "Will-I-not?" His steps were hard, bare feet jarring on the stone stairs.

The large entry hall was in chaos, filled with their guards, men in the Count's livery, medics. A man, or a body, Cordelia could not tell which, in the black fatigue uniform of the night guards, was laid out on the tessalated pavement, a medic at his head. Both were soaked from the rain, and smeared with mud. Bloodstained water pooled beneath them, and the medic's bootsoles squeaked in it.

Commander Illyan, beads of water gleaming in his hair from the foggy drizzle, was just coming in the front door with an aide, saying, "Let me know as soon as the techs get here with the kirilian detector. Meantime keep everyone off that wall and out of the alley. My lord!" he cried when he saw Vorkosigan. "Thank God you're all right!"

Vorkosigan growled in his throat, wordlessly. A knot of men surrounded the prisoner, who was leaning face to the wall, one hand over his head and the other held stiffly to his side at an odd angle. Droushnakovi stood near, wearing a wet shift. A wicked-looking metal crossbow dangled gleaming from her hand, evidently the weapon that had been used to fire the gas grenade through their window. She bore a livid mark on her face, and stanched a nosebleed with her other hand. Blood stained her nightgown here and there. Koudelka was there, too, leaning on his sword, one leg dragging. He wore a wet and muddy uniform and bedroom slippers, and a sour look on his face.

"I'd have had him," he was snapping, evidently

continuing an ongoing argument, "if you hadn't come running up and shouting at me—"

"Oh, really!" Droushnakovi snapped back. "Well, pardon me, but I don't see it that way. Seems to me he had you, laid out flat on the ground. If I hadn't seen his legs going up the wall—"

"Stuff it! It's Lord Vorkosigan!" hissed another guard. The knot of men turned, to step back before his face.

"How did he get in?" began Vorkosigan, and stopped. The man was wearing the black fatigues of the Service. "Surely not one of your men, Illyan!" His voice grated, metal on stone.

"My lord, we've got to have him alive, to question him," said Illyan uneasily at Vorkosigan's shoulder, half-hypnotized by the same look that had made the guards recoil. "There may be more to the conspiracy. You can't . . ."

The prisoner turned, then, to face his captors. A guard started forward to shove him back into position against the wall, but Vorkosigan motioned him away. Cordelia could not see Vorkosigan's face, standing behind him in that moment, but his shoulders lost their murderous tension, and the rage drained out of his backbone, leaving only a gutter-smear of pain. Above the insignialess black collar was the ravaged face of Evon Vorhalas.

"Oh, not *both* of them," breathed Cordelia.

Hatred hastened the rhythm of Vorhalas's breathing as he glared at his intended victim. "You bastard. You snake-cold bastard. Sitting there cold as stone while they hacked off his head. Did you feel a thing? Or did you enjoy it, my Lord Regent? I swore I'd get you then."

There was a long silence, then Vorkosigan leaned close to him, one arm extended past his head for support against the wall. He whispered hoarsely, "You missed me, Evon."

Vorhalas spat in his face, spittle bloody from his injured mouth. Vorkosigan made no move to wipe it away. "You missed my wife," he went on in a slow soft cadence. "But you got my son. Did you dream of sweet revenge? You have it. Look at her eyes, Evon. A man could drown in those sea-grey eyes. I'll be looking at them every day for

the rest of my life. So eat vengeance, Evon. Drink it.
Fondle it. Wrap it round you in the night watch. It's all
yours. I will it all to you. For myself, I've gorged it to
the gagging point, and have lost my stomach for it."

Vorhalas looked up, then, for the first time, past him
to Cordelia. She thought of the child in her belly, his delicate girdering of new cartilagenous bones perhaps even
now beginning to rot, twist, slough, but could not hate
Vorhalas, although she tried to for a moment. She couldn't
even find him baffling. She had a sense, as of a second
sight, that she could see right through his wounded spirit
the way doctors saw through a wounded body with their
diagnostic viewers. Every twist and tear and emotional
abrasion, every young cancer of resentment growing from
them, and above all the great gash of his brother's death
seemed red-lined in her mind's eye.

"He didn't enjoy it, Evon," she said. "What would you
have had from him? Do you even know?"

"A little human pity," he snarled. "He could have saved
Carl. Even then he could have. I thought at first that was
why he had come."

"Oh, God," said Vorkosigan. He looked sick at the flashing vision of the rise and fall of hopes these words conjured. "I don't play theater with lives, Evon!"

Vorhalas held his hatred like a shield before him. "Go
to hell."

Vorkosigan sighed, and pushed away from the wall. The
doctor was lingering to chivvy them to the waiting vehicle
for the trip to the Imperial Military Hospital. "Take him
away, Illyan," said Vorkosigan wearily.

"Wait," said Cordelia. "I need to know—I need to ask
him something."

Vorhalas eyed her sullenly.

"Was this the result you intended? I mean, when you
chose that particular weapon? That specific poison?"

He looked away from her, speaking to the far wall. "It
was what I could grab, going through the armory. I didn't
think you could identify it, and get the antidote all the
way from ImpMil in time. . . ."

"You relieve me of a burden," she whispered.

"The antidote came from the Imperial Residence," Vorkosigan explained. "A quarter of the distance. The Emperor's infirmary there has everything. As for identification . . . I was there, at the destruction of the Karian mutiny. Just about your age, I think, or a little younger. The smell brought it all back, just now. Boys coughing out their lungs in red blobs. . . ." He seemed to shrink into himself, into the past.

"I didn't intend your death particularly. You were just in the way, between me and him." Vorhalas gestured blindly at her swollen torso. "It wasn't the result I intended. I meant to kill him. I didn't even know for sure that you shared the same room at night." He was looking everywhere, now, except her face. "I never thought about killing your . . ."

"Look at me," she croaked, "and say the word out loud."

"Baby," he whispered, and burst into sudden, shocking sobs.

Vorkosigan stepped back, beside her. "Wish you hadn't done that," he whispered. "Reminds me of his brother. Why am I death to that family?"

"Still want him to eat vengeance?"

He leaned his forehead on her shoulder, briefly. "Not even that. You empty us all out, dear Captain. But, oh . . ." His hand reached out as if to cup her belly, then drew back in consciousness of their ring of silent watchers. He straightened. "Bring me a full report in the morning, Illyan," he said, "at the hospital."

He took her by the arm as they turned to follow the doctor. She could not tell if it was to support her or himself.

She was surrounded by helpers at the Imperial Military Hospital complex, carried along as on a river. Doctors, nurses, corpsmen, guards. Aral was separated from her at the door, and it made her uneasy and alone in the crowd. She said very little to them, empty courtesies, automatic as levers. She wished for shock to take her consciousness, numbness, reality-denying madness, hallucinations, anything. Instead she just felt tired.

The baby was moving within her, flutters, kneading turns; evidently the teratogenic antidote was a very slow-acting poison. They were still granted a little time together, it seemed, and she loved him through her skin, her fingertips moving in a slow massage over her abdomen. *Welcome, my son, to Barrayar, the abode of cannibals; this place didn't even wait the usual eighteen or twenty years to eat you.* Ravenous planet.

She was bedded down in a luxurious private room in a VIP wing, hastily cleared for their exclusive use. She was relieved to discover Vorkosigan had been ensconced just across the hall. Dressed already in green military-issue pajamas, he came promptly over to see her tucked into bed. She managed a small smile for him, but did not attempt to sit up. The force of gravity was pulling her down into the center of the world. Only the rigidity of the bed, the building, the planet's crust, held her up against it, not her will at all.

He was trailed by an anxious corpsman, saying, "Remember, sir, try not to talk so much, till after the doctor's had a chance to give your throat the irrigation treatment."

The grey light of dawn was making the windows pale. He sat on the edge of the bed and took her hand, rubbing it. "You're cold, dear Captain," he whispered hoarsely. She nodded. Her chest ached, her throat was raw, and her sinuses burned.

"I should never have let them talk me into taking the job," he went on. "So sorry . . ."

"I talked you into it, too. You tried to warn me. Not your fault. It seemed right for you. Is right."

He shook his head. "Don't talk. Makes scar tissue on the vocal cords."

She gave vent to a joyless "Ha!" and laid a finger across his lips as he started to speak again. He nodded, resigned, and they remained looking at each other for a time. He pushed her tangled hair back gently from her face, and

she captured the broad hand to hold against her cheek
for comfort, until he was hunted out by a posse of doctors and technicians and driven off for a treatment. "We'll
be in to see you shortly, Milady," their chieftain promised ominously.

They returned after a while, to make her gargle a nasty
pink fluid, and breathe into a machine, then rumbled out
again. A female nurse brought her breakfast, which she
did not touch.

Then a committee of grim-faced doctors entered her
room. The one who had come from the Imperial Residence in the night was now smartly groomed and neatly
dressed in civilian clothes. Her own personal physician
was flanked by a younger, black-browed man in Service
greens with captain's tabs on his collar. She gazed at their
three faces and thought of Cerberus.

Her man introduced the stranger. "This is Captain
Vaagen, of the Imperial Military Hospital's research facility.
He's our resident expert on military poisons."

"Inventing them, or cleaning up after them, Captain?"
Cordelia asked.

"Both, Milady." He stood at a sort of aggressive parade
rest.

Her own man had the look about his eyes of someone
who had drawn the short straw, although his lips smiled.
"My Lord Regent has asked me to inform you of the schedule of treatments, and so on. I'm afraid," he cleared his
throat, "that it would be best if we scheduled the abortion
promptly. It is already unusually late in your pregnancy for
it, and it would be as well for your recovery to relieve you
of the physiological strain as soon as possible."

"Is there nothing that can be done?" she asked hopelessly, already knowing the answer from their faces.

"I'm afraid not," said her man sadly. The man from
the Imperial Residence nodded confirmation.

"I ran a literature search," said the captain unexpectedly, staring out the window, "and there was that calcium
experiment. True, the results they got weren't particularly
heartening—"

"I thought we'd agreed not to bring that up," glared the Residence man.

"Vaagen, that's cruel," said her own man. "You're just raising false hopes. You can't make the Regent's wife into one of your hapless experimental animals for a lot of untried shots in the dark. You have your permission from the Regent for the autopsy—leave it at that."

Her world turned right-side-up again in a second, as she looked at the face of the man with ideas. She knew the type; half-right, half-cocked, half-successful, flitting from one monomania to another like a bee pollinating flowers, gathering little fruit but leaving seeds behind. She was nothing to him, personally, but the raw material for a monograph. The risks she took did not appall his imagination, she was not a person but a disease state. She smiled upon him, slowly, wildly, knowing him then for her ally in the enemy camp.

"How do you do, Dr. Vaagen? How would you like to write the paper of a lifetime?"

The Residence man barked a laugh. "She's got your number, Vaagen."

He smiled back, astonished to be so instantly understood. "You realize, I can't guarantee any results. . . ."

"Results!" interrupted her man. "My God, you'd better let her know what your idea of results is. Or show her the pictures—no, don't do that. Milady," he turned to her, "the treatment he's discussing was last tried twenty years ago. It did irreparable damage to the mothers. And the results—the very best results you could hope for would be a twisted cripple. Perhaps much worse. Indescribably worse."

"Jellyfish describes it pretty well," said Vaagen.

"You're inhuman, Vaagen!" snapped her man, with a glance her way to check the distress quotient.

"A viable jellyfish, Dr. Vaagen?" asked Cordelia, intent.

"Mm. Maybe," he replied, inhibited by his colleagues' angry glares. "But there is the difficulty of what happens to the mothers when the treatment is applied in vivo."

"So, can't you do it in vitro?" Cordelia asked the obvious question.

Vaagen shot a glance of triumph at her man. "It would certainly open up a number of possible lines of experiment, if it could be arranged," he murmured to the ceiling.

"In vitro?" said the Residence man, puzzled. "How?"

"What, how?" said Cordelia. "You've got seventeen Escobaran-manufactured uterine replicators stored in a closet around here somewhere, carried home from the war." She turned excitedly to Vaagen. "Do you happen to know a Dr. Henri?"

Vaagen nodded. "We've worked together."

"Then you know all about them!"

"Well—not exactly all. But, ah—in fact, he informs me that they are available. But you understand, I'm not an obstetrician."

"You certainly aren't," said her man. "Milady, this man isn't even a physician. He's only a biochemist."

"But you're an obstetrician," she pointed out. "So we have the whole team, then. Dr. Henri, and, um, Captain Vaagen here for Piotr Miles, and you, for the transfer."

His lips were compressed, and his eyes held a very strange expression. It took her a moment to identify it as fear. "I can't do the transfer, Milady," he said. "I don't know how. Nobody on Barrayar has ever done one."

"You don't advise it, then?"

"Definitely not. The possibility of permanent damage— you can, after all, begin again in a few months, if the soft-tissue scarring doesn't extend to testicular—ahem. You can begin again. I am your doctor, and that is my considered opinion."

"Yes, if somebody else doesn't knock Aral off in the meantime. I must remember this is Barrayar, where they are so in love with death they bury men who are still twitching. *Are* you willing to try the operation?"

He drew himself up in dignity. "No, Milady. And that's final."

"Very well." She pointed a finger at her doctor, "You're

out," and shifted it to Vaagen, "you're in. You are now in charge of this case. I rely on you to find me a surgeon—or a medical student, or a horse doctor, or *somebody* who's willing to try. And then you can experiment to your heart's content."

Vaagen looked mildly triumphant; her former man looked furious. "We had better see what my Lord Regent has to say, before you carry his wife off on this wave of criminally false optimism."

Vaagen looked a little less triumphant.

"You thinking of charging over there right now?" asked Cordelia.

"I'm sorry, Milady," said the Residence man, "but I think we'd do best to quash this thing right now. You don't know Captain Vaagen's reputation. Sorry to be so blunt, Vaagen, but you're an empire builder, and this time you've gone too far."

"Are you ambitious for a research wing, Captain Vaagen?" Cordelia inquired.

He shrugged, embarrassed rather than outraged, so she knew the Residence man's words to be at least half true. She gathered Vaagen in by eye, willing to possess him body, mind, and soul, but especially mind, and wondering how best to fire his imagination in her service.

"You shall have an institute, if you can bring this off. You tell him," she jerked her head in the direction of the hall, toward Aral's room, "*I* said so."

Variously discomfited, angry, and hopeful, they withdrew. Cordelia lay back on the bed and whistled a little soundless tune, her fingertips continuing their slow abdominal massage. Gravity had ceased to exist.

CHAPTER NINE

She slept at last, toward the middle of the day, and woke disoriented. She squinted at the afternoon light slanting through the hospital room's windows. The grey rain had gone away. She touched her belly, for grief and reassurance, and rolled over to find Count Piotr sitting at her bedside.

He was dressed in his country clothes, old uniform trousers, plain shirt, a jacket that he wore only at Vorkosigan Surleau. He must have come up directly to ImpMil. His thin lips smiled anxiously at her. His eyes looked tired and worried.

"Dear girl. You need not wake up for me."

"That's all right." She blinked away blear from her eyes, feeling older than the old man. "Is there something to drink?"

He hastily poured her cold water from the bedside basin spigot, and watched her swallow. "More?"

"That's enough. Have you seen Aral yet?"

He patted her hand. "I've talked to Aral already. He's resting now. I am so sorry, Cordelia."

"It may not be as bad as we feared at first. There's

137

still a chance. A hope. Did Aral tell you about the uterine replicator?"

"Something. But the damage has already been done, surely. Irrevocable damage."

"Damage, yes. How irrevocable it is, no one knows. Not even Captain Vaagen."

"Yes, I met Vaagen a little while ago." Piotr frowned. "A pushing sort of fellow. New Man type."

"Barrayar needs its new men. And women. Its technologically trained generation."

"Oh, yes. We fought and slaved to create them. They are absolutely necessary. They know it, too, some of them." A hint of self-aware irony softened his mouth. "But this operation you're proposing, this placental transfer . . . it doesn't sound too safe."

"On Beta Colony, it would be routine." Cordelia shrugged. *We are not, of course, on Beta Colony.*

"But something more straightforward, better understood—you would be ready to begin again much sooner. In the long run, you might actually lose less time."

"Time . . . isn't what I'm worried about losing." A meaningless concept, now she thought of it. She lost 26.7 hours every Barrayaran day. "Anyway, I'm never going through *that* again. I'm not a slow learner, sir."

A flicker of alarm crossed his face. "You'll change your mind, when you feel better. What does matter now—I've talked to Captain Vaagen. There seemed no question in his mind there is great damage."

"Well, yes. The unknown is whether there can be great repairs."

"Dear girl." His worried smile grew tenser. "Just so. If only the fetus were a girl . . . or even a second son . . . we could afford to indulge your understandable, even laudable, maternal emotions. But this thing, if it lived, would be *Count Vorkosigan* someday. We cannot afford to have a deformed *Count Vorkosigan.*" He sat back, as if he had just made some cogent point.

Cordelia wrinkled her brow. "Who is we?"

"House Vorkosigan. We are one of the oldest great

houses on Barrayar. Never, perhaps, the richest, seldom
the strongest, but what we've lacked in wealth we've made
up in honor. Nine generations of Vor warriors. This would
be a horrible end to come to, after nine generations, don't
you see?"

"House Vorkosigan, at this point in time, consists of
two individuals, you and Aral," Cordelia observed, both
amused and disturbed. "And Counts Vorkosigan have come
to horrible ends throughout your history. You've been
blown up, shot, starved, drowned, burned alive, beheaded,
diseased, and demented. The only thing you've never done
is die in bed. I thought horrors were your stock in trade."

He returned her a pained smile. "But we've never been
mutants."

"I think you need to talk to Vaagen again. The fetal
damage he described was teratogenic, not genetic, if I
understand him correctly."

"But people will think it's a mutant."

"What the devil do you care what some ignorant prole
thinks?"

"Other Vor, dear."

"Vor, prole, they're equally ignorant, I assure you."

His hands twitched. He opened his mouth, closed it
again, frowned, and said more sharply, "A Count
Vorkosigan has never been an experimental laboratory
animal, either."

"There you go, then. He serves Barrayar even before
he's born. Not a bad start on a life of honor." Perhaps
some good would come of it, in the end, some knowledge gained; if not help for themselves, then for some
other parents' grief. The more she thought about it, the
more right her decision felt, on more than one level.

Piotr jerked his head back. "For all you Betans seem
soft, you have an appalling cold-blooded streak in you."

"Rational streak, sir. Rationality has its merits. You
Barrayarans ought to try it sometime." She bit her tongue.
"But we run ahead of ourselves, I think, sir. There are
lots of d—" *dangers,* "difficulties yet to come. A placental
transfer this late in pregnancy is tricky even for galactics.

I admit, I wish there were time to import a more experienced surgeon. But there's not."

"Yes . . . yes . . . it may yet die, you're right. No need to . . . but I'm afraid for you, too, girl. Is it worth it?"

Was what worth what? How could she know? Her lungs burned. She smiled wearily at him, and shook her head, which ached with tight pressure in her temples and neck.

"Father," came a raspy voice from the doorway. Aral leaned there, in his green pajamas, a portable oxygenator stuck up his nose. How long had he stood there? "I think Cordelia needs to rest."

Their eyes met, over Piotr. *Bless you, love. . . .*

"Yes, of course." Count Piotr gathered himself together, and creaked to his feet. "I'm sorry, you're quite correct." He pressed Cordelia's hand one more time, firmly, with his dry old-man's grip. "Sleep. You'll be able to think more clearly later."

"Father."

"You shouldn't be out of bed, should you?" said Piotr, drawn off. "Go back and lie down, boy. . . ." His voice drifted away, across the corridor.

Aral returned later, after Count Piotr had finally left.

"Was Father bothering you?" he asked, looking grim. She held out her hand to him, and he sat beside her. She transferred her head from her pillow to his lap, her cheek on the firm-muscled leg beneath the thin pajama, and he stroked her hair.

"No more than usual," she sighed.

"I feared he was upsetting you."

"It's not that I'm not upset. It's just that I'm too tired to run up and down the corridor screaming."

"Ah. He did upset you."

"Yes." She hesitated. "In a way, he has a point. I was so afraid for so long, waiting for the blow to fall, from somewhere, nowhere, anywhere. Then came last night, and the worst was done, over . . . except it's not over. If the blow had been more complete, I could stop, quit now. But this is going to go on and on." She rubbed her cheek against the cloth. "Did Illyan come up with anything new? I thought I heard his voice out there, earlier."

His hand continued to stroke her hair, in even rhythm. "He'd finished the preliminary fast-penta interrogation of Evon Vorhalas. He's now investigating the old armory where Evon stole the soltoxin. It appears Evon might not have equipped himself so ad hoc unilaterally as he claimed. An ordnance major in charge there has disappeared, AWOL. Illyan's not certain yet if the man was eliminated, to clear Evon's path, or if he actually helped Evon, and has gone into hiding."

"He might just be afraid. If it was dereliction."

"He'd better be afraid. If he had any conscious connivance in this . . ." His hand clenched in her hair, he became aware of the pull, muttered, "Sorry," and continued petting. Cordelia, feeling very like an injured animal, crept deeper into his lap, her hand on his knee.

"About Father—if he upsets you again, send him to me. You shouldn't have to deal with him. I told him it was your decision."

"My decision?" Her hand rested, without moving. "Not our decision?"

He hesitated. "Whatever you want, I'll support you."

"But what do you want? Something you're not telling me?"

"I can't help understanding his fears. But . . . there's something I haven't discussed with him yet, nor am I going to. The next child may not be so easy to come by as the first."

Easy? You call this easy?

He went on, "One of the lesser-known side effects of soltoxin poisoning is testicular scarring, on the micro-level. It could reduce fertility below the point of no return. Or so my examining physician warns me."

"Nonsense," said Cordelia. "All you need is any two somatic cells and a replicator. Your little finger and my big toe, if that's all they can scrape off the walls after the next bomb, could go on reproducing little Vorkosigans into the next century. However many our survivors choose to afford."

"But not naturally. Not without leaving Barrayar."

"Or changing Barrayar. *Dammit.*" His hand jerked back at the bite in her tone. "If only I had *insisted* on using the replicator in the first place, the baby need never have been at risk. I knew it was safer, I knew it was there—" Her voice broke.

"Sh. Sh. If only I had . . . not taken the job. Kept you at Vorkosigan Surleau. Pardoned that murderous idiot Carl, for God's sake. If only we'd slept in separate rooms . . ."

"No!" Her hand tightened on his knee. "And I refuse to go live in some bomb shelter for the next fifteen years. Aral, this place has to change. This is unbearable." *If only I had never come here.*

If only. If only. If only.

The operating room seemed clean and bright, if not so copiously equipped as galactic standard. Cordelia, wafting on her float pallet, turned her head sideways to take in as much detail as she could. Lights, monitors, an operating table with a catch-basin set beneath it, a tech checking a bubbling tank of clear yellow fluid. This was not, she told herself sternly, the point of no return. This was simply the next logical step.

Captain Vaagen and Dr. Henri stood sterile-garbed and waiting, beyond the operating table. Next to them sat the portable uterine replicator, a metal and plastic canister half a meter tall, studded with control panels and access ports. The lights on its sides glowed green and amber. Cleaned, sterilized, its nutrient and oxygen tanks re-charged and ready . . . Cordelia eyed it with profound relief. The primitive Barrayaran back-to-the-apes style gestation was nothing but the utter failure of reason to triumph over emotion. She'd so wanted to please, to fit in, to try to become Barrayaran. . . . *And so my child pays the price. Never again.*

Dr. Ritter, the surgeon, was tall and dark-haired, with olive skin and long lean hands. Cordelia had liked his hands the first moment she saw them. Steady. Ritter and a medtech now positioned her over the operating table, and shifted the float pallet out from under her. Dr. Ritter smiled reassuringly. "You're doing fine."

Of course I'm fine, we haven't even started yet, Cordelia thought irritably. Dr. Ritter was palpably nervous, though the tension somehow stopped at his elbows. The surgeon was a friend of Vaagen's, whom Vaagen had strong-armed into this, after they'd spent a day running through a list of more experienced men who had refused to touch the case.

Vaagen had explained it to Cordelia. "What do you call four big bravos with clubs in a dark alley?"

"What?"

"A Vor lord's malpractice suit." He'd chuckled. Vaagen's sense of humor was acid-black. Cordelia could have hugged him for it. He'd been the only person to crack a joke in her presence in the last three days, possibly the most rational and honest person she'd met since she'd left Beta Colony. She was glad he was here.

They rolled her to her side, and touched her spine with the medical stun. A tingle, and her cold feet felt suddenly warm. Her legs went abruptly inert, like bags of lard.

"Can you feel that?" asked Dr. Ritter.

"Feel what?"

"Good." He nodded to the tech, and they straightened her out. The tech uncovered her stomach, and turned on the sterilizer-field. The surgeon palpated her, cross-checking the holovid monitors for the infant's exact position within her.

"Are you sure you wouldn't rather be asleep through this?" Dr. Ritter asked her for the last time.

"No. I want to watch. This is my first child being born." *Maybe my only child being born.*

He smiled wanly. "Brave girl."

Girl, hell, I'm older than you. Dr. Ritter, she sensed, would rather not be watched. Tough.

Dr. Ritter paused, taking one last glance around as if mentally checklisting the readiness of his tools and people. And will and nerve, Cordelia guessed.

"Come on, Ritter my man, let's get this over with," said Vaagen, tapping his fingers impatiently. His tone was a peculiar mix, a little sarcastic prodding lilt over an underlying warmth of genuine encouragement. "My scans show bone sloughing already under way. If the disintegration gets too far advanced, I'll have no matrix left to build from. Cut now, chew your nails later."

"Chew your own nails, Vaagen," said the surgeon genially. "Jog my elbow again and I'll have my medtech put a speculum down your throat."

Very old friends, Cordelia gauged. But the surgeon raised his hands, took a breath and a grip on his vibra-scalpel, and sliced her belly open in one perfectly controlled stroke. The medtech followed his motion smoothly with the surgical hand-tractor, clamping blood vessels; scarcely a cat-scratch of blood escaped. Cordelia felt pressure but no pain. Other cuts laid open her uterus.

A placental transfer was vastly more demanding than a straightforward cesarian section. The fragile placenta must be chemically and hormonally persuaded to release from the blood-vessel-enriched uterus, without damaging too many of its multitude of tiny villi, then floated free from the uterine wall in a running bath of highly oxygenated nutrient solution. The replicator sponge then had to be slipped into place between the placenta and the uterine wall, and the placenta's villi at least partially induced to re-interdigitate on its new matrix, before the whole mess could be lifted from the living body of the mother and placed in the replicator. The more advanced the pregnancy, the more difficult the transfer.

The umbilical cord between placenta and infant was monitored, and extra oxygen injected by hypospray as needed. On Beta Colony, a nifty little device would do this; here, an anxious tech hovered.

The tech began running the clear bright yellow solution-bath into her uterus. It filled her, and ran over, trickling pink-tinged down her sides and into the catch basin. The surgeon was now working, in effect, underwater. No question about it, a placental transfer was a messy operation.

"Sponge," called the surgeon softly, and Vaagen and Henri trundled the uterine replicator to her side, and strung out the matrix sponge from it on its feed lines. The surgeon fiddled interminably with a tiny hand-tractor, his hands out of Cordelia's line of sight as she peered down cross-eyed over her chest to her rounded—so-barely-rounded—belly. She shivered. Ritter was sweating.

"Doctor . . ." A tech pointed to something on a vid monitor.

"Mm," said Ritter, glancing up, then continuing fiddling. The techs murmured, Vaagen and Henri murmured, calm, professional, reassuring . . . she was so cold. . . .

The fluid trickling over the white dam of her skin changed abruptly from pink-tinged to bright, bright red, a splashing flow, much faster than the input feed was emitting.

"*Clamp* that," hissed the surgeon.

Cordelia caught just a glimpse, beneath a membrane, of tiny arms, legs, a wet dark head, wriggling on the surgeon's gloved hands, no larger than a half-drowned kitten. "Vaagen! Take this thing of yours *now* if you want it!" snapped Ritter. Vaagen plunged his gloved hands into her belly as dark whorls clouded Cordelia's vision, her head aching, exploding in sudden sparkling flashes. The blackness ballooned out, overwhelming her. The last thing she heard was the surgeon's despairing sibilant voice, "Oh, *shit* . . . !"

Her dreams were foggy with pain. The worst part was the choking. She choked and choked, and wept for lack of air. Her throat was full of obstructions, and she clawed at it, until her hands were bound. She dreamed of Vorrutyer's tortures, then, multiplied and extended into insane complications that went on for hours. A demented Bothari knelt on her chest, and she could get no air at all.

When she finally woke clear-headed, it was like breaking up out of some underground prison-hell into God's own light. Her relief was so profound she wept again, a muted whimper and a wetness in her eyes. She could breathe, although it pained her; she was bruised and aching and unable to move. But she could breathe. That was enough.

"Sh. Sh." A thick warm finger touched her eyelids, wiping away the moisture. "It's all right."

"Izzit?" She blinked and squinted. It was night, artificial light making warm pools in the room. Aral's face wavered over hers. "Izzit . . . tonight? Wha' happened?"

"Sh. You've been very, very sick. You had a violent hemorrhage during the placental transfer. Your heart stopped twice." He moistened his lips and went on. "The trauma, on top of the poisoning, flared into soltoxin pneumonia. You had a very bad day yesterday, but you're over the worst, off the respirator."

"How . . . long?"

"Three days."

"Ah. Baby, Aral. Diddit work? Details!"

"It went all right. Vaagen reports the transfer was successful. They lost about thirty percent of the placental function, but Henri compensated with an enriched and increased oxy-solution flow, and all seems to be well, or as well as can be expected. The baby's still alive, anyway. Vaagen has started his first calcium-treatment experiment, and promises us a baseline report soon." He caressed her forehead. "Vaagen has priority-access to any equipment, supplies, or techs he cares to requisition, including outside consultants. He has an advising civilian pediatrician, plus Henri. Vaagen himself knows more about our military poisons than any man, on Barrayar or off it. We can do no more, right now. So rest, love."

"Baby—where?"

"Ah—you can see where, if you wish." He helped her lift her head, and pointed out the window. "See that second building, with the red lights on the roof? That's the biochemistry research facility. Vaagen and Henri's lab is on the third floor."

"Oh, I recognize it now. Saw it from the other side, the day we collected Elena."

"That's right." His face softened. "Good to have you

back, dear Captain. Seeing you that sick . . . I haven't
felt that helpless and useless since I was eleven years old."

That was the year Mad Yuri's death squad had
murdered his mother and brother. "Sh," she said in turn.
"No, no . . . s'all right now."

They took away all the rest of the tubes piercing her
body the next morning, except for the oxygen. Days of
quiet routine followed. Her recovery was less interrupted
than Aral's. What seemed troops of men, headed by
Minister Vortala, came to see him at all hours. He had
a secured comconsole installed in his room, over medical protests. Koudelka joined him eight hours a day, in
the makeshift office.

Koudelka seemed very quiet, as depressed as everyone else in the wake of the disaster. Though not as morbid
as anyone who'd had to do with their failed Security. Even
Illyan shrank, when he saw her.

Aral walked her carefully up and down the corridor
a couple of times a day. The vibra-scalpel had made a
cleaner cut through her abdomen than, say, your average sabre-thrust, but it was no less deep. The healing
scar ached less than her lungs, though. Or her heart.
Her belly was not so much flat as flaccid, but definitely
no longer occupied. She was alone, uninhabited, she was
herself again, after five months of that strange doubled
existence.

Dr. Henri came with a float chair one day, and took
her on a short trip over to his laboratory, to see where
the replicator was safely installed. She watched her baby
moving in the vid scans, and studied the team's technical readouts and reports. Their subject's nerves, skin, and
eyes tested out encouragingly, though Henri was not so
sure about hearing, because of the tiny bones in the ear.
Henri and Vaagen were properly trained scientists, almost
Betan in their outlook, and she blessed them silently and
thanked them aloud, and returned to her room feeling
enormously better.

When Captain Vaagen burst into her room the next

afternoon, however, her heart sank. His face was thunderously dark, his lips tight and harsh.

"What's wrong, Captain?" she asked urgently. "That second calcium run—did it fail?"

"Too early to tell. No, your baby's the same, Milady. Our trouble is with your in-law."

"Beg pardon?"

"General Count Vorkosigan came to see us this morning."

"Oh! He came to see the baby? Oh, good. He's so disturbed by all this new life-technology. Maybe he's finally starting to work past those emotional blocks. He embraces the new death-technologies readily enough, old Vor warrior that he is. . . ."

"I wouldn't get too optimistic about him, if I were you, Milady." He took a deep breath, taking refuge in a formality of stance, just black, not black-humored this time. "Dr. Henri had the same idea you did. We showed the General all around the lab, went over the equipment, explained our treatment theories. We were absolutely honest, as we've been with you. Maybe too honest. He wanted to know what results we were going to get. Hell, we don't know. And so we said.

"After some beating around the bush, hinting . . . well, to cut it short, the General first asked, then ordered, then tried to bribe Dr. Henri to open the stopcock. To destroy the fetus. The mutation, he calls it. We threw him the hell out. He swore he'd be back."

She was shaking, down in her belly, though she kept her face blank. "I see."

"I want that old man kept *out* of my lab, Milady. And I don't care how you do it. I don't need this kind of crap coming down. Not from that high up."

"I'll see . . . wait here." She wrapped her robe around her own green pajamas more tightly, seated her oxygen tube more firmly, and walked carefully across the corridor. Aral, half-casual in uniform trousers and a shirt, sat at a small table by his window. The only sign of his continued patient-hood was the oxygen tube up his nose, treatment for his own lingering soltoxin pneumonia. He was conferring with a man while Koudelka took notes. The man was not, thank God, Piotr, but merely some ministerial secretary of Vortala's.

"Aral. I need you."

"Can it wait?"

"No."

He rose from his chair with a brief "Excuse me a moment, gentlemen," and trod across the hall in her wake. Cordelia closed the door behind them.

"Captain Vaagen, please tell Aral what you just told me."

Vaagen, looking a degree more nervous, repeated his tale. To his credit, he did not soften the details. A weight seemed to settle on Aral's shoulders as he listened, rounding and hunching them.

"Thank you, Captain. You were correct to report this. I will take care of it immediately."

"That's all?" Vaagen glanced at Cordelia in doubt.

She opened her palm to him. "You heard the man."

Vaagen shrugged, and saluted himself out.

"You don't doubt his story?" asked Cordelia.

"I've been listening to the Count my father's thoughts on this subject for a week, love."

"You argued?"

"He argued. I just listened."

Aral returned to his own room, and asked Koudelka and the secretary to wait in the corridor. Cordelia sat on his bed and watched as he punched up codes on his comconsole.

"Lord Vorkosigan here. I wish to speak simultaneously to the Security chief, Imperial Military Hospital, and Commander Simon Illyan. Get them both on, please."

A brief wait, as each man was located. Judging from the fuzzy background in the vid, the ImpMil man was in his office somewhere in the hospital complex. They tracked Illyan down at a forensic laboratory in ImpSec HQ.

"Gentlemen." Aral's face was quite expressionless. "I wish to revoke a Security clearance." Each man attentively prepared to make notes on their respective comconsoles.

"General Count Piotr Vorkosigan is to be denied access to Building Six, Biochemical Research, Imperial Military Hospital, until further notice. Notice from me personally."

Illyan hesitated. "Sir—General Vorkosigan has absolute clearance, by Imperial order. He's had it for years. I need an Imperial order to countermand it."

"That's precisely what this is, Illyan." A trace of impatience rasped in Vorkosigan's voice. "By my order, Aral Vorkosigan, Regent to His Imperial Majesty Gregor Vorbarra. Is that official enough?"

Illyan whistled softly, but his face snapped to blankness at Vorkosigan's frown. "Yes, sir. Understood. Is there anything else?"

"That's all. Just that one building."

"Sir . . ." the hospital security commander said, "what if . . . General Vorkosigan refuses to halt when ordered?"

Cordelia could just picture it, some poor young guard being mowed down flat by all that history. . . .

"If your security people are indeed so overwhelmed by one old man, they may use force up to and including stunner fire," said Aral tiredly. "Dismissed. Thank you."

The ImpMil man nodded cautiously, and disconnected.

Illyan lingered in doubt a moment. "Is that a good idea, at his age? Stunning can be bad for the heart. And he's not going to like it one bit, when we tell him there's someplace he can't go. By the way, why—?" Aral merely stared coldly at him, till he gulped, "Yes, sir," saluted, and signed off.

Aral sat back, gazing pensively at the blank space where the vid images had glowed. He glanced up at Cordelia, and his lips twisted, a grimace of irony and pain. "He is an old man," he said at last.

"The old man just tried to kill your son. What's left of your son."

"I see his view. I see his fears."

"Do you see mine, too?"

"Yes. Both."

"When push comes to shove—if he tries to go back there—"

"He is my past." He met her eyes. "You are my future.

The rest of my life belongs to the future. I swear by my word as Vorkosigan."

Cordelia sighed, and rubbed her aching neck, her aching eyes.

Koudelka rattled at the door, and stuck his head surreptitiously within. "Sir? The minister's secretary wants to know—"

"In a minute, Lieutenant." Vorkosigan waved him back out.

"Let's blow out of this place," said Cordelia suddenly.

"Milady?"

"ImpMil, and ImpSec, and ImpEverything, is giving me a bad case of ImpClaustrophobia. Let's go down to Vorkosigan Surleau for a few days. You'll recover better there yourself, it will be harder for all your dedicated minions," she jerked her head at the corridor, "to get at you, there. Just you and me, boy." Would it work? Suppose they retired to the scene of their summer happiness, and it wasn't there anymore? Drowned in the autumn rains . . . She could feel the desperation in herself, seeking their lost balance, some solid center.

His brows rose in approval. "Outstanding idea, dear Captain. We'll take the old man along."

"Oh, must we—oh. Yes, I see. Quite. By all means."

CHAPTER TEN

Cordelia woke slowly, stretched, and clutched the magnificent silky feather-stuffed comforter to her. The other side of the bed was empty—she touched the dented pillow—cold and empty. Aral must have tiptoed out early. She luxuriated in the sensation of finally having enough sleep, not waking to that stunned exhaustion that had clotted her mind and body for so long. This made the third night in a row she'd slept well, warmed by her husband's body, both of them gladly rid of the irritating oxygen-fittings on their faces.

Their corner room, on the second floor of the old stone converted barracks, was cool this morning, and very quiet. The front window opened onto the bright green lawn, descending into mist that hid the lake and the village and hills of the farther shore. The damp morning felt comfortable, felt right, proper contrast to the feather comforter. When she sat up, the new pink scar on her abdomen only twinged.

Droushnakovi poked her head around the doorframe. "Milady?" she called softly, then saw Cordelia sitting up, bare feet hung out over the edge of the bed. Cordelia swung her feet back and forth, experimentally, encouraging circulation. "Oh, good, you're awake." Drou shouldered her way through the door, bearing a large and promising tray. She wore one of her more comfortable dresses, with a wide swinging skirt, and a warm padded vest with embroidery. Her footsteps sounded on the wide wooden floorboards, then were muffled on the handwoven rug as she crossed the room.

"I'm hungry," said Cordelia in wonder, as the aromas from the tray tickled her nose. "I think that's the first time in three weeks." Three weeks, since that night of horrors at Vorkosigan House.

Drou smiled, and set the tray down at the table by the front window. Cordelia found robe and slippers, and made for the coffeepot. Drou hovered, seeming ready to catch her if she fell over, but Cordelia did not feel nearly so shaky today. She seated herself and reached for steaming groats and butter, and a pitcher of hot syrup the Barrayarans made from boiled-down tree sap. Wonderful food.

"Have you eaten, Drou? Want some coffee? What time is it?"

The bodyguard shook her blonde head. "I'm fine, Milady. It's about elevenses."

Droushnakovi had been part of the assumed background, for the past several days here at Vorkosigan Surleau. Cordelia found herself really looking at the girl for almost the first time since she'd left ImpMil. Drou was attentive and alert as ever, but with an underlying tension, that same bad-guard-slink—perhaps it was only because she was feeling better herself, but Cordelia selfishly wanted the people around her to be feeling better, too, if only not to drag her back down.

"I'm feeling so much less thick, today. I talked to Captain Vaagen yesterday, on the vid. He thinks he's seen the first signs of molecular re-calcification in little Piotr Miles. Very encouraging, if you know how to interpret Vaagen. He doesn't offer false hopes, but what little he does say, you can rely on."

Drou glanced up from her lap, fixing a responding

smile on her downcast features. She shook her head. "Uterine replicators seem so strange to me. So alien."

"Not so strange as what evolution laid on us, ad lib empirical," Cordelia grinned back. "Thank God for technology and rational design. I know whereof I speak, now."

"Milady . . . how did you first know you were pregnant? Did you miss a monthly?"

"A menstrual period? No, actually." She thought back to last summer. This very room, that unmade bed in fact. She and Aral could begin sharing intimacies there again soon, though with some loss of piquancy without reproduction as a goal. "Aral and I thought we were all settled here, last summer. He was retired, I was retired . . . no impediments. I was on the verge of being old for the organic method, which seemed the only one available here on Barrayar; more to the point, he wanted to start soon. So a few weeks after we were married, I went and had my contraceptive implant removed. Made me feel very wicked; at home I couldn't have had it taken out without buying a license."

"Really?" Drou listened with openmouthed fascination.

"Yes, it's a Betan legal requirement. You have to qualify for a parent's license first. I've had my implant since I was fourteen. I had a menstrual period once then, I remember. We turn them off till they're needed. I got my implant, and my hymen cut, and my ears pierced, and had my coming-out party. . . ."

"You didn't . . . start doing sex when you were fourteen, did you?" Droushnakovi's voice was hushed.

"I could have. But it takes two, y'know. I didn't find a real lover till later." Cordelia was ashamed to admit how much later. She'd been so socially inept, back then. . . . *And you haven't changed much,* she admitted wryly to herself.

"I didn't think it would happen so fast," Cordelia went on. "I thought we'd be in for several months of earnest and delightful experiment. But we caught the baby first try. So I still haven't had a menstrual period, here on Barrayar."

"First try," echoed Drou. Her lip curled in introspective dismay. "How did you know you'd . . . caught? The nausea?"

"Fatigue, before nausea. But it was the little blue dots . . ." Her voice faltered, as she studied the girl's twisted-up features. "Drou, are all these questions academic, or do you have some more personal interest in the answers?"

Her face almost crumpled. "Personal," she choked out.

"Oh." Cordelia sat back. "D'you . . . want to talk about it?"

"No . . . I don't know. . . ."

"I presume that means yes," Cordelia sighed. Ah, yes. Just like playing Mama Captain to sixty Betan scientists back on Survey, though queries about pregnancy were perhaps the one interpersonal trouble they'd never laid in her lap. But given the Really Dumb Stuff that rational and select group had sprung on her from time to time, the feral Barrayaran version ought to be just . . . "You know I'll be glad to help you any way I can."

"It was the night of the soltoxin attack," she sniffled. "I couldn't sleep. I went down to the refectory kitchen to get something to eat. On the way back upstairs I noticed a light on in the library. Lieutenant Koudelka was in there. He couldn't sleep either."

Kou, eh? Oh, good, good. This might be all right after all. Cordelia smiled in genuine encouragement. "Yes?"

"We . . . I . . . he . . . kissed me."

"I trust you kissed him back?"

"You sound like you *approve.*"

"I do. You are two of my favorite people, you and Kou. If only you'd get your heads straight . . . but go on, there has to be more." Unless Drou was more ignorant than Cordelia believed possible.

"We . . . we . . . we . . ."

"Screwed?" Cordelia suggested hopefully.

"Yes, Milady." Drou turned scarlet, and swallowed. "Kou seemed so happy . . . for a few minutes. I was so happy for him, so excited, I didn't care how much it hurt."

Ah, yes, the barbaric Barrayaran custom of introducing their women to sex with the pain of unanesthesized defloration. Though considering how much pain their reproductive methods later entailed, perhaps it constituted fair warning. But Kou, in the glimpses she'd had of him, hadn't seemed as happy as a new lover ought to be either. What were these two doing to each other? "Go on."

"I thought I saw a movement in the back garden, out the door from the library. Then came the crash upstairs— oh, Milady! I'm so sorry! If I'd been guarding you, instead of doing *that*—"

"Whoa, girl! You were off-duty. If you hadn't been doing *that*, you'd have been in bed asleep. No way is the soltoxin attack your fault, yours or Kou's. In fact, if you hadn't been up and, and more or less dressed, the would-be assassin might have gotten away." *And we wouldn't be anticipating yet another public beheading, or whatever, God help us.* One part of Cordelia wished they'd gone for seconds, and never looked out the damned window. But Droushnakovi had enough consequences to deal with right now without those mortal complications.

"But if only—"

"*If onlys* have been thick in the air around here, these last weeks. I think it's time to replace them with some *Now-we-go-ons*, frankly." Cordelia's mind caught up with herself at last. Drou was Barrayaran; Drou therefore didn't have a contraceptive implant. It didn't sound like that idiot Kou had offered an alternative, either. Drou had therefore spent the last three weeks wondering . . . "Would you like to try one of my little blue dots? I have lots left."

"Blue dots?"

"Yes, I started to tell you. I have a packet of these little diagnostic strips. Bought them in Vorbarr Sultana last summer at an import shop. You pee on one, and if the dot turns blue, you're in. I only used up three, last summer." Cordelia went to her dresser drawer, and rooted through it for the obsolete supplies. "Here." She handed one to Drou. "Go relieve yourself. And your mind."

"Do they work so soon?"

"After five days." Cordelia held up her hand. "Promise."

Staring worriedly at the little strip of paper, Droushnakovi vanished into Cordelia and Aral's bathroom, off the bedroom. She emerged in a few minutes. Her face was glum, her shoulders slumped.

What does this mean? Cordelia wondered in exasperation. "Well?"

"It stayed white."

"Then you aren't pregnant."

"Guess not."

"I can't tell if you're glad or sorry. Believe me, if you want to have a baby, you'd do much better to wait a couple years till they get a bit more medical technology on-line around here." Though the organic method had been fascinating, for a time. . . .

"I don't want . . . I want . . . I don't know . . . Kou's hardly spoken to me since that night. I didn't want to be pregnant, it would destroy me, and yet I thought maybe he would, would . . . be as excited and happy about it as he was about the sex, maybe. Maybe he'd come back and—oh, things were going so well, and now they're so spoiled!" Her hands were clenched, face white, teeth gritted.

Cry, so I can breathe, girl. But Droushnakovi regained her self-control. "I'm sorry, Milady. I didn't mean to spill all this stupidity on you."

Stupidity, yes, but not unilateral stupidity. Something this screwed up had to have taken a committee. "So what is the matter with Kou? I thought he was just suffering from soltoxin-guilt, like everyone else in the household." *From Aral and myself on down.*

"I don't know, Milady."

"Have you tried something really radical, like asking him?"

"He *hides*, when he sees me coming."

Cordelia sighed, and turned her attention to getting dressed. Real clothes, not patient robes, today. There in the back of Aral's closet were her tan trousers from her old Survey uniform, hung up. Curiously, she tried them on. Not only did they fasten, they were loose. She *had* been sick.

Rather aggressively, she left them on, and chose a long-sleeved flowered smock-top to go with them. Very comfortable. She smiled at her slim, if pale, profile in the mirror.

"Ah, dear Captain." Aral stuck his head in the bedroom door. "You're up." He glanced at Droushnakovi. "You're both here. Better still. I think I need your help, Cordelia. In fact, I'm certain of it." Aral's eyes were alight with the strangest expression. Amazement, bemusement, worry? He let himself in. He was wearing his standard gear for off-duty time at Vorkosigan Surleau, old uniform trousers and a civilian shirt. He was trailed by a tense and miserable Koudelka, dressed in neat black fatigues with his red lieutenant's tabs bright on the collar. He clutched his swordstick. Drou backed to the wall, and crossed her arms.

"Lieutenant Koudelka—he tells me—wishes to make a confession. He is also, I suspect, hoping for absolution," said Aral.

"I don't deserve that, sir," Koudelka muttered. "But I couldn't live with myself anymore. This has to come out." He stared at the floor, meeting no one's eyes. Droushnakovi watched him breathlessly. Aral eased over and sat on the edge of the bed beside Cordelia.

"Hold on to your hat," he murmured to her out of the corner of his mouth. "This one took *me* by surprise."

"I think I may be way ahead of you."

"That wouldn't be a first." He raised his voice. "Go ahead, Lieutenant. This won't be any easier for being dragged out."

"Drou—Miss Droushnakovi—I came to turn myself in. And to apologize. No, that sounds trivial, and believe me, I don't think it trivial. You deserve more than apology, I owe you expiation. Whatever you want. But I'm sorry, so *sorry* I raped you."

Droushnakovi's mouth fell open for a full three seconds, then shut so hard Cordelia could hear her teeth snap. "*What?!*"

Koudelka flinched, but never looked up. "Sorry . . . sorry," he mumbled.

"You. Think. You. What?!" gasped Droushnakovi, horrified and outraged. "You think you could—oh!" She stood rigid now, hands clenched, breathing fast. "Kou, you oaf! You idiot! You moron! You-you-you—" Her words sputtered off. Her whole body was shaking. Cordelia watched in utter fascination. Aral rubbed his lips thoughtfully.

Droushnakovi stalked over to Koudelka and kicked his swordstick out of his hand. He almost fell, with a startled "Huh?", clutching at it and missing as it clattered across the floor.

Drou slammed him expertly into the wall, and paralyzed him with a nerve thrust, her fingers jammed up into his solar plexus. His breath stopped.

"You *goon.* Do you think you could lay a hand on me without my permission? Oh! To be so, to be so, so, so—" Her baffled words dissolved into a scream of outrage, right next to his ear. He spasmed.

"Please don't break my secretary, Drou, the repairs are expensive," said Aral mildly.

"Oh!" She whirled away, releasing Koudelka. He staggered and fell to his knees. Hands over her face, biting her fingers, she stomped out the door, slamming it behind her. Only then did she sob, sharp breaths retreating up the hallway. Another door slammed. Silence.

"I'm sorry, Kou," said Aral into the long lull. "But it doesn't look as though your self-accusation stands up in court."

"I don't understand." Kou shook his head, crawled after his swordstick, and climbed very shakily to his feet.

"Do I gather you are both talking about what happened between you the night of the soltoxin attack?" Cordelia asked.

"Yes, Milady. I was sitting up in the library. Couldn't sleep, thought I'd run over some figures. She came in. We sat, talked. . . . Suddenly I found myself . . . well . . . it was the first time I'd been functional since I was hit by the nerve disruptor. I thought it might be another year, or *forever*—I panicked, I just panicked. I . . . took her . . . right there. Never asked, never said a word. And then came the crash from upstairs, and we both ran out into the back garden and . . . she never accused me, next day. I waited and waited."

"But if he didn't rape her, why did she get so angry just now?" asked Aral.

"But she's been mad," said Koudelka. "The looks she's given me, these last three weeks . . ."

"The looks were fear, Kou," Cordelia advised him.

"Yes, that's what I thought."

"Because she was afraid she was *pregnant,* not because she was afraid of *you,*" Cordelia clarified.

"Oh." Koudelka's voice went small.

"She's not, as it happens." (Kou echoed himself with another small "Oh.") "But she's mad at you now, and I don't blame her."

"But if she doesn't think I—what reason?"

"You don't see it?" She frowned at Aral. "You either?"

"Well . . ."

"It's because you just insulted her, Kou. Not then, but right now, in this room. And not just in slighting her combat prowess. What you just said revealed to her, for the first time, that you were so intent on *yourself* that night, you never saw *her* at all. Bad, Kou. Very bad. You owe her a profound apology. Here she was, giving her Barrayaran all to you, and you so little appreciated what she was doing, you didn't even perceive it."

His head came up suddenly. "Gave me? Like some charity?"

"Gift of the gods, more like," murmured Aral, lost in some appreciation of his own.

"I'm not a—" Koudelka's head swiveled toward the door. "Are you saying I should run after her?"

"Crawl, actually, if I were you," recommended Aral. "Crawl fast. Slither under her door, go belly-up, let her stomp on you till she gets it out of her system. Then apologize some more. You may yet save the situation." Aral's eyes were openly alight with amusement now.

"What do you call that? Total surrender?" said Kou indignantly.

"No. I'd call it winning." His voice grew a shade cooler. "I've seen the war between men and women descend to scorched-earth heroics. Pyres of pride. You don't want to go down that road. I guarantee it."

"You're—Milady! You're laughing at me! Stop!"

"Then stop making yourself ridiculous," said Cordelia sharply. "Get your head out of your ass. Think for sixty consecutive seconds about somebody besides yourself."

"Milady. Milord." His teeth were gritted now with frozen dignity. He bowed himself out, well slapped. But he turned the wrong way in the hallway, the opposite direction to which Droushnakovi had fled, and clattered down the end stairs.

Aral shook his head helplessly, as Koudelka's footsteps faded. A splutter escaped him.

Cordelia punched him softly on the arm. "Stop that! It's not funny to them." Their eyes met; she sniggered, then caught her breath firmly. "Good heavens, I think he *wanted* to be a rapist. Odd ambition. Has he been hanging around with Bothari too much?"

This slightly sick joke sobered them both. Aral looked thoughtful. "I think . . . Kou was flattering his self-doubts. But his remorse was sincere."

"Sincere, but a trifle smug. I think we may have coddled his self-doubts long enough. It may be time to kick his tail."

Aral's shoulders slumped wearily. "He owes her, no doubt. Yet what should I order him to do? It's worthless, if he doesn't pay freely."

Cordelia growled agreement.

It wasn't until lunch that Cordelia noticed something missing from their little world.

"Where's the Count?" she asked Aral, as they found the table set only for two by Piotr's housekeeper, in a front dining room overlooking the lake. The day had failed to warm. The earlier mist had risen only to clot into low scudding grey clouds, windy and chilly. Cordelia had added an old black fatigue jacket of Aral's over her flowered blouse.

"I thought he went to the stables. For a training session with that new dressage prospect of his," said Aral, also regarding the table uneasily. "That's what he told me he was going to do."

The housekeeper, bringing in soup, volunteered, "No, m'lord. He went off in the groundcar early, with two of his men."

"Oh. Excuse me." Aral nodded to Cordelia and rose, and exited the dining room to the back hall. One of the storerooms on the back side of the house, wedged into the slope, had been converted into a secured comm center, with a double-scrambled comconsole and a full-time ImpSec guard outside its door. Aral's footsteps echoed down the hall in that direction.

Cordelia took one bite of soup, which went down like liquid lead, set her spoon aside, and waited. She could hear Aral's voice, in the quiet house, and electronically tinged responses in some stranger's tones, but too muffled for her to make out the words. After what seemed a small eternity, though in fact the soup was still hot, Aral returned, bleak-faced.

"Did he go up there?" Cordelia asked. "To ImpMil?"

"Yes. He's been and left. It's all right." His heavy jaw was set.

"Meaning, the baby's all right?"

"Yes. He was denied admittance, he argued awhile, he left. Nothing worse." He began glumly spooning soup.

The Count returned a few hours later. Cordelia heard the fine whine of his groundcar pass up the drive and around the north end of the house, pause, a canopy open and close, and the car continue on to the garages, sited over the crest of the hill near the stables. She was sitting with Aral in the front room with the new big windows. He had been engrossed in some government report on his handviewer, but at the sound of the closing canopy put it on "pause" and waited with her, listening, as hard footsteps passed rapidly around the house and up the front steps. Aral's mouth was taut with unpleased anticipation, his eyes grim. Cordelia shrank back in her chair, and steeled her nerves.

Count Piotr swung into their room, and stood, feet planted. He was formally dressed in his old uniform with his general's rank insignia. "There you are." The liveried man trailing him took one uneasy glance at Aral and Cordelia, and removed himself without waiting to be dismissed. Count Piotr didn't even notice him go.

Piotr focused on Aral first. "You. You *dared* to shame me in public. Entrap me."

"You shamed yourself, I fear, sir. If you had not gone down that path, you would not have found that trap."

Piotr's tight jaw worked this one over, the lines in his face grooved deep. Anger; embarrassment struggling with self-righteousness. Embarrassed as only one in the wrong can be. *He doubts himself,* Cordelia realized. A thread of hope. *Let us not lose that thread, it may be our only way out of this labyrinth.*

The self-rightousness took ascendance. "I shouldn't have to be doing this," snarled Piotr. "It's women's work. Guarding our genome."

"Was women's work, in the Time of Isolation," said Aral in level tones. "When the only answer to mutation was infanticide. Now there are other answers."

"How *strange* women must have felt about their pregnancies, never knowing if there was life or death at the end of them," Cordelia mused. One sip from that cup was all she desired for a lifetime, and yet Barrayaran women had drained it to the dregs over and over . . . the wonder was not that their descendants' culture was chaotic, but that it wasn't more completely insane.

"You fail all of us when you fail to control her," said Piotr. "How do you imagine you can run a planet when you cannot run your own household?"

One corner of Aral's mouth twisted up slightly. "Indeed, she is difficult to control. She escaped me twice. Her voluntary return still astounds me."

"Awake to your duties! To me as your Count if not as your father. You are liege-sworn to me. Do you choose to obey this off-worlder woman before me?"

"Yes." Aral looked him straight in the eye. His voice

fell to a whisper. "That is the proper order of things." Piotr flinched. Aral added dryly, "Attempting to switch the issue from infanticide to obedience will not help you, sir. You taught me specious-rhetoric-chopping yourself."

"In the old days, you could have been beheaded for less insolence."

"Yes, the present setup is a little peculiar. As a count's heir, my hands are between yours, but as your Regent, your hands are between mine. Oath-stalemate. In the old days we could have broken the deadlock with a nice little war." He grinned back, or at least bared his teeth. Cordelia's mind gyrated, *One day only: The Irresistible Force Meets the Immovable Object. Tickets, five marks.*

The door to the hallway swung open, and Lieutenant Koudelka peered nervously within. "Sir? Sorry to interrupt. I'm having trouble with the comconsole. It's down again."

"What sort of trouble, Lieutenant?" Vorkosigan asked, wrenching his attention around with an effort. "The intermittency?"

"It's just not working."

"It was fine a few hours ago. Check the power supply."

"Did that, sir."

"Call a tech."

"I can't, without the comconsole."

"Ah, yes. Get the guard commander to open it up for you, then, see if the trouble is anything obvious. Then send for a tech on his clear-link."

"Yes, sir." Koudelka backed out, after a wary glance at the three tense people still frozen in their places waiting for him to withdraw.

The Count wouldn't quit. "I swear, I will disown it. That thing in the can at ImpMil. Utterly disinherit it."

"Not an operative threat, sir. You can only directly disown me. By an Imperial order. Which you would have to humbly petition, ah . . . *me*, for." His edged smile gleamed. "I would, of course, grant it to you."

The muscles in Piotr's jaw jumped. Not the irresistible force and the immovable object after all, but the irresistible force and some fluid sea; Piotr's blows kept failing to land, splashing past helplessly. Mental judo. He was off-balance, and flailed for his center, striking out wildly now. "Think of Barrayar. Think of the example you're setting."

"Oh," breathed Aral, "that I have." He paused. "We have never led from the rear, you or I. Where a Vorkosigan goes, maybe others might not find it so impossible to follow. A little personal . . . social engineering."

"Maybe for galactics. But our society can't afford this luxury. We barely hold our own as it is. We cannot carry the deadweight of millions of dysfunctionals!"

"Millions?" Aral raised a brow. "Now you extrapolate from one to infinity. A weak argument, sir, unworthy of you."

"And surely," said Cordelia quietly, "how much is bearable each individual, carrying his or her own burden, must decide."

Piotr swung on her. "Yes, and who is paying for all this, eh? The Imperium. Vaagen's laboratory is budgeted under military research. All Barrayar is paying for prolonging the life of your monster."

Discomfited, Cordelia replied, "Perhaps it will prove a better investment than you think."

Piotr snorted, his head lowered mulishly, hunched between his skinny shoulders. He stared through Cordelia at Aral. "You are determined to lay this thing on me. On my house. I cannot persuade you otherwise, I cannot order you . . . very well. You're so set on change, here's a change for you. I don't want my name on that thing. I can deny you that, if nothing else."

Aral's lips were pinched, nostrils flaring. But he never moved in his seat. The viewer glowed on, forgotten in his still hands. He held his hands quiet and totally controlled, not permitting them to clench. "Very well, sir."

"Call him Miles Naismith Vorkosigan, then," said Cordelia, feigning calm over a sick and trembling belly. "My father will not begrudge it."

"Your father is dead," snapped Piotr.

Smeared to bright plasma in a shuttle accident more

than a decade ago . . . She sometimes fancied, when she closed her eyes, that she could still sense his death imprinted on her retina in magenta and teal. "Not wholly. Not while I live, and remember."

Piotr looked as if she'd just hit him in his Barrayaran stomach. Barrayaran ceremonies for the dead approached ancestor-worship, as if remembrance could keep the souls alive. Did his own mortality run chill in his veins today? He had gone too far, and knew it, but could not back down. "Nothing, nothing wakes you up! Try this, then." He straddled the floor, boots planted, and glared at Aral. "Get out of my house. Both houses, Vorkosigan House, too. Take your woman and remove yourself. Today!"

Aral's eyes flicked only once around his childhood home. He set the viewer carefully aside, and stood. "Very well, sir."

Piotr's anger was anguished. "You'd throw away your home for this?!"

"My home is not a place. It is a person, sir," Aral said gravely. Then added reluctantly, "People."

Meaning Piotr, as well as Cordelia. She sat bent over, aching with the tension. Was the old man stone? Even now Aral offered him gestures of courtesy that nearly stopped her heart.

"You will return your rents and revenues to the District purse," said Piotr desperately.

"As you wish, sir." Aral headed for the door.

Piotr's voice went smaller. "Where will you live?"

"Illyan has been urging me for some time to move to the Imperial Residence, for security reasons. Evon Vorhalas has persuaded me Illyan is right."

Cordelia had risen when Aral did. She went now to the window and stared out over the moody grey, green, and brown landscape. Whitecaps foamed on the pewter water of the lake. The Barrayaran winter was going to be so cold. . . .

"So, you set yourself up with Imperial airs after all, eh?" jibed Piotr. "Is that what this is, hubris?"

Aral grimaced in profound irritation. "On the contrary,

sir. If I'm to have no income but my admiral's half-pay, I cannot afford to pass up rent-free quarters."

A movement in the scudding clouds caught Cordelia's eye. She squinted uneasily. "What's wrong with that lightflyer?" she murmured half to herself.

The speck grew, jinking oddly. It trailed smoke. It stuttered over the lake, straight at them. "God, I wonder if it's full of bombs?"

"What?" said Aral and Piotr together, and stepped quickly to the window with her, Aral on her right hand, Piotr on her left.

"It has ImpSec markings," said Aral.

Piotr's old eyes narrowed. "Ah?"

Cordelia mentally planned a sprint down the back hall and out the end door. There was a bit of a ditch on the other side of the drive, if they went flat in it maybe . . . but the lightflyer was slowing at the end of its trajectory. It wobbled toward a landing on the front lawn. Men in Vorkosigan livery and ImpSec green and black cautiously surrounded it. The flyer's damage was clearly visible now, a plasma-slagged hole, black smears of soot, warped control surfaces—it was a miracle it flew at all.

"Who—?" said Aral.

Piotr's squint sharpened as a glimpse of the pilot winked through the damaged canopy. "Ye gods, it's Negri!"

"But who's that with—come on!" Aral flung over his shoulder, running out the door. They charged in his wake, around into the front hall, bursting out the door and churning down the green slope.

The guards had to pry open the warped canopy. Negri fell into their arms. They laid him on the grass. He had a grotesque burn a meter long on the left side of his body and thigh, his green uniform melted and charred away to reveal bleeding white bubbles, cracked-open flesh. He shivered uncontrollably.

The short figure strapped into the passenger seat was Emperor Gregor. The five-year-old boy was weeping in terror, not loudly, just muffled, gulping, suppressed whimpers. Such self-control in one so young seemed sinister

to Cordelia. He should be screaming. She felt like screaming. He wore ordinary play-clothes, a soft shirt and pants
in dark blue. He was missing one shoe. An ImpSec guard
unhooked his seat belt and dragged him out of the flyer.
He cringed from the man and stared at Negri in utter
horror and confusion. *Did you think adults were inde-
structible, child?* Cordelia grieved.

Kou and Drou materialized from their separate holes
in the house, to goggle along with the rest of the guards.
Gregor spotted Droushnakovi, and flew to her like an
arrow, to wind his hands tightly in her skirt. "Droushie,
help!" His crying dared to become audible, then. She
wrapped her arms around him and lifted him up.

Aral knelt by the injured ImpSec chief. "Negri, what
happened?"

Negri reached up and grabbed his jacket with his
working right hand. "He's trying for a coup—in the capital.
His troops took ImpSec, took the comm center—why
didn't you respond? HQ surrounded, infiltrated—bad
fighting now at the Imperial Residence. We were on to
him—about to arrest—he panicked. Struck too soon. I
think he has Kareen—"

Piotr demanded, "Who has, Negri, who?"

"Vordarian."

Aral nodded grimly. "Yes . . ."

"You—take the boy," gasped Negri. "He's almost on top
of us . . ." His shivers oscillated into convulsions, his eyes
rolling back whitely. His breath stuttered in resonant
chokes. His brown eyes refocused in sudden intensity.
"Tell Ezar—" The convulsions took him again, racking his
thick body. Then they stopped. *All stop.* He was no longer
breathing.

CHAPTER ELEVEN

"Sir," said Koudelka urgently to Vorkosigan, "the secured comconsole was sabotaged." The ImpSec guard commander at his elbow nodded confirmation. "I was just coming to tell you. . . ." Koudelka glanced fearfully at Negri's body, laid out on the grass. Two ImpSec men now knelt beside it frantically applying first aid: heart massage, oxygen, and hypospray injections. But the body remained flaccid under their pummeling, the face waxy and inert. Cordelia had seen death before, and recognized the symptoms. *No good, fellows, you won't call this one back. Not this time. He's gone to deliver that last message to Ezar in person.* Negri's last report . . .

"What time-frame on the sabotage?" demanded Vorkosigan. "Delayed or immediate?"

"It looked like immediate," reported the guard commander. "No sign of a timer or device. Somebody just broke open the back and smashed it up inside."

Everyone's eyes went to the ImpSec man who had been assigned the guard post outside the comconsole room. He stood, dressed like most of the others in black fatigues, disarmed between two of his fellows. They had followed their commander out when the uproar began

169

on the front lawn. The prisoner's face was about the same lead-grey color as Negri's, but animated by flickering fear.

"And?" Vorkosigan said to the guard commander.

"He denies doing it," shrugged the commander. "Naturally."

Vorkosigan looked at the arrestee. "Who went in after me?"

The guard stared around wildly. He pointed abruptly at Droushnakovi, still holding the whimpering Gregor. "Her."

"I never!" said Drou indignantly. Her clutch tightened.

Vorkosigan's teeth closed. "Well, I don't need fast-penta to know that one of you is lying. No time now. Commander, arrest them both. We'll sort it out later." Vorkosigan's eyes anxiously scanned the northern horizon. "You," he pointed to another ImpSec man, "assemble every piece of transport you can find. We evacuate immediately. You," this to one of Piotr's armsmen, "go warn them in the village. Kou, grab the files, take a plasma arc and finish melting down that comconsole, and get back to me."

Koudelka, with one anguished look back over his shoulder at Droushanakovi, stumped off toward the house. Drou stood stiffly, stunned and angry and frightened, the cold wind fluttering her skirts. Her brows drew down at Vorkosigan. She scarcely noticed Koudelka's departure.

"You going to Hassadar first?" said Piotr to his son in a strange mild tone.

"Right."

Hassadar, the Vorkosigan's District capital: Imperial troops were quartered there. A loyal garrison?

"Not planning to hold it, I trust," said Piotr.

"Of course not. Hassadar," Vorkosigan's wolf-grin winked on and off, "shall be my first gift to Commodore Vordarian."

Piotr nodded, as if satisfied. Cordelia's head spun. Despite Negri's surprise, neither Piotr nor Aral seemed at all panicked. No wasted motion; no wasted words.

"You," said Aral to Piotr in an undertone, "take the boy." Piotr nodded. "Meet us—no. Don't tell even me where. You contact us."

"Right."

"Take Cordelia."

Piotr's mouth opened; it closed saying only, "Ah."

"And Sergeant Bothari. For Cordelia. Drou being—temporarily—off duty."

"I must have Esterhazy, then," said Piotr.

"I'll want the rest of your men," said Aral.

"Right." Piotr took his Armsman Esterhazy aside, and spoke to him in low tones; Esterhazy departed upslope at a dead run. Men were scattering in every direction, as their orders proliferated down their command chain. Piotr called another liveried retainer to him, and told him to take his groundcar and start driving west.

"How far, m'lord?"

"As far as your ingenuity can take you. Then escape if you can, and rejoin m'lord Regent, eh?"

The man nodded, and galloped off like Esterhazy.

"Sergeant, you will obey Lady Vorkosigan's voice as my own," Aral told Bothari.

"Always, my lord."

"I want that lightflyer." Piotr nodded to Negri's damaged vehicle, which, while no longer smoking, did not look very airworthy to Cordelia. Not nearly ready for wild flight, jinking or diving to evade determined enemies . . . *It's in about as good a shape for this as I am,* she feared. "And Negri," Piotr continued.

"He would appreciate that," said Aral.

"I am certain of it." Piotr nodded shortly, and turned to the first-aid squad. "Leave off, boys, it's no damn good by now." He directed them instead to load the body into the lightflyer.

Aral turned to Cordelia last, at last, for the first time. "Dear Captain . . ." The same sere expression had been fixed on his face since Negri had fallen out of the lightflyer.

"Aral, was this a surprise to anyone but me?"

"I didn't want to worry you with it, when you were so sick." His lips thinned. "We'd found Vordarian was conspiring, at HQ and elsewhere. Illyan's investigation was inspired. Top security people must have that sort of intuition, I suppose. But to convict a man of Vordarian's magnitude and connections of treason, we needed the hardest of evidence. The Council of Counts as a body is highly intolerant of central Imperial interference with their members. We couldn't take a mere vaporplot before them.

"But Negri called me last night with the word he had his evidence in hand, enough to move on at last. He needed an Imperial order from me to arrest a ruling District Count. I was supposed to go up to Vorbarr Sultana tonight and oversee the operation. Clearly, Vordarian was warned. His original move wasn't planned for another month, preferably right after my successful assassination."

"But—"

"Go, now." He pushed her toward the lightflyer. "Vordarian's troops will be here in minutes. You must get away. No matter what else he holds, he can't make himself secure while Gregor stays free."

"Aral—" Her voice came out a stupid squeak; she swallowed what felt like freeze-dried chunks of spit. She wanted to gabble a thousand questions, ten thousand protests. "Take care."

"You, too." A last light flared in his eyes, but his face was already distant, lost to the driving internal rhythm of tactical calculation. No time.

Aral went to take Gregor from Drou's arms, whispering something to her; reluctantly, she released the boy to him. They piled into the lightflyer, Bothari at the controls, Cordelia jammed into the back beside Negri's corpse, Gregor dumped into her lap. The boy made no noise at all, but only shivered. His eyes were wide and shocky, turned up to hers. Her arms encircled him automatically. He did not cling back, but wrapped his arms around his own torso. Negri, lolling, feared nothing now, and she almost envied him.

"Did you see what happened to your mother, Gregor?" Cordelia murmured to him.

"The soldiers took her." His voice was thin and flat. The overloaded lightflyer hiccoughed into the air, and

Bothari aimed it generally upslope, wavering only meters from the ground. It whined and moaned and rattled. Cordelia did, too, internally. She twisted around to stare back through the distorted canopy for a look—a last look?—at Aral, who had turned away and was double-timing toward the driveway where his soldiers were assembling a motly collection of vehicles, personal and governmental. *Why aren't we taking one of those?*

"When you clear the second ridge—if you can—turn right, Sergeant," Piotr directed Bothari. "Follow the creek."

Branches slashed at the canopy, as Bothari flew less than a meter above the trickling water and sharp rocks.

"Land in that little space there and kill the power," ordered Piotr. "Everyone, strip off any powered items you may be carrying." He divested his chrono and a comm link. Cordelia shed her chrono.

Bothari, easing the flyer down beside the creek beneath some Earth-import trees that had only half-shed their leaves, asked, "Does that include weapons, m'lord?"

"Especially weapons, Sergeant. The charge unit on a stunner shows up on a scanner like a torch. A plasma arc power cell lights it up like a bloody bonfire."

Bothari fished two of each from his person, plus other useful gear; a hand-tractor, his comm link, his chrono, some kind of small medical diagnostic device. "My knife, too, m'lord?"

"Vibra-knife?"

"No, just steel."

"Keep that." Piotr hunched over the lightflyer's controls and began re-programming the automatic pilot. "Everyone out. Sergeant, jam the canopy half-open."

Bothari managed this task with a pebble crammed forcibly into the canopy's seating-groove, then whirled at a sound from the undergrowth.

"It's me," came Armsman Esterhazy's breathless voice. Esterhazy, age forty, a mere stripling beside some of Piotr's other grizzled veterans, kept himself in top shape; he'd been hustling indeed, to get so puffed. "I have them, my lord."

The "them" in question turned out to be four of Piotr's horses, tied together by lines attached to the metal bars in their mouths the Barrayarans called "bits." Cordelia thought it a very small control surface for such a large piece of transport. The big beasts twitched and stamped and shook their jingling heads, red nostrils round and flaring, ominous bulky shapes in the vegetation.

Piotr finished re-programming the autopilot. "Bothari, here," he said. Together, they manhandled Negri's corpse back to the pilot's seat and strapped it in. Bothari powered the lightflyer up and jumped out. It lurched into the air, nearly crashing into a tree, and lumbered back over the ridge. Piotr, standing watching it rise, muttered under his breath, "Salute him for me, Negri."

"Where are you sending him?" Cordelia asked. *Valhalla?*

"Bottom of the lake," said Piotr, with some satisfaction. "*That* will puzzle them."

"Won't whoever follows trace it? Hoist it back out?"

"Eventually. But it should go down in the two-hundred-meter-deep section. It will take them time. And they won't know at first when it went down, nor how many bodies are missing from it. They'll have to search that whole section of the lake bottom, to be sure that Gregor isn't stuck in it. And negative evidence is never quite conclusive, eh? They won't *know*, even then. Mount up, troops, we're on our way." He headed purposefully toward his animals.

Cordelia trailed doubtfully. Horses. Would one call them slaves, symbionts, or commensals? The one toward which Esterhazy aimed her stood five feet high at the top. He stuck its lines into her hands and turned away. Its saddle was at the level of her chin, and how was she supposed to levitate up there? The horse looked much larger, at this range, than when idling around decoratively at a distance in its pasture. The brown fur-covered skin of its shoulder shuddered suddenly. *Oh, God, they've given me a defective one, it's going into convulsions*—a small mew escaped her.

Bothari had climbed atop his, somehow. He at least was not overpowered by the size of the animal. Given his height he made the full-sized beast look like a pony. City-bred, Bothari was no horseman, and seemed all knees and elbows despite what cavalry training Piotr had managed to inflict on him in the months of his service. But he was clearly in control of his mount, however awkward and rough his motions.

"You're point-man, Sergeant," Piotr told him. "I want us strung out to the limit of mutual visibility. No bunching up. Start up the trails for the flat rock—you know the place—and wait for us."

Bothari jerked his horse's head around and kicked at its sides, and clattered off up the woodland path at the seat-thumping pace called a *canter*.

Supposedly-creaky Piotr swung up into his saddle in one fluid motion; Esterhazy handed Gregor up to him, and Piotr held the boy in front of him. Gregor had actually seemed to cheer up at the sight of the horses, Cordelia could not imagine why. Piotr appeared to do nothing at all, but his horse arranged itself neatly ready to start up the trail—*telepathy*, Cordelia decided wildly. *They've mutated into telepaths here and never told me . . .* or maybe it was the horse that was telepathic.

"Come on, woman, you're next," Piotr snapped impatiently.

Desperately, Cordelia stuck her foot through the whatchamacallit foot-holder, *stirrup*, grabbed, and heaved. The saddle slid slowly around the horse's belly, and Cordelia with it, till she was clinging underneath among a forest of horse legs. She fell to the ground with a thump, and scrambled out of the way. The horse twisted its neck around and peered at her, in a dismay much milder than her own, then stuck its rubbery lips to the ground and began nibbling up weeds.

"Oh, God," Piotr groaned in exasperation.

Esterhazy dismounted again, and hurried to her elbow to help her up. "Milady. Are you all right? Sorry, that was my fault, should have re-checked, uh—haven't you ever ridden before?"

"Never," Cordelia confessed. He hastily pulled off the saddle, straightened it back around, and fastened it more tightly. "Maybe I can walk. Or run." *Or slit my wrists. Aral, why did you send me off with these madmen?*

"It's not that hard, Milady," Esterhazy promised her. "Your horse will follow the others. Rose is the gentlest mare in the stables. Doesn't she have a sweet face?"

Malevolent brown eyes with purple centers ignored Cordelia. "I can't." Her breath caught in a sob, the first of this ungodly day.

Piotr glanced at the sky, and back over his shoulder. "Useless Betan frill," he snarled at her. "Don't tell *me* you've never ridden astride." His teeth bared. "Just pretend it's my son."

"Here, give me your knee," said Esterhazy after an anxious look at the Count, cupping his hands.

Take the whole damned leg. She was shaking with anger and fear. She glared at Piotr, and grabbed again at the saddle. Somehow, Esterhazy managed to boost her aboard. She clung like grim death, deciding after one glance not to look down.

Esterhazy tossed her reins to Piotr, who caught them with an easy wrist-flick and took her horse in tow. The trail became a kaleidoscope of trees, rocks, sucking mud puddles, whipping branches, all whirling and bumping past. Her belly began to ache, her new scar twinging. *If that bleeding starts again inside* . . . They went on, and on, and on.

They bumped down at last from a canter to a walk. She blinked, red-faced and wheezing and dizzy-sick. They had climbed, somehow, to a clearing overlooking the lake, having circled behind the broad shallow inlet that lay to the left of the Vorkosigan property. As her vision cleared, she could make out the little green patch in the general red-brown background that was the sloping lawn of the old stone house. Across the water lay the tiny village.

Bothari was there before them, waiting, hunkered down in the scrub out of sight, his blowing horse tied to a tree. He rose silently, and approached them, to stare worriedly at Cordelia. She half-fell, half-slid, off into his arms.

"You go too fast for her, m'lord. She's still sick."

Piotr snorted. "She'll be a lot sicker if Vordarian's squads overtake us."

"I'll manage," gasped Cordelia, bent over. "In a minute. Just. Give me. A minute." The breeze, chilling down as the autumn sun slanted toward evening, lapped her hot skin. The sky had greyed over to a solid shadowless milk-color. Gradually, she was able to straighten against the abdominal pain. Esterhazy arrived at the clearing, bringing up the rear at a less hectic pace.

Bothari nodded to the distant green patch. "There they are."

Piotr squinted; Cordelia stared. A couple of flyers were landing on the lawn. Not Aral's equipment. Men boiled out of them like black ants in their military fatigues, maybe one or two bright flecks of maroon and gold among them, and a few spots of officer's dark green. *Great. Our friends and our enemies are all wearing the same uniforms. What do we do, shoot them all and let God sort them out?*

Piotr looked sour indeed. Were they smashing his home, down there, tearing the place apart looking for the refugees?

"Won't they be able to tell, when they count the horses missing from the stable, where we've gone and how?" asked Cordelia.

"I let them all out, Milady," said Esterhazy. "At least they'll all have a chance, that way. I don't know how many we'll get back."

"Most of them will hang around, I'm afraid," said Piotr. "Hoping for their grain. I wish they had the sense to scatter. God knows what viciousness those vandals will come up with, if they're cheated of all their other prey."

A trio of flyers was landing around the perimeter of the little village. Armed men disembarked, and vanished among the houses.

"I hope Zai warned them all in time," muttered Esterhazy.

"Why would they bother those poor people?" asked Cordelia. "What do they want there?"

"Us, Milady," said Esterhazy grimly. At her confused look he went on, "Us armsmen. Our families. They're on a hostage-hunt down there."

Esterhazy had a wife and two children in the capital, Cordelia recalled. And what was happening to them right now? Had anyone passed them a warning? Esterhazy looked like he was wondering that, too.

"No doubt Vordarian will play the hostage game," said Piotr. "He's in for it now. He must win, or die."

Sergeant Bothari's narrow jaw worked, as he stared through the murky air. Had anyone remembered to warn Mistress Hysopi?

"They'll be starting their air-search shortly," said Piotr. "Time to get under cover. I'll go first. Sergeant, lead her."

He turned his horse and vanished into the undergrowth, following a path so faint Cordelia could not have recognized it as one. It took Bothari and Esterhazy together to lift her back aboard her transport. Piotr chose a walk for the pace, not for her sake, Cordelia suspected, but for his sweat-darkened animals. After that first hideous gallop, a walk was like a reprieve. At first.

They rode among trees and scrub, along a ravine, over a ridge, the horses' hooves scraping over stone. Her ears strained for the whine of flyers overhead. When one came, Bothari led her on a wild and head-spinning slide down into a ravine, where they dismounted and cowered under a rock ledge for minutes, until the whine faded. Getting back out of the ravine was even more difficult. They had to lead the horses up, Bothari practically seeming to hoist his along the precarious scrubby slope.

It grew darker, and colder, and windier. Two hours became three, four, five, and the smoky darkness turned pitchy. They bunched up with the horses nose to tail, trying not to lose Piotr. It began to rain, a sad black drizzle that made Cordelia's saddle even slipperier.

Around midnight they came to a clearing, hardly less black than the shadows, and Piotr at last called a halt. Cordelia sat against a tree, stunned with exhaustion, nerve-strung, holding Gregor. Bothari split a ration bar he'd been carrying in his pocket, their only food, between Cordelia and Gregor. With Bothari's uniform jacket wrapped around him, Gregor finally overcame the chill enough to sleep. Cordelia's legs went pins and needles, beneath him, but at least he was a lump of warmth.

Where was Aral, by now? For that matter, where were they? Cordelia hoped Piotr knew. They could not have made more than five kilometers an hour at most, with all that up and down and switch-back doubling. Did Piotr really imagine they were going to elude their pursuers this way?

Piotr, who had sat for a while under his own tree a few meters off, got up and went into the scrub to piss, then came back to peer at Gregor in the dimness. "Is he asleep?"

"Yes. Amazingly."

"Mm. Youth," Piotr grunted. Envy?

His tone was not so hostile as earlier, and Cordelia ventured, "Do you suppose Aral is in Hassadar by now?" She could not quite bring herself to say, *Do you suppose he ever made it to Hassadar?*

"He'll have been and gone by now."

"I thought he would raise its garrison."

"Raise and disperse, in a hundred different directions. And which squad has the Emperor? Vordarian won't know. But with luck, that traitor will be lured into occupying Hassadar."

"Luck?"

"A small but worthy diversion. Hassadar has no strategic value to speak of for either side. But Vordarian must divert a part of his—surely finite number of—loyal troops to hold it, deep in a hostile territory with a long guerilla tradition. We'll get good intelligence of everything they do there, but the population will be opaque to them.

"And it's my capital. He occupies a count's district capital with Imperial troops—all my brother counts must pause and think about that one. *Am I next?* Aral probably went on to Tanery Base Shuttleport. He must open an independent line of communication with the space-based forces, if Vordarian has truly choked off Imperial Headquarters. The spacers' choice of loyalties will be critical. I predict a severe outbreak of technical difficulties in their comm rooms, while the ship commanders scramble to figure out which is going to be the winning side." Piotr emitted a macabre chuckle, in the shadows. "Vordarian is too young to remember Mad Emperor Yuri's War. Too bad for him. He's gained sufficient advantage, with his quick start, I'd loathe to grant him more."

"How fast . . . did it all happen?"

"Fast. There was no hint of any trouble when I was up to the capital at noon. It must have broken out right after I left."

A chill that had nothing to do with the rain fell between them briefly, as both remembered why Piotr had made that journey this day.

"Does the capital . . . have great strategic value?" Cordelia asked, changing the subject, unwilling to break open that raw issue again.

"In some wars it would. Not this one. This is not a war for territory. I wonder if Vordarian realizes that? It's a war for loyalties, for the minds of men. No material object in it has more than a passing tactical importance. Vorbarr Sultana is a communications center, though, and communication is much. But not the only center. Collateral circulation will serve."

We have no communications at all, thought Cordelia dully. Out here in the woods in the rain. "But if Vordarian holds the Imperial Military Headquarters right now . . ."

"What he holds right now, unless I miss my guess, is a very large building full of chaos. I doubt a quarter of the men are at their posts, and half of them are plotting sabotage to benefit whatever side they secretly favor. The rest are out running for cover, or trying to get their families out of town."

"Will Captain Vorpatril be all—will Vordarian bother Lord and Lady Vorpatril, do you think?" Alys Vorpatril's pregnancy was very close to term. When she had visited

Cordelia at ImpMil—only ten days ago?—her gliding walk
had become a heavy flatfooted waddle, her belly a swaying
high arc. Her doctor promised her a big boy. Ivan, he
was to be named. His nursery was completely equipped
and fully decorated, she had groaned, shifting her stomach
uncomfortably in her lap, and *now* would be a good
time. . . .

Now was not a good time anymore.

"Padma Vorpatril will head the list. The hunt will be
up for him, all right. He and Aral are the last descendants of Prince Xav, now, if anybody's fool enough to start
up that damned succession-debate again. Or if anything
does happen to Gregor." He bit down on this last line
as if he might hold back fate with his teeth.

"Lady Vorpatril and the baby, too?"

"Perhaps not Alys Vorpatril. The boy, definitely."

Not exactly a separable matter, just at the moment.

The wind had died down at last. Cordelia could hear
the horses' teeth tearing up plants, a steady *munch-munch-
munch*.

"Won't the horses show up on thermal sensors? And
us, too, despite dumping our power cells. I don't see how
they can miss us for long." Were troops up there right
now, eyes in the clouds?

"Oh, all the people and beasts in these hills will show
up on their thermal sensors, once they start aiming them
in the right direction."

"All? I hadn't seen any."

"We've passed about twenty little homesteads, so far
tonight. All the people, and their cows, and their goats,
and their red deer, and their horses, and their children.
We're straws in a haystack. Still, it will be well for us to
split up soon. If we can make it to the trail at the base
of Amie Pass before mid-morning, I have an idea or two."

By the time Bothari shoved her back atop Rose, the
deep blackness was greying. Pre-dawn light seeped into
the woods as they began to move again. Tree branches
were charcoal stokes in the dripping mist. She clung to
her saddle in silent misery, towed along by Bothari. Gregor

actually still slept, for the first twenty minutes of the ride, openmouthed and limp and pale in Piotr's grip.

The growing light revealed the night's ravages. Bothari and Esterhazy were both muddy and scuffed, beard-peppered, their brown-and-silver uniforms rumpled. Bothari, having given up his jacket to Gregor, went in shirtsleeves. The open round collar of his shirt made him look like a condemned criminal being led to the beheading-block. Piotr's general's dress greens had survived fairly well, but his stubbled red-eyed face above it was like a derelict's. Cordelia felt herself a hopeless tangle, with her wet tendrils of hair, mishmash of old clothing and house slippers.

It could be worse. I could still be pregnant. At least if I die, I die singly now. Was little Miles safer than she right now? Anonymous in his replicator on some shelf in Vaagen and Henri's restricted laboratory? She could pray so, even if she couldn't believe so. *You Barrayaran bastards had better leave my boy alone.*

They zigzagged up a long slope. The horses blew like bellows even though just walking: getting balky, stumbling over roots and rocks. They came to a halt at the bottom of a little hollow. Both horses and people drank from the murky stream. Esterhazy loosened girths again. He scratched under the horses' headbands, and they butted against him, nuzzling his empty pockets for tidbits. He murmured apologies and little encouragements to them. "It's all right, Rosie, you can rest at the end of the day. Just a few more hours." It was more briefing than anybody had bothered to give Cordelia.

Esterhazy left the horses to Bothari and accompanied Piotr into the woods, scrabbling up the slope. Gregor busied himself in an attempt to gather vegetation and hand-feed it to the animals. They lipped at the native Barrayaran plants and let them fall messily from their mouths, unpalatable. Gregor kept picking the wads up and offering them again, trying to shove them in around the horses' bits.

"What's the Count up to, do you know?" Cordelia asked Bothari.

He shrugged. "Gone to make contact with somebody. *This* won't do." A jerk of his head in no particular direction indicated their night of beating around in the brush.

Cordelia could only agree. She lay back and listened for lightflyers, but heard only the babble of water in the little stream, echoed by the gurgles of her empty stomach. She was galvanized into motion once, to keep the hungry Gregor from sampling some of the possibly-toxic plants himself.

"But the horses ate these ones," he protested.

"No!" Cordelia shuddered, detailed visions of unfavorable biochemical and histamine reactions dancing in a molecular crack-the-whip through her head. "It's one of the first habits you have to learn for Betan Astronomical Survey, you know. Never put strange things in your mouth till they've been cleared by the lab. In fact, avoid touching your eyes, mouth, and mucous membranes."

Gregor, unconsciously compelled, promptly rubbed his nose and eyes. Cordelia sighed, and sat back down. She sucked on her tongue, thinking about that stream water and hoping Gregor wouldn't point out her inconsistency. Gregor threw pebbles into the pools.

Fully an hour later, Esterhazy returned. "Come on." They merely led the horses this time, sure sign of a steep climb to come. Cordelia scrambled, and scraped her hands. The horses' haunches heaved. Over the crest, down, up again, and they came out on a muddy double trail carved through the forest.

"Where are we?" asked Cordelia.

"Aime Pass Road, Milady," supplied Esterhazy.

"This is a road?" Cordelia muttered in dismay, staring up and down it. Piotr stood a little way off, with another old man holding the reins of a sturdy little black-and-white horse.

The horse was considerably better groomed than the old man. Its white coat was bright and its black coat shiny. Its mane and tail were brushed to feather-softness. Its feet and fetlocks were wet and dark, though, and its belly flecked with fresh mud. In addition to an old cavalry saddle like Piotr's horse's, the pinto bore four large saddle-bags, a pair in front and a pair behind, and a bedroll.

The old man, as unshaven as Piotr, wore an Imperial Postal Service jacket so weatherworn its blue had turned grey. This was supplemented by odd bits of other old uniforms: a black fatigue shirt, an ancient pair of trousers from a set of dress greens, worn but well-oiled officer's knee-high riding boots on his bent bowlegs. He also wore a non-regulation felt hat with a few dried flowers stuck in its faded print headband. He smacked his black-stained lips and stared at Cordelia. He was missing several teeth; the rest were long and yellow-brown.

The old man's gaze fell on Gregor, holding Cordelia's hand. "So that's him, eh? Huh. Not much." He spat reflectively into the weeds by the side of the path.

"Might do in time," asserted Piotr. "If he gets time."

"I'll see what I can do, Gen'ral."

Piotr grinned, as if at some private joke. "You have any rations on you?"

"'Course." The old man smirked, and turned to rummage in one of his saddlebags. He came up with a package of raisins in a discarded plastic flimsy, some little cakes of brownish crystals wrapped in leaves, and what looked like a handful of strips of leather, again in a twist made of a used plastic flimsy. Cordelia caught a heading, *Update of Postal Regluations C6.77a, modified 6/17. File Immediately In Permanent Files.*

Piotr looked the stores over judiciously. "Dried goat?" He nodded toward the leathery mess.

"Mostly," said the old man.

"We'll take half. And the raisins. Save the maple sugar for the children." Piotr popped one cube in his mouth, though. "I'll find you in maybe three days, maybe a week. You remember the drill from Yuri's War, eh?"

"Oh, yes," drawled the old man.

"Sergeant." Piotr waved Bothari to him. "You go with the Major, here. Take *her*, and the boy. He'll take you to ground. Lie low till I come get you."

"Yes, m'lord," Bothari intoned flatly. Only his flickering eyes betrayed his uneasiness.

"What we got here, Gen'ral?" inquired the old man, looking up at Bothari. "New one?"

"A city boy," said Piotr. "Belongs to my son. Doesn't talk much. He's good at throats, though. He'll do."

"Aye? Good."

Piotr was moving a lot more slowly. He waited for Esterhazy to give him a leg up on his horse. He settled into his saddle with a sigh, his back temporarily curved in an uncharacteristic slump. "Damn, but I'm getting old for this sort of thing."

Thoughtfully, the man Piotr had called the Major reached into a side pocket and pulled out a leather pouch. "Want my gum-leaf, Gen'ral? A better chew than goat, if not as long-lasting."

Piotr brightened. "Ah. I would be most grateful. But not your whole pouch, man." Piotr dug among the pressed dried leaves that filled the container, and crumbled himself off a generous half, which he stuffed in his breast pocket. He put a wad in his cheek, and returned the pouch with a sincere salute. Gum-leaf was a mild stimulant; Cordelia had never seen Piotr chew it in Vorbarr Sultana.

"Take care of m'lord's horses," called Esterhazy rather desperately to Bothari. "They're not machines, remember. "

Bothari grunted something noncommittal, as the Count and Esterhazy headed their animals back down the trail. They were out of sight in a few moments. A profound quiet descended.

CHAPTER TWELVE

The Major put Gregor, comfortably padded by the bed-roll and saddlebags, up behind him. Cordelia faced one more climb onto that torture-device for humans and horses called a saddle. She would never have made it without Bothari. The Major took her reins this time, and Rose and his horse walked side by side with a lot less jerking of the bridle. Bothari dropped back, trailing watchfully.

"So," said the old man after a time, with a sideways look at her, "you're the new Lady Vorkosigan."

Cordelia, rumpled and filthy, smiled back desperately. "Yes. Ah, Count Piotr didn't mention your name, Major . . . ?"

"Amor Klyeuvi, Milady. But folks up here just call me Kly."

"And, uh . . . what are you?" Besides some mountain kobold Piotr had conjured out of the ground.

He smiled, an expression more repellent than attractive given the state of his teeth. "I'm the Imperial Mail, Milady. I ride the circuit through these hills, out of Vorkosigan Surleau, every ten days. Been at it for eighteen years. There are grown kids up here with kids of their own who never knew me as anything but Kly the Mail."

"I thought mail went to these parts by lightflyer."

"They're phasing them in. But the flyers don't go to every house, just to these central drop-points. No courtesy to it, anymore." He spat disgust and gum-leaf. "But if the General'll hold 'em off another two years here, I'll make my last twenty, and be a triple-twenty-years Service man. I retired with my double-twenty, see."

"From what branch, Major Klyuevi?"

"Imperial Rangers." He watched slyly for her reaction; she rewarded him with impressed raised brows. "I was a throat-cutter, not a tech. 'S why I could never go higher than major. Got my start at age fourteen, in these mountains, running rings around the Cetagandans with the General and Ezar. Never did get back to school after that. Just training courses. The Service passed me by, in time."

"Not entirely, it seems," said Cordelia, staring around the apparently unpeopled wilderness.

"No . . ." His breath became a purse-lipped sigh, as he glanced back over his shoulder at Gregor in meditative unease.

"Did Piotr tell you what happened yesterday afternoon?"

"Yo. I left the lake day-before-yesterday morning. Missed all the excitement. I expect the news will catch up with me before noon."

"Is . . . anything else likely to catch up with us by then?"

"We'll just have to see." He added more hesitantly, "You'll have to get out of those clothes, Milady. The name VORKOSIGAN, A., in big block letters over your jacket-pocket isn't any too anonymous."

Cordelia glanced down at Aral's black fatigue shirt, quelled.

"My lord's livery sticks out like a flag, too," Kly added, looking back at Bothari. "But you'll pass well enough, in the right clothes. I'll see what I can do, in a bit here."

Cordelia sagged, her belly aching in anticipation of rest. Refuge. But at what price to those who gave her refuge? "Will helping us put you in danger?"

His tufted grey brow rose. "Belike." His tone did not invite further comment on the topic.

She had to bring her tired mind back on-line somehow, if she was to be asset and not hazard to everyone around her. "That gum-leaf of yours. Does it work anything like coffee?"

"Oh, better than coffee, Milady."

"Can I try some?" Shyness lowered her voice; it might be too intimate a request.

His cheeks creased in a dry grin. "Only backcountry sticks like me chew gum-leaf, Milady. Pretty Vor ladies from the capital wouldn't be caught dead with it in their pearly teeth."

"I'm not pretty, I'm not a lady, and I'm not from the capital. And I'd kill for coffee right now. I'll try it."

He let his reins drop to his steadily plodding horse's neck, rummaged in his blue-grey jacket pocket, and pulled out his pouch. He broke off a chunk, in none-too-clean fingers, and leaned across.

She regarded it a doubtful moment, dark and leafy in her palm. *Never put strange organics in your mouth till they've been cleared by the lab.* She lapped it up. The wad was made self-sticking by a bit of maple syrup, but after her saliva washed away the first startling sweetness, the flavor was pleasantly bitter and astringent. It seemed to peel away the night's film coating her teeth, a real improvement. She straightened.

Kly regarded her with bemusement. "So what are you, off-worlder not-a-lady?"

"I was an astrocartographer. Then a Survey captain. Then a soldier, then a POW, then a refugee. And then I was a wife, and then I was a mother. I don't know what I'm going to be next," she answered honestly, around the gum-leaf. *Pray not* widow.

"Mother? I'd heard you were pregnant, but . . . didn't you lose your baby to the soltoxin?" He eyed her waist in confusion.

"Not yet. He still has a fighting chance. Though it seems a little uneven, to match him against all of Barrayar just yet. . . . He was born prematurely. By surgical section." (She decided not to try to explain the uterine replicator.) "He's at the Imperial Military Hospital. In Vorbarr Sultana. Which for all I know has just been captured by Vordarian's rebel forces . . ." She shivered. Vaagen's lab was classified, nothing to draw anyone's attention. Miles was all right, all right, all right, and one crack in that thin shell of conviction would hatch out hysteria. . . . Aral, now, Aral could take care of himself if anyone could. So how had he been so caught-out, eh, eh? No question, ImpSec was riddled with treason. They couldn't trust anyone around here, and where was Illyan? Trapped in Vorbarr Sultana? Or was he Vordarian's quisling? No . . . Cut off, more likely. Like Kareen. Like Padma and Alys Vorpatril. Life racing death . . .

"No one will bother the hospital," said Kly, watching her face.

"I—yes. Right."

"Why did you come to Barrayar, off-worlder?"

"I wanted to have children." A humorless laugh puffed from her lips. "Do you have any children, Kly the Mail?"

"Not so far as I know."

"You were very wise."

"Oh . . ." His face grew distant. "I don't know. Since my old woman died, 's been pretty quiet. Some men I know, their children have been a great trouble to them. Ezar. Piotr. Don't know who will burn the offerings on my grave. M' niece, maybe."

Cordelia glanced at Gregor, riding along atop the saddlebags and listening. Gregor had lit the taper to Ezar's great funeral offering-pyre, his hand guided by Aral's.

They rode on up the road, climbing. Four times Kly ducked up side-trails, while Cordelia, Bothari, and Gregor waited out of sight. On the third of these delivery-runs Kly returned with a bundle including an old skirt, a pair of worn trousers, and some grain for the tired horses. Cordelia, still chilled, put the skirt on over her old Survey trousers. Bothari exchanged his conspicuous brown uniform pants with the silver stripe down the side for the hillman's cast-offs. The pants were too short, riding ankle-high, giving him the look of a sinister scarecrow. Bothari's uniform and Cordelia's black fatigue shirt were bundled out of sight in an empty mailbag. Kly solved the problem of Gregor's missing shoe by simply stripping off the remaining one and letting the boy go barefoot, and concealing his too-nice blue suit beneath a man's oversize shirt with the sleeves rolled up. Man, woman, child, they looked a haggard, ragged little hill family.

They made the top of Amie Pass and started back down. Occasionally folk waited by the roadside for Kly; he passed on verbal messages, rattling them off in what sounded to Cordelia to be verbatim style. He distributed letters on paper and cheap vocodisks, their self-playbacks tinny and thin. Twice he paused to read letters to apparently illiterate recipients, and once to a blind man guided by a small girl. Cordelia grew twitchier with each mild encounter, drained by nervous exhaustion. *Will that fellow betray us? What do we look like to that woman? At least the blind man can't describe us. . . .*

Toward dusk, Kly returned from one of his side-loops to gaze up and down the silent shadowed wilderness trail and declare, "This place is just too crowded." It was a measure of Cordelia's overstrain that she found herself mentally agreeing with him.

He looked her over, worry in his eyes. "Think you can go on for another four hours, Milady?"

What's the alternative? Sit by this mud puddle and weep till we're captured? She struggled to her feet, pushing up from the log she'd been perched on waiting their guide's return. "That depends on what's at the end of four more hours of this."

"My place. I usually spend this night at my niece's, near here. My route ends about another ten hours farther on, when I'm making my deliveries, but if we go straight up we can do it in four. I can double back to this point by tomorrow morning and keep my schedule as usual. Real quiet-like. Nothing to remark on."

What does "straight up" mean? But Kly was clearly right; their whole safety lay in their anonymity, their invisibility. The sooner they were out of sight, the better. "Lead on, Major."

It took six hours. Bothari's horse went lame, short of their goal. He dismounted and towed it. It limped and tossed its head. Cordelia walked, too, to ease her raw legs and to keep herself warm and awake in the chilling darkness. Gregor fell asleep and fell off, cried for his mother, then fell asleep again when Kly moved him around to his front to keep a better grip. The last climb stole Cordelia's breath and made her heart race, even though she hung on to Rose's stirrup for help. Both horses moved like old women with arthritis, stumping along jerkily; only the animals' innate gregariousness kept them following Kly's hardy pinto.

The climb became a drop, suddenly, over a ridge and into a great vale. The woods grew thin and ragged, interspersed with mountain meadows. Cordelia could feel the spaces stretching out around her, true mountain scale at last, vast gulfs of shadow, huge bulks of stone, silent as eternity. Three snowflakes melted on her staring, upturned face. At the edge of a vague patch of trees, Kly halted. "End of the line, folks."

Cordelia sleepwalked Gregor into the tiny shack, felt her way to a cot, and rolled him onto it. He whimpered in his sleep as she dragged the blankets over him. She stood swaying, numb-brained, then in a last burst of lucidity kicked off her slippers and climbed in with him. His feet were cold as a cryo-corpse's. As she warmed them against her body his shivering gradually relaxed into deeper sleep. Dimly, she was aware that Kly—Bothari—somebody, had started a fire in the fireplace. Poor Bothari, he'd been awake every bit as long as she had. In a quite military sense, he was her man; she should see that he ate, cared for his feet, slept . . . she should, she should. . . .

Cordelia snapped awake, to discover that the movement that had roused her was Gregor, sitting up beside her and rubbing his eyes in bleary disorientation. Light streamed in through two dirty windows on either side of the wooden front door. The shack, or cabin—two of the walls were made of whole logs stacked up—was only a single room. In the grey stone fireplace at one end a kettle and a covered pot sat on a grating over a bed of glowing coals. Cordelia reminded herself again that wood represented poverty, not wealth, here. They must have passed ten million trees yesterday.

She sat up, and gasped from the pain in her muscles. She straightened her legs. The bed was a rope net strung on a frame and supporting first a straw-stuffed mattress, then a feather-stuffed one. She and Gregor were warm, at least, in their nest. The air of the room was dusty-smelling, tinged with a pleasant edge of wood smoke.

Booted footsteps sounded on the boards of the porch outside, and Cordelia grasped Gregor's arm in sudden panic. She couldn't run—that black iron fireplace poker would make a pretty poor weapon against a stunner or nerve disruptor—but the steps were Bothari's. He slipped through the door along with a puff of outside air. His crudely sewn tan cloth jacket must be a borrowing from Kly, judging from the way his bony wrists stuck out beyond the turned-down sleeve cuffs. He'd pass for a hillman easily, as long as he kept his urban-accented mouth shut.

He nodded at them. "Milady. Sire." He knelt by the fireplace, glanced under the pot lid, and tested the kettle's temperature by cupping a big hand a few centimeters above it. "There's groats, and syrup," he said. "Hot water. Herb tea. Dried fruit. No butter."

"What's happening?" Cordelia rubbed her face awake, and swung her legs overboard, planning a stumble toward that herb tea.

"Not much. The Major rested his horse a while, and left before light, to keep his schedule. It's been real quiet, since."

"Did you get any sleep yet?"

"Couple of hours, I think."

The tea had to wait while Cordelia escorted the Emperor downslope to Kly's outhouse. Gregor wrinkled his nose, and eyed the adult-sized seat nervously. Back on the cabin porch Cordelia supervised hand and face washing over a dented metal basin.

The view from the porch, once she'd toweled her face dry and vision clear, was stunning. Half of Vorkosigan's District seemed spread out below, the brown foothills, the green- and yellow-specked peopled plains beyond. "Is that our lake?" Cordelia nodded to a glint of silver in the hills, near the limits of her vision.

"I think so," said Bothari, squinting.

So far, to have come this fast on foot. So fearfully near, in a lightflyer . . . Well, at least you could see whatever was coming.

The hot groats and syrup, served on a cracked white plate, tasted wonderful. Cordelia guzzled herb tea, and realized she'd become dangerously dehydrated. She tried to encourage Gregor to drink, but he didn't like the astringent taste of the tea. Bothari looked almost suffused with shame, that he couldn't produce milk out of the air at his Emperor's direct request. Cordelia solved the dilemma by sweetening the tea with syrup, rendering it acceptable.

By the time they finished breakfast, washed up the few utensils and dishes, and flung the bit of wash water over the porch rail, the porch had warmed enough in the morning sun to make sitting tolerable.

"Why don't you take over the bed, Sergeant. I'll keep watch. Ah . . . did Kly have any suggestions what we should do, if somebody hostile drops down on us here before he gets back? It kind of looks like we've run out of places to run to."

"Not quite, Milady. There's a set of caves, up in that patch of woods in back. An old guerilla cache. Kly took me back last night to see the entrance."

Cordelia sighed. "Right. Get some sleep, Sergeant, we'll surely need you later."

She sat in the sun in one of the wooden chairs, resting her body if not her mind. Her eyes and ears strained for the whine of a distant lightflyer or heavy aircar. She tied Gregor's feet up with makeshift rag shoes, and he wandered about examining things. She accompanied him on a visit to the shed to see the horses. The Sergeant's beast was still very lame, and Rose was moving as little as possible, but they had fodder in a rick and water from a little stream that ran across the end of their enclosure. Kly's other horse, a lean and fit-looking sorrel, seemed to tolerate the equine invasion, only nipping when Rose edged too close to its side of the hayrick.

Cordelia and Gregor sat on the porch steps as the sun passed zenith, comfortably warm now. The only sound in the vast vale besides a breeze in the branches was Bothari's snores, resonating through the cabin walls. Deciding this was as relaxed as they were likely to get, Cordelia at last dared quiz Gregor on his view—her only eyewitness report—of the coup in the capital. It wasn't much help; Gregor's five-year-old eyes saw the *what* well enough, it was the *whys* that escaped him. On a higher level, she had the same problem, Cordelia admitted ruefully to herself.

"The soldiers came. The colonel told Mama and me to come with him. One of our liveried men came in. The colonel shot him."

"Stunner, or nerve disruptor?"

"Nerve disruptor. Blue fire. He fell down. They took us to the Marble Courtyard. They had aircars. Then Captain Negri ran in, with some men. A soldier grabbed me, and Mama grabbed me back, and that's what happened to my shoe. It came off in her hand. I should have . . . fastened it tighter, in the morning. Then Captain Negri shot the soldier who was carrying me, and some soldiers shot Captain Negri—"

"Plasma arc? Is that when he got that horrible burn?" Cordelia asked. She tried to keep her tone very calm.

Gregor nodded mutely. "Some soldiers took Mama, those other ones, not Negri's ones. Captain Negri picked me up and ran. We went through the tunnels, under the Residence, and came out in a garage. We went in the lightflyer. They shot at us. Captain Negri kept telling me to shut up, to be quiet. We flew and flew, and he kept yelling at me to be quiet, but I *was*. And then we landed by the lake." Gregor was trembling again.

"Mm." Kareen spun in vivid detail in Cordelia's head, despite the simplicity of Gregor's account. That serene face, wrenched into screaming rage and terror as they tore the son she'd borne the Barrayaran hard way from her grip, leaving . . . nothing but a shoe, of all their precarious life and illusory possessions. So Vordarian's troops had Kareen. As hostage? Victim? Alive or dead?

"Do you think Mama's all right?"

"Sure." Cordelia shifted uncomfortably. "She's a very valuable lady. They won't hurt her." *Till it becomes expedient for them to do so.*

"She was crying."

"Yes." She could feel that same knot in her own belly. The mental flash she'd shied from all day yesterday burst in her brain. Boots, kicking open a secured laboratory door. Kicking over desks, tables. No faces, just boots. Gun butts sweeping delicate glassware and computerized monitors from benches into a tangled smash on the floor. A uterine replicator rudely jerked open, its sterile seals slashed, its contents dumped pell-mell wetly on the tiles . . . no need even for the traditional murderous swing by the heels of infant head against the nearest concrete wall, Miles was so little the boots could just *step* on him and smash him to jam. . . . She drew in her breath.

Miles is all right. Anonymous, just like us. We are very small, and very quiet, and safe. Shut up, keep quiet, kid. She hugged Gregor tightly. "My little boy is in the capital, too, same as your Mama. And you're with me. We'll look out for each other. You bet."

After supper, and still no sign of Kly, Cordelia said, "Show me that cave, Sergeant."

Kly kept a box of cold lights atop his mantel. Bothari cracked one, and led Cordelia and Gregor up into the woods on a faint stony path. He made a menacing will-o'-the-wisp, with the bright green-tinged light shining from the tube between his fingers.

The area near the cave mouth showed signs of having once been cleared, though recent overgrowth was closing back in. The entrance was by no means hidden, a yawning black hole twice the height of Bothari and wide enough to edge a lightflyer through. Immediately within, the roof rose and walls flared to create a dusty cavern. Whole patrols could camp therein, and had, in the distant past, judging from the antique litter. Bunk niches were carved in the rock, and names and initials and dates and crude comments covered the walls.

A cold fire-pit in the center was matched by a blackened vent-hole above, which had once provided exit for the smoke. A ghostly crowd of hillmen, guerilla soldiers, seemed to hover in Cordelia's mind's eye, eating, joking, spitting gum-leaf, cleaning their weapons and planning their next foray. Ranger spies came and went, ghosts among the ghosts, to place their precious blood-won information before their young general, who spread his maps out on that flat rock over there. . . . She shook the vision from her head, and took the light and explored the niches. At least five traversable exits led off from the cavern, three of which showed signs of having been heavily traveled.

"Did Kly say where these went, or where they came out, Sergeant?"

"Not exactly, Milady. He did say the passages went back for kilometers, into the hills. He was late, and in a hurry to get on."

"Is it a vertical or horizontal system, did he say?"

"Beg pardon, Milady?"

"All on one strata, or with unexpected big drops? Are there lots of blind alleys? Which path were we supposed to take? Are there underground streams?"

"I think he expected to be leading us, if we went in. He started to explain, then said it was too complicated."

She frowned, contemplating the possibilities. She'd done a bit of cave work in her Survey training, enough to grasp what the term *respect for the hazards* meant. Vents, drops, cracks, labyrinthine cross-passages . . . plus, here, the unexpected rise and fall of water, not a matter of much concern on Beta Colony. It had rained last night. Sensors were not much help in finding a lost cave explorer. And whose sensors? If the system was as extensive as Kly suggested, it could absorb hundreds of searchers. . . . Her frown changed to a slow smile.

"Sergeant, let's camp here tonight."

Gregor liked the cave, especially when Cordelia described the history of the place. He rattled around the cavern whispering military dialogue to himself like "Zap, zap, zap!", climbed in and out of all the niches, and tried to sound out the rude words carved in the walls. Bothari lit a small fire in the pit and spread a bedroll for Gregor and Cordelia, taking the night watch for himself. Cordelia set a second bedroll, wrapped around trail snacks and supplies, in a grabbable bundle near the entrance. She arranged the black fatigue jacket with the name VORKOSIGAN, A., artistically in a niche, as if used to sit upon and keep someone's haunches from the cold stone and then temporarily forgotten when the sitter rose. Last of all Bothari brought up their lame and useless horses, re-saddled and bridled, and tethered them just outside.

Cordelia emerged from the widest passage, where she'd dropped an almost-spent cold light a quarter kilometer along, over a rope-strung ten-meter cliff. The rope was natural fiber, and very old and brittle. She'd elected not to test it.

"I don't quite get it, Milady," said Bothari. "With the horses abandoned out there, if anyone comes looking they'll find us at once, and know exactly where we've gone."

"Find this, yes," said Cordelia. "Know where we've gone, no. Because without Kly, there is no way I'm taking Gregor down into this labyrinth. But the best way to look like we were here is to actually be here for a bit."

Bothari's flat eyes lit in understanding at last, as he gazed around at the five black entrances at their various levels. "Ah!"

"That means we also need to find a real bolt-hole.

Somewhere up in the woods, where we can cut across to the trail Kly brought us up yesterday. Wish we'd done this in daylight."

"I see what you mean, Milady. I'll scout."

"Please do, Sergeant."

Taking their trail bundle, he disappeared into the dim woods. Cordelia tucked Gregor into the bedroll, then perched outside among the rocks above the cave mouth and kept watch. She could see the vale, stretched out greyly below the tops of the trees, and make out Kly's cabin roof. No smoke rose now from its chimney. Beneath the stone, no remote thermal sensor would find their new fire, though the smell of it hung in the chill air, detectable to nearby noses. She watched for moving lights in the sky till the stars were a watery blur in her eyes.

Bothari returned after a very long time. "I have a spot. Shall we move now?"

"Not yet. Kly might still show up." *First.*

"Your turn to sleep, then, Milady."

"Oh, yes." The evening's exertions had only partly warmed the acid fatigue from her muscles. Leaving Bothari on the limestone outcrop in the starlight like a guardian gargoyle, she crawled in with Gregor. Eventually, she slept.

She woke with the grey light of dawn making the cavern entrance a luminous misty oval. Bothari made hot tea, and they shared cold lumps of pan bread left from last night, and nibbled dried fruit.

"I'll watch some more," Bothari volunteered. "I can't sleep so good without my medication anyway."

"Medication?" said Cordelia.

"Yeah, I left my pills at Vorkosigan Surleau. I can feel it clearing out of my system. Things seem sharper."

Cordelia chased a suddenly very lumpy bite of bread with a swallow of hot tea. But were his psychoactive drugs truly therapeutic, or merely political in their effect? "Let me know if you are experiencing any kind of difficulty, Sergeant," she said cautiously.

"Not so far. Except it's getting harder to sleep. They

suppress dreams." He took his tea and wandered back to his post.

Cordelia carefully refrained from cleaning up their campsite. She did escort Gregor to the nearest rivulet for a personal washup. They were certainly acquiring an authentic hill-folk aroma. They returned to the cavern, where Cordelia rested a while on the bedroll. She must insist on relieving Bothari soon. Come on, Kly. . . .

Bothari's tense low voice reverberated in the cavern. "Milady. Sire. Time to go."

"Kly?"

"No."

Cordelia rolled to her feet, kicked the pre-arranged pile of dirt over the last coals of their fire, grabbed Gregor, and hustled him out the cave mouth. He looked suddenly frightened and sickly. Bothari was pulling the bridles off the horses, loosing them and tossing the gear on the pile with the saddles. Cordelia pulled herself up beside the cave and snatched one quick glimpse over the treetops. A flyer had landed in front of Kly's cabin. Two black-uniformed soldiers were circling to the right and left. A third disappeared under the porch roof. Faint and delayed in the distance came the bang of Kly's front door being kicked open. Only soldiers, no hillman-guides or hillman-prisoners in that flyer. No sign of Kly.

They took to the woods at a jog, Bothari boosting up and carrying Gregor piggyback. Rose made to follow them, and Cordelia whirled to wave her arms and whisper frantically, "No! Go away, idiot beast!" to spook her off. Rose hesitated, then turned to stay by her lame companion.

Their run was steady, unpanicked. Bothari had his route all picked out, taking advantage of sheltering rocks and trees and water-carved steps. They scrambled up, down, up, but just when she thought her lungs would burst and their pursuers must spot them, Bothari vanished along a steep rock face.

"Over here, Milady!"

He'd found a thin, horizontal crack in the rocks, half a meter high and three meters deep. She rolled in beside

him to find the niche shielded by solid rock everywhere
but the front, and that almost blocked by fallen stone.
Their bedroll and supplies waited.

"No wonder," Cordelia gasped, "the Cetagandans had
trouble up here." A thermal sensor would have to be
aimed straight in, to pick them up, from a point twenty
meters in the air out over the ravine. The place was
riddled with hundreds of similar crannies.

"Even better." Bothari pulled a pair of antique field
glasses, looted from Kly's cabin, from their bedroll. "We
can see them."

The glasses were nothing but binocular tubes with slid-
ing glass lenses, purely passive light-collectors. They must
have dated from the Time of Isolation. The magnifica-
tion was poor by modern standards, no UV or infrared
boost, no rangefinder pulse . . . no power cell to leak
detectable energy traces. Flat on her belly, chin in the
rubble, Cordelia could glimpse the distant cavern entrance
on the slope rising beyond the ravine and a knife-backed
ridge. When she said, "Now we must be *very* quiet," pale
Gregor practically went fetal.

The black-clad scanner men found the horses at last,
though it seemed to take them forever. Then they found
the cave mouth. The tiny figures gesticulated excitedly
to each other, ran in and out, and called the flyer, which
landed outside the entrance with much crackling of shrubbery. Four men entered; eventually, one came back out.
In time, another flyer landed. Then a lift van arrived, and
disgorged a whole patrol. The mountain mouth ate them
all. Another lift van came, and men set up lights, a field
generator, comm links.

Cordelia made a nest of the bedroll for Gregor, and
fed him little snacks and sips from their water bottle.
Bothari stretched out in the back of the niche with the
thinnest blanket folded under his head, otherwise seeming
impervious to the stone. While Bothari dozed, Cordelia
kept careful count of the net flow of hunters. By mid-
afternoon, she calculated that some forty men had gone
below and not come up again.

Two men were brought out strapped to float pallets, loaded into a medical-evacuation lifter, and flown away. A lightflyer made a bad landing in the crowded area, toppled downslope, and crunched into a tree. Yet more men became involved in extracting, righting, and repairing it. By dusk over sixty men had been sucked down the drain. A whole company drawn away from the capital, not pursuing refugees, not available to root out the secrets of ImpMil . . . it wasn't enough to make a real difference, surely.

It's a start.

Cordelia and Bothari and Gregor slipped from the niche in the gloaming, cleared the ravines, and made their way silently through the woods. It was nearly full dark when they came to the edge of the trees and struck Kly's trail. As they crossed over the ridge edging the vale, Cordelia looked back. The area by the cave mouth was marked by searchlights, stabbing up through the mists. Lightflyers whined in and out of the site.

They dropped over the ridge and slithered down the slope that had so nearly killed her to climb, hanging on to Rose's stirrup two days ago. Fully five kilometers down the trail, in a rocky region of treeless scrub, Bothari came to an abrupt halt. "Sh. Milady, listen."

Voices. Men's voices, not far off, but strangely hollow. Cordelia stared into the darkness, but no lights moved. Nothing moved. They crouched beside the trail, senses straining.

Bothari crept off, head tilted, following his ears. After a few moments Cordelia and Gregor cautiously followed. She found Bothari kneeling by a striated outcrop. He motioned her closer.

"It's a vent," he announced in a whisper. "Listen."

The voices were much clearer now, sharp cadences, angry gutturals punctuated by swearing in two or three languages.

"Goddammit, I know we went left back at that third turn."

"That wasn't the third turn, that was the fourth."

"We re-crossed the stream."

"It wasn't the same friggin' stream, *sabaki!*"

"*Merde. Perdu!*"

"Lieutenant, you're an idiot!"

"Corporal, you're out of line!"

"This cold light's not going to last the hour. See, it's fading."

"Well, don't shake it up, you moron, when it glows brighter it goes faster."

"Give me that—!"

Bothari's teeth gleamed in the darkness. It was the first smile Cordelia had seen crack his face in months. Silently, he saluted her. They tiptoed softly away, into the chill of the Dendarii night.

Back on the trail, Bothari sighed deeply. "If only I'd had a grenade to drop down that vent. Their search parties would still be shooting at each other this time next week."

CHAPTER THIRTEEN

Four hours down the night trail, the distinctive black and white horse loomed out of the dark. Kly was a shadow aboard it, but his thick profile and battered hat were instantly recognizable.

"Bothari!" The name huffed from Kly's mouth. "We live. Grace of God."

Bothari's voice was flat. "What happened to you, Major?"

"I almost ran into one of Vordarian's squads at a cabin I was delivering mail to. They're actually trying to go over these hills house by house. Dosing everyone they meet with fast-penta. They must be bringing the drug in by the barrel."

"We expected you back last night," said Cordelia. She tried not to let her tone sound too accusing.

The felt hat bobbed as Kly gave her a weary nod of greeting. "Would've been, except for Vordarian's bloody patrol. I didn't dare let them question me. I spent a day and a night, dodging 'em. Sent my niece's husband to get you. But when he got to my place this morning, Vordarian's men were all over. I figured we'd lost everything. But when they were still all over by nightfall, I took heart. They wouldn't still be looking for you if they'd found you. Figured I'd better get my ass up here and do some scouting myself. This is beyond hope."

Kly turned his horse around, heading back down the trail. "Here, Sergeant, put the boy up."

"I can carry the boy. Think you'd better give m'lady a lift. She's about out."

Too true. It was a measure of Cordelia's exhaustion that she went willingly to Kly's horse. Between them, Bothari and Kly shoved her aboard, perched astraddle on the pinto's warm rump. They started off, Cordelia gripping the mailman's coat.

"What happened to you?" Kly asked in turn.

Cordelia let Bothari answer, in his short sentences made even shorter by his burdened stride, as he carried Gregor piggyback. When he got to a mention of the men heard down the vent, Kly barked a laugh, then clapped a hand over his mouth. "They'll be weeks getting out of there. Good work, Sergeant!"

"It was Lady Vorkosigan's idea."

"Oh?" Kly twisted around to glance back over his shoulder at Cordelia, clinging wanly.

"Aral and Piotr both seemed to think diversion worthwhile," Cordelia explained. "I gather Vordarian has limited reserves."

"You think like a soldier, m'lady." Kly sounded approving.

Cordelia wrinkled her brow in dismay. What an appalling compliment. The last thing she wanted was to start thinking like a soldier, playing their game by their rules. The hallucinatory military world-view was horribly infectious, though, immersed in it as she was now. *How long can I tread water?*

Kly led them on another two hours of night marching, striking out on unfamiliar trails. In deep pre-dawn dark they came to a shack, or house. It seemed to be of similar construction to Kly's place, but more extensive, with rooms built on and other rooms built on to the additions. A light from a tiny flame, some sort of greasy homemade candle, burned in a window.

An old woman in a nightgown and jacket, her grey hair in a braid down her back, came to the door and motioned them within. Another old man—but younger than Kly—took the horse out of sight toward a shed. Kly made to go with him.

"Is it safe here?" Cordelia asked dizzily. *Where is here?*

Kly shrugged. "They searched here day before yesterday. Before I sent for m' nephew-in-law. Checked it off clean."

The old woman snorted, surly memory in her eye.

"What with the caves, and all the unchecked homesteads, and the lake, it'll be a while before they get around to re-checking. They're still searching the lake bottom, I hear, they've flown in all kinds of equipment. It's as safe as any." He went off after his horse.

Meaning, as unsafe as any. Bothari was already taking his boots off. His feet must be bad. Her feet were a mess, her slippers walked to flinders, and Gregor's rag shoes utterly destroyed. She'd never felt so near the end of all endurance, bone-weary, blood-weary, though she'd done much longer hikes before. It was as if her truncated pregnancy had drained life itself out of her, to pass it on to another. She let herself be guided, fed bread and cheese and milk and put to bed in a little side room, herself on one narrow cot and drooping Gregor on another. She would believe in safety tonight the way Barrayaran children believed in Father Frost at Winterfair, true because she desperately wanted it to be.

The next day a raggedy boy of about ten appeared out of the woods, riding Kly's sorrel horse bareback with a rope halter. Kly made Cordelia, Gregor, and Bothari hide out of sight while he paid the boy off with a few coins, and Sonia, Kly's aged niece, packed him some sweet cakes to speed him on his way. Gregor peeked wistfully out the corner of one curtained window as the child vanished again.

"I didn't dare go myself," Kly explained to Cordelia. "Vordarian has three platoons of men up there now." A wheezing chuckle escaped him at some inner vision. "But the boy knows nothing but that the old mailman was sick and needed his re-mount."

"They didn't fast-penta that child, did they?"

"Oh, yes."

"They dared!"

Kly's black-stained lips compressed in sympathy with her outrage. "If he can't get hold of Gregor, Vordarian's coup is likely doomed. And he knows it. There's not much he wouldn't dare to do, at this point." He paused. "You can be glad fast-penta has replaced torture, eh?"

Kly's nephew-in-law helped him saddle up the sorrel, and buckle on the mailbags. The mailman adjusted his hat, and climbed up.

"If I don't keep my schedule, it will be near-impossible for the Gen'ral to contact me," he explained. "Got to go, I'm late already. I'll be back. You and the boy stay inside, out of sight, as much as you can, m'lady." He turned his horse toward the bare-branched woods. The animal blended quickly into the red-brown native scrub.

Cordelia found Kly's last advice all too easy to follow. She spent most of the next four days in her cot-bed. The dull silence of hours went by in a fog, a relapse into the frightening fatigue she'd experienced after the placental transfer operation and its near-lethal complications. Conversation provided no diversion. The hill-folk were as laconic as Bothari. It was the threat of fast-penta, Cordelia thought. The less you knew, the less you could tell. The old woman Sonia's eyes probed Cordelia curiously, but she never asked anything beyond, "You hungry?" Cordelia didn't even know her last name.

Baths. After the first one, Cordelia did not ask again. The old couple worked all afternoon to haul and heat enough water for herself and Gregor. Their simple meals were nearly as much labor. No *Pull Tab To Heat Contents* up here. Technology, a woman's best friend. Unless the technology appeared in the form of a nerve disruptor in the hand of some dead-eyed soldier hunting you down carelessly as an animal.

Cordelia counted over the days since the coup, since all hell had broken loose. What was happening in the larger world? What response from the space forces, from planetary embassies, from conquered Komarr? Would Komarr seize the chaos to revolt, or had Vordarian taken them by surprise too? *Aral, what are you doing out there?*

Sonia, though she asked no questions, would now and then return from outings and drop bits of local news. Vordarian's troops, headquartered in Piotr's residence, were close to abandoning the search of the lake bottom. Hassadar was sealed, but refugees escaped in a trickle; someone's children, smuggled out, had arrived to stay with relatives nearby. At Vorkosigan Surleau most of Piotr's armsmen's families had escaped except Armsman Vogti's wife and very aged mother, who had been taken away in a groundcar, no one knew where.

"And, oh yes, very strange," Sonia added. "They took Karla Hysopi. That hardly makes sense. She was only the widow of a retired regular Service sergeant, what use do they expect to make of her?"

Cordelia froze. "Did they take the baby, too?"

"Baby? Donnia didn't say about a baby. Grandchild, was it?"

Bothari was sitting by the window sharpening his knife on Sonia's kitchen whetstone. His hand paused in mid-stroke. He looked up to meet Cordelia's alarmed eyes. Beyond a tightening of his jaw his face did not change expression, yet the sudden increase of tension in his body made Cordelia's stomach knot. He looked back down at what he was doing, and took a longer, firmer stroke that hissed along the whetstone like water on coals.

"Maybe . . . Kly will know something more, when he comes back," Cordelia quavered.

"Belike," said Sonia doubtfully.

At last, on schedule, on the evening of the seventh day, Kly rode into the clearing on his sorrel horse. A few minutes later Armsman Esterhazy rode in behind him. He was dressed in hillman's togs, and his mount was a lean and spindle-shanked hill horse, not one of Piotr's big glossy beasts. They put their horses away and came in to a dinner Sonia had apparently fixed this night of Kly's rounds for eighteen years.

After dinner they pulled up chairs to the stone fireplace, and Kly and Esterhazy briefed Cordelia and Bothari in low tones. Gregor sat by Cordelia's feet.

"Since Vordarian has greatly widened his search area," Esterhazy began, "Count and Lord Vorkosigan have decided that the mountains are still the best place to hide Gregor. As the search radius grows enemy forces will be spread thinner and thinner."

"Locally, Vordarian's forces are still hunting up and down the caves," Kly put in. "There's about two hundred men still up there. But as soon as they finish finding each other, I expect they'll pull out. I hear they've given up on finding you in there, Milady. Tomorrow, Sire," Kly glanced down and addressed Gregor directly, "Armsman Esterhazy will take you to a new place, a lot like this one. You'll have a new name for a while, for pretend. And Armsman Esterhazy will pretend he's your da. Think you can do that?"

Gregor's hand tightened on Cordelia's skirt. "Will Lady Vorkosigan pretend she's my ma?"

"We're going to take Lady Vorkosigan back to Lord Vorkosigan, at Tanery Base Shuttleport." At Gregor's alarmed look Kly added, "There's a pony, where you're going. And goats. The lady there might teach you how to milk the goats."

Gregor looked doubtful, but did not fuss further, though the next morning as he was put up behind Esterhazy on the shaggy horse he looked near to tears.

Cordelia said anxiously, "Take care of him, Armsman."

Esterhazy gave her a driven look. "He's my Emperor, Milady. He holds my oath."

"He's also a little boy, Armsman. Emperor is . . . a delusion you all have in your heads. Take care of the Emperor for Piotr, yes, but you take care of Gregor for me, eh?"

Esterhazy met her eyes. His voice softened. "My little boy is four, Milady."

He did understand, then. Cordelia swallowed relief and grief. "Have you . . . heard anything from the capital? About your family?"

"Not yet," said Esterhazy bleakly.

"I'll keep my ears open. Do what I can."

"Thank you." He gave her a nod, not as retainer to his lady, but as one parent to another. No other word seemed necessary.

Bothari was out of earshot, having returned to the cabin to pack up their few supplies. Cordelia went to Kly's stirrup, as he prepared to swing his black and white horse about and lead Esterhazy and Gregor on their way. "Major. Sonia passed on a rumor that Vordarian's troops took Mistress Hysopi. Bothari had hired her to foster his baby girl. Do you know if they took Elena—the baby—too?"

Kly lowered his voice. " 'Twas the other way around, as I have it. They went for the baby, Karla Hysopi raised hell, so they took her too even though she wasn't on the list."

"Do you know where?"

He shook his head. "Somewhere in Vorbarr Sultana. Belike your husband's Intelligence will know exactly, by now."

"Have you told the Sergeant yet?"

"His brother armsman told him, last night."

"Ah."

Gregor looked back over his shoulder at her as they rode away, until they were obscured from sight by the tree-boles.

For three days Kly's nephew guided them through the mountains, Bothari on foot leading Cordelia on a bony-hipped little hill horse with a sheepskin pad cinched to its back. On the third afternoon, they came to a cabin which sheltered a skinny youth who led them to a shed that held, wonder of wonders, a rickety lightflyer. He loaded up the backseat with Cordelia and six jugs of maple syrup. Bothari shook hands silently with Kly's nephew, who mounted the little horse and vanished into the woods.

Under Bothari's narrow eye, the skinny youth coaxed
his vehicle into the air. Brushing treetops, they followed
ravines and ridges up over the snow-frosted spine of the
mountains and down the other side, out of Vorkosigan's
District. They came at dusk to a little market town. The
youth brought his flyer down in a side street. Cordelia
and Bothari helped him carry his gurgling produce to a
small grocer's shop, where he bartered the syrup for
coffee, flour, soap, and power cells.

Upon returning to his lightflyer, they found that a
battered groundtruck had pulled up and parked behind
it. The youth exchanged no more than a nod with its
driver, who hopped out and slid the door to the cargo
bay aside for Bothari and Cordelia. The bay was a quarter
full of fiber sacks of cabbages. They did not make very
good pillows, though Bothari did his best to arrange
Cordelia a nest of them as the truck rocked along above
the dismally uneven roads. Bothari then sat wedged
against the side of the cargo bay and compulsively polished the edge of his knife to molecular sharpness with
a makeshift strop, a bit of leather he'd begged from Sonia.
Four hours of this and Cordelia was ready to start talking to the cabbages.

The truck thumped to a halt at last. The door slid
aside, and first Bothari then Cordelia emerged to find
themselves in the middle of nowhere: a gravel-surfaced
road over a culvert, in the dark, in the country, in an
unfamiliar district of unknown loyalties.

"They'll pick you up at Kilometer Marker Ninety-six,"
the truck driver said, pointing to a white smudge in the
dimness that appeared to be merely a painted rock.

"When?" asked Cordelia desperately. For that matter,
who were *they*?

"Don't know." The man returned to his truck and drove
off in a spray of gravel from the hoverfan, as if he were
already pursued.

Cordelia perched on the painted boulder and wondered
morbidly which side was going to leap out of the night
first, and by what test she might tell them apart. Time

passed, and she entertained an even more depressed vision
of no one picking them up at all.

But at last a darkened lightflyer floated down out of the
night sky, its engines pitched to eerie near-silence. Its
landing feet crunched in the gravel. Bothari crouched
beside her, his useless knife gripped in his hand. But the
man awkwardly levering himself up out of the passenger
seat was Lieutenant Koudelka. "Milady?" he called uncertainly to the two human scarecrows. "Sergeant?" A breath
of pure delight puffed from Cordelia as she recognized the
pilot's blonde head as Droushnakovi. *My home is not a
place, it is people, sir. . . .*

With Bothari's hand on her elbow, at Koudelka's anxious gesture Cordelia fell gratefully into the padded
backseat of the flyer. Droushnakovi cast a dark look over
her shoulder at Bothari, wrinkled her nose, and asked,
"Are you all right, Milady?"

"Better than I expected, really. Go, go."

The canopy sealed, and they rose into the air. Vent fans
powered up, cycling filtered air. Colored lights from the
control interface highlighted Kou's and Drou's faces. A
technological cocoon. Cordelia glanced at systems readouts over Droushnakovi's shoulder, and then up through
the canopy; yes, dark shapes paced them, guardian military
flyers. Bothari saw them, too, his eyes narrowing in approval. Some fraction of tension eased from his body.

"Good to see you two—" some subtle cue of their body
language, some hidden reserve, kept Cordelia from adding
together again. "I gather you got that accusation about
the comconsole sabotage straightened out in good order?"

"As soon as we got the chance to stop and fast-penta
that guard corporal, Milady," Droushnakovi answered. "He
didn't have the nerve to suicide before questioning."

"He was the saboteur?"

"Yes," answered Koudelka. "He'd intended to escape
to Vordarian's troops when they arrived to capture us.
Vordarian apparently suborned him months ago."

"That accounts for our security problems. Or does it?"

"He passed information about our route, the day of

the sonic grenade attempt." Koudelka rubbed at his sinuses in memory.

"So it was Vordarian behind that!"

"Confirmed. But the guard doesn't seem to have known anything about the soltoxin. We turned him inside out. He wasn't a high-level conspirator, just a tool."

Nasty flow of thought, but, "Has Illyan reported in yet?"

"Not yet. Admiral Vorkosigan hopes he may be hiding in the capital, if he wasn't killed in the first fighting."

"Hm. Well, you'll be glad to know Gregor's all right—"

Koudelka held up an interrupting hand. "Excuse me, Milady. The Admiral ordered—you and the Sergeant are not to debrief anything about Gregor to anyone except Count Piotr or himself."

"All right. Damn fast-penta. How is Aral?"

"He's well, Milady. He ordered me to bring you up to date on the strategic situation—"

Screw the strategic situation, what about my baby? Alas, the two seemed inextricably intertwined.

"—and answer any questions you had."

Very well. "What about our baby? Pi—Miles?"

"We've heard nothing bad, Milady."

"What does that mean?"

"It means we've heard nothing," Droushnakovi put in glumly.

Koudelka shot her an irate look, which she shrugged off with a twitch of one shoulder.

"No news may be good news," Koudelka went on. "While it's true Vordarian holds the capital—"

"And therefore ImpMil, yes," said Cordelia.

"And he's publicizing names of hostages related to anyone in our command structure, there's been no mention of, of your child, in the lists. The Admiral thinks Vordarian simply doesn't realize that what went into the replicator was viable. Doesn't know what he's got."

"Yet," bit off Cordelia.

"Yet," Koudelka conceded reluctantly.

"All right. Go on."

"The overall situation isn't as bad as we feared at first.

Vordarian holds Vorbarr Sultana, his own District and its military bases, and he's put troops in Vorkosigan's District, but he only has about five district counts who are his committed allies. About thirty of the other counts were caught in the capital, and we can't tell their real allegiance while Vordarian holds guns to their heads. Most of the twenty-three remaining Districts have reiterated their oaths to my Lord Regent. Though a couple are waffling, who have relatives in the capital or who are in dicey strategic positions as potential battlefields."

"And the space forces?"

"I was just coming to them, yes, Milady. Over half of their supplies come up from the shuttleports in Vordarian's District. For the moment, they're still holding out for a clear result rather than moving in to create one. But they've refused to openly endorse Vordarian. It's a balance, and whoever can tip it their way first will start a landslide. Admiral Vorkosigan seems awfully confident." Cordelia was not sure from the lieutenant's tone if he altogether shared that confidence. "But then, he has to. For morale. He says Vordarian lost the war the hour Negri got away with Gregor, and the rest is just maneuvering to limit the losses. But Vordarian holds Princess Kareen."

"Doubtless one of the losses Aral is anxious to limit. Is she all right? Vordarian's goons haven't abused her?"

"Not as far as we know. She seems to be under house arrest in her own rooms in the Imperial Residence. Several of the more important hostages have been secluded there."

"I see." She glanced sideways in the dim cabin at Bothari, who did not change expression. She waited for him to ask after Elena, but he said nothing. Droushnakovi stared bleakly into the night, at the mention of Kareen.

Had Kou and Drou made up? They seemed cool, civil, all duty and on duty. But whatever surface apologies had passed, Cordelia sensed no healing in them. The secret adoration and will-to-trust was all gone from the blue eyes that now and then flicked from the control interface to the man in the passenger seat. Drou's glances were merely wary.

Lights glowed ahead on the ground, the spatter of a middle-sized city, and beyond it, the jumbled geometrics of a sprawling military shuttleport. Drou went through code-check after code-check, as they approached. They spiraled down to a pad that lit for them, peopled with armed guards. Their guard-flyers passed on overhead to their own landing zones.

The guards surrounded them as they exited the flyer, and escorted them as fast as Koudelka's pace would permit to a lift tube. They went down, took a slide-walk, and went down again through blast doors. Tanery Base clearly featured a hardened underground command post. Welcome to the bunker. And yet a throat-catching whiff of familiarity shook Cordelia for a terrifying moment of confusion and loss. Beta Colony did a lot better on the interior decorating than these barren corridors, but she might have descended to the utility level of some buried Betan city, safe and cool. . . . *I want to go home.*

There were three green-uniformed officers, talking in a corridor. One was Aral. He saw her. "Thank you, dismissed, gentlemen," he said in the middle of someone's sentence, then more consciously, "We'll continue this shortly." But they lingered to goggle.

He looked no worse than tired. Her heart ached to look at him, and yet . . . *Following you has brought me here. Not to the Barrayar of my hopes, but to the Barrayar of my fears.*

With a voiceless "Ha!" he embraced her, hard to him. She hugged him back. *This is a good thing. Go away, World.* But when she looked up the World was still waiting, in the form of seven watchers all with agendas.

He held her away, and scanned her anxiously up and down. "You look terrible, dear Captain."

At least he was polite enough not to say, You *smell* terrible. "Nothing a bath won't cure."

"That is not what I meant. Sickbay for you, before anything." He turned to find Sergeant Bothari first in line.

"Sir, I must report in to my lord Count," Bothari said.

"Father's not here. He's on a diplomatic mission from

me to some of his old cronies. Here, you, Kou—take
Bothari and set him up with quarters, food chits, passes,
and clothes. I'll want your personal report immediately
I've seen to Cordelia, Sergeant."

"Yes, sir." Koudelka led Bothari away.

"Bothari was amazing," Cordelia confided to Aral.
"No—that's unjust. Bothari was Bothari, and I shouldn't
have been amazed at all. We wouldn't have made it without him."

Aral nodded, smiling a little. "I thought he would do
for you."

"He did indeed."

Droushnakovi, taking up her old position at Cordelia's
elbow the moment Bothari vacated it, shook her head in
doubt, and followed along as Aral steered Cordelia down
the corridor. The rest of the parade followed less certainly.

"Hear any more about Illyan?" Cordelia asked.

"Not yet. Did Kou brief you?"

"A sketch, enough for now. I don't suppose any more
word's come in on Padma and Alys Vorpatril, then, either?"

He shook his head regretfully. "But neither are they
on the list of Vordarian's confirmed captures. I think
they're hiding in the city. Vordarian's side is leaking
information like a sieve, we'd know if any arrest that
important had happened. I can only wonder if our own
arrangements are so porous. That's the trouble with these
damned civil affrays, everybody has a brother—"

A voice from down the corridor hailed loudly, "Sir! Oh,
sir!" Only Cordelia felt Aral flinch, his arm jerking under
her hand.

An HQ staffer led a tall man in black fatigues with
colonel's tabs on the collar toward them. "There you are,
sir. Colonel Gerould is here from Marigrad."

"Oh. Good. I have to see this man now. . . ." Aral
looked around hurriedly, and his eye fell on Droushnakovi.
"Drou, please escort Cordelia to the infirmary for me. Get
her checked, get her—get her everything."

The colonel was no HQ desk pilot. He looked, in fact,
as if he'd just flown in from some front line, wherever

the "front" was in this war for loyalties. His fatigues were dirty and wrinkled and looked slept-in, their smoke-stink eclipsing Cordelia's mountain-reek. His face was lined with fatigue. But he looked only grim, not beaten. "The fighting in Marigrad has gone house-to-house, Admiral," he reported without preamble.

Vorkosigan grimaced. "Then I want to hopscotch it. Come with me to the tactics room—*what* is that on your arm, Colonel?"

A wide piece of white cloth and a narrower strip of brown circled the officer's black upper left sleeve. "ID, sir. We couldn't tell who we were shooting at, up close. Vordarian's people are wearing red and yellow, 's as close as they could come to maroon and gold, I guess. That's supposed to be brown and silver for Vorkosigan, of course."

"That's what I was afraid of." Vorkosigan looked extremely stern. "Take it off. Burn it. And pass the word down the line. You already have a uniform, Colonel, issued to you by the Emperor. That's who you're fighting for. Let the traitors alter their uniforms."

The colonel looked shocked at Vorkosigan's vehemence, but, after a beat, enlightened; he stripped the cloth hastily from his arm and stuffed it in his pocket. "Right, sir."

Aral let go of Cordelia's hand with a palpable effort. "I'll meet you in our quarters, love. Later."

Later in the week, at this rate. Cordelia shook her head helplessly, took in one last view of his stocky form as if her intensity could somehow digitize and store him for retrieval, and followed Droushnakovi into Tanery Base's underground warren. At least with Drou, Cordelia was able to overrule Vorkosigan's itinerary and insist on a bath first. Almost as good, she found half a dozen new outfits in her correct size, betraying Drou's palace-trained good taste, waiting for her in a closet in Aral's quarters.

The base doctor had no charts; Cordelia's medical records were of course all behind enemy lines in Vorbarr Sultana at present. He shook his head and keyed up a new form on his report panel. "I'm sorry, Lady Vorkosigan. We'll simply have to begin at the beginning. Please bear with me. Do I understand correctly you've had some sort of female trouble?"

No, most of my troubles have been with males. Cordelia bit her tongue. "I had a placental transfer, let me see, three plus," she had to count it up on her fingers, "about five weeks ago."

"Excuse me, a what?"

"I gave birth by surgical section. It did not go well."

"I see. Five weeks post-partum." He made a note. "And what is your present complaint?"

I don't like Barrayar, I want to go home, my father-in-law wants to murder my baby, half my friends are running for their lives, and I can't get ten minutes alone with my husband, whom you people are consuming before my eyes, my feet hurt, my head hurts, my soul hurts . . . it was all too complicated. The poor man just wanted something to put in his blank, not an essay. "Fatigue," Cordelia managed at last.

"Ah." He brightened, and entered this factoid on his report panel. "Post-partum fatigue. This is normal." He looked up and regarded her earnestly. "Have you considered starting an exercise program, Lady Vorkosigan?"

CHAPTER FOURTEEN

"Who are Vordarian's men?" Cordelia asked Aral in frustration. "I've been running from them for weeks, but it's like I've only glimpsed them in a rearview mirror. Know your enemy and all that. Where does he get this endless supply of goons?"

"Oh, not endless." Aral smiled slightly, and took another bite of stew. They were—miracle!—alone at last, in his simple underground senior officer's apartment. Their supper had been brought in on a tray by a batman, and spread on a low table between them. Aral had then, to Cordelia's relief, ejected this hovering minion with a "Thank you, Corporal, that will be all."

Aral swallowed his bite and continued, "Who are they? For the most part, anyone who was caught with an officer up along his chain of command who elected Vordarian's side, and who hasn't worked up the nerve, or in some cases the wit, to either frag the officer or desert his unit and report in elsewhere. And obedience and unit cohesion is deeply inculcated in these men. 'When the going gets rough, stick to your unit' is literally drilled into them. So the unfortunate fact that their officer is leading them into treason makes clinging to

218

their squad-brothers even more natural. Besides," he
grinned bleakly, "it's only treason if Vordarian loses."

"And is Vordarian losing?"

"As long as I live, and keep Gregor alive, Vordarian
cannot win." He nodded in conviction. "Vordarian is
imputing crimes to me as fast as he can invent them. Most
serious is the rumor he's floating that I've made away with
Gregor and seek the Imperium for myself. I judge this a ploy
to smoke out Gregor's hiding place. He knows that Gregor's
not with me. Or he'd be tempted to lob a nuclear in here."

Cordelia's lips curled in aversion. "So does he want to
capture Gregor, or kill him?"

"Kill only if he can't capture. I will, when the time is
right, produce Gregor."

"Why not right now?"

He sat back with a tired sigh, and pushed away his tray
with a few bites of stew and a ragged bread shred still
left in his bowl. "Because I wish to see how many of
Vordarian's forces I can woo back to my side before the
denoument. Desert to me is not quite the right term . . . come
over, maybe. I don't wish to inaugurate my second year
of office with four thousand military executions. All below
a certain rank can be given a blanket pardon on the
grounds that they were oath-bound to follow their officers,
but I want to save as many of the senior men as I can.
Five district counts and Vordarian are doomed now, no
hope for them. *Damn* him for starting this."

"What are Vordarian's troops doing? Is this a sitzkrieg?"

"Not quite. He's wasting a lot of his time and mine,
trying to gain a couple of useless strong points, like the
supply depot at Marigrad. We oblige and draw him in,
or out. It keeps Vordarian's commanders occupied, and
their minds off the real high ground, which are the space-
based forces. If only I had Kanzian!"

"Have your intelligence people located him yet?" The
admired Admiral Kanzian was one of the two men in the
Barrayaran High Command whom Vorkosigan regarded
as his superiors in strategy. Kanzian was an advanced space
operations specialist; the space-based forces had great faith

in him. "No horse manure stuck on *his* boots," was the way Kou had once expressed it, to Cordelia's amusement.

"No, but Vordarian doesn't have him either. He's vanished. Hope to God he wasn't caught in some stupid street cross-fire and is lying unidentified on a slab somewhere. What a waste that would be."

"Would going up help? To sway the space forces?"

"Why d'you think I'm troubling to hold Tanery Base? I've considered the pros and cons of moving my field HQ aboard ship. I think not yet; it could be misinterpreted as the first step in running away."

Running away. What a seductive thought. Far, far away from all this lunacy, till it was all reduced to the single dimension of a minor filler in some galactic news vid. But . . . run away from Aral? She studied him, as he sat back on the padded sofa, staring at but not seeing the remains of his supper. A weary middle-aged man in a green uniform, of no particular handsomeness (except perhaps for the sharp grey eyes); a hungry intellect at constant internal war with fear-driven aggression, each fueled by a lifetime crowded with bizarre experience, Barrayaran experience. *You should have fallen in love with a happy man, if you wanted happiness. But no, you had to fall for the breathtaking beauty of pain.* . . .

The two shall be made one flesh. How literal that ancient pious mouthing had turned out to be. One little scrap of flesh, prisoned in a uterine replicator behind enemy lines, bound them now like siamese twins. And if little Miles died, would that bond be slashed?

"What . . . what are we doing about Vordarian's hostages?"

He sighed. "That is the hard nut in the center. Stripped of everything else, as we are gradually doing, Vordarian still holds over twenty district counts and Kareen. And several hundred lesser folk."

"Such as Elena?"

"Yes. And the city of Vorbarr Sultana itself, for that matter. He could threaten to atomize the city, at the end, to get passage off-planet. I've toyed with the idea of dealing. Have him assassinated later. Can't just let him go free, it would be unjust to all those who've died already in loyalty to me. What burning could satisfy those betrayed souls? No.

"So we're planning various rescue-raid options, for the end. The moment when the shift in men and loyalties reaches critical mass, and Vordarian really starts to panic. Meanwhile we wait. In the end . . . I'll sacrifice hostages before I'll let Vordarian win." His unseeing stare was black, now.

"Even Kareen?" *All the hostages? Even the tiniest?*

"Even Kareen. She is Vor. She understands."

"The surest proof I am not Vor," said Cordelia glumly. "I don't understand any of this . . . stylized madness. I think you should all be in therapy, every last one of you."

He smiled slightly. "Do you think Beta Colony could be persuaded to send us a battalion of psychiatrists as humanitarian aid? The one you had that last argument with, perhaps?"

Cordelia snorted. Well, Barrayaran history did have a sort of weird dramatic beauty, in the abstract, at a distance. A passion play. It was close-up that the stupidity of it all became more palpable, dissolving like a mosaic into meaningless squares.

Cordelia hesitated, then asked, "Are we playing the hostage game?" She was not sure she wanted to hear the answer.

Vorkosigan shook his head. "No. That's been my toughest argument, all week, to look men in the eye who have wives and children up in the capital, and say No." He arranged his cutlery neatly on his tray, in its original pattern, and added in a meditative tone, "But they aren't looking widely enough. This is not, so far, a revolution, merely a palace coup. The population is inert, or rather, lying low, except for some informers. Vordarian is making his appeals to the elite conservatives, old Vor, and the military. The Count can't count. The new technoculture is producing plebe progressives as fast as our schools can crank them out. They are the majority of the future. I wish to give them some method besides colored armbands to distinguish the good guys from the bad guys. Moral suasion is a more powerful force than Vordarian suspects. What old Earth general said that the moral is to the physical as three to one? Oh, Napoleon, that was it. Too bad he didn't follow his own advice. I'd put it as five to one, for this particular war."

"But do your powers balance? What about the physical?"

Vorkosigan shrugged. "We each have access to enough weapons to lay Barrayar waste. Raw power is not really the issue. But my legitimacy is an enormous advantage, as long as weapons must be manned. Hence Vordarian's attempts to undercut that legitimacy with his accusations about my doing away with Gregor. I propose to catch him in his lie."

Cordelia shivered. "You know, I don't think I would care to be on Vordarian's side."

"Oh, there are still a few ways he could win. My death is entailed in all of them. Without me as a focus, the only Regent annointed by the late Ezar, what's to choose? Vordarian's claim is then as good as anyone's. If he killed me, and got possession of Gregor, or vice versa, he could conceivably consolidate from there. Till the next coup, and train of revolts and vengeance-killings rebounding into the indefinite future . . ." His eyes narrowed, as he contemplated this dark vision. "That's my worst nightmare. That this war won't stop if we lose, till another Dorca Vorbarra the Just arises to put an end to another Bloody Century. God knows when. Frankly, I don't see a man of that calibre among my generation."

Check your mirror, thought Cordelia somberly.

"Ah, so *that's* why you wanted me to see the doctor first," Cordelia teased Aral that night. The doctor, once Cordelia had adjusted a few of his confused assumptions, had examined her meticulously, changed his prescription from exercise to rest, and cleared her to resume marital relations, with caution. Aral merely grinned, and made love to her as if she were spun glass. His own recovery from the soltoxin was nearly complete, she judged from this. He slept like a rock, only warmer, till the comconsole woke them at dawn. There must have been some military conspiracy at work, for it not to have lit up before then. Cordelia pictured some understaffer confiding to Kou, "Yeah, let's let the Old Man get laid, maybe he'll mellow out. . . ."

Still, the miserable fatigue-fog lifted faster this time. Within a day, with Droushnakovi for escort, Cordelia was up and exploring her new surroundings.

She ran across Bothari in the base gymnasium. Count Piotr had not yet returned, so once he'd debriefed to Aral Bothari had no duties either. "Got to keep in training," he told her shortly.

"You been sleeping?"

"Not much," he said, and resumed his running. Compulsively, too long, far past the optimum effect-for-time-spent trade-off. He sweated to fill time and kill thought, and Cordelia silently wished him luck.

She caught up on the details of the war from Aral and Kou and the controlled newsvids. What counts were allied, who was known hostage and where, what units were deployed on each side and which were ripped apart and scattered to both; where fighting had taken place, what damages, which commanders had renewed oath . . . knowledge without power. No more, she judged, than her intellectualized version of Bothari's endless running; and even less useful for distracting her mind from unbroken concentration on all the horrors and disasters, past or impending, that she could presently do nothing about.

She preferred her military history with more temporal displacement. A century or two in the past, say. She imagined some cool future scholar looking through a time-telescope at her, and gave him a mental rude gesture. Anyway, she now realized, the military histories she'd read had left out the most important part; they never told what happened to people's babies.

No—they were all babies, out there. Every mother's son in a black uniform. One of Aral's reminiscences floated up in her memory, velvet voice rumbling, "It was about that time that soldiers started looking like children to me. . . ."

She pushed away from the vidconsole, and went to search the bathroom for medication for pain.

On the third day she passed Lieutenant Koudelka in a corridor, stumping along at a near run, his face flushed with excitement.

"What's up, Kou?"

"Illyan's here. And he's brought Kanzian with him!"

Cordelia followed him to a briefing room. Droushnakovi had to lengthen even her long stride to keep up. Aral, flanked by two staffers, sat with his hands clasped on the table before him, listening with utmost attention. Commander Illyan sat on the edge of the table, swinging one leg in rhythm to his voice. A bandage on his left arm was stained with yellow seepage. He was pale and dirty, but his eyes shone in triumph, gilded with a touch of fever. He wore civilian gear that looked as if it had been stolen out of someone's laundry, and then rolled downhill in.

An older man was sitting beside Illyan—a staffer handed the man a drink, which Cordelia recognized as a potassium-salts-laced fruit-flavored pick-me-up for the metabolically depleted. He tasted it dutifully, and made a face, looking as if he would have preferred some more old-fashioned revivifier such as brandy. Overweight and undertall, greying where he was not balding, Admiral Kanzian was not a very martial-looking man. He looked grandfatherly—though only if one's grandfather was a research professor. His face was held together with an intensity of intellect that seemed to give the term "military science" real clout. Cordelia had met him in uniform; his air of quiet authority seemed unaffected by civilian shirt and slacks that might have come from the same laundry basket as Illyan's.

Illyan was saying, "—and then we spent the next night in the cellar. Vordarian's squad came back the next morning, but—Milady!"

His grin of greeting was blunted by a flash of guilt, as he glanced to and away from her waist. She'd rather he kept piffling on, excited, about his adventures, but her arrival seemed to deflate him, ghost of his most notable failure at his banquet of victory.

"Wonderful to see you both, Simon, Admiral." They exchanged nods; Kanzian made to rise, but was unanimously waved back to his seat, which made his lip twist in bemusement. Aral signed her to sit next to him.

Illyan continued in a more clipped fashion. His past two weeks of hide-and-seek with Vordarian's forces seemed to parallel Cordelia's, though in the far more complex setting of the seized capital. But Cordelia recognized the familiar terrors under his plain words. He brought his tale swiftly up to the present moment. Kanzian nodded an occasional confirmation.

"Well done, Simon," said Vorkosigan when Illyan concluded. He nodded toward Kanzian. "Extremely well done."

Illyan smiled. "Thought you'd like it, sir."

Vorkosigan turned to Kanzian. "As soon as you feel able, I would like to brief you in the tac room, sir."

"Thank you, my lord. I've been out of communications—except for Vordarian's newscasts—since I escaped Headquarters. Though there was much to be deduced from what we did see. By the way, I commend your strategy of restraint. Good so far. But you're close to its limits."

"So I've sensed, sir."

"What's Jolly Nolly doing at Jumppoint Station One?"

"Not answering his tightbeam. Last week his understaffers were offering an amazing array of excuses, but their ingenuity finally dried up."

"Ha. I can just picture it. His colitis must be in wonderful form. I'll bet not all of those 'indisposeds' were lies. I think I should begin with a private chat with Admiral Knollys, just the two of us."

"I would appreciate that, sir."

"We will discuss the inevitabilities of time. And the defects of a potential commander who bases an entire strategy on an assassination he then does not succeed in carrying out." Kanzian frowned judgmentally. "Not well constructed, to let your whole war turn on one event. Vordarian always did have a tendency to pop off."

Cordelia, aside, caught Illyan's eye. "Simon. Did you pick up any information at all, while you were trapped in Vorbarr Sultana, about the Imperial Military Hospital? Vaagen and Henri's lab?" *My baby?*

Regretfully, he shook his head. "No, Milady." Illyan glanced in turn at Vorkosigan. "My lord, is it true about Captain Negri's death? We'd only had it from rumor, and Vordarian's propaganda broadcasts. Thought it might have been a lie."

"Negri is dead. Unfortunately." Vorkosigan grimaced.

Illyan sat upright in alarm. "And the Emperor, too?"

"Gregor is safe and well."

Illyan slumped again. "Thank God. Where?"

"Elsewhere," said Vorkosigan dryly.

"Oh. Quite, sir. Beg pardon."

"As soon as you've hit sickbay and the showers, Simon, I have some housecleaning chores for you," Vorkosigan continued. "I want to know just exactly how ImpSec was blindsided by Vordarian's coup. I have no wish to malign the dead—and God knows the man paid for his mistakes—but Negri's old personal system for running ImpSec, with all his little secret compartments shared only with Ezar, has to be taken completely apart. Every component, every man re-examined, before it's all put back together. That will be your first job as the new Chief of Imperial Security. Captain Illyan."

Illyan's face went from pale-tired to green-white. "Sir— you want me to step into *Negri's* shoes?"

"Shake them out, first," Vorkosigan advised dryly. "And with dispatch, if you please. I cannot produce the Emperor until ImpSec is again fit to guard him."

"Yes, sir." Illyan's voice was thin with his staggerment.

Kanzian levered out of his seat, shrugging off the help of an anxious staff officer. Aral squeezed Cordelia's hand under the table, and rose to accompany the nucleus of

his new General Staff. As they all exited, Kou grinned
over his shoulder at Cordelia and whispered, "Things are
looking up, eh?"

She smiled bleakly back at him. Vorkosigan's words
echoed in her head. *When the shift in men and loyalties
reaches the critical point, and Vordarian starts to
panic* . . .

The trickle of refugees appearing at Tanery Base became
a steady stream, as the week wore on. The most spectacular
after Kanzian was the breakout of Prime Minister Vortala
from Vordarian's house arrest. He arrived with several
wounded liveried men and a hair-raising tale of bribery,
trickery, chase, and exchange-of-fire. Two lesser Imperial
Ministers also turned up, one on foot. Morale rose with
each notable addition; the base's atmosphere grew electric
with anticipation of action. The question exchanged by
staffers in corridors became not, "Who's come in?" but
"Who's come in this morning?" Cordelia tried to appear
cheered by it all, hugging her dread to her private mind.
Vorkosigan grew both pleased and tenser.

As instructed, Cordelia rested a lot in Vorkosigan's
quarters. All too soon she felt re-energized enough to start
beating on the walls. She then tried varying the prescription with a few experimental push-ups and knee-bends
(but not sit-ups). She was just contemplating the merits
and drawbacks of going to join Bothari in the gym, when
the comconsole chimed.

Koudelka's apprehensive face appeared over the vid
plate. "Milady, m'lord requests you join him now in Briefing
Room Seven. Something's come in he wants you to see."

Cordelia's stomach twisted. "All right. On my way."

An array of men were waiting in Briefing Room Seven,
clustered around a vidconsole in low-voiced debate. Staffers, Kanzian, Minister Vortala himself. Vorkosigan looked
up and gave her a brief, unfelt smile.

"Cordelia. I'd like your opinion on something that's
come in."

Flattering, but, "What sort of something?"

"Vordarian's latest special report has a new twist. Kou, replay the vid, please."

Vordarian's propaganda broadcasts from the capital were mostly subjects for derision, among Vorkosigan's men. Their faces looked rather more serious, this time.

Vordarian appeared in what was recognizably one of the state rooms of the Imperial Residence, the formal and serene Blue Room. Ezar Vorbarra used to make his rare public pronouncements from that background. Vorkosigan frowned.

Vordarian, in full dress greens, was seated on an ivory silk sofa, Princess Kareen at his side. Her dark hair was pulled back severely from her oval face with jeweled combs. She wore a striking black gown, somber and formal.

Vordarian spoke only a few earnest words, invoking the viewers' attention. Then the vid cut away to the great chamber of the Council of Counts at Vorhartung Castle. The vid zoomed in on the Lord Guardian of the Speaker's circle, dressed in his full regalia. The vid did not show what, besides its own pickup, was aimed at the Lord Guardian's head, but something in his repeated looks, just to one side instead of directly at the focus, made Cordelia place a lethally armed man, or maybe a squad, in that unseen position.

The Lord Guardian raised a plastic flimsy, and began, "I quote—due to the—"

"Ah, slick!" murmured Vortala, and Koudelka paused the vid to say, "I beg your pardon, Minister?"

"The I-quote—he's just legally distanced himself from the words about to come off that flimsy and out his mouth. Didn't catch that, the first time. Good, Georgos, good," Vortala addressed the paralyzed figure. "Go on, Lieutenant, I didn't mean to interrupt."

The holovid image continued, "—vile murder of the child-Emperor Gregor Vorbarra, and betrayal of his sacred oaths by the would-be usurper Vorkosigan, the Council of Counts declares the false Regent faithless, outcast, stripped of powers and outlawed. This day the Council of Counts confirms Commodore Count Vidal Vordarian as Prime Minister and acting Regent for Dowager-Princess Kareen Vorbarra, forming an emergency caretaker government until such time as a new heir may be found and confirmed by the Council of Counts and Council of Ministers in full council assembled."

He continued with further legalities, as the vid panned the chamber. "Freeze it, Koudelka," Vortala demanded. His lips moved as he counted. "Ha! Not even one-third present. He doesn't have near a quorum. Who does he think he's fooling?"

"Desperate man, desperate measures," Kanzian murmured as the holo continued at Koudelka's touch.

"Watch Kareen," Vorkosigan said to Cordelia.

The holo cut back to Vordarian and the Princess. Vordarian went on in such mealy terms, it took Cordelia a moment to unravel the fact that in the phrase "personal protector," Vordarian was announcing an engagement of marriage. His hand closed earnestly over Kareen's, though his eye contact was reserved for the holovid. Kareen lifted her hand to receive a ring without changing her calm expression in the slightest. The vid closed with solemn music. The End. They were thankfully spared Betan-style post-mortem commentary; apparently, nobody ever asked the Barrayaran-in-the-street much of anything, at least until major rioting raised the volume to a level no one dared ignore.

"How would you analyze Kareen's reaction?" Aral asked Cordelia.

Cordelia's brows rose. "What reaction? How, analyze? She never said a word!"

"Just so. Does she looked drugged to you? Or under compulsion? Or was that real assent? Is she duped by Vordarian's propaganda, or what?" Frustrated, Vorkosigan eyed the space where the woman's image had lately been. "She's always been reserved, but that was the most unreadable performance I've ever seen."

"Run it again, Kou," said Cordelia. She had him stop at the best views of Kareen. She studied the frozen face, scarcely less animate than when the holo was running.

"She doesn't look woozy or sedated. And her eyes don't look aside the way the Speaker's did."

"Nobody threatening her with a weapon?" Vortala guessed.

"Or perhaps she simply doesn't care," Cordelia suggested grimly.

"Assent, or compulsion?" Vorkosigan repeated.

"Maybe neither. She's been dealing with this sort of nonsense all her adult life . . . what do you expect of her? She survived three years of marriage with Serg, before Ezar sheltered her. She must be a bona fide expert in guessing what not to say and when not to say it."

"But to publicly submit to Vordarian—if she thinks he's responsible for Gregor's death . . ."

"Yes, what does she believe? If she truly thinks her son is dead—even if she doesn't believe you killed him— then all she has left to look out for is her own survival. Why risk that survival for some dramatic futility, if it won't help Gregor? What does she owe you, owe us, after all? We've all failed her, as far as she knows."

Vorkosigan winced.

Cordelia went on, "Vordarian's been controlling her access to information, surely. She may even be convinced he's winning. She's a survivor; she's survived Serg and Ezar, so far. Maybe she means to survive you and Vordarian both. Maybe the only revenge she thinks she'll ever get is to live long enough to spit on all your graves."

One of the staff officers muttered, "But she's Vor. She should have defied him."

Cordelia favored him with a glittery grin. "Oh, but you never know what any Barrayaran woman thinks by what she says in front of Barrayaran men. Honesty is not exactly rewarded, you know."

The staffer gave her an unsettled look. Drou smiled sourly. Vorkosigan blew out his breath. Koudelka blinked.

"So, Vordarian gets tired of waiting and appoints himself Regent," Vortala murmured.

"And Prime Minister," Vorkosigan pointed out in return. "Indeed, he swells."

"Why not go straight for the Imperium?" asked the staff officer.

"Testing the waters," said Kanzian.

"It's coming, later in the script," opined Vortala.

"Or maybe sooner, if we force his hand a bit," suggested Kanzian. "The last and fatal step. We must consider how to rattle him just a little more."

"Not much longer," Vorkosigan said firmly.

The ghostly mask of Kareen's face hung before Cordelia's mind's eye all that day, and returned at her waking the next morning. What did Kareen think? What did Kareen feel, for that matter? Perhaps she was as numb as the evidence suggested. Perhaps she was biding her time. Perhaps she was all for Vordarian. *If I knew what she believed, I'd know what she was doing. If I knew what she was doing, I'd know what she believed.*

Too many unknowns in this equation. *If I were Kareen . . .* Was this a valid analogy? Could Cordelia reason from herself to another? Could anyone? They had likenesses, Kareen and herself, both women, near in age, mothers of endangered sons. . . . Cordelia took Gregor's shoe from her meager pile of mountain souvenirs, and turned it in her hand. *Mama grabbed me back, but my shoe came off in her hand. I should have fastened it tighter. . . .* Maybe she should trust her own judgment. Maybe she knew exactly what Kareen was thinking.

When the comconsole chimed, close to the time of yesterday's call, Cordelia shot to answer it. A new broadcast from the capital, new evidence, something to break that circle of unreason? But the face that materialized over the vidplate was not Koudelka, but a stranger with Intelligence insignia on his collar.

"Lady Vorkosigan?" he began deferentially.

"Yes?"

"I'm Major Sircoj, duty-officer at the main portal. It's my job to screen everyone new reporting in, men who've left traitor-units and so on, and to collect any new intelligence they've brought with them. We had a man turn up half an hour ago who says he escaped the capital, who refuses to voluntarily debrief. We've confirmed his claim that he's had anti-interrogation conditioning—if we try to fast-penta him, it'll kill him. He keeps asking—actually, insisting—to speak with you. He could be an assassin."

Cordelia's heart pounded. She leaned into the holovid as if she might climb through it. "Did he bring anything with him?" she demanded breathlessly. "Like a canister, about half a meter high—lots of blinking lights, and big red letters on top that say This End Up? Looks mysterious as hell, guaranteed to send any security guard into fits—his name, Major!"

"He brought nothing but the clothes he's standing in. He's not in good shape. His name is Vaagen, Captain Vaagen."

"I'll be right there."

"No, Milady! The man is practically raving. Could be dangerous, I can't let you—"

She left him talking to an empty room. Droushnakovi had to break into a run to catch up with her. Cordelia made it to the main portal Security offices in less than seven minutes, and paused in the corridor to catch her breath. To catch her soul, that wanted to fly out her mouth. Calm. Calm. Raving apparently cut no ice with Sircoj.

She lifted her chin and entered the office. "Tell Major Sircoj that Lady Vorkosigan is here to see him," she told the clerk, who raised impressed brows and obediently bent to his comconsole.

Sircoj appeared in a few endless minutes—through *that* door, Cordelia mentally marked his route. "I must see Captain Vaagen."

"Milady, he could be dangerous," Sircoj began exactly where she'd cut him off before. "He could be programmed in some unexpected way."

Cordelia considered unexpectedly grabbing Sircoj by the throat and attempting to squeeze reason into him. Impractical. She took a deep breath. "What will you let me do? Can I at least see him on vid?"

Sircoj looked thoughtful. "That might be all right. A cross-check on our identification, and we can record. Very well."

He took her into another room, and keyed up a monitor viewer. Her breath blew out with a small moan.

Vaagen was alone in a holding room, pacing from wall to wall. He wore green uniform trousers and a brown-stained white shirt. He was terribly changed from the trim and energetic scientist she'd last seen in his lab at ImpMil. Both his eyes were ringed with red-purple blotches, one lid swollen nearly shut; the slit glowed a frightening blood-scarlet. He moved bent-over. Bathless, sleepless, swollen lips . . .

"You get a medtech for that man!" Cordelia realized she'd yelled when Sircoj jumped.

"He's been triaged. His condition is not life-threatening. We can start treating him just as soon as he's security-cleared," said Sircoj doggedly.

"Then you put him on-line with me," Cordelia said through set teeth. "Drou, go back to the office, call Aral. Tell him what's going on."

Sircoj looked worried at this, but stuck valiantly to his procedures. More endless seconds, while someone went back to the prison-area and took Vaagen to a comconsole.

His face came up over the plate at last; Cordelia could see her own face reflected in the passionate intensity in his. Connected at last.

"Vaagen! What happened?"

"Milady!" His hands clenched, trembling, as he leaned on them toward the vid pickup. "The idiots, the morons, the ignorant, stupid—" he sputtered into helpless obscenities, then caught his breath and began again, quickly, concisely, as if her image might be snatched away again at any moment.

"We thought we might be all right at first, after the first two days' fighting trailed off. We hid the replicator at ImpMil, but nobody came. We lay low, and took turns sleeping in the lab. Then Henri managed to smuggle his wife out of town, and we both stayed. We tried to continue the treatments in secret. Thought we might wait it out, wait till rescue. Things had to break, one way or another. . . .

"We'd almost stopped expecting them, but they came. Last—yesterday." He rubbed a hand through his hair as if seeking some connection between real-time and nightmare-time, where clocks ran crazy. "Vordarian's squad. Came looking for the replicator. We locked the lab, they broke in. Demanded it. We refused, refused to talk, they couldn't fast-penta either of us. So they beat us up. Beat him to *death*, like street scum, like he was nobody, all that intelligence, all that education, all that promise *wasted*, dropped by some mumbling moron swinging a gun butt. . . ." Tears were running down his face.

Cordelia stood white and stricken; bad, bad attack of defective deja vu. She'd played the lab scene in her head already a thousand times, but she'd never seen Dr. Henri dead on the floor, nor Vaagen beaten senseless.

"Then they ripped into the lab. Everything, all the treatment records. All Henri's work on burns, gone. They didn't have to do that. All gone for nothing!" His voice cracked, hoarse with fury.

"Did they . . . find the replicator? Dump it out?" She could see it; she had seen it over and over, spilling. . . .

"They found it, finally. But then they took it. And then let *me* go." He shook his head from side to side.

"Took it," she repeated stupidly. Why? What sense, to take the technology and not the techs? "And let you go. To run to us, I suppose. To give us the word."

"You have it, Milady."

"Where, do you suppose? Where did they take it?"

Vorkosigan's voice spoke beside her. "The Imperial Residence, most likely. All the best hostages are being kept there. I'll put Intelligence right on it." He stood, feet planted, grey-faced. "It seems we're not the only side turning up the pressure."

CHAPTER FIFTEEN

Within two minutes of Vorkosigan's arrival at main portal Security, Captain Vaagen was flat on a float pallet and on his way to the infirmary, with the top trauma doctor on the base being paged for rendezvous. Cordelia reflected bitterly on the nature of chain of command; all truth and reason and urgent need were not enough, apparently, to lend causal power to one outside that chain.

Further interrogation of the scientist had to wait on his medical treatment. Vorkosigan used the time to put Illyan and his department on the new problem. Cordelia used the time to pace in circles in the infirmary's waiting area. Droushnakovi watched her in silent worry, not so foolish as to offer up reassurances they both knew to be empty.

At last the trauma man emerged from surgery to announce Vaagen conscious and oriented enough for a brief—he emphasized the brief—questioning. Aral came, trailing Koudelka and Illyan, and they all trooped in to find Vaagen in an infirmary bed, with his eye patched and an IV running fluids and meds.

Vaagen's hoarse and weary voice added a few horrific

details, but nothing to change the word-picture he'd first given Cordelia.

Illyan listened with steady attention. "Our people at the Residence confirm," he reported when Vaagen ran down, depressed whisper trailing to silence. "The replicator was apparently brought in yesterday, and has been placed in the most heavily guarded wing, near Princess Kareen's quarters. Our loyalists don't know what it is, they think it's some kind of a device, maybe a bomb to take out the Residence and everyone in it in the final battle."

Vaagen snorted, coughed, and winced.

"Do they have anyone tending it?" Cordelia asked the question no one else had, so far. "A doctor, a medtech, anyone?"

Illyan frowned. "I don't know, Milady. I can try to find out, but every extra communication endangers our people up there."

"Mm."

"The treatment's interrupted anyway," Vaagen muttered. His hand fiddled with the edge of his sheet. "Bitched to hell."

"I realize you've lost your notes, but could you . . . reconstruct your work?" Cordelia asked diffidently. "If you got the replicator back, that is. Take up where you left off."

"It wouldn't be where we left off, by the time we got it back. And it wasn't all in my head. Some of it was in Henri's."

Cordelia took a deep breath. "As I recall, these Escobaran portable replicators run on a two-week service cycle. When did you last recharge the power, and change the filters and add nutrients?"

"Power cell's good for months," Vaagen corrected. "Filters are more of a problem. But the nutrient solution will be the first limiting factor it'll hit. At its hyped-up metabolic rate, the fetus would starve a couple of days before the system choked on its waste. Breakdown products might overload the filters pretty soon after lean-tissue metabolism began, though."

She avoided Aral's gaze and looked straight at Vaagen, who looked straight back with his one good eye, more than physical pain in his face. "And when did you and Henri last service the replicator?"

"The fourteenth."

"Less than six days left," Cordelia whispered, appalled.

"About . . . about that. What day is this?" Vaagen looked around in an uncharacteristic uncertainty that hurt Cordelia's heart to watch.

"The time limit applies only if it's not being properly taken care of," Aral put in. "The Residence physician, Kareen and Gregor's man—wouldn't he realize something was needed?"

"Sir," Illyan said, "the Princess's physician was reported killed in the first day's fighting at the Residence. Two cross-confirmations—I have to consider it certain."

"They could let Miles die out of sheer ignorance up there," Cordelia realized in dismay. "As well as on purpose." Even one of their own secret loyalists, under the heroic impression he was defusing a bomb, could be a menace to her child.

Vaagen twisted in his sheets. Aral caught Cordelia's eye, and jerked his head toward the door. "Thank you, Captain Vaagen. You have done us extraordinary service. Beyond duty."

"Screw duty," Vaagen muttered. "Bitched to hell . . . damned ignorant goons . . ."

They withdrew, to leave Vaagen to his unrestful recovery. Vorkosigan dispatched Illyan to his multiplied duties.

Cordelia faced Aral. "Now what?"

His lips were a flat, hard line, his eyes half-absent with calculation, the same calculations she was running, Cordelia guessed, complicated by a thousand added factors she could only imagine. He said slowly, "Nothing's changed, really. From before."

"It is changed. Whatever the difference there is between being in hiding, and being a prisoner. But why did Vordarian wait till now for this capture? If he was ignorant of Miles's existence before this, who told him of it? Kareen, maybe, when she decided to cooperate?"

Droushnakovi looked sick at this suggestion.

Aral said, "Maybe Vordarian's playing with us. Maybe he was always keeping the replicator in reserve, till he most needed a new lever."

"Our son. In reserve," Cordelia corrected. She stared into those half-there grey eyes, willing *See me, Aral!* "We have to talk about this." She towed him down the corridor to the nearest private room, a doctors' conference chamber, and turned up the lights. Obediently, he seated himself at the table, Kou at his elbow, and waited for her. She sat down opposite him. *We've always sat on the same side, before. . . .* Drou stood behind her.

Aral watched her warily. "Yes, Cordelia?"

"What's going on in your head?" she demanded. "Where are we, in this?"

"I . . . regret. In hindsight. Regret not sending a raid earlier. The Residence is a far more difficult fortress to penetrate right now than the military hospital, dangerous as a raid on ImpMil would have been. And yet . . . I could not change that choice. When men on my own staff were asked to wait and sweat, I could not risk men and expend resources for my private benefit. Miles's . . . position, gave me the power to demand their loyalty in the face of Vordarian's pressure. They knew I asked no risk of them and theirs I was unwilling to share myself."

"But now the situation's changed," Cordelia pointed out. "Now you aren't sharing the same risks. Their relatives have all the time there is. Miles has only six days, minus the time we spend arguing." She could feel that clock ticking, in her head.

He said nothing.

"Aral . . . in all our time here, what favor have I ever asked of you, of your official powers?"

A sad half-smile quirked across his lips, and vanished. His eyes were wholly on her, now. "Nothing," he whispered. They both sat tensely, leaning toward the other, his elbows planted and hands clasped near his chin, her hands out flat before her, controlled.

"I'm asking now."

"Now," he said after a long hesitation, "is an extremely delicate time, in the overall strategic situation. We are right now engaged in secret negotiations with two of Vordarian's top commanders to sell him out. The space forces are about to commit. We are on the verge of being able to shut Vordarian down without a major set-battle."

Cordelia's thought was diverted just long enough to wonder how many of Vorkosigan's commanders were secretly negotiating right now to sell *them* out. Time would tell. Time.

Vorkosigan continued, "If—*if* we bring this negotiation off as I wish, we will be in a position to rescue most of the hostages in one major surprise raid, from a direction Vordarian does not expect."

"I'm not asking for a big raid."

"No. But I'm telling you that a small raid, particularly if things went wrong, might seriously interfere with the success of the larger, later one."

"Might."

"Might." He tilted his head in concession to the uncertainty.

"Time?"

"About ten days."

"Not good enough."

"No. I will try to speed things up. But you understand—if I botch this chance, this timing, several thousand men could pay for my mistakes with their lives."

She understood clearly. "All right. Suppose we leave the armies of Barrayar out of this for the moment. Let me go. With maybe a liveried man or two, and pinpoint—downright hypodermic—secrecy. A totally private effort."

His hands slapped to the table, and he sputtered, "No! God, Cordelia!"

"Do you doubt my competence?" she asked dangerously. *I sure do.* Now was not the moment to admit this, however. "Is that 'Dear Captain' just a pet name for a pet, or did you mean it?"

"I have seen you do extraordinary things—"

You've also seen me fall flat on my face, so?

"—but you are not expendable. God. That really would make me terminally crazy. To wait, not knowing . . ."

"You ask that of me. To wait, unknowing. You ask it every day."

"You are stronger than I. You are strong beyond reason."

"Flattering. Not convincing."

His thought circled hers; she could see it in his knife-keen eyes. "No. No haring off on your own. I forbid it, Cordelia. Flat, absolutely. Put it right out of your mind. I cannot risk you both."

"You do. In this."

His jaw clamped; his head lowered. Message received and understood. Koudelka, sitting worriedly beside him, glanced back and forth between the two of them in consternation. Cordelia could sense the pressure of Drou's hand, white-tight on the back of her chair.

Vorkosigan looked like something being ground between two great stones; she had no desire to see him smeared to powder. In a moment, he would demand her word to confine herself to Base, to dare no risk.

She opened her hand, curving up on the tabletop. "I would choose differently. But no one appointed me Regent of Barrayar."

The tension ran out of him with a sigh. "Insufficient imagination." *A common failing, among Barrayarans, my love.*

Returning to Aral's quarters, Cordelia found Count Piotr in the corridor, just turning away from their door. He was quite changed from the exhausted wild man who'd left her on a mountain trail. Now he was dressed in the sort of quietly upper-class clothes favored by retired Vor lords and senior Imperial ministers; neat trousers, polished half-boots, an elaborate tunic. Bothari loomed at his shoulder, once again costumed in his formal brown-and-silver livery. Bothari carried a thick coat folded over his arm, by which Cordelia deduced Piotr had just blown in from his diplomatic mission to some fellow District count to the wintery north of Vordarian's holdings. Vorkosigan's people certainly seemed to be able to move at will now, outside the heartlands held by Vordarian.

"Ah. Cordelia." Piotr gave her a formal, cautious nod; not reopening hostilities here. That was fine with Cordelia. She was not sure she had any will to fight left in her gnawed-out heart.

"Good day, sir. Was your trip a success?"

"Indeed it was. Where is Aral?"

"Gone to Sector Intelligence, I believe, to consult with Illyan about the most recent reports from Vorbarr Sultana."

"Ah? What's happening?"

"Captain Vaagen turned up at our door. He'd been beaten half-senseless, but he still somehow made it from the capital—it seems Vordarian finally woke up to the fact that he had another hostage. His squad looted Miles's replicator from ImpMil, and took it back to the Imperial Residence. I expect we'll hear more from him soon about it, but he's doubtless waited to give us the full pleasure of Captain Vaagen's tale, first."

Piotr threw back his head in a sharp, bitter laugh. "Now *there's* an empty threat."

Cordelia unclenched her jaw long enough to say, "What do you mean, sir?" She knew perfectly well what he meant, but she wanted to see him run to his limit. *All the way, damn you; spit it all out.*

His lips twitched, half frown, half smile. "I mean Vordarian inadvertently offers House Vorkosigan a service. I'm sure he doesn't realize it."

You wouldn't say that if Aral were standing here, old man. Did you set this up? God, she couldn't say that to him—"Did you set this up?" Cordelia demanded tightly.

Piotr's head jerked back. "I don't deal with traitors!"

"He's of your Old Vor party. Your true allegiance. You always said Aral was too damned progressive."

"You dare accuse me—!" His outrage edged into plain rage.

Her rage was shadowing her vision with red. "I know you are an attempted murderer, why not an attempted traitor, too? I can only hope your incompetence holds good."

His voice was breathy with fury. "Too far!"

"No, old man. Not nearly far enough."

Drou looked absolutely terrorized. Bothari's face was a stony blank. Piotr's hand twitched, as if he wanted to strike her. Bothari watched that hand, his eyes glittering oddly, shifting.

"While dumping that mutant out of its can is the best favor Vidal Vordarian could do me, I am hardly likely to let him know it," Piotr bit out. "It will be far more amusing to watch him try to play a joker as if it were an ace, and then wonder what went wrong. Aral knows—I imagine he's relieved as hell, to have Vordarian do his job for him. Or have you bewitched him into planning something spectacularly stupid?"

"Aral's doing nothing."

"Oh, good boy. I was wondering if you'd stolen his spine permanently. He is Barrayaran after all."

"So it seems," she said woodenly. She was shaking. Piotr was not in much better case.

"This is a side-issue," he said, as much to himself as her, trying to regain his self-control. "I have major issues to pursue with the Lord Regent. Farewell, Milady." He tilted his head in ironic effort, and turned away.

"Have a nice day," she snarled to his back, and flung herself through the door into Aral's quarters.

She paced for twenty minutes, back and forth, before she trusted herself enough to speak even to Drou, who had squeezed into a corner seat as if trying to make herself small.

"You don't really think Count Piotr is a traitor, do you, Milady?" Droushnakovi asked, when Cordelia's steps finally slowed.

Cordelia shook her head. "No . . . no. I just wanted

to hurt him back. This place is getting to me. Has gotten to me." Wearily, she sank into a seat and leaned her head back against the padding. After a silence she added, "Aral's right. I have no right to risk. No, that's not quite correct. I have no right to *failure*. And I don't trust myself anymore. I don't know what's happened to my edge. Lost it in a strange land." *I can't remember. Can't remember how I did it.* She and Bothari were twins, right enough, two personalities separately but equally crippled by an overdose of Barrayar.

"Milady . . ." Droushnakovi plucked at her skirts, looking down into her lap. "I was in Imperial Residence Security for three years."

"Yes . . ." Her heart lurched, gulped. As an exercise in self-discipline, Cordelia closed her eyes and did not open them again. "Tell me about that, Drou."

"Negri trained me himself. Because I was Kareen's body servant, he always said I would be the last barrier between Kareen and Gregor and—and anything that was bad enough to get that far. He showed me everything about the Residence. He used to drill me about it. He showed me things I don't think he showed anybody else. We had five emergency escape routes worked out, in our disaster drills. Two of them were common Security procedure. One of them he showed only to a few top staffers like Illyan. The other two—I don't know that anybody knew about them but Negri and Emperor Ezar. And I'm thinking . . ." she moistened her lips, "a secret route out of something ought to be an equally secret route in. Don't you think?"

"Your reasoning interests me extremely, Drou. As Aral might say. Go on." Cordelia still did not open her eyes.

"That's about it. If I could somehow get to the Residence, I bet I could get in. If Vordarian's just taken over all the standard Security arrangements and beefed them up."

"And get back out?"

"Why not?"

Cordelia found she had to remember to breathe. "Who do you work for, Drou?"

"Captain—" she started to answer, but slowed self-consciously. "Negri. But he's dead. Commander—Captain Illyan, now, I suppose."

"Let me rephrase that." Cordelia opened her eyes at last. "Who did you put your life on the line for?"

"Kareen. And Gregor, of course. They were kind of the same thing."

"Still are. This mother bets." She caught Drou's blue gaze. "And Kareen gave you to me."

"To be my mentor. We thought you were a soldier."

"Never. But that doesn't mean I never fought." Cordelia paused. "What do you want to trade for, Drou? Your life in my hand—I shall not say oath-sworn, that's for those other idiots—for what?"

"Kareen," Droushnakovi answered steadily. "I've watched them, here, gradually reclassifying her as expendable. Every day for three years, I put my life on the line because I believed that her life was important. You watch someone that closely for that long, you don't have too many illusions about her. Now they seem to think I should just switch off my loyalty, like some guard-machine. There's something wrong with that. I want to—to at least try for Kareen. In exchange for that—whatever you will, Milady."

"Ah." Cordelia rubbed her lips. "That seems . . . equitable. One expendable life for another. Kareen for Miles." She sank down in the chair in deep meditation.

First you see it. Then you do it. "It's not enough." Cordelia shook her head at last. "We need . . . someone who knows the city. Someone with muscle, for backup. A weapons-man, a sleepless eye. I need a friend." The corners of her lips turned up in a very small smile. "Closer than a brother." She rose and walked to the comconsole.

"You asked to see me, Milady?" said Sergeant Bothari.
"Yes. Please come in."

Senior officers' quarters did not intimidate Bothari, but his brow furrowed nonetheless as Cordelia gestured him to a seat. She took Aral's usual spot across the low table from him. Drou sat again in the corner, watching in reserved silence.

Cordelia regarded Bothari, who regarded her in return. He looked all right physically, though his face was grooved with tension. She sensed, as with a third eye, frustrated energies coursing through his body; arcs of rage, nets of control, a tangled electric knot of dangerous sexuality under it all. Reverberating energies, building up and up without release, in desperate need of ordered action lest they break out wildly on their own. She blinked, and refocused on his less terrifying surface; a tired-looking ugly man in an elegant brown uniform.

To her surprise, Bothari began. "Milady. Have you heard anything new about Elena?"

Wondering why I called you here? To her shame, she had almost forgotten Elena. "Nothing new, I'm afraid. She is reported being kept along with Mistress Hysopi in that downtown hotel that Vordarian's Security commandeered when they ran out of cells, with a lot of other second- and third-tier hostages. She hasn't been moved to the Residence or anything." Elena was not, unlike Kareen, in the direct line of Cordelia's secret mission. If he asked, how much dare she promise?

"I was sorry to hear about your son, Milady."

"My mutant, as Piotr would say." She watched him; she could read his shoulders and spine and gut better than that blank beaky face.

"About Count Piotr," he said, and stopped. His hands hooked each other, between his knees, and flexed. "I had thought to speak to the admiral. I hadn't thought to speak to you. I should have thought of you."

"Always." *Now what?*

"Man came up to me yesterday. In the gym. Not in uniform, no rank or nametag. He offered me Elena. Elena's life, if I would assassinate Count Piotr."

"How tempting," Cordelia choked, before she could stop herself. "What, uh, guarantees did he offer?"

"That question came to me, pretty shortly. There I would be, in deep shit, maybe executed, and who would care for a, a dead man's bastard then? I figured it for a cheat, just another cheat. I went back to look for him, been on the lookout, but I never spotted him since." He sighed. "It almost seems like a hallucination, now."

The expression on Drou's face was a study in the deepest unreassurance, but fortunately Bothari was turned away from her and did not notice. Cordelia shot her a small quelling frown.

"Have you been having hallucinations?" Cordelia asked.

"I don't think so. Just bad dreams. I try not to sleep."

"I . . . have a dilemma of my own," Cordelia said. "As you heard me tell Piotr."

"Yes, Milady."

"Had you heard about the time limit?"

"Time limit?"

"If it's not serviced, the replicator will start to fail to support Miles in less than six days. Aral argues that Miles is in no more danger than any of his staffers' families. I disagree."

"Behind his back, I've heard some say otherwise."

"Ah?"

"They say it's a cheat. The admiral's son is some sort of mutant, non-viable, while they risk whole children."

"I don't think he realizes . . . anyone says that."

"Who would repeat it to his face?"

"Very few. Maybe not even Illyan." Though Piotr probably wouldn't fail to pass it on, if he picked it up. "Dammit! No one, on either side, would hesitate to dump that replicator." She brooded, and began again. "Sergeant. Who do you work for?"

"I am oath-sworn Armsman to Count Piotr," Bothari recited the obvious. He was watching her closely now, a weird smile tugging at one corner of his mouth.

"Let me rephrase that. I know the official penalties for an armsman going AWOL are fearsome. But suppose—"

"Milady." He held up a hand; she paused in mid-breath. "Do you remember, back on the front lawn at Vorkosigan Surleau when we were loading Negri's body into the lightflyer, when my Lord Regent told me to obey your voice as his own?"

Cordelia's brows went up. "Yes . . . ?"

"He never countermanded that order."

"Sergeant," she breathed at last, "I'd never have guessed you for a barracks-lawyer."

His smile grew a millimeter tighter. "Your voice is as the voice of the Emperor himself. Technically."

"Is it, now," she whispered in delight. Her nails dug into her palms.

He leaned forward, his hands now held rock-still between his knees. "So, Milady. What were you saying?"

The motor pool staging bay was an echoing low vault, its shadows slashed by the lights from a glass-walled office. Cordelia stood waiting in the darkened lift tube portal, Drou at her shoulder, and watched through the distant rectangle of glass as Bothari negotiated with the transport officer. General Vorkosigan's Armsman was signing out a vehicle for his oath-lord. The passes and IDs Bothari had been issued apparently worked just fine. The motor pool man fed Bothari's cards to his computer, took Bothari's palm print on his sensor-pad, and dispatched orders with snap and hustle.

Would this simple plan work? Cordelia wondered desperately. And if it didn't, what alternative had they? Their planned route sketched itself in her mind, red light-lines snaking over a map. Not north toward their goal, but due south first, by groundcar into the next loyal District. Ditch the distinctive government vehicle, take the monorail west to yet another District, then northwest to another; then due east into Count Vorinnis's neutral zone, focus of so much diplomatic attention from both sides. Piotr's comment echoed in her memory, "I swear, Aral, if Vorinnis doesn't quit trying to play both ends against the middle, you ought to hang him higher than Vordarian when this is over." Then into the capital District itself, then, somehow, into the sealed city. A daunting number of kilometers to cover. Three times the distance of the direct route.

So much time. Her heart swung north like a compass needle.

The first and last Districts would be the worst. Aral's forces could be almost more inimical to this excursion than Vordarian's. Her head spun with the cumulative impossibility of it all.

Step by step, she told herself firmly. One step at a time. Just get off Tanery Base; that, they could do. Divide the infinite future into five-minute blocks, and take them one by one.

There, the first five minutes down already, and a swift and shining general staff car appeared from underground storage. A small victory, in reward for a little patience and daring. What might great patience and daring yet bring?

Judiciously, Bothari inspected the vehicle, as if in doubt that it was quite fit for his master. The transport officer waited anxiously, and seemed to deflate with relief when the great general's Armsman, after running his hand over the canopy and frowning at some minute speck of dust, gave it a grudging acceptance. Bothari brought the vehicle around to the lift tube portal and parked it, neatly blocking the office's view of the entering passengers.

Drou bent to pick up their satchel, packed with a very odd variety of clothing including Bothari's and Cordelia's mountain souvenirs, and their thin assortment of weapons. Bothari set the polarization on the rear canopy to mirror-reflection, and raised it.

"Milady!" Lieutenant Koudelka's anxious voice called from the lift tube entry behind them. "What are you doing?"

Cordelia's teeth closed on vile words. She converted her savage expression to a light, surprised smile, and turned. "Hello, Kou. What's up?"

He frowned, looking at her, at Droushnakovi, at the satchel. "I asked first." He was out of breath; he must have been chasing them down for some minutes, after not finding her in Aral's quarters. An ill-timed errand.

Cordelia kept her smile fixed, as her mind blinked on a vision of a Security team piling out of the lift tube to arrest her, or at least her plans. "We're . . . going into town."

. His lips thinned in skepticism. "Oh? Does the Admiral know? Where's Illyan's outer-perimeter team, then?"

"Gone on ahead," said Cordelia blandly.

The vague plausibility actually raised a flicker of doubt in his eyes. Alas, only for a moment. "Now, wait just a bloody minute—"

"Lieutenant," Sergeant Bothari interrupted. "Take a look at this." He gestured toward the rear passenger compartment of the staff car.

Koudelka leaned to look. "What?" he said impatiently.

Cordelia winced as Bothari's open hand chopped down across the back of Koudelka's neck, and winced again at the heavy *thud* of Koudelka's head hitting the far side of the compartment's interior after a powerful boost-assist to neck and belt by Bothari. His swordstick clattered to the pavement.

"In." Bothari's voice was a strained low growl, accompanied by a quick glance across the bay toward the glass-walled transport office.

Droushnakovi flung the satchel into the compartment and dove in after Koudelka, shoving his long loose limbs out of the way. Cordelia grabbed up the stick and piled in after. Bothari stood back, saluted, closed the mirrored canopy, and entered the driver's compartment.

They started smoothly. Cordelia had to control irrational panic as Bothari stopped at the first checkpoint. She could see and hear the guards so clearly, it was difficult to remember they saw only the reflections of their own hard eyes. But apparently General Piotr could indeed pass anywhere at will. How pleasant, to be General Piotr. Though in these trying times, probably not even Piotr could have entered Tanery Base without that rear canopy being opened and scanned. The final gate crew that waved them out was busily engaged in just such an inspection of a large incoming convoy of freight haulers. Their timing was just as Cordelia had planned and prayed.

Cordelia and Droushnakovi finally got the sprawling

Koudelka straightened up between them. His first alarming flaccidity was passing off. He blinked and moaned. Koudelka's head, neck, and upper torso were of the few areas of his body not rewired; Cordelia trusted nothing inorganic was broken.

Droushnakovi's voice was taut with worry. "What'll we do with him?"

"We can't dump him out on the road, he'd run back and give the word," said Cordelia. "Yet if we cinched him to a tree out of sight somewhere, there's a chance he might not be found . . . we'd better tie him up, he's coming around."

"I can handle him."

"He's had enough handling, I'm afraid."

Droushnakovi managed to immobilize Koudelka's hands with a twisted scarf from the satchel; she was quite good at clever knots.

"He might prove useful," mused Cordelia.

"He'll betray us," frowned Droushnakovi.

"Maybe not. Not once we're in enemy territory. Once the only way out is forward."

Koudelka's eyes stopped jerking, following some invisible starry blur, and came at last into focus. Both his pupils were still the same size, Cordelia was relieved to note.

"Milady—Cordelia," he croaked. His hands yanked futilely at the silky bonds. "This is crazy. You'll run right into Vordarian's forces. And then Vordarian will have two handles on the Admiral, instead of just one. And you and Bothari know where the Emperor is!"

"Was," corrected Cordelia. "A week ago. He's been moved since then, I'm sure. And Aral has demonstrated his capacity to resist Vordarian's leverage, I think. Don't underestimate him."

"Sergeant Bothari!" Koudelka leaned forward, appealing into the intercom. The front canopy was also silvered, now.

"Yes, Lieutenant?" Bothari's bass monotone returned.

"I order you to turn this vehicle around."

A slight pause. "I'm not in the Imperial Service anymore, sir. Retired."

"Piotr didn't order this! You're Count Piotr's man."

A longer pause; a lower tone. "No. I am Lady Vorkosigan's dog."

"You're off your meds!"

How such could travel over a purely audio link Cordelia was not sure, but a canine grin hung in the air before them.

"Come on, Kou," Cordelia coaxed. "Back me. Come for luck. Come for life. Come for the adrenaline rush."

Droushnakovi leaned over, a sharp smile on her lips, to breathe in Koudelka's other ear, "Look at it this way, Kou. Who else is ever going to give you a chance at field combat?"

His eyes shifted, right and left, between his two captors. The pitch of the groundcar's power-whine rose, as they arrowed into the growing twilight.

CHAPTER SIXTEEN

Illegal vegetables. Cordelia sat in bemused contemplation between sacks of cauliflower and boxes of cultivated
brillberries as the creaking hovertruck coughed along.
Southern vegetables, that flowed toward Vorbarr Sultana
on a covert route just like hers. She was half-certain that
under that pile were a few sacks of the same green cabbages she'd traveled with two or three weeks ago, migrat-
ing according to the strange economic pressures of the
war.

The Districts controlled by Vordarian were now under
strict interdiction by the Districts loyal to Vorkosigan.
Though starvation was still a long way off, food prices in
the capital of Vorbarr Sultana had skyrocketed, in the face
of hoarding and the coming winter. So poor men were
inspired to take chances. And a poor man already taking
a chance was not averse to adding a few unlisted passengers to his load, for a bribe.

It was Koudelka who'd generated the scheme, abandoning his urgent disapproval, drawn in to their
strategizing almost despite himself. It was Koudelka who'd
found the produce wholesale warehouses in the town in
Vorinnis's District, and cruised the loading docks for

independents striking out with their loads. Though it was
Bothari who'd ruled the size of the bribe, pitifully small
to Cordelia's mind, but just right for the parts they now
played of desperate countryfolk.

"My father was a grocer," Koudelka had explained
stiffly, when selling his scheme to them. "I know what
I'm doing."

Cordelia had puzzled for a moment what his wary
glance at Droushnakovi meant, till she recalled Drou's
father was a soldier. Kou had talked of his sister and
widowed mother, but it was not till that moment that
Cordelia realized Kou had edited his father from his
reminiscences out of social embarrassment, not any lack
of love between them. Koudelka had vetoed the choice
of a meat truck for transport: "It's more likely to be
stopped by Vordarian's guards," he'd explained, "so they
can shake down the driver for steaks." Cordelia wasn't sure
if he was speaking from military or food service experience, or both. In any case, she was grateful not to ride
with grisly refrigerated carcasses.

They dressed for their parts as best they could, pool-
ing the satchel and the clothes they stood in. Bothari and
Koudelka played two recently discharged vets, looking to
better their sorry lot, and Cordelia and Drou two
countrywomen co-scheming with them. The women were
decked in a realistically odd combination of worn mountain dress and upper-class castoffs apparently acquired
from some secondhand shop. They managed the right
touch of mis-fittedness, of women not wearing originals,
by trading garments.

Cordelia's eyes closed in exhaustion, though sleep was
far from her. Time ticked in her brain. It had taken them
two days to get this far. So close to their goal, so far from
success . . . Her eyes snapped open again when the truck
halted and thumped to the ground.

Bothari eased through the opening to the driver's
compartment. "We get out here," he called lowly. They
all filed through, dropping to the city curb. Their breath
smoked in the chill. It was pre-dawn dark, with fewer

lights about than Cordelia thought there ought to be. Bothari waved the transport on.

"Didn't think we should ride all the way in to the Central Market," Bothari grunted. "Driver says Vorbohn's municipal guards are thick there this time of day, when the new stocks come in."

"Are they anticipating food riots?" Cordelia asked.

"No doubt, plus they like to get theirs first," said Koudelka. "Vordarian's going to have to put the army in soon, before the black market sucks all the food out of the rationing system." Kou, in the moments he forgot to pretend himself an artificial Vor, displayed an amazing and detailed grasp of black-market economics. Or, how *had* a grocer bought his son the education to gain entry to the fiercely competitive Imperial Military Academy? Cordelia grinned under her breath, and looked up and down the street. It was an old section of town, pre-dating lift tubes, no buildings more than six flights high. Shabby, with plumbing and electricity and light-pipes cut into the architecture, added as afterthoughts.

Bothari led off, seeming to know where he was going. The maintenance did not improve, in their direction of transit. Streets and alleys narrowed, channeling a moist aroma of decay, with an occasional whiff of urine. Lights grew fewer. Drou's shoulders hunched. Koudelka gripped his stick.

Bothari paused before a narrow, ill-lit doorway bearing a hand-lettered sign, *Rooms*. "This'll do." The door, an ancient non-automatic that swung on hinges, was locked. He rattled it, then knocked. After a long time, a little door within the door opened, and suspicious eyes stared out.

"Whatcha want?"

"Room."

"At this hour? Not damned likely."

Bothari pulled Drou forward. The stripe of light from the opening played over her face.

"Huh," grunted the door-muffled voice. "Well . . ." Some clinking of chains, the grind of metal, and the door swung open.

They all huddled in to a narrow hallway featuring stairs, a desk, and an archway leading back to a darkened chamber. Their host grew even grumpier when he learned they desired only one room among the four of them. Yet he did not question it; apparently their real desperation lent their pose of poverty a genuine edge. With the two women and especially Koudelka in the party, no one seemed to leap to identify them as secret agents.

They settled into a cramped, cheap upstairs room, giving Kou and Drou first shot at the beds. As dawn seeped through the window, Cordelia followed Bothari back downstairs to forage.

"I should have realized we'd need to bring rations, to a city under siege," Cordelia muttered.

"It's not that bad yet," said Bothari. "Ah—best you don't talk, Milady. Your accent."

"Right. In that case, strike up a conversation with this fellow, if you can. I want to hear the local view of things."

They found the innkeeper, or whatever he was, in the little room beyond the archway, which, judging from a counter and a couple of battered tables with chairs, doubled as a bar and a dining room. The man reluctantly sold them some seal-packed food and bottled drinks at inflated prices, while complaining about the rationing and angling for information about them.

"I been planning this trip for months," said Bothari, leaning on the bar, "and the damned war's bitched it."

The innkeep made an encouraging noise, one entrepreneur to another. "Oh? What's your strat?"

Bothari licked his lips, eyes narrowing in thought. "You saw that blonde?"

"Yo?"

"Virgin."

"No way. Too old."

"Oh, yeah. She can pass for class, that one. We were gonna sell it to some Vor lord at Winterfair. Get us a grubstake. But they've all skipped town. Could try for a rich merchant, I guess. But she won't like it. I promised her a real lord."

Cordelia hid her mouth behind her hand, and tried not to emit any attention-drawing noises. It was an excellent thing Drou was not there to learn Bothari's idea of a cover story. Good God. Did Barrayaran men actually pay for the privilege of committing that bit of sexual torture upon uninitiated women?

The 'keep glanced at Cordelia. "You leave her alone with your partner without her duenna, you could lose what you came to sell."

"Naw," said Bothari. "He would if he could, but he took a nerve-disruptor bolt, once. Below the belt, like. He's out on medical discharge."

"What're you out on?"

"Discharged without prejudice."

This was a code-phrase for, Quit or be housed in the stockade, as Cordelia understood it, the ultimate fate of chronic troublemakers who fell just, but only just, short of felony.

"You put up with a spastic?" The 'keep jerked his head, indicating their upstairs room and its inhabitants.

"He's the brains of the outfit."

"Not too many brains, to come up here and try to do that bit of business now."

"Yeah. I think I could've had a better price for that same piece of meat here if I'd had her butchered and dressed."

"You got that right," snorted the 'keep glumly, eyeing the food piled on the counter before Cordelia.

"She's too good to waste, though. Guess I'll have to find something else, till this mess blows over. Kill some time. Somebody may be hiring muscle. . . ." Bothari let this trail off. Was he running out of inspiration?

The 'keep studied him with interest. "Yo? I've had something in my eye I could use a, like, agent for. Been afraid for a week somebody else'd go after it first. You could be just what I need."

"Yo?"

The 'keep leaned forward across the bar, confidentially. "Count Vordarian's boys are giving out some fat rewards, down at ImpSec, for information-leading-to. Now, I wouldn't normally mess with ImpSec whoever was running it this week, but there's a strange fellow down the street who's taken a room. And he keeps to it, 'cept when he goes out for food, more food than one man might eat . . . he's got someone in there with him no one ever sees. And he sure isn't one of us. I can't help thinking he might be . . . worth something to somebody, eh?"

Bothari frowned judiciously. "Could be dangerous. Admiral Vorkosigan blows back into town, they'll be looking real hard for that little list of informers. And you have an address."

"But you don't, seems. If you'd front it, I could give you a ten percent split. I think he's big, that fellow. He's sure scared."

Bothari shook his head. "I been out-country, and I came up here—can't you smell it, here in the city? Defeat, man. Vordarian's people look downright morbid to me. I'd think real carefully 'bout that list, if I was you."

The 'keep's lips tightened in frustration. "One way or another, opportunity's not going to last."

Cordelia grabbed for Bothari's ear to whisper, "Play along. Find out who it is. Could be an ally." After a moment's thought she added, "Ask for fifty percent."

Bothari straightened, nodded. "Fifty-fifty," he said to the 'keep. "For the risk."

The 'keep frowned at Cordelia, but respectfully. He said reluctantly, "Fifty percent of something's better than a hundred percent of nothing, I suppose."

"Can you get me a look at this fellow?" asked Bothari. "Maybe."

"Here, woman." Bothari piled the packages in Cordelia's arms. "Take these back to the room."

Cordelia cleared her throat, and tried for an imitation mountain accent. "You be careful belike. City man'll take you."

Bothari favored the 'keep with an alarming grin. "Ah, he wouldn't try and cheat an old vet. More than once."

The 'keep smiled back nervously.

❖   ❖   ❖

Cordelia dozed uneasily, and jerked awake as Bothari returned to their little room. He checked the hallway carefully before closing the door behind him. He looked grim.

"Well, Sergeant? What did you find out?" What if their fellow-hider turned out to be someone as strategically important as, say, Admiral Kanzian? The thought frightened her. How could she resist being turned aside from her personal mission if some greater good were too crystal-clear. . . . Kou on a pallet on the floor, and Drou on the other cot, both blinking sleep, sat up on their elbows to listen.

"It's Lord Vorpatril. Lady Vorpatril, too."

"Oh, no." She sat upright. "Are you certain?"

"Oh, yes."

Kou scrubbed at his scalp, hair bent with sleep. "Did you make contact with them?"

"Not yet."

"Why not?"

"It's Lady Vorkosigan's call. Whether to divert from our primary mission."

And to think she'd wished for command. "Do they seem all right?"

"Alive, lying low. But—that git downstairs can't have been the only one to spot them. I've spiked him for now, but somebody else could get greedy any time."

"Any sign of the baby?"

He shook his head. "She hasn't had it yet."

"It's late! She was due over two weeks ago. How hellish." She paused. "Do you think we could escape the city together?"

"The more people in a party, the more conspicuous," Bothari said slowly. "And I caught a glimpse of Lady Vorpatril. She's real conspicuous. People'd notice her."

"I don't see how joining us now would improve their position. Their cover's worked for several weeks. If we succeed at the Residence, maybe we can try for them on the way back. Certainly have Illyan send loyalist agents

to help them, if we get back . . ." Damn. If she were
an official raid, she'd have just the contacts the Vorpatrils
needed. But then, if she were an offical raid, she doubtless
would not have come this way. She sat thinking. "No. No
contact yet. But we'd better do something to discourage
your friend downstairs."

"I have," said Bothari. "Told him I knew where I could
get a better price, and not risk my head later. We may
be able to bribe him to help us."

"You'd trust him?" said Droushnakovi doubtfully.

Bothari grimaced. "As far as I can see him. I'll try to
keep an eye on him, while we're here. 'Nother thing. I
caught a broadcast on his vid in the back room. Vordarian
had himself declared Emperor last night."

Kou swore. "So he's finally gone and done it."

"But what does it mean?" asked Cordelia. "Does he
feel himself strong, or is it a move of desperation?"

"Last-ditch ploy to try to sway the space forces, I'd
guess," said Kou.

"Will it really attract more men than it offends?"

Kou shook his head. "We have a real fear of chaos,
on Barrayar. We've tried it. It's nasty. The Imperium has
been identified as a source of order ever since Dorca
Vorbarra broke the power of the warring counts and
unified the planet. Emperor is a real power-word, here."

"Not to me," Cordelia sighed. "Let's get some rest.
Maybe by this time tomorrow it'll all be over." Hopeful/
gruesome thought, depending on how it was construed.
She counted the hours over for the thousandth time, one
day left to penetrate the Residence, two to get back to
Vorkosigan's territories . . . not much to spare. She felt
as if she was flying, faster and faster. And running out
of turning room.

Last chance to call the whole thing off. A fine mist-
ing rain had brought early dusk to the city. Cordelia stared
out the dirty window into the slick street, striped with
the reflections of a few sickly amber-haloed streetlights.
Only a few bundled shapes hurried along, heads down.

It was as if war and the winter had inhaled autumn's last breath, and blew back out a deathly silence. *Nerves,* Cordelia told herself, straightened her back, and led her little party downstairs.

The desk was deserted. Cordelia was just deciding to skip such formalities as checking out—they had, after all, paid in advance—when the 'keep came stomping in through the front door, shaking cold drops from his jacket and swearing. He spotted Bothari.

"You! It's all your fault, you gutless git. We missed it, we bloody missed it, and now someone else will collect. That reward could've been mine, should've been mine—"

The 'keep's invective was cut off with a thump as Bothari pinned him to the wall. The man's toes stretched for the floor as Bothari's suddenly feral face leaned into his. *"What happened?"*

"One of Vordarian's squads picked up that fellow. Looks like he led them back to his partner, too." The 'keep's voice wavered between anger and fear. "They've got them both, and I've got nothing!"

"Got them?" Cordelia repeated sickly.

"Picking 'em off right now, damn it."

There might still be a chance, Cordelia realized. Command decision or tactical compulsion, it hardly mattered now. She grabbed a stunner out of the satchel; Bothari stepped back and she buzzed the 'keep where he stood openmouthed. Bothari shoved his inert form behind the desk. "We have to try for them. Drou, break out the rest of the weapons. Sergeant, lead us there. Go!"

And so she found herself running down the street toward a scene any right-minded Barrayaran would run the other way to avoid, a night-arrest by security forces. Drou kept up with Bothari; Koudelka, burdened with the satchel, lagged behind. Cordelia wished the mist were thicker.

The Vorpatrils' bolt-hole turned out to be two blocks down and one over, in a shabby narrow building much like the one they'd spent the day in. Bothari held up a hand, and they peered cautiously around the corner, then drew back. Two Security groundcars were parked out front of the little hostel, covering the entrance. But for themselves, the area was strangely deserted. Koudelka came panting up behind.

"Droushnakovi," said Bothari, "circle around. Get a cross-fire position covering the other side of those groundcars. Watch out, they're sure to have men at the back door."

Yes, street tactics were clearly Bothari's call. Drou nodded, checked her weapons' charges, and walked as if casually across the corner, not even turning her head. Once out of the enemy's line of sight, she flowed into a silent run.

"We got to get a better position," Bothari muttered, risking his head once more around the corner. "Can't bloody see."

"A man and a woman walk down the street," Cordelia visualized desperately. "They stop to talk in a doorway. They goggle curiously at the security men, who are engrossed in their arrest—would we pass?"

"Not for long," said Bothari, "once they spot our energy weapons on their area scanners. But we'd last longer than two men. It's going to move fast, when it moves. Might pass just long enough. Lieutenant, cover us from here. Have the plasma arc ready, it's all we've got to stop a vehicle."

Bothari shoved his nerve disruptor out of sight under his jacket. Cordelia tucked her stunner in the waistband of her skirt, and lightly took Bothari's arm. They strolled around the corner.

This was a really stupid idea, Cordelia decided, matching steps to Bothari's booted stride. They should have set up hours ago, if they'd been going to try an ambush like this. Or they should have hooked Padma and Alys out hours ago. And yet—how long ago had Padma been spotted? Might they have fallen into some long-laid trap, and gone down together? *No might-have-beens. Pay attention to the now.*

Bothari's steps slowed, as they approached a deep shadowed doorway. He swung her in, and leaned with his arm on the wall, close to her. They were near enough now to the arrest scene to catch voices. Snatches of crackle from the comm links carried clearly in the damp air.

Just in time. Despite the shabby shirt and trousers, Cordelia readily recognized the dark-haired man pinned against the groundcar by one guard as Captain Vorpatril. His face was marred with a grated, bleeding contusion and swollen lips, pulled back in a stereotypical fast-penta-induced smile. The smile slipped to anguish, and back again, and his giggles choked on moans.

Black-clad security men were bundling a woman out the hostel door and into the street. The security team's attention was drawn to her; Cordelia's and Bothari's, too.

Alys Vorpatril wore only a nightgown and robe, with her feet jammed bare into flat shoes. Her dark hair was loose, flowing down wildly around her white face; she looked a fair madwoman. She was indeed conspicuously pregnant, black robe falling open around her white-gowned belly. The guard manhandling her had her arms locked behind her; her legs splayed for balance against his backward pull.

The guard commander, a full colonel, checked a report panel. "That's it, then. The lord and the heir." His eye locked to Alys Vorpatril's abdomen; he shook his head as if to clear it, and spoke into his comm link. "Pull back, boys, we're done here."

"What the hell are we supposed to do about this, Colonel?" asked his lieutenant uneasily. His voice blended fascination with dismay as he walked over to Lady Vorpatril and lifted her gown high. She had gained weight, these last two months; her chin and breasts were rounded, thighs thickened, belly padded out. He poked a curious finger deep into that soft white flesh. She stood silent, trembling, face on fire with rage at his liberty and eyes glistening dark with tears of fear. "Our orders are to kill the lord and the heir. It doesn't say her. Are we supposed to sit around and wait? Squeeze? Cut her open? Or," his voice went persuasive, "maybe just take her back to HQ?"

The guard holding her from behind grinned and ground his hips into her buttocks, mock-thrusts of unmistakable meaning. "We don't have to take her straight back, do we? I mean, this is Vor meat. What a chance."

The colonel stared at him, and spat disgust. "Corporal, you're perverted."

Cordelia realized with a shock that Bothari's riveted attention to the scene before them was no longer tactical. He was deeply aroused. His eyes seemed to glaze as she watched; his lips parted.

The guard colonel pocketed his comm link, and drew his nerve disruptor. "No." He shook his head. "We make this quick and clean. Step aside, Corporal."

Strange mercies . . .

The guard expertly popped Alys's knees and shoved her down, stepping back. Her hands flung out to the pavement, too late to save her swollen belly from a hard smack. Padma Vorpatril moaned through his fast-penta haze. The guard colonel raised his nerve disruptor and hesitated, as if uncertain whether to aim it at her head or torso.

"*Kill them,*" Cordelia hissed in Bothari's ear, jerked out her stunner, and fired.

Bothari snapped not only awake, but over into some berserker mode; his nerve disruptor bolt hit the guard colonel at the same moment as Cordelia's stunner beam did, though she had drawn first. Then he was moving, a dark blur leaping behind a parked vehicle. He snapped off shots, blue crackles that electrified the air; two more guards fell as the rest took cover behind their groundcars.

Alys Vorpatril, still on the pavement, curled up in a tight ball, trying to cover her abdomen with her arms and legs. Padma Vorpatril, penta-drunk, staggered bewilderedly toward her, arms out, apparently with some similar idea in mind. The guard lieutenant, rolling on the pavement toward cover, aimed his nerve disruptor at the distraught man.

The guard lieutenant's pause for accuracy was fatal; Droushnakovi's nerve disruptor cross-fire and Cordelia's stunner beam intersected upon his body—a millisecond too late. His nerve disruptor bolt took Padma Vorpatril squarely in the back of his head. Blue sparks danced, dark hair sparked orange, and Padma's body arced in a violent convulsion and fell twitching. Alys Vorpatril wailed, a short sharp cry cut off by a gasp. On her hands and knees, she seemed momentarily frozen between trying to crawl toward him, or away.

Droushnakovi's cross-fire vantage was perfect. The last guard was killed while still trying to raise the canopy of the armored groundcar. A driver, shielded inside the second vehicle, prudently chose to try and speed away. Koudelka's plasma arc bolt, set on high power, blasted into the groundcar as it accelerated past the corner. It skidded wildly, dragging an edge and trailing sparks, and crashed into the side of a brick building.

Yes, and didn't my whole strategy for this mission turn on our staying invisible? Cordelia thought dizzily, and ran forward. She and Droushnakovi reached Alys Vorpatril at the same moment; together they hoisted the shuddering woman to her feet.

"We have to get out of here," said Bothari, rising from his firing-crouch and coming toward them.

"No shit," agreed Koudelka, limping up and staring around at the sudden and spectacular carnage. The street was amazingly quiet. Not for long, Cordelia suspected.

"This way." Bothari pointed up an alley, narrow and dark. "Run."

"Shouldn't we try to take that car?" Cordelia gestured to the body-draped vehicle.

"No. Traceable. And it can't fit where we're going."

Cordelia was not sure if the wild-faced, weeping Alys was able to run anywhere, but she stuck her stunner back in her waistband and took one of the pregnant woman's arms. Drou took the other, and together they guided her in the sergeant's wake. At least Koudelka was no longer the slowest of the party.

Alys was crying, yet not hysterical; she glanced only once over her shoulder at her husband's body, then concentrated grimly on trying to run. She did not run well. She was hopelessly unbalanced, her arms wrapping her belly in an attempt to take up the shocks of her heavy footsteps. "Cordelia," she gasped. An acknowledgment of recognition; there was no time or breath for demands of explanation.

They had not lurched more than three blocks when Cordelia began to hear sirens from the area they were fleeing. But Bothari seemed controlled again, unpanicked. They traversed another narrow alley, and Cordelia realized they had crossed into a region of the city with no streetlights, or indeed any lights at all. Her eyes strained in the misty shadows.

Alys stopped suddenly, and Cordelia skidded to a halt, almost jerking the woman off her feet. Alys stood for half a minute, bent over, gasping.

Cordelia realized that beneath its deceptive padding of fat, Alys's abdomen was hard as a rock; the back of her robe was soaking wet. "Are you going into labor?" she asked. She didn't know why she made that a question, the answer was obvious.

"This has been going on—for a day and a half," Alys blurted. She seemed unable to straighten. "I think my water broke back there, when that bastard knocked me down. Unless it's blood—should have passed out by now, if all that was blood—it hurts so much worse, now. . . ." Her breath slowed; she pulled her shoulders back with effort.

"How much longer?" asked Kou in alarm.

"How should I know? I've never done this before. Your guess is as good as mine," Lady Vorpatril snapped. Hot anger to warm cold fear. It wasn't enough warmth, a candle against a blizzard.

"Not much longer, I'd say," came Bothari's voice out of the dark. "We'd better go to ground. Come on."

Lady Vorpatril could no longer run, but managed a rapid waddle, stopping helplessly every two minutes. Then every one minute.

"Not going to make it all the way," muttered Bothari. "Wait here." He disappeared up a side—alley? The passages all seemed alleys here, cold and stinking, much too

narrow for groundcars. They had passed exactly two
people in the maze, huddled to one side of a passage in
a heap, and stepped carefully around them.

"Can you do anything to, like, hold back?" asked Kou,
watching Lady Vorpatril double over again. "We ought
to . . . try and get a doctor or something."

"That's what that idiot Padma went out for," Alys
ground out. "I begged him not to go . . . oh, God!" After
another moment she added, in a surprisingly conversa-
tional tone, "The next time you're vomiting your guts out,
Kou, let me suggest you just close your mouth and swallow hard . . . it's not exactly a voluntary reflex!" She
straightened again, shivering violently.

"She doesn't need a doctor, she needs a flat spot,"
Bothari spoke from the shadows. "This way."

He led them a short distance to a wooden door, formerly
nailed shut in an ancient solid stuccoed wall. Judging from
the fresh splinters, he'd just kicked it open. Once inside,
with the door pulled tight-shut again, Droushnakovi at last
dared pull a hand-light from the satchel. It illuminated a
small, empty, dirty room. Bothari swiftly prowled its peri-
meters. Two inner doors had been broken open long ago,
but beyond them all was soundless and lightless and apparently deserted. "It'll have to do," said Bothari.

Cordelia wondered what the hell to do next. She knew
all about placental transfers and surgical sections now, but
for so-called normal births she had only theory to go on.
Alys Vorpatril probably had even less grasp of the biol-
ogy, Drou less still, and Kou was downright useless. "Has
anyone here ever actually been in on one of these,
before?"

"Not I," muttered Alys. Their looks met in rather too
clear an understanding.

"You're not alone," said Cordelia stoutly. Confidence
should lead to relaxation, should lead to something. "We'll
all help."

Bothari said—oddly reluctantly—"My mother used to
do a spot of midwifery. Sometimes she'd drag me along
to help. There's not that much to it."

Cordelia controlled her brows. That was the first time she'd heard the sergeant say word one about either of his parents.

The sergeant sighed, clearly realizing from their array of looks that he'd just put himself in charge. "Lend me your jacket, Kou."

Koudelka divested the garment gallantly, and made to wrap it around the shaking Lady Vorpatril. He looked a little more dismayed when the sergeant put his own jacket around Lady Vorpatril's shoulders, then made her lie down on the floor and spread Koudelka's jacket under her hips. She looked less pale, lying down, less like she was about to pass out. But her breath stopped, then she cried out, as her abdominal muscles locked again.

"Stay with me, Lady Vorkosigan," Bothari murmured to Cordelia. For what? Cordelia wondered, then realized why as he knelt and gently pushed up Alys Vorpatril's nightgown. *He wants me for a control mechanism.* But the killing seemed to have bled off that horrifying wave of lust that had so distorted his face, back in the street. His gaze now was only normally interested. Fortunately, Alys Vorpatril was too self-absorbed to notice that Bothari's attempt at an expression of medical coolness was not wholly successful.

"Baby's head's not showing yet," he reported. "But soon."

Another spasm, and he looked around vaguely and added, "I don't think you'd better scream, Lady Vorpatril. They'll be looking by now."

She nodded understanding, and waved a desperate hand; Drou, catching on, rolled up a bit of cloth into a rag rope, and gave it to her to bite.

And so the tableau hung, for spasm after uterine spasm. Alys looked utterly wrung, crying very quietly, unable to stop her body's repeated attempts to turn itself inside out long enough to catch either breath or balance. The baby's head crowned, dark haired, but seemed unable to go further.

"How long is this supposed to take?" asked Kou, in a

voice that tried to sound measured, but came out very worried.

"I think he likes it where he is," said Bothari. "Doesn't want to come out in the cold." This joke actually got through to Alys; her sobbing breath didn't change, but her eyes flashed in a moment of gratitude. Bothari crouched, frowned judiciously, hunkered around to her side, placed a big hand on her belly, and waited for the next spasm. Then he leaned.

The infant's head popped out, between Lady Vorpatril's bloody thighs, quick as that.

"There," said the sergeant, sounding rather satisfied. Koudelka looked thoroughly impressed.

Cordelia caught the head between her hands, and eased the body out with the next contraction. The baby boy coughed twice, sneezed like a kitten in the awed silence, inhaled, grew pinker, and emitted a nerve-shattering wail. Cordelia nearly dropped him.

Bothari swore at the noise. "Give me your swordstick, Kou."

Lady Vorpatril looked up wildly. "No! Give him back to me, I'll make him be quiet!"

"Wasn't what I had in mind," said Bothari with some dignity. "Though it's an idea," he added as the wails went on. He pulled out the plasma arc and heated the sword briefly, on low power. Sterilizing it, Cordelia realized.

Placenta followed cord on the next contraction, a messy heap on Kou's jacket. She stared with covert fascination at the spent version of the supportive organ that had been of so much concern in her own case. *Time. This rescue's taken so much time. What are Miles's chances down to now?* Had she just traded her son's life for little Ivan's? Not-so-little Ivan, actually, no wonder he'd given his mother so much trouble. Alys must be blessed with an unusually wide pelvic arch, or she'd never have made it though this nightmare night alive.

After the cord drained white, Bothari cut it with the sterilized blade, and Cordelia self-knotted the rubbery thing as best she could. She mopped off the baby and wrapped him in their spare clean shirt, and handed him at last into Alys's outstretched arms.

Alys looked at the baby and began crying again, muffled sobs. "Padma said . . . I'd have the best doctors. Padma said . . . there'd be no pain. Padma said he'd stay with me . . . damn you, Padma!" She clutched Padma's son to her. In an altered tone of mild surprise, she added, "Ow!" Infant mouth had found her breast, and apparently had a grip like a barracuda.

"Good reflexes," observed Bothari.

CHAPTER SEVENTEEN

"For God's sake, Bothari, we can't take her in *there*," hissed Koudelka.

They stood in an alley deep in the maze of the caravanserai. A thick-walled building bulked an unusual three stories high in the cold, wet darkness. High on its stuccoed face, scabrous with peeling paint, yellow light glinted through carved shutters. An oil lamp burned dimly above a wooden door, the only entrance Cordelia could see.

"Can't leave her out here. She needs heat," replied the sergeant. He carried Lady Vorpatril in his arms; she clung to him, wan and shivering. "It's a slow night anyway. Late. They're closing down."

"What is this place?" asked Droushnakovi.

Koudelka cleared his throat. "Back in the Time of Isolation, when this was the center of Vorbarr Sultana, it was a lord's Residence. One of the minor Vorbarra princes, I think. That's why it's built like a fortress. Now it's a . . . sort of inn."

Oh, so this is your whorehouse, Kou, Cordelia managed not to blurt out. Instead she addressed Bothari, "Is it safe? Or is it likely to be stocked with informers like that last place?"

"Safe for a few hours," Bothari judged. "A few hours is all we have anyway." He set Lady Vorpatril down, handing her off to Droushnakovi, and slipped inside after a muffled conversation through the door with some guardian. Cordelia tucked little Ivan more firmly to her, tugging her jacket over him for all the warmth she could share. Fortunately, he had slept quietly through their several-minutes hike from the abandoned building to this place. In a few moments Bothari returned, and motioned them to follow.

They passed through an entryway, almost like a stone tunnel, with narrow slits in the walls and holes every half-meter above. "For defense, in the old days," whispered Koudelka, and Droushnakovi nodded understanding. No arrows or boiling oil awaited them tonight, though. A man as tall as Bothari, but wider, locked the door again behind them.

They came out in a large, dim room that had been converted into some sort of bar/dining room. It was occupied only by two dispirited-looking women in robes and a man snoring with his head on the table. As usual, an extravagant fireplace glowed with coals of wood.

They had a guide, or hostess. A rangy woman beckoned them silently toward the stairs. Fifteen years ago, or even ten years ago, she might have achieved a leggy aquiline look; now she was bony and faded, mis-clad in a gaudy magenta robe with drooping ruffles that seemed to echo her inherent sadness. Bothari swept up Lady Vorpatril and carried her up the steep stairs. Koudelka stared around uneasily, and seemed to brighten slightly upon not finding someone.

The woman led them to a room off an upstairs hallway. "Change the sheets," muttered Bothari, and the woman nodded and vanished. Bothari did not set the exhausted Lady Vorpatril down. The woman returned in a few minutes, and whisked off the bed's rumpled coverings and replaced them with fresh linens. Bothari laid Lady Vorpatril in the bed and backed up. Cordelia tucked the sleeping infant in her arm, and Lady Vorpatril managed a grateful nod.

The—housewoman, Cordelia decided she would think of her—stared with a spark of interest at the baby. "That's a new one. Big boy, eh?" her voice swung to a tentative coo.

"Two weeks old," stated Bothari in a repelling tone.

The woman snorted, hands on hips. "I do my bit of midwifery, Bothari. Two hours, more like."

Bothari shot Cordelia an odd look, almost a flash of fear. The housewoman held up a hand to ward off his frown. "Whatever you say."

"We should let her sleep," said Bothari, "till we're sure she isn't going to bleed."

"Yes, but not alone," said Cordelia. "In case she wakes up disoriented in a strange place." In the range of strange, Cordelia suspected, this place qualified as downright alien for the Vor woman.

"I'll sit with her a while," volunteered Droushnakovi. She glowered suspiciously at the housewoman, who was apparently leaning too near the baby for her taste. Cordelia didn't think Drou was at all fooled by Koudelka's pretense that they had stumbled into some sort of museum. Nor would Lady Vorpatril be, once she'd rested enough to regain her wits.

Droushnakovi plunked down in a shabby padded armchair, wrinkling her nose at its musty smell. The others withdrew from the room. Koudelka went off to find whatever this old building used for a lavatory, and to try and buy them some food. An underlying tang to the air suggested to Cordelia that nothing in the caravanserai was hooked up to the municipal sewerage. No central heating, either. At Bothari's frown, the housewoman made herself scarce.

A sofa, a couple of chairs, and a low table occupied a space at the end of the hall, lit by a red-shaded battery-driven lamp. Wearily, Bothari and Cordelia sat there. With the pressure off for a moment, not fighting the strain, Bothari looked ragged. Cordelia had no idea what she looked like, but she was certain it wasn't her best.

"Do they have whores on Beta Colony?" Bothari asked suddenly.

Cordelia fought mental whiplash. His voice was so tired the question sounded almost casual, except that Bothari never made casual conversation. How much had tonight's violent events disturbed his precarious balance, stressed his peculiar fault lines? "Well . . . we have the L.P.S.T.s," she answered cautiously. "I guess they fill some of the same social functions."

"Ellpee Estees?"

"Licensed Practical Sexuality Therapists. You have to pass the government boards, and get a license. You're required to have at least an associate degree in psychotherapy. Except that all three sexes take up the profession. The hermaphrodites make the most money, they're very popular with the tourists. It's not . . . not a high social status job, but neither are they dregs. I don't think we have dregs on Beta Colony, we sort of stop at the lower middle class. It's like . . ." she paused, struggling for a cultural translation, "sort of like being a hairdresser, on Barrayar. Delivering a personal service to professional standards, with a bit of art and craft."

She'd actually managed to boggle Bothari, surely a first. His brow wrinkled. "Only Betans would think you needed a bleeding university degree. . . . Do *women* hire them?"

"Sure. Couples, too. The . . . the teaching element is rather more emphasized, there."

He shook his head, and hesitated. He shot her a sidelong look. "My mother was a whore." His tone was curiously distant. He waited.

"I'd . . . about figured that out."

"Don't know why she didn't abort me. She could have, she did those as well as midwifery. Maybe she was looking to her old age. She used to sell me to her customers."

Cordelia choked. "Now . . . now *that* would not have been allowed, on Beta Colony."

"I can't remember much about that time. I ran away when I was twelve, when I got big enough to beat up her damned customers. Ran with the gangs, till I was sixteen, passed for eighteen, and lied my way into the

Service. Then I was out of here." His palms slid across
each other, indicating how slick and fast his escape.

"The Service must have seemed like heaven, in com-
parison."

"Till I met Vorrutyer." He stared around vaguely.
"There were more people around here, back then. It's
almost dead here now." His voice went meditative.
"There's a great deal of my life I can't remember very
well. It's like I'm all . . . patchy. Yet there are some things
I want to forget and can't."

She wasn't about to ask, What? But she made an
I-am-listening noise, down in her throat.

"Don't know who my father was. Being a bastard here
is damn near as bad as being a mutant."

" 'Bastard' is used as a negative description of a personality, but it doesn't really have an objective meaning,
in the Betan context. Unlicensed children aren't the same
thing, and they're so rare, they're dealt with on a case-
by-case basis." *Why is he telling me all this? What does
he want of me? When he started, he seemed almost fearful;
now he looks almost contented. What did I say right?* She
sighed.

To her secret relief, Koudelka returned about then,
bearing actual fresh sandwiches of bread and cheese, and
bottled beer. Cordelia was glad for the beer; she'd have
been dubious of the water in this place. She chased her
first bite with a grateful swallow, and said, "Kou, we have
to re-arrange our strategy."

He settled awkwardly beside her, listening seriously.
"Yes?"

"We obviously can't take Lady Vorpatril and the baby
with us. And we can't leave her here. We left five corpses
and a burning groundcar for Vordarian's security. They're
going to be searching this area in earnest. But for just
a little while longer, they will still be hunting for a very
pregnant woman. It gives us a time window. We have to
split up."

He filled a hesitant moment with a bite of sandwich.
"Will you go with her, then, Milady?"

She shook her head. "I must go with the Residence team. If only because I'm the only one who can say, This is impossible now, it's time to quit. Drou is absolutely required, and I need Bothari." *And, in some strange way, Bothari needs me.* "That leaves you."

His lips compressed bitterly. "At least I won't slow you down."

"You're not a default choice," she said sharply. "Your ingenuity got us in to Vorbarr Sultana. I think it can get Lady Vorpatril out. You're her best shot."

"But it feels like you're running into danger, and I'm running away."

"A dangerous illusion. Kou, think. If Vordarian's goons catch her again, they'll show her no mercy. Nor you, nor especially the baby. There is no 'safer.' Only mortal necessity, and logic, and the absolute need to keep your head."

He sighed. "I'll try, Milady."

" 'Try' is not good enough. Padma Vorpatril 'tried.' You bloody *succeed*, Kou."

He nodded slowly. "Yes, Milady."

Bothari left to scrounge clothing for Kou's new persona of poor-young-husband-and-father. "Customers are always leaving things," he remarked. Cordelia wondered what he could collect here in the way of street clothes for Lady Vorpatril. Kou took food in to Lady Vorpatril and Drou. He returned with a very bleak expression on his face, and settled again beside Cordelia.

After a time he said, "I guess I understand now why Drou was so worried about being pregnant."

"Do you?" said Cordelia.

"Lady Vorpatril's troubles make mine look . . . pretty small. God, that looked painful."

"Mm. But the pain only lasts a day." She rubbed her scar. "Or a few weeks. I don't think that's it."

"What is, then?"

"It's . . . a transcendental act. Making life. I thought about that, when I was carrying Miles. 'By this act, I bring one death into the world.' One birth, one death, and all the pain and acts of will between. I didn't understand certain Oriental mystic symbols like the Death-mother, Kali, till I realized it wasn't mystic at all, just plain fact. A Barrayaran-style sexual 'accident' can start a chain of causality that doesn't stop till the end of time. Our children change us . . . whether they live or not. Even though your child turned out to be chimerical this time, Drou was touched by that change. Weren't you?"

He shook his head in bafflement. "I wasn't thinking about all that. I just wanted to be normal. Like other men."

"I think your instincts are all right. They're just not enough. I don't suppose you could get your instincts and your intellect working together for once, instead of at cross-purposes?"

He snorted. "I don't know. I don't know . . . how to get through to her now. I said I was sorry."

"It's not all right between you two, is it?"

"No."

"You know what's bothered me most, on the journey up here?" said Cordelia.

"No . . ."

"I couldn't say goodbye to Aral. If . . . anything happens to me—or to him, for that matter—it will leave something hanging, unraveled, between us. And no way to ever make it right."

"Mm." He folded a little more into himself, slumped in the chair.

She meditated a bit. "What have you tried besides 'I'm sorry'? How about, 'How do you feel? Are you all right? Can I help? I love you,' there's a classic. Words of one syllable. Mostly questions, now I think on it. Shows an interest in starting a conversation, y'know?"

He smiled sadly. "I don't think she wants to talk to me anymore."

"Suppose," she leaned her head back, and stared unseeing down the hallway. "Suppose things hadn't taken such a wrong turn, that night. Suppose you hadn't panicked. Suppose that idiot Evon Vorhalas hadn't interrupted with his little horror show." There was a thought. Too painful, that might-not-have-been. "Drop back to square one. There you were, cuddling happily." Aral had used that word, cuddling. It hurt too much to think of Aral just now, too. "You part friends, you wake up the next morning, er, aching with unrequited love . . . what happens next, on Barrayar?"

"A go-between."

"Ah?"

"Her parents, or mine, would hire a go-between. And then they'd, well, arrange things."

"And you do what?"

He shrugged. "Show up on time for the wedding and pay the bill, I guess. Actually, the parents pay the bill."

No wonder the man was at a loss. "Did you want a wedding? Not just to get laid?"

"Yes! But . . . Milady, I'm just about half a man, on a good day. Her family'd take one look at me and laugh."

"Have you ever met her family? Have they met you?"

"No . . ."

"Kou, are you listening to yourself?"

He looked rather shamefaced. "Well . . ."

"A go-between. Huh." She stood up.

"Where are you going?" he asked nervously.

"Between," she said firmly. She marched down the hall to Lady Vorpatril's door, and stuck her head in. Droushnakovi was sitting watching the sleeping woman. Two beers and the sandwiches sat untouched on a bedside table.

Cordelia slipped within, and closed the door gently. "You know," she murmured, "good soldiers never pass up a chance to eat or sleep. They never know how much they'll be called on to do, before the next chance."

"I'm not hungry." Drou too had a folded-in look, as if caught in some trap within herself.

"Want to talk about it?"

She grimaced uncertainly, and moved away from the bed to a settee in the far corner of the room. Cordelia sat beside her. "Tonight," she said lowly, "was the first time I was ever in a real fight."

"You did well. You found your position, you reacted—"

"No." Droushnakovi made a bitter hand-chopping gesture. "I didn't."

"Oh? It looked good to me."

"I ran around behind the building—stunned the two security men waiting at the back door. They never saw me. I got to my position, at the building's corner. I watched those men, tormenting Lady Vorpatril in the street. Insulting and staring and pushing and poking at her . . . it made me so angry, I switched to my nerve disruptor. I wanted to kill them. Then the firing started. And . . . and I hesitated. And Lord Vorpatril died because of it. My fault—"

"Whoa, girl! That goon who shot Padma Vorpatril wasn't the only one taking aim at him. Padma was so penta-soaked and confused, he wasn't even trying to take cover. They must have double-dosed him, to force him to lead them back to Alys. He might as easily have died from another shot, or blundered into our own cross-fire."

"Sergeant Bothari didn't hesitate," Droushnakovi said flatly.

"No," agreed Cordelia.

"Sergeant Bothari doesn't waste energy feeling . . . sorry, for the enemy, either."

"No. Do you?"

"I feel sick."

"You kill two total strangers, and expect to feel jolly?"

"Bothari does."

"Yes. Bothari enjoyed it. But Bothari is not, even by Barrayaran standards, a sane man. Do you aspire to be a monster?"

"You call him that!"

"Oh, but he's *my* monster. My good dog." She always had trouble explaining Bothari, sometimes even to herself. Cordelia wondered if Droushnakovi knew the Earth-historical origin of the term, scapegoat. The sacrificial animal that was released yearly into the wilderness, to carry the sins of its community away . . . Bothari was surely her beast of burden; she saw clearly what he did for her. She was less certain what she did for him, except that he seemed to find it desperately important. "I, for one, am glad you are heartsick. Two pathological killers in my service would be an excess. Treasure that nausea, Drou."

She shook her head. "I think maybe I'm in the wrong trade."

"Maybe. Maybe not. Think what a monstrous thing an army of Botharis would be. Any community's arm of force—military, police, security—needs people in it who can do the necessary evil, and yet not be made evil by it. To do only the necessary, and no more. To constantly question the assumptions, to stop the slide into atrocity."

"The way that security colonel quashed that obscene corporal."

"Yes. Or the way that lieutenant questioned the colonel . . . I wish we might have saved him," Cordelia sighed.

Drou frowned deeply, into her lap.

"Kou thought you were angry with him," said Cordelia.

"Kou?" Droushnakovi looked up dimly. "Oh, yes, he was just in here. Did he want something?"

Cordelia smiled. "Just like Kou, to imagine all your unhappiness must center on him." Her smile faded. "I'm going to send him with Lady Vorpatril, to try and smuggle her and the baby out. We'll go our separate ways as soon as she's able to walk."

Drou's face grew worried. "He'll be in terrible danger. Vordarian's people will be rabid over losing her and the young lord tonight."

Yes, there was still a Lord Vorpatril to disturb Vordarian's genealogical calculations, wasn't there? Insane system, that made an infant seem a mortal danger to a grown man. "There's no safety for anybody, till this vile war is ended. Tell me. Do you still love Kou? I know you're over your initial starry-eyed infatuation. You see his faults. Egocentric, and with a bug in his brain about his injuries, and terribly worried about his masculinity. But he's not stupid. There's hope for him. He has an interesting life ahead of him, in the Regent's service." Assuming they all lived through the next forty-eight hours. A passionate desire to live was a good thing to instill in her agents, Cordelia thought. "Do you want him?"

"I'm . . . bound to him, now. I don't know how to explain . . . I gave him my virginity. Who else would have me? I'd be ashamed—"

"Forget that! After we bring off this raid, you're going to be covered in so much glory, men will be lining up for the status of courting you. You'll have your pick. In Aral's household, you'll have a chance to meet the best. What do you want? A general? An Imperial minister? A Vor lordling? An off-world ambassador? Your only problem will be choosing, since Barrayaran custom stingily only allows you one husband at a time. A clumsy young lieutenant hasn't got a prayer of competing with all those polished seniors."

Droushnakovi smiled, a bit skeptically, at Cordelia's painted vision. "Who says Kou won't be a general himself someday?" she said softly. She sighed, her brow creasing. "Yes. I still want him. But . . . I guess I'm afraid he'll hurt me again."

Cordelia thought that one over. "Probably. Aral and I hurt each other all the time."

"Oh, not you two, Milady! You seem so, so perfect."

"Think, Drou. Can you imagine what mental state Aral is in right this minute, because of my actions? I can. I do."

"Oh."

"But pain . . . seems to me an insufficient reason not to embrace life. Being dead is quite painless. Pain, like time, is going to come on regardless. Question is, what glorious moments can you win from life in addition to the pain?"

"I'm not sure I follow that, Milady. But . . . I have a picture, in my head. Of me and Kou, on a beach, all alone. It's so warm. And when he looks at me, he sees me, really sees me, and loves me. . . ."

Cordelia pursed her lips. "Yeah . . . that'll do. Come with me."

The girl rose obediently. Cordelia led her back in to

the hall, forcefully arranged Kou at one end of the sofa, sat Drou down on the other, and plopped down between them. "Drou, Kou has a few things to say to you. Since you apparently speak different languages, he's asked me to be his interpreter."

Kou made an embarrassed negative motion over Cordelia's head.

"That hand signal means, I'd rather blow up the rest of my life than look like a fool for five minutes. Ignore it," Cordelia said. "Now, let me see. Who begins?"

There was a short silence. "Did I mention I'm also playing the parts of both your parents? I think I shall begin by being Kou's Ma. Well, son, and have you met any nice girls yet? You're almost twenty-six, you know. I saw that vid," she added in her own voice as Kou choked. "I have her style, eh? And her content. And Kou says, Yes, Ma, there's this gorgeous girl. Young, tall, smart—and Kou's Ma says, Tee hee! And hires me, your friendly neighborhood go-between. And I go to your father, Drou, and say, there's this young man. Imperial lieutenant, personal secretary to the Lord Regent, war hero, slated for the inside track at Imperial HQ—and he says, Say no more! We'll take him. Tee-hee. And—"

"I think he'll have more to say than that!" interrupted Kou.

Cordelia turned to Droushnakovi. "What Kou just said was, he thinks your family won't like him 'cause he's a crip."

"No!" said Drou indignantly. "That's not so—"

Cordelia held up a restraining hand. "As your go-between, Kou, let me tell you. When one's only lovely daughter points and says firmly, Da, I want *that* one, a prudent Da responds only, Yes, dear. I admit, the three large brothers may be harder to convince. Make her cry, and you could have a serious problem in the back alley. By which I presume you haven't complained to them yet, Drou?"

She stifled an involuntary giggle. "No!"

Kou looked as if this was a new and daunting thought.

"See," said Cordelia, "you can still evade fraternal retribution, Kou, if you scramble." She turned to Drou. "I know he's been a lout, but I promise you, he's a trainable lout."

"I *said* I was sorry," said Kou, sounding stung.

Drou stiffened. "Yes. Repeatedly," she said coldly.

"And *there* we come to the heart of the matter," Cordelia said slowly, seriously. "What Kou actually means, Drou, is that he isn't a bit sorry. The moment was wonderful, you were wonderful, and he wants to do it again. And again and again, with nobody but you, forever, socially approved and uninterrupted. Is that right, Kou?"

Kou looked stunned. "Well—yes!"

Drou blinked. "But . . . that's what I wanted you to say!"

"It was?" He peered over Cordelia's head.

This go-between system may have some real merits. But also its limits. Cordelia rose from between them, and glanced at her chrono. The humor drained from her spirit. "You have a little time yet. You can say a lot in a little time, if you stick to words of one syllable."

CHAPTER EIGHTEEN

Pre-dawn in the alleys of the caravanserai was not so pitchy-black as night in the mountains. The foggy night sky reflected back a faint amber glow from the surrounding city. The faces of her friends were grey blurs, like the very earliest of ancient photographs; Cordelia tried not to think, *Like the faces of the dead.*

Lady Vorpatril, cleaned and fed and rested a few hours, was still none too steady, but she could walk on her own. The housewoman had contributed some surprisingly sober clothes for her, a calf-length grey skirt and sweaters against the cold. Koudelka had exchanged all his military gear for loose trousers, old shoes, and a jacket to replace the one that had suffered from its emergency obstetrical use. He carried baby Lord Ivan, now makeshift-diapered and warmly wrapped, completing the picture of a timid little family trying to make it out of town to the wife's parents in the country before the fighting started. Cordelia had seen hundreds of refugees just like them, in passing, on her way into Vorbarr Sultana.

Koudelka inspected his little group, ending with a frowning look at the swordstick in his hand. Even when seen as a mere cane, the satin wood, polished steel ferrule, and inlaid grip did not look very middle-class. Koudelka sighed. "Drou, can you hide this somehow? It's conspicuous as hell with this outfit, and more of a hindrance than a help when I'm trying to carry this baby."

Droushnakovi nodded, and knelt and wrapped the stick in a shirt, and stuffed it into the satchel. Cordelia remembered what had happened the last time Kou had carried that stick down to the caravanserai, and stared nervously into the shadows. "How likely are we to be jumped by someone, at this hour? We don't look rich, certainly."

"Some would kill you for your clothes," said Bothari glumly, "with winter coming on. But it's safer than usual. Vordarian's troops have been sweeping the quarter for 'volunteers,' to help dig those bomb shelters in the city parks."

"I never thought I'd approve of slave labor," Cordelia groaned.

"It's nonsense anyway," Koudelka said. "Tearing up the parks. Even if completed they wouldn't shelter enough people. But it looks impressive, and it sets up Lord Vorkosigan as a threat, in people's minds."

"Besides," Bothari lifted his jacket to reveal the silvered gleam of his nerve disruptor, "this time I've got the right weapon."

This was it, then. Cordelia embraced Alys Vorpatril, who hugged her back, murmuring, "God help you, Cordelia. And God rot Vidal Vordarian in hell."

"Go safely. See you back at Tanery Base, eh?" Cordelia glanced at Koudelka. "Live, and so confound our enemies."

"We'll tr—we will, Milady," said Koudelka. Gravely, he saluted Droushnakovi. There was no irony in the military courtesy, though perhaps a last tinge of envy. She returned him a slow nod of understanding. Neither chose to confuse the moment with further words. The two groups parted in the clammy darkness. Drou watched over her shoulder till Koudelka and Lady Vorpatril turned out of sight, then picked up the pace.

They passed from black alleys to lit streets, from

deserted darkness to occasional other human forms,
hurrying about early winter morning business. Everybody
seemed to cross streets to avoid everybody else, and
Cordelia felt a little less noticeable. She stiffened inwardly
when a municipal guard groundcar drove slowly past them,
but it did not stop.

They paused, across the street, to be certain their target
building had been unlocked for the morning. The structure was multi-storied, in the utilitarian style of the building boom that had come on the heels of Ezar Vorbarra's
ascent to power and stability thirty-plus years ago. It was
commercial, not governmental; they crossed the lobby,
entered the lift tubes, and descended unimpeded.

Drou began seriously looking over her shoulder when
they reached the sub-basement. "*Now* we look out of
place." Bothari kept watch as she bent and forced a lock
to a utility tunnel. She led them down it, taking two cross-
turns. The passage was clearly used frequently, as the
lights remained on. Cordelia's ears strained for footsteps
not their own.

An access cover was bolted to the floor. Droushnakovi
loosened it quickly. "Hang and drop. It's not much more
than two meters. It'll likely be wet."

Cordelia slid into the dark circle, landing with a splash.
She lit her hand-light. The water, slick and black and
shimmering, came to her booted ankles in the synthacrete
tube. It was icy cold. Bothari followed. Drou knelt on his
shoulders, to coax the cover back into place, then splashed
down beside her. "There's about half a kilometer of this
storm sewer. Come on," she whispered. This close to their
goal, Cordelia needed no urging to hurry.

At the half-kilometer, they climbed into a darkened
orifice high on the curving wall that led to a much older
and smaller tunnel, made of time-blackened brick. Knees
and backs bent, they shuffled along. It must be particularly painful for Bothari, Cordelia reflected. Drou slowed,
and began tapping on the tunnel's roof with the steel ferrule of Koudelka's stick. When the ticks became hollow
tocks, she stopped. "Here. It's meant to swing downward.

Watch it." She released the sheath, and slid the blade carefully between a line of slimy bricks. A click, and the false-brick-lined panel flopped down, nearly cracking her head. She returned the sword to its casing. "Up." She pulled herself through.

They followed to find themselves in another ancient drain, even narrower. It sloped more steeply upward. They crouched along, their clothes brushing the sides and picking up damp stains. Drou rose suddenly, and clambered out over a pile of broken bricks into a dark, pillared chamber.

"What is this place?" whispered Cordelia. "Too big for a tunnel . . ."

"The old stables," Drou whispered back. "We're under the Residence grounds, now."

"It doesn't sound so secret to me. Surely they must appear in old drawings and elevations. People—Security—must know this is here." Cordelia stared into the dim, musty recesses, past pale arches picked out by their wavering hand-lights.

"Yes, but this is the cellar of the *old* old stables. Not Dorca's, but Dorca's great-uncle's. He kept over three hundred horses. They burned down in a spectacular fire about two hundred years ago, and instead of rebuilding on the site, they knocked them flat and put up the *new* old stables on the east side, downwind. Those got converted to staff apartments in Dorca's day. Most of the hostages are being kept over there now." Drou marched firmly forward, as if sure of her ground. "We're to the north of the main Residence now, under the gardens Ezar designed. Ezar apparently found this old cellar and arranged this passage with Negri, thirty years ago. A bolt-hole that even their own Security didn't know about. Trusting, eh?"

"Thank you, Ezar," Cordelia murmured wryly.

"Once we're out of Ezar's passage, the real risk starts," the girl commented.

Yes, they could still pull out now, retrace their steps and no one the wiser. *Why have these people so blithely handed me the right to risk their lives? God, I hate command.* Something skittered in the shadows, and some-where, water dripped.

"Here," said Droushnakovi, shining her light on a pile of boxes. "Ezar's cache. Clothes, weapons, money—Captain Negri had me add some women's and boy's clothes to it just last year, at the time of the Escobar invasion. He was keyed up for trouble about it, but the riots never reached here. My clothes should only be a little big for you."

They discarded their beslimed street clothes. Droushnakovi shook out clean dresses, suitable for senior Residence womenservants too superior for menial's uni-forms; the girl had worn them for just such service. Bothari unbundled his black fatigue uniform again from the satchel, and donned it, adding correct Imperial Security insignia. From a distance he made a proper guard, though he was perhaps a little too rumpled to pass inspection up close. As Drou had promised, a complete array of weapons lay fully charged in sealed cases. Cordelia chose a fresh stunner, as did Drou; their eyes met. "No hesitation this time, eh?" Cordelia murmured. Drou nodded grimly. Bothari took one of each, stunner, nerve disruptor, and plasma arc. Cordelia trusted he wouldn't clank when he walked.

"You can't fire that thing indoors," Droushnakovi objected to the plasma arc.

"You never know," shrugged Bothari.

After a moment's thought, Cordelia added the swordstick, tightening a loop of her belt around its grip. A serious weapon it wasn't, but it had proved an unex-pectedly useful tool on this trip. *For luck.* Then from the last depths of the satchel, Cordelia pulled what she pri-vately considered to be the most potent weapon of all.

"A shoe?" said Droushnakovi blankly.

"Gregor's shoe. For when we make contact with Kareen. I rather fancy she still has the other." Cordelia nested it deeply in the inner pocket of one of Drou's Vorbarra-crested boleros, worn over Cordelia's dress to complete the picture of an inner Residence worker.

When their preparations were as complete as possible,

Drou led them again into narrowing darkness. "Now we're under the Residence itself," she whispered, turning sideways. "We go up this ladder, between the walls. It was added after, there's not much space."

This proved an understatement. Cordelia sucked in her breath and climbed after her, sandwiched flat between two walls, trying not to accidently touch or thump. The ladder was made, naturally, of wood. Her head throbbed with exhaustion and adrenaline. She mentally measured the width. Getting the uterine replicator back down this ladder was going to be a bitch. She told herself sternly to think positively, then decided that was positive. *Why am I doing this? I could be back at Tanery Base with Aral right now, letting these Barrayarans kill each other all day long, if it is their pleasure. . . .*

Above her, Drou stepped aside onto some sort of tiny ledge, a mere board. When Cordelia came up beside her, she gestured "stop" and extinguished her hand-light. Drou touched some silent latch mechanism, and a wall panel swung outward before them. Clearly, everything had been kept well oiled right up to Ezar's death.

They looked out into the old Emperor's bedchamber. They had expected it to be empty. Drou's mouth opened in a voiceless O of dismay and horror.

Ezar's huge old carved wooden bed, the one he'd for-God's-sake *died* in, was occupied. A shaded light, dimmed to an orange glow, cast highlight and shadow across two bare-torsoed, sleeping forms. Even in this foreshortened view, Cordelia instantly recognized the dish-face and moustache of Vidal Vordarian. He sprawled across four-fifths of the bed, his heavy arm flung possessively across Princess Kareen. Her dark hair was tumbled on the pillow. She slept in a tight, tiny ball in the upper corner of the bed, facing outward, white arms clutched to her chest, nearly in danger of falling out.

Well, we're reached Kareen. But there's a hitch. Cordelia shivered with the impulse to shoot Vordarian in his sleep. But the energy discharge must set off alarms. Until she had Miles's replicator in her hand, she was not ready to run for it. She motioned Drou to close the panel again, and breathed "Down," to Bothari, waiting beneath her. They reversed their painstaking four-flight climb. Back in the tunnel, Cordelia turned to face the girl, who was crying quite silently.

"She's sold out to him," Droushnakovi whispered, her voice shaking with grief and revulsion.

"If you'll explain to me what power-base you imagine she has to resist the man right now, I'd be interested to hear it," said Cordelia tartly. "What do you expect her to do, fling herself out a window to avoid a fate worse than death? She did fates worse than death with Serg, I don't think they hold any more emotion for her."

"But if only we'd got here sooner, I might—we might have saved her."

"We still might."

"But she's really sold out!"

"Do people lie in their sleep?" asked Cordelia. At Drou's confused look, she explained. "She didn't look like a lover to me. She lay like a prisoner. I promised we'd try for her, and we will." *Time.* "But we'll go for Miles first. Let's try the second exit."

"We'll have to pass through more monitored corridors," Droushnakovi warned.

"Can't be helped. If we wait, this place will start waking up, and we'll hit more people."

"They're coming on duty in the kitchens right now," sighed Drou. "I used to stop in for coffee and hot pastries, some days."

Alas, a commando raid could not knock off for breakfast. This was it. Go or no-go? Was it bravery, or stupidity, that drove her on? It couldn't be bravery, she was sick with fear, the same hot acid nausea she'd felt just before combat during the Escobar war. Familiarity with the sensation didn't help. *If I do not act, my child will die.* She would simply have to do without courage. "Now," Cordelia decided. "There will be no better chance."

Up the narrow ladder again. The second panel opened in the old Emperor's private office. To Cordelia's relief it still remained dark and unused, untouched since it had been cleaned out and locked after Ezar's death last spring. His comconsole desk, with all its Security overrides, was disconnected, wiped of secrets, dead as its owner. The windows were still dark, with the tardy winter morning.

Kou's stick banged against Cordelia's calf as she strode across the room. It did look odd, hitched to her waist too obviously like a sword. On a bureau in the office was a wide antique tray holding a flat ceramic bowl, typical of the knickknacks that cluttered the Residence. Cordelia laid the stick across the tray and lifted it solemnly, servant-fashion.

Droushnakovi nodded approval. "Carry it halfway between your waist and your chest," she whispered. "And keep your spine straight, they always told me."

Cordelia nodded. They closed the panel behind them, straightened themselves, and entered the lower corridor of the north wing.

Two Residence serving women and a security guard. At first glance, they looked perfectly natural in this setting, even in these troubled times. A guard corporal standing duty at the foot of the Petite Stairway at the corridor's west end came to attention at the sight of Bothari's ImpSec and rank tabs; they exchanged salutes. They were passing out of sight up around the stairs' curve before he looked again, harder. Cordelia steeled herself not to break into a panicked run. A subtle piece of misdirection; the two women couldn't be a threat, they were already guarded. That their guard could be the threat, might escape the corporal for minutes yet.

They turned into the upper corridor. There. Behind *that* door, according to the loyalists' reports, Vordarian kept the captured replicator. Right under his eye. Perhaps as a human shield; any explosive dropped on Vordarian's quarters must kill tiny Miles as well. Or did the Barrayaran think of her damaged child as human?

Another guard stood outside that door. He stared at them suspiciously, his hand touching his sidearm. Cordelia and Droushnakovi walked on by without turning their heads. Bothari's exchanged salute flowed smoothly into a clip to the man's jaw that snapped his head back into the wall. Bothari caught him before he dropped. They swung the door open and dragged the guard inside; Bothari took his place in the corridor. Silently, Drou closed the door.

Cordelia stared wildly around the little chamber, looking for automatic monitors. The room might formerly have been a bedroom of the sort once slept in by bodyservants to be near their Vorish masters, or perhaps an unusually large wardrobe; it didn't even have a window overlooking some dull inner court. The portable uterine replicator sat on a cloth-covered table in the exact center of the room. Its lights still glowed their reassuring greens and ambers. No feral red eyes warned of malfunction yet. A breath half-agony, half-relief, tore from Cordelia's lips at the sight of it.

Droushnakovi gazed around the room unhappily.

"What's wrong, Drou?" whispered Cordelia.

"Too easy," the girl muttered.

"We're not done yet. Say 'easy' an hour from now." She licked her lips, shaken by secret subliminal agreement with Droushnakovi's evaluation. No help for it. Grab and go. Speed, not secrecy, was their hope now.

She set the tray down on the table, reached for the replicator's carrying handle, and stopped. Something, something wrong . . . she stared more closely at the readouts. The oxygenation monitor wasn't even functioning. Though its indicator light glowed green, the nutrient fluid level read 00.00. *Empty.*

Cordelia's mouth opened in a silent wail. Her stomach churned. She leaned closer, eyes devouring all the illogical hash of false readouts. Her hagridden nightmare, made suddenly and horribly real—had they dumped it on the floor, into a drain, down a toilet? Had Miles died quickly, mercifully smashed, or had they let the tiny infant, bereft of life-support, twitch to death in agony while they watched? Perhaps they hadn't even bothered to watch. . . .

The serial number. Look at the serial number. A hopeless hope, but . . . she forced her blurring eyes to focus, her racing mind to try and remember. She had fingered that number, pensively, back in Vaagen and Henri's lab, meditating upon this piece of technology and the distant world that had created it—and this number didn't match. Not the same replicator, not Miles's! One of the sixteen others, used to bait this trap.

Her heart sank. How many other traps were laid? She pictured herself running frantically from replicator to replicator, like a distraught child in some cruel game of keep-away, searching. . . . *I shall go mad.*

No. Wherever the real replicator was, it was near to Vordarian's person. Of that, she was sure. She knelt beside the table, putting her head down a moment to fight the blood-drained black balloons that clouded her vision and threatened to empty her mind of consciousness. She lifted the cloth. *There.* A pressure-sensor. Was this Vordarian's own clever idea? Slick and vicious. Drou bent to follow her gesture.

"A trap," whispered Cordelia. "Lift the replicator, and the alarms go off."

"If we disarm it—"

"No. Don't bother. It's false bait. Not the right replicator. It's an empty, with the controls buggered to make it look like it's running." Cordelia tried to think clearly through the pounding in her skull. "We'll have to retrace our steps. Back down, and up. I hadn't expected to encounter Vordarian here. But I guarantee he'll know where Miles is. A little old-fashioned interrogation. We'll be working against time. When the alarm goes up—"

Footsteps thudded in the corridor, and shouts. The chirping buzz of stunner fire. Swearing, Bothari flung himself backward through the door. "That's done it. They've spotted us."

When the alarm goes up, it's all over, Cordelia's thought completed itself, in a vertigo of loss. No window, one door, and they'd just lost control of their only exit. Vordarian's trap had worked after all. *May Vidal Vordarian rot in hell. . . .*

Droushnakovi clutched her stunner. "We won't surrender you, Milady. We'll fight to the end."

"Rubbish," snapped Cordelia. "There's nothing our deaths would buy here but the deaths of a few more of Vordarian's goons. Meaningless."

"You mean we should just quit?"

"Suicidal glory is the luxury of the irresponsible. We're not giving up. We're waiting for a better opportunity to win. Which we can't take if we're stunned or nerve-fried." Of course, if that had been the real replicator on the table . . . she was insane enough by now to sacrifice these people's lives for her son's, Cordelia reflected ruefully, but not yet mad enough to trade them for nothing. She hadn't grown that Barrayaran yet.

"You give yourself to Vordarian as a hostage," Bothari warned.

"Vordarian has held me hostage since the day he took Miles," Cordelia said sadly. "This changes nothing."

A few minutes of shouted negotiations through the door accomplished their surrender, despite the hair-trigger nerves of the security guards. They tossed out their weapons. The guards ran a scan for power packs to be sure, then four of them piled into the little room to frisk their new prisoners. Two more waited outside as backup. Cordelia made no sudden moves to startle them. A guard frowned puzzlement when the interesting lump in Cordelia's vest turned out to be only a child's shoe. He laid it on the table next to the tray.

The commander, a man in the maroon and gold Vordarian livery, spoke into his wrist comm. "Yes. We're secured here. Tell m'lord. No, he said to wake him. You want to explain why you didn't? Thank you."

The guards did not prod them into the corridor, but waited. The still-unconscious man Bothari had clipped was dragged out. The guards placed Cordelia, arms outstretched to the wall and legs straddled, in a row with Bothari and Droushnakovi. She was dizzy with despair. But Kareen would come to her sometime, even as a prisoner. Must come to her. All she needed was thirty seconds with Kareen, maybe less. *When I see Kareen, you are a dead man, Vordarian. You may walk and talk and give orders, unconscious of your demise for weeks, but I'll seal your fate as surely as you've sealed my son's.*

The reason for the wait materialized at last; Vordarian himself, in green uniform trousers and slippers, bare-chested, shouldered his way through the doorway. He was followed by Princess Kareen, clutching a dark red velvet robe around her. Cordelia's heart hammered at a doubled rate. *Now?*

"So. The trap worked," Vordarian began complacently, but added a genuinely shocked "Huh!" as Cordelia pushed away from the wall and turned to face him. A hand signal stopped a guard from shoving her back into position. The shock on Vordarian's face gave way to a wolfish grin. "My God, did it work! Excellent!" Kareen, hovering behind him, stared at Cordelia in bewildered astonishment.

MY trap worked, Cordelia thought, stunned with her opportunity. *Watch me. . . .*

"That's the thing, my lord," said the liveried man, not at all happily. "It didn't work. We didn't pick this party up at the outer perimeter of the Residence and clear their way, they just bloody turned up—without triggering anything. That shouldn't have happened. If I hadn't come along looking for Roget, we might not have spotted 'em."

Vordarian shrugged, too delighted by the magnitude of his prey to issue some trifling censure. "Fast-penta that frill," he pointed at Droushnakovi, "and I imagine you'll find out how. She used to work in Residence Security."

Droushnakovi glowered over her shoulder at Princess Kareen in hurt accusation; Kareen unconsciously pulled her robe up more closely about her neck, her dark eyes full of equally hurt question.

"Well," said Vordarian, still smiling at Cordelia, "is my Lord Vorkosigan so thin of troops he sends his wife to do their work? We cannot lose." He smiled at his guards, who smiled back.

Damn, I wish I'd shot this lout in his sleep. "What have you done with my son, Vordarian?"

Vordarian said through his teeth, "An outworlder frill will never gain power on Barrayar by scheming to give a mutant the Imperium. That, I guarantee."

"Is that the official line, now? I don't want power. I just object to idiots having power over me."

Behind Vordarian, Kareen's lips quirked sadly. *Yes, listen to me, Kareen!*

"Where's my son, Vordarian?" Cordelia repeated doggedly.

"He's Emperor Vidal now," Kareen remarked, her glance going back and forth between them, "if he can keep it."

"I will," Vordarian promised. "Aral Vorkosigan has no better a blood-claim than my own. And I will protect where Vorkosigan's party has failed. Protect and preserve the real Barrayar." His head shifted; apparently this assertion was directed over his shoulder to Kareen.

"We have not failed," Cordelia whispered, meeting Kareen's eyes. *Now.* She lifted the shoe from the table, and stretched out her arm with it; Kareen's eyes widened. She darted forward and grabbed it. Cordelia's hand spasmed like a dying runner's giving up the baton in some mortal relay race. Fierce certainty bloomed like fire in her soul. *I have you now, Vordarian.* The sudden movement sent a ripple through the armed guards. Kareen examined the shoe with passionate intensity, turning it in her hands. Vordarian's brows rose in bafflement, then he dismissed Kareen from his attention and turned to his liveried guard commander.

"We'll keep all three of these prisoners here in the Residence. I'll personally attend the fast-penta interrogations. This is a spectacular opportunity—"

Kareen's face, when she lifted it again to Cordelia, was terrible with hope.

Yes, thought Cordelia. *You were betrayed. Lied to. Your son lives; you must move and think and feel again, no more the walking numbness of a dead spirit* beyond pain. This is no gift I've brought you. It is a curse.

"Kareen," said Cordelia softly, "where is my son?"

"The replicator is on a shelf in the oak wardrobe, in the old Emperor's bedchamber," Kareen replied steadily, locking her eyes to Cordelia's. "Where is mine?"

Cordelia's heart melted in gratitude for her curse, live pain. "Safe and well, when I last saw him, as long as this pretender," she jerked her head at Vordarian, "doesn't find out where. Gregor misses you. He sends his love." Her words might have been spikes, pounded into Kareen's body.

That got Vordarian's attention. "Gregor is at the bottom of a lake, killed in the flyer crash with that traitor Negri," he said roughly. "The most insidious lie is the one you want to hear. Guard yourself, my lady Kareen. I could not save him, but I will avenge him. I promise you that."

Uh-oh. Wait, Kareen. Cordelia bit her lip. *Not here. Too dangerous. Wait your best opportunity. Wait till the bastard's asleep, at least*—but if even a Betan hesitated to shoot her enemy sleeping, how much less a Vor? *She is true Vor. . . .*

An unfriendly smile crinkled Kareen's lips. Her eyes were alight. "This has never been immersed," she said softly.

Cordelia heard the murderous undertones ringing like a bell; Vordarian, apparently, only heard the breathiness of some girlish grief. He glanced at the shoe, not grasping its message, and shook his head as if to clear it of static. "You'll bear another son someday," he promised her kindly. "Our son."

Wait, wait, wait, Cordelia screamed inside.

"Never," whispered Kareen. She stepped back beside the guard in the doorway, snatched his nerve disruptor from his open holster, aimed it point-blank at Vordarian, and fired.

The startled guard knocked her hand up; the shot went wide, crackling into the ceiling. Vordarian dove behind the table, the only furniture in the room, rolling. His liveried man, in pure spinal reflex, snapped up his nerve disruptor and fired. Kareen's face muscles locked in death-agony as the blue fire washed around her head; her mouth pulled open in a last soundless cry. *Wait*, Cordelia's thought wailed.

Vordarian, utterly horrified, bellowed "No!", scrambled to his feet, and tore a nerve disruptor from the hand of another guard. The liveried man, realizing the enormity of his error, tossed his weapon away as if to divorce himself from his action. Vordarian shot him.

The room tilted around her. Cordelia's hand locked around the hilt of the swordstick and triggered its sheath flying into the head of one guard, then brought the blade smartly down across Vordarian's weapon-wrist. He screamed, and blood and the nerve disruptor flew wide. Droushnakovi was already diving for the first discarded nerve disruptor. Bothari just took his target out with one lethal hand-blow to the neck. Cordelia slammed the door shut against the guards in the corridor, surging forward. A stunner charge buzzed into the walls, then three blue bolts in rapid succession from Droushnakovi took out the last of Vordarian's men.

"*Grab* him," Cordelia yelled to Bothari. Vordarian, shaking, his left hand clamped around his half-severed right wrist, was in poor condition to resist, though he kicked and shouted. His blood ran the color of Kareen's robe. Bothari locked Vordarian's head in a firm grip, nerve disruptor pressed to his skull.

"Out of here," snarled Cordelia, and kicked the door back open. "To the Emperor's chamber." *To Miles.* Vordarian's other guards, preparing to fire, held back at the sight of their master.

"Back off!" Bothari roared, and they fell away from the door. Cordelia grabbed Droushnakovi by the arm, and they stepped over Kareen's body. Her ivory limbs lay muddled in the red fabric, abstractly beautiful forms even in death. The women kept Bothari and Vordarian between themselves and Vordarian's troops, and retreated down the corridor.

"Pull that plasma arc out of my holster and start firing,"

Bothari savagely directed Cordelia. Yes; Bothari had managed to retrieve it in the melee, probably why his body count hadn't been higher.

"You can't set fire to the *Residence*," Drou gasped in horror.

A fortune in antiquities and Barrayaran historical artifacts were housed in this wing alone, no doubt. Cordelia grinned wildly, grabbed the weapon, and fired back down the corridor. Wooden furniture, wooden parquetry, and age-dry tapestries roared into flame as the beam's searing fingers touched them.

Burn, you. Burn for Kareen. Pile a death-offering to match her courage and agony, blazing higher and higher— As they reached the door of the old Emperor's bedchamber, she fired the hallway in the opposite direction for good measure. *THAT for what you've done to me, and to my boy*—the flames should hold back pursuit for a few minutes. She felt as though her body were floating, light as air. *Is this how Bothari feels, when he kills?*

Droushnakovi went for the wall panel to the secret ladder. She was functioning steadily now, as if her hands belonged to a different body than her tear-ravaged face. Cordelia dropped the sword on the bed and raced straight for the huge old carved oak wardrobe that stood against the near wall, and flung its doors wide. Green and amber lights glowed in the dim recesses of the center shelf. *God, don't let it be another decoy. . . .* Cordelia wrapped her arms around the canister and lifted it out into the light. The right weight, this time, heavy with fluids; the right readouts, the right numbers. The right one.

Thank you, Kareen. I didn't mean to kill you. Surely she was mad. She didn't feel anything, no grief or remorse, though her heart was racing and her breath came in gasps. A shocky combat-high, that immortal rush that made men charge machine guns. So this was what the war-addicts came for.

Vordarian was still struggling against Bothari's grip, swearing horribly. "You won't escape!" He stopped bucking, and tried to catch Cordelia's eyes. He took a deep breath. "Think, Lady Vorkosigan. You'll never make it. You must have me for a shield, but you can't carry me stunned. Conscious, I'll fight you every meter of the way. My men will be all over you, out there." His head jerked toward the window. "Stun us all and take you prisoner." His voice went persuasive. "Surrender now, and you'll save your lives. That one's life, too, if it means so much to you." He nodded to the replicator Cordelia held in her arms. Her steps were heavier than Alys Vorpatril's, now.

"I never gave orders for that fool Vorhalas to kill Vorkosigan's heir," Vordarian continued desperately into her silence. Blood leaked rapidly between his fingers. "It was only his father, with his fatal progressive policies, who threatened Barrayar. Your son might have inherited the Countship from Piotr with my goodwill. Piotr should never have been divided from his party of true allegiance. It's a crime, what Lord Aral has put Piotr through—"

So. It was you. Even at the very beginning. Blood loss and shock were making a jerky parody of Vordarian's usual smooth delivery of political argument. It was as if he sensed he could talk his way out of retribution, if only he hit on the right key words. Somehow, Cordelia doubted he would. Vordarian was not gaudily evil like Vorrutyer had been, not personally degraded like Serg; yet evil had flowed from him nonetheless, not from his vices, but from his virtues: the courage of his conservative convictions, his passion for Kareen. Cordelia's head ached, vilely.

"We'd never proved you were behind Evon Vorhalas," Cordelia said quietly. "Thank you for the information."

That shut him up, for a moment. His eyes shifted uneasily to the door, soon to burst inward, ignited by the inferno behind it.

"Dead, I'm no use to you as a hostage," he said, drawing himself up in dignity.

"'You're no use to me at all, Emperor Vidal," said Cordelia frankly. "There are at least five thousand casualties in this war so far. Now that Kareen is dead, how long will you keep fighting?"

"Forever," he snarled whitely. "I will avenge her— avenge them all—"

Wrong answer, Cordelia thought, with a curious light-headed sadness. "Bothari." He was at her side instantly. "Pick up that sword." He did so. She set the replicator on the floor and laid her hand briefly atop his; wrapped around the hilt. "Bothari, execute this man for me, please." Her tone sounded weirdly serene in her own ears, as if she'd just asked Bothari to pass the butter. Murder didn't really require hysterics.

"Yes, Milady," Bothari intoned, and lifted the blade. His eyes gleamed with joy.

"What?" yelped Vordarian in astonishment. "You're a Betan! You can't do—"

The flashing stroke cut off his words, his head, and his life. It was really extremely neat, despite the last spurts of blood from the stump of his neck. Vorkosigan should have loaned Bothari's services the day they'd executed Carl Vorhalas. All that upper body strength, combined with that extraordinary steel . . . the bemused gyration of her thought snapped back to near-reality as Bothari fell to his knees with the body, dropping the swordstick and clutching his head. He screamed. It was as if Vordarian's death cry had been forced out of Bothari's throat.

She dropped beside him, suddenly afraid again, though she'd been numb to fear, white-out overloaded, ever since Kareen had grabbed for the nerve disruptor and triggered all this chaos. Keyed by similar stimuli, Bothari was having the forbidden flashback, Cordelia guessed, to the mutinous throat-cutting that the Barrayaran high command had decreed he must forget. She cursed herself for not forseeing this possibility. Would it kill him?

"This door is hot as hell," Droushnakovi, white and shaken, reported from beside it. "Milady, we have to get out of here *now.*"

Bothari was gasping raggedly, hands still pressed to his head, yet even as she watched his breathing grew marginally less disrupted. She left him, to crawl blindly over the floor. She needed something, something moisture-proof. . . .

There, at the bottom of the wardrobe, was a sturdy plastic bag containing several pairs of Kareen's shoes, no doubt hastily transported by some maidservant when Vordarian had Imperially decreed Kareen move in with him. Cordelia emptied out the shoes, stumbled back around the bed, and collected Vordarian's head from the place where it had rolled to a stop. It was heavy, but not so heavy as the uterine replicator. She pulled the drawstrings tight.

"Drou. You're in the best shape. Carry the replicator. Start down. Don't drop it." If she dropped Vordarian, Cordelia decided, it would scarcely do him further harm.

Droushnakovi nodded and grabbed up both the replicator and the abandoned swordstick. Cordelia wasn't sure if she retrieved the latter for its newly acquired historical value, or from some fractured sense of obligation for one of Kou's possessions. Cordelia coaxed Bothari to his feet. Cool air was rushing up out of the panel opening, drawn by the fire beyond the door. It would make a neat flue, till the burning wall crashed in and blocked the entry. Vordarian's people were going to have a very puzzling time, poking through the embers and wondering where they'd gone.

The descent was nightmarish, in the compressed space, with Bothari whimpering below her feet. She could carry the bag neither beside nor in front of her, so had to balance it on one shoulder and go one-handed, palm slapping down the rungs and her wrist aching.

Once on the level, she prodded the weeping Bothari ruthlessly forward, and wouldn't let him stop till they came again to Ezar's cache in the ancient stable cellar.

"Is he all right?" Droushnakovi asked nervously, as Bothari sat down with his head between his knees.

"He has a headache," said Cordelia. "It may take a while to pass off."

Droushnakovi asked even more diffidently, "Are *you* all right, Milady?"

Cordelia couldn't help it; she laughed. She choked down the hysteria as Drou began to look really scared. "No."

CHAPTER NINETEEN

Ezar's cache included a crate of currency, Barrayaran marks of various denominations. It also included a choice of IDs tailored to Drou, not all of which were obsolete. Cordelia put the two together, and sent Drou out to purchase a used groundcar. Cordelia waited by the cache while Bothari slowly uncurled from his tight fetal ball of pain, recovering enough to walk.

Getting back out of Vorbarr Sultana had always been the weak part of her plan, Cordelia felt, perhaps because she'd never really believed they'd get this far. Travel was tightly restricted, as Vordarian sought to keep the city from collapsing under him should its frightened populace attempt to stream away. The monorail required passes and cross-checks. Lightflyers were absolutely forbidden, targets of opportunity for trigger-happy guards. Groundcars had to cross multiple roadblocks. Foot travel was too slow for her burdened and exhausted party. There were no good choices.

After an eternity, pale Drou returned, to lead them back through the tunnels and out to an obscure side street. The city was dusted with sooty snow. From the direction of the Residence, a kilometer off, a darker cloud

boiled up to mix with the winter-grey sky; the fierce fire
was still not under control, apparently. How long would
Vordarian's decapitated command structure keep functioning? Had word of his death leaked out yet?

As instructed, Drou had found a very plain and
unobtrusive old groundcar, though there had been enough
funds to buy the most luxurious new vehicle the city still
held. Cordelia wanted to save that reserve for the checkpoints.

But the checkpoints were not as bad as Cordelia had
feared. Indeed, the first was empty, its guards pulled back,
perhaps, to fight the fire or seal the perimeter of the
Residence. The second was crowded with vehicles and impatient drivers. The inspectors were perfunctory and nervous,
distracted and half-paralyzed by who-knew-what rumors
coming from downtown. A fat wad of currency, handed
out under Drou's perfect false ID, disappeared into a
guard's pocket. He waved Drou through, driving her "sick
uncle" home. Bothari looked sick enough, for sure,
huddled under a blanket that also hid the replicator. At
the last checkpoint Drou "repeated" a likely version of
a rumor of Vordarian's death, and the worried guard
deserted on the spot, shedding his uniform in favor of
a civilian overcoat and vanishing down a side street.

They zigzagged over bad side roads all afternoon to
reach Vorinnis's neutral District, where the aged groundcar
died of a fractured power-train. They abandoned it and
took to the monorail system then, Cordelia driving her
exhausted little party on, racing the clock in her head.
At midnight, they reported in at the first military instal-
lation over the next loyalist border, a supply depot. It took
Drou several minutes of argument with the night duty
officer to persuade him to 1) identify them, 2) let them
in, and 3) let them use the military comm net to call
Tanery Base to demand transport. At that point the D.O.
abruptly became a lot more efficient. A high-speed air
shuttle with a hot pilot was scrambled to pick them up.

Approaching Tanery Base at dawn from the air,
Cordelia felt the most unpleasant flash of deja vu. It was

so like her first arrival from the mountains, she had the sense of being caught in a time loop. Perhaps she'd died and gone to hell, and her eternal torment would be to repeat the last three weeks' events over and over, endlessly. She shivered.

Droushnakovi watched her with concern. The exhausted Bothari dozed, in the air shuttle's passenger cabin. Illyan's two ImpSec men, identical twins for all Cordelia could tell to Vordarian's ones they'd murdered back at the Residence, maintained a nervous silence. Cordelia held the uterine replicator possessively on her lap. The plastic bag sat between her feet. She was irrationally unable to let either item out of her sight, though it was clear Drou would much rather the bag had ridden in the luggage compartment.

The air shuttle touched neatly down on its landing pad, and its engines whined to silence.

"I want Captain Vaagen, and I want him *now*," Cordelia repeated for the fifth time as Illyan's men led them underground into the Security debriefing area.

"Yes, Milady. He's on his way," the ImpSec man assured her again. She glowered suspiciously at him.

Cautiously, the ImpSec men relieved them of their personal arsenal. Cordelia didn't blame them; she wouldn't have trusted her wild-looking crew with charged weapons either. Thanks to Ezar's cache the women were not ill dressed, though there had been nothing in Bothari's size, so he'd retained his smoked and stinking black fatigues. Fortunately the dried blood spatters didn't show much. But all their faces were hollow-eyed, grooved and shadowed. Cordelia shivered, and Bothari's hands and eyelids twitched, and Droushnakovi had a distressing tendency to start crying, silently, at random moments, stopping as suddenly as she started.

At long last—only minutes, Cordelia told herself firmly—Captain Vaagen appeared, a tech at his side. He wore undress greens, and his steps were quick, up to Vaagen-speed again. The only residue of his injuries seemed to be a black patch over his eye; on him, it looked good, giving him a fine piratical air. Cordelia trusted the patch was only a temporary part of ongoing treatment.

"Milady!" He managed a smile, the first to shift those facial muscles in a while, Cordelia sensed. His one eye gleamed triumph. "You got it!"

"I hope so, Captain." She held up the replicator, which she had refused to let the ImpSec men touch. "I hope we're in time. There aren't any red lights yet, but there was a warning beeper. I shut it off, it was driving me crazy."

He looked the device over, checking key readouts. "Good. Good. Nutrient reservoir is very low, but not quite depleted yet. Filters still functioning, uric acid level high but not over tolerance—I think it's all right, Milady. Alive, that is. What this interruption has done to my calcification treatments will take more time to determine. We'll be in the infirmary. I should be able to begin servicing it within the hour."

"Do you have everything you need there? Supplies?"

His white teeth flashed. "Lord Vorkosigan had me begin setting up a lab the day after you left. Just in case, he said."

Aral, I love you. "Thank you. Go, go." She surrendered the replicator into Vaagen's hands, and he hurried out with it.

She sat back down like a marionette with the strings cut. Now she could allow herself to feel the full weight of her exhaustion. But she could not stop quite yet. She had one very important debriefing yet to accomplish. And not to these hovering ImpSec twits, who pestered her— she closed her eyes and pointedly ignored them, letting Drou stammer out answers to their foolish questions.

Desire warred with dread. She wanted Aral. She had defied Aral, most openly. Had it touched his honor, scorched his—admittedly, unusually flexible—Barrayaran male ego beyond tolerance? Would she be frozen out of his trust forever? No, that suspicion was surely unjust. But his public credibility among his peers, part of the delicate psychology of power—had she damaged it? Would some damnable unforseen political consequence rebound

out of all this, back on their heads? Did she care? Yes,
she decided sadly. It was hell to be so tired, and still care.

"Kou!"

Drou's cry snapped Cordelia's eyes open. Koudelka was
limping into the main portal Security debriefing office.
Good Lord, the man was back in uniform, shaved and
sharp. Only the grey rings under his eyes were non-
regulation.

Kou and Drou's reunion, Cordelia was delighted to note,
was not in the least military. The staff soldier was instantly
plastered all over with tall and grubby blonde, exchanging muffled un-regulation greetings like *darling, love, thank
God, safe, sweet.* . . . The ImpSec men turned away uncomfortably from the blast of naked emotion radiating from
their faces. Cordelia basked in it. A far more sensible way
to greet a friend than all that moronic saluting.

They parted only to see each other better, still holding hands. "You made it," chortled Droushnakovi. "How
long have you—is Lady Vorpatril—?"

"We only made it in about two hours ahead of you," Kou
said breathlessly, reoxygenating after a heroic kiss. "Lady
Vorpatril and the young lord are bedded down in the
infirmary. The doctor says she's suffering mainly from stress
and exhaustion. She was incredible. We had a couple of
bad moments, getting past Vordarian's Security, but she
never cracked. And you—you did it! I passed Vaagen in
the corridor, with the replicator—you rescued m'lord's son!"

Droushnakovi's shoulders sagged. "But we lost Princess
Kareen."

"Oh." He touched her lips. "Don't tell me—Lord
Vorkosigan instructed me to bring you all to him the
instant you arrived. Debrief to him before anyone. I'll take
you to him now." He waved away the ImpSec men like
flies, something Cordelia had been longing to do.

Bothari had to help her rise. She gathered up the
yellow plastic bag. She noted ironically that it bore the
name and logo of one of the capital's most exclusive
women's clothiers. *Kareen encompasses you at last, you
bastard.*

"What's that?" asked Kou.

"Yes, Lieutenant," the urgent ImpSec man put in, "please—she's refused to let us examine it in any way. By regulations, we shouldn't let her carry it into the base."

Cordelia pulled open the top of the bag and held it out for Kou's inspection. He peered within.

"*Shit.*" The ImpSec men surged forward as Koudelka jumped back. He waved them down. "I . . . I see," he swallowed. "Yes, Admiral Vorkosigan will certainly want to see *that.*"

"Lieutenant, what should I put on my inventory?" the ImpSec man—whined, Cordelia decided, was what he was doing. "I have to register it, if it's going in."

"Let him cover his ass, Kou," Cordelia sighed.

Kou peeked again, his lips twisting into a very crooked grin. "It's all right. Put it down as a Winterfair gift for Admiral Vorkosigan. From his wife."

"Oh, Kou," Drou held out his sword. "I saved this. But we lost the casing, I'm sorry."

Kou took it, looked at the bag, made the connection, and carried it more carefully. "That's . . . that's all right. Thank you."

"I'll take it back to Siegling's and get a duplicate casing made," Cordelia promised.

The ImpSec men gave way before Admiral Vorkosigan's top aide. Kou led Cordelia, Bothari, and Drou into the base. Cordelia pulled the drawstring tight, and let the bag swing from her hand.

"We're going down to the Staff level. The admiral's been in a sealed meeting for the last hour. Two of Vordarian's top officers came in secretly last night. Negotiating to sell him out. The best hostage-rescue plan hinges on their cooperation."

"Did they know about this yet?" Cordelia held up the bag.

"I don't think so, Milady. You've just changed everything." His grin grew feral, and his uneven stride lengthened.

"I expect that raid is still going to be required,"

Cordelia sighed. "Even in collapse, Vordarian's side is still dangerous. Maybe more dangerous, in their desperation." She thought of that downtown Vorbarr Sultana hotel, where Bothari's baby girl Elena was, as far as she knew, still housed. Lesser hostages. Could she persuade Aral to apportion a few more resources for lesser hostages? Alas, she had probably not put all the soldiers out of work even yet. *I tried. God, I tried.*

They went down, and down, to the nerve center of Tanery Base. They came to a highly secured conference chamber; a lethally armed squad stood ramrod-guard outside it. Koudelka wafted them past. The doors slid aside, and closed again behind them.

Cordelia took in the tableau, that paused to look back up at her from around the polished table. Aral was in the center, of course. Illyan and Count Piotr flanked him on either side. Prime Minister Vortala was there, and Kanzian, and some other senior staffers all in formal dress greens. The two double-traitors sat across, with their aides. Clouds of witnesses. She wanted to be alone with Aral, be rid of the whole bloody mob of them. *Soon.*

Aral's eyes locked to hers in silent agony. His lips curled in an utterly ironic smile. That was all; and yet her stomach warmed with confidence again, sure of him. No frost. It was going to be all right. They were in step again, and a torrent of words and hard embraces could not have communicated it any better. Embraces would come, though, the grey eyes promised. Her own lips curved up for the first time since—when?

Count Piotr's hand slapped down hard upon the table. "Good God, woman, where have you *been*?" he cried furiously.

A morbid lunacy overtook her. She smiled fiercely at him, and held up the bag. "Shopping."

For a second, the old man nearly believed her; conflicting expressions whiplashed over his face, astonishment, disbelief, then anger as it penetrated he was being mocked.

"Want to see what I bought?" Cordelia continued, still

floating. She yanked the bag's top open, and rolled
Vordarian's head out across the table. Fortunately, it had
ceased leaking some hours back. It stopped faceup before
him, lips grinning, drying eyes staring.

Piotr's mouth fell open. Kanzian jumped, the staffers swore, and one of Vordarian's traitors actually fell
out of his chair, recoiling. Vortala pursed his lips and
raised his brows. Koudelka, grimly proud of his key role
in stage-managing this historic moment in one-
upsmanship, laid the swordstick on the table as further
evidence. Illyan puffed, and grinned triumphantly through
his shock.

Aral was perfect. His eyes widened only briefly, then
he rested his chin on his hands and gazed over his father's
shoulder with an expression of cool interest. "But of
course," he breathed. "Every Vor lady goes to the capital to shop."

"I paid too much for it," Cordelia confessed.

"That, too, is traditional." A sardonic smile quirked his
lips.

"Kareen is dead. Shot in the melee. I couldn't save her."

He opened his hand, as if to let the nascent black
humor fall through his fingers. "I see." He raised his eyes
again to hers, as if asking *Are you all right?*, and apparently finding the answer, *No.*

"Gentlemen. If you will be pleased to excuse your-
selves for a few minutes. I wish to be alone with my
wife."

In the shuffle of the men rising to their feet, Cordelia
caught a mutter, "Brave man . . ."

She nailed Vordarian's men by eye, as they backed from
the table. "Officers. I recommend that when this conference resumes, you surrender unconditionally upon Lord
Vorkosigan's mercy. He may still have some." *I certainly
don't*, was the unspoken cap to that. "I'm tired of your
stupid war. End it."

Piotr edged past her. She smiled bitterly at him. He
grimaced uneasily back. "It appears I underestimated you,"
he murmured.

"Don't you ever . . . cross me again. And stay away from my son."

A look from Vorkosigan held back her outpouring of rage, quivering on the lip of her cup. She and Piotr exchanged wary nods, like the vestigial bows of two duelists.

"Kou," said Vorkosigan, staring bemusedly at the grisly object lying by his elbow. "Will you please arrange for this thing to be removed to the base morgue. I don't fancy it as a table decoration. It will have to be stored till it can be buried with the rest of him. Wherever that may be."

"Sure you don't want to leave it there to inspire Vordarian's staffers to come to terms?" said Kou.

"No," said Vorkosigan firmly. "It's had a sufficiently salutary effect already."

Gingerly, Kou took the bag from Cordelia, opened it, and used it to capture Vordarian's head without actually touching it.

Aral's eye took in her weary team, Droushnakovi's grief, Bothari's compulsive twitching. "Drou. Sergeant. You are dismissed to wash and eat. Report back to me in my quarters after we finish here."

Droushnakovi nodded, and the sergeant saluted, and they followed Koudelka out.

Cordelia fell into Aral's arms as the door sighed shut, into his lap, catching him as he rose for her. They both landed with enough force to threaten the balance of the chair. They embraced each other so tightly, they had to back off to manage a kiss.

"Don't you ever," he husked, "pull a stunt like that again."

"Don't you ever let it become necessary, again."

"Deal."

He held her face away from his, between his hands, his eyes devouring her. "I was so afraid for you, I forgot to be afraid for your enemies. I should have remembered. Dear Captain."

"I couldn't have done a thing, alone. Drou was my eyes, Bothari my right arm, Koudelka our feet. You must forgive Kou for going AWOL. We sort of kidnapped him."

"So I heard."

"Did he tell you about your cousin Padma?"

"Yes," a grieved sigh. He stared back through time. "Padma and I were the only survivors of Mad Yuri's massacre of Prince Xav's descendants, that day. I was eleven. Padma was one, a baby . . . I always thought of him as the baby, ever after. Tried to watch out for him . . . Now I'm the only one left. Yuri's work is almost done."

"Bothari's Elena. She must be rescued. She's a lot more important than that barn full of counts at the Residence."

"We're working on that right now," he promised. "Top priority, now that you've removed Emperor Vidal from consideration." He paused, smiling slowly. "I fear you've shocked my Barrayarans, love."

"Why? Did they think they had a monopoly on savagery? Those were Vordarian's last words. 'You're a Betan. You can't do.' "

"Do what?"

"*This*, I suppose he would have said. If he'd had the chance."

"A lurid trophy, to carry on the monorail. Suppose someone had asked you to open your bag?"

"I would have."

"Are you . . . quite all right, love?" His mouth was serious, under his smile.

"Meaning, have I lost my grip? Yes, a little. More than a little." Her hands still shook, as they had for a day, a continuing tremula that did not pass off. "It seemed . . . necessary, to bring Vordarian's head along. I hadn't actually thought about mounting it on the wall of Vorkosigan House along with your father's hunting trophies, though it's an idea. I don't think I consciously realized why I was hanging on to it till I walked into this room. If I'd staggered in here empty-handed and told all those men I'd killed Vordarian, and undeclared their little war, who'd have believed me? Besides you."

"Illyan, perhaps. He's seen you in action before. The others . . . you're quite right."

"I think I also had some idea stuck in my mind from ancient history. Didn't they used to publicly display the bodies of slain rulers, to scotch pretenders? It seemed appropriate. Though Vordarian was almost a side-issue, from my point of view."

"Your ImpSec escort reported to me you'd recovered the replicator. Was it still working?"

"Vaagen has it now, checking it. Miles is alive. Damage unknown. Oh. It seems Vordarian had some hand in setting up Evon Vorhalas. Not directly, through some agent."

"Illyan suspected it." His arms tightened around her.

"About Bothari," she said. "He's not in good shape. Way overstressed. He needs real treatment, medical, not political. That memory wipe was a horror show."

"At the time, it saved his life. My compromise with Ezar. I had no power then. I can do better now."

"You'd better. He's fixated on me like a dog. His words. And I've used him like one. I owe him . . . everything. But he scares me. Why *me*?"

Vorkosigan looked very thoughtful. "Bothari . . . does not have a good sense of self. No strong center. When I first met him, at his most ill, his personality was close to separating into multiples. If he were better educated, not so damaged, he would have made an ideal spy, a deep-penetration mole. He's a chameleon. A mirror. He becomes whatever is required of him. Not a conscious process, I don't think. Piotr expects a loyal retainer, and Bothari plays the part, deadpan as you please. Vorrutyer wanted a monster, and Bothari became his torturer. And victim. I demanded a good soldier, and he became one for me. You . . ." his voice softened, "you are the only person I know who looks at Bothari and sees a hero. So he becomes one for you. He clings to you because you create him a greater man than he ever dreamed of being."

"Aral, that's crazed."

"Ah?" He nuzzled her hair. "But he's not the only man you have that peculiar effect upon. Dear Captain."

"I'm afraid I'm not in much better shape than Bothari. I botched it, and Kareen died. Who will tell Gregor? If it weren't for Miles, I'd quit. You keep Piotr off me, or I swear, next time I'll try and take him apart." She was shaking again.

"Sh." He rocked her, a little. "I think you can at least leave the mopping up to me, eh? Will you trust me again? We'll make something of these sacrifices. Not vain."

"I feel dirty. I feel sick."

"Yes. Most sane people do, coming in off a combat mission. It's a very familiar state of mind." He paused. "But if a Betan can become so Barrayaran, maybe it's not so impossible for Barrayarans to become a little more Betan. Change *is* possible."

"Change is inevitable," she asserted. "But you can't manage it Ezar's way. This isn't Ezar's era anymore. You have to find your own way. Remake this world into one Miles can survive in. And Elena. And Ivan. And Gregor."

"As you will, Milady."

On the third day after Vordarian's death, the capital fell to loyal Imperial troops; if not without a shot being fired, at least not nearly so bloodily as Cordelia had feared. Only two pockets of resistance, at ImpSec and at the Residence itself, had to be cleared out by ground troops. The downtown hotel with its hostages was surrendered intact by its garrison, after hours of intense covert negotiations. Piotr gave Bothari a one-day leave to personally retrieve his child and her fosterer and escort them home. Cordelia slept through the night for the first time since her return.

Evon Vorhalas had been commanding ground troops for Vordarian in the capital, in charge of the last defense of the space communications center in the military headquarters complex. He died in the final flurry of fighting, shot by his own men when he spurned an offer of amnesty in return for their surrender. In a way, Cordelia was relieved. The traditional punishment for treason upon the part of a Vor lord was public exposure and death by starvation. The late Emperor Ezar had not hesitated to maintain the gruesome tradition. Cordelia could only pray that Gregor's reign would see the custom end.

Without Vordarian to hold it together, his rebel coalition shattered rapidly into disparate factions. An extreme conservative Vor lord in the city of Federstok raised his standard and declared himself Emperor, succeeding Vordarian; his pretendership lasted somewhat less than thirty hours. In an eastern coastal District belonging to one of Vordarian's allies, the Count suicided upon capture. An anti-Vor group declared an independent republic in the chaos. The new Count, an infantry colonel from a collateral family line who had never anticipated such honors falling upon him, took instant and effective exception to this violent swing to the over-progressive. Vorkosigan left it to him and his District militia, reserving Imperial troops for "non-District-internal matters."

"You can't go halfway and stop," Piotr muttered forebodingly, at this delicacy.

"One step at a time," Vorkosigan returned grimly, "I can walk around the world. Watch me."

On the fifth day, Gregor was returned to the capital. Vorkosigan and Cordelia together undertook to tell him of the death of Kareen. He cried in bewilderment. When he quieted, he was taken for a ride in a groundcar with a transparent force-screen, reviewing some troops; in fact, the troops were reviewing him, that he might be seen to be alive, finally dispelling Vordarian's rumors of his death. Cordelia rode with him. His silent shockiness hurt her to the heart, but it was better from her point of view than parading him first and then telling him. If she'd had to endure his repeated queries of when he would see his mother again, all during the ride, she would have broken down herself.

The funeral for Kareen was public, though much less elaborate than it would have been in less chaotic circumstances. Gregor was required to light an offering pyre for the second time in a year. Vorkosigan asked

Cordelia to guide Gregor's hand with the torch. This part of the funeral ceremony seemed almost redundant, after what she'd done to the Residence. Cordelia added a thick lock of her own hair to the pile. Gregor clung close to her.

"Are they going to kill me, too?" he whispered to her. He didn't sound frightened, just morbidly curious. Father, grandfather, mother, all gone in a year; no wonder he felt targeted, confused though his understanding of death was at his age.

"No," she said firmly. Her arm tightened around his shoulders. "I won't let them." God help her, this baseless assurance actually seemed to console him.

I'll look after your boy, Kareen, Cordelia thought as the flames rose up. The oath was more costly than any gift being burned, for it bound her life unbreakably to Barrayar. But the heat on her face eased the pain in her head, a little.

Cordelia's own soul felt like an exhausted snail, shelled in a glassy numbness. She crept like an automaton through the rest of the ceremony, though there were flashes when her surroundings made no sense at all. The assorted Barrayaran Vor reacted to her with a frozen, deep formality. *They doubtless figure me for crazy-dangerous, a madwoman let out of the attic by overindulgent relations.* It finally dawned on her that their exaggerated courtesies signified *respect.*

It made her furious. All Kareen's courage of endurance had bought her nothing, Lady Vorpatril's brave and bloody birth-giving was taken for granted, but whack off some idiot's head and you were really somebody, by God—!

It took Aral an hour, when they returned to his quarters, to calm her down, and then she had a crying jag. He stuck it out.

"Are you going to use this?" she asked him, when sheer weariness returned her to a semblance of coherence. "This, this . . . amazing new *status* of mine?" How she loathed the word, acid in her mouth.

"I'll use anything," he vowed quietly, "if it will help

me put Gregor on the throne in fifteen years a sane and competent man, heading a stable government. Use you, me, whatever it takes. To pay this much, then fail, would not be tolerable."

She sighed, and put her hand in his. "In case of accident, donate my remaining body parts, too. It's the Betan way. Waste not."

His lip curled up helplessly. Face-to-face, they rested their foreheads together for a moment, bracing each other. "Want not."

Her silent promise to Kareen was made policy when she and Aral, as a couple, were officially appointed Gregor's guardians by the Council of Counts. This was legally distinct somehow from Aral's guardianship of the Imperium as Regent. Prime Minister Vortala took time to lecture her and make it clear her new duties involved no political powers. She did have economic functions, including trusteeship of certain Vorbarra holdings that were separate from Imperial properties, appending strictly to Gregor's title as Count Vorbarra. And by Aral's delegation, she was given oversight of the Emperor's household. And education.

"But, Aral," said Cordelia, stunned. "Vortala emphasized I was to have no power."

"Vortala . . . is not all-wise. Let's just say, he has a little trouble recognizing as such some forms of power which are not synonymous with force. Your window of opportunity is narrow, though; at age twelve Gregor will enter a pre-Academy preparatory school."

"But do they realize . . . ?"

"I do. And you do. It's enough."

CHAPTER TWENTY

One of Cordelia's first orders was to assign Droushnakovi back to Gregor's person, for his emotional continuity. This did not mean giving up the girl's company, a comfort to which Cordelia had grown deeply accustomed, because upon Illyan's renewed insistence Aral finally took up living quarters in the Imperial Residence. It eased Cordelia's heart, when Drou and Kou were wed a month after Winterfair.

Cordelia offered herself as a go-between for the two families. For some reason, Kou and Drou both turned the offer down, hastily, though with profuse thanks. Given the bewildering pitfalls of Barrayaran social custom, Cordelia was just as happy to leave it to the experienced elderly lady the couple did contract.

Cordelia saw Alys Vorpatril often, exchanging domestic visits. Baby Lord Ivan was, if not exactly a comfort to Alys, certainly a distraction in her slow recovery from her physical ordeal. He grew rapidly despite a tendency to fussiness, an iatrogenic trait, Cordelia realized after a while, triggered by Alys's fussing over him. Ivan should have three or four sibs to divide her attention among, Cordelia decided, watching Alys burp him on her shoulder while planning aloud his educational attack, come age eighteen, upon the formidable Imperial Military Academy entrance examinations.

Alys Vorpatril was drawn off her embittered mourning for Padma and her planning of Ivan's life down to the last detail, when she was given a look at a picture of the wedding dress Drou was drooling over.

"No, no, no!" she cried, recoiling. "All that lace—you would look as furry as a big white bear. Silk, dear, long falls of silk is what you need—" and she was off. Motherless, sisterless Drou could scarcely have found a more knowledgeable bridal consultant. Lady Vorpatril ended by making the dress one of her several presents, to be sure of its aesthetic perfection, along with a "little holiday cottage" which turned out to be a substantial house on the eastern seashore. Come summer, Drou's beach dream would come true. Cordelia grinned, and purchased the girl a nightgown and robe with enough tiers of lace layered on them to satiate the most frill-starved soul.

Aral lent the hall: the Imperial Residence's Red Room and adjacent ballroom, the one with the beautiful marquetry floor, which to Cordelia's immense relief had escaped the fire. In theory, this magnificent gesture was required to ease Illyan's Security headaches, as Cordelia and Aral were to stand among the principal witnesses. Personally, Cordelia thought converting ImpSec into wedding caterers a promising turn of events.

Aral looked over the guest list and smiled. "Do you realize," he said to Cordelia, "every class is represented? A year ago this event, here, would not have been possible. The grocer's son and the non-com's daughter. They bought it with blood, but maybe next year it can be bought with peaceful achievement. Medicine, education, engineering, entrepreneurship—shall we have a party for librarians?"

"Won't those terrible Vorish crones all Piotr's friends are married to complain about social over-progressiveness?"

"With Alys Vorpatril behind this? They wouldn't dare."

The affair grew from there. By a week in advance Kou

and Drou were considering eloping out of sheer panic, having lost all control of everything whatsoever to their eager helpers. But the Imperial Residence's staff brought it all together with practiced ease. The senior housewoman flew about, chortling, "And here I was afraid we weren't going to have anything to do, once the admiral moved in, but those dreadful boring General Staff dinners."

The day and hour came at last. A large circle made of colored groats was laid out on the floor of the Red Room, encompassed by a star with a variable number of points, one for each parent or principal witness to stand at: in this case, four. In Barrayaran custom a couple married themselves, speaking their vows within the circle, requiring neither priest nor magistrate. Practically, a coach, called appropriately enough the Coach, stood outside the circle and read the script for the fainthearted or faint-headed to repeat. This dispensed with the need for higher neural functions such as learning and memory on the part of the stressed couple. Lost motor coordination was supplied by a friend each, who steered them to the circle. It was all very practical, Cordelia decided, as well as splendid.

With a grin and a flourish Aral placed her at her assigned star point, as if setting out a bouquet, and took his own place. Lady Vorpatril had insisted on a new gown for Cordelia, a sweeping length of blue and white with red floral accents, color-coordinated with Aral's ultra-formal parade red-and-blues. Drou's proud and nervous father also wore his red-and-blues and held down his point. Strange to think of the military, which Cordelia normally associated with totalitarian impulses, as the spearhead of egalitarianism on Barrayar. The Cetagandans' gift, Aral called it; their invasion had first forced the promotion of talent regardless of origin, and the waves of that change were still traveling through Barrayaran society.

Sergeant Droushnakovi was a shorter, slighter man than Cordelia had expected. Either Drou's mother's genes, better nutrition, or both had boosted all his children up taller than himself. All three brothers, from the captain to the corporal, had been broken loose from their military assignments to attend, and stood now in the big outer circle of other witnesses along with Kou's excited younger sister. Kou's mother stood on the star's last point, crying and smiling, in a blue dress so color-perfect Cordelia decided Alys Vorpatril must have somehow gotten to her, too.

Koudelka marched in first, propped by his stick with its new cover and Sergeant Bothari. Sergeant Bothari wore the most glittery version of Piotr's brown and silver livery, and whispered helpful, horribly suggestive advice like "If you feel really nauseous, Lieutenant, put your head down." The very thought turned Kou's face greener, an extraordinary color-contrast with his red-and-blues that Lady Vorpatril would no doubt have disapproved.

Heads turned. *Oh, my.* Alys Vorpatril had been absolutely right about Drou's gown. She swept in, as stunningly graceful as a sailing ship, a tall clean perfection of form and function, ivory silk, gold hair, blue eyes, white, blue, and red flowers, so that when she stepped up beside Kou one suddenly realized how tall he must be. Alys Vorpatril, in silver-grey, released Drou at the circle's edge with a gesture like some hunting goddess releasing a white falcon, to soar and settle on Kou's outstretched arm.

Kou and Drou made it through their oaths without stammering or passing out, and managed to conceal their mutual embarrassment at the public declaration of their despised first names, Clement and Ludmilla.

("My brothers used to call me Lud," Drou had confided to Cordelia during the practice yesterday. "Rhymes with mud. Also thud, blood, crud, dud, and cud."

"You'll always be Drou to me," Kou had promised.)

As senior witness Aral then broke the circle of groats with a sweep of one booted foot and let them out, and the music, dancing, eating and drinking began.

The buffet was incredible, the music live, and the drinking . . . traditional. After the first formal glass of the good wine Piotr'd sent on, Cordelia drifted up to Kou and murmured a few words about Betan research on the detrimental effects of ethanol on sexual function, after which he switched to water.

"Cruel woman," Aral whispered in her ear, laughing.

"Not to Drou, I'm not," she murmured back.

She was formally introduced to the brothers, now brothers-in-law, who regarded her with that awed respect that made her teeth grind. Though her jaw eased a bit when a rhyming brother was waved to silence by Dad to make room for some comment by the bride on the topic of hand-weapons. "Quiet, Jos," Sergeant Droushnakovi told his son. "You've never handled a nerve disruptor in combat." Drou blinked, then smiled, a gleam in her eye.

Cordelia seized a moment with Bothari, whom she saw all too seldom now that Aral had split his household from Piotr's.

"How is Elena doing, now she's back home? Has Mistress Hysopi recovered from it all yet?"

"They're well, Milady," Bothari ducked his head, and almost-smiled. "I visited about five days ago, when Count Piotr went down to check on his horses. Elena, um, creeps. Put her down and look away a minute, you look back and she's moved. . . ." He frowned. "I hope Carla Hysopi stays alert."

"She saw Elena safely through Vordarian's war, I suspect she'll handle crawling with equal ease. Courageous woman. She should be in line for some of those medals they're handing out."

Bothari's brow wrinkled. "Don't know they'd mean much to her."

"Mm. She does understand she can call on me for anything she needs, I trust. Any time."

"Yes, Milady. But we're doing all right for the moment." A flash of pride, there, in that statement of sufficiency. "It's very quiet down at Vorkosigan Surleau, in the winter. Clean. A right and proper place for a baby." *Not like the place I grew up in,* Cordelia could almost hear him add. "I mean her to have everything right and proper. Even her da."

"How are you doing, yourself?"

"The new med is better. Anyway, my head doesn't feel

like it's stuffed with fog anymore. And I sleep at night. Besides that I can't tell what it's doing."

Its job, apparently; he seemed relaxed and calm, almost free of that sinister edginess. Though he was still the first person in the room to look over to the buffet and ask, "Is *he* supposed to be up?"

Gregor, in pajamas, was creeping along the edge of the culinary array, trying to look invisible and nail down a few goodies before he was spotted and taken away again. Cordelia got to him first, before he was either stepped on by an unwary guest, or recaptured by Security forces in the persons of the breathless maidservant and terrified bodyguard who were supposed to be filling in for Drou. They were followed up by a paper-white Simon Illyan. Fortunately for Illyan's heart, Gregor had apparently only been formally missing for about sixty seconds. Gregor shrank into her skirts as the hyperventilating adults loomed over him.

Drou, who had noticed Illyan touch his comm, turn pale, and start to move, checked in by sheer force of habit. "What's the matter?"

"How'd he get away?" snarled Illyan to Gregor's keepers, who stammered out something inaudible about *thought he was asleep* and *never took my eyes off.*

"He's not away," Cordelia put in tartly. "This is his home. He ought to be at least able to walk about inside, or why do you keep all those bloody useless guards on the walls out there?"

"Droushie, can't I come to your party?" Gregor asked plaintively, casting around desperately for an authority to outrank Illyan.

Drou looked at Illyan, who looked disapproving. Cordelia broke the deadlock without hesitation. "Yes, you can."

So, under Cordelia's supervision, the Emperor danced with the bride, ate three cream cakes, and was carried away to bed satisfied. Fifteen minutes was all he'd wanted, poor kid.

The party rolled on, elated. "Dance, Milady?" Aral inquired hopefully at her elbow.

Dare she try it? They were playing the restrained rhythms of the mirror-dance—surely she couldn't go too wrong. She nodded, and Aral drained his glass and led her onto the polished marquetry. Step, slide, gesture: concentrating, she made an interesting and unexpected discovery. Either partner could lead, and if the dancers were alert and sharp, the watchers couldn't tell the difference. She tried some dips and slides of her own, and Aral followed smoothly. Back and forth the lead passed like a ball between them, the game growing ever more absorbing, until they ran out of music and breath.

The last snows of winter were melting from the streets of Vorbarr Sultana when Captain Vaagen called from ImpMil for Cordelia.

"It's time, Milady. I've done all I can do in vitro. The placenta is ten months old and clearly senescing. The machine can't be boosted any more to compensate."

"When, then?"

"Tomorrow would be good."

She barely slept that night. They all trooped down to the Imperial Military Hospital the next morning, Aral, Cordelia, Count Piotr flanked by Bothari. Cordelia was not at all sure she wanted Piotr present, but until the old man did them all the convenience of dropping dead, she was stuck with him. Maybe one more appeal to reason, one more presentation of the facts, one more try, would do the trick. Their unresolved antagonism grieved Aral; at least let the onus for fueling it fall on Piotr, not herself. *Do your worst, old man. You have no future except through me. My son will light your offering pyre.* She was glad to see Bothari again, though.

Vaagen's new laboratory was an entire floor in the most up-to-date building in the complex. Cordelia'd had him moved from his old lab on account of ghosts, having come in for one of her frequent visits soon after their return to Vorbarr Sultana to find him in a state of near-paralysis, unable to work. Every time he entered the room, he'd said, Dr. Henri's violent and senseless death replayed in his memory. He could not step on the floor near the place where Henri's body had fallen, but had to walk wide around; little noises made him jump and twitch. "I am a man of reason," he'd said hoarsely. "This superstitious nonsense means nothing to me." So Cordelia had helped him burn a private offering to Henri in a brazier on the lab floor, and disguised the move as a promotion.

The new lab was bright and spacious and free of revenant spirits. Cordelia found a mob of men waiting when Vaagen ushered her in: researchers assigned to Vaagen to explore replicator technology, interested civilian obstetricians including Dr. Ritter, Miles's own pediatrician-to-be, and his consulting surgeon. The changing of the guard. Mere parents needed determination to elbow their way in.

Vaagen bustled about, happily important. He still wore his eyepatch, but promised Cordelia he would take the time for the last round of surgery to restore his vision very soon now. A tech trundled out the uterine replicator and Vaagen paused, as if trying to figure out how to put the proper drama and ceremony into what Cordelia knew for a very simple event. He settled on turning it into a technical lecture for his colleagues, detailing the composition of the hormone solutions as he injected them into the appropriate feed-lines, interpreting readouts, describing the placental separation going on within the replicator, the similarities and differences between replicator and body births. There were several differences Vaagen didn't mention. *Alys Vorpatril should see this,* Cordelia thought.

Vaagen looked up to see her watching him, paused self-consciously, and smiled. "Lady Vorkosigan." He gestured to the replicator's latch-seals. "Would you care to do the honors?"

She reached, hesitated, and looked around for Aral. There he was, solemn and attentive at the edge of the crowd. "Aral?"

He strode forward. "Are you sure?"

"If you can open a picnic cooler, you can do this." They each took a latch and raised them in unison, breaking the

sterile seal, and lifted the top off. Dr. Ritter moved in
with a vibra-scalpel, cutting through the thick felt mat of
nutrient tubing with a touch so delicate the silvery
amniotic sac beneath was unscored, then cut Miles free
of his last bit of biological packaging, clearing his mouth
and nose of fluids before his first surprised inhalation.
Aral's arm, around her, tightened so hard it hurt. A
muffled laugh, no more than a breath, broke from his lips;
he swallowed and blinked to bring his features, suffused
with elation and pain, back under strict control.

Happy birthday, thought Cordelia. *Good color . . .*

Unfortunately, that was about all that was really good.
The contrast with baby Ivan was overwhelming. Despite
the extra weeks of gestation, ten months to Ivan's nine-
and-a-half, Miles was barely half Ivan's size at birth, and
far more wizened and wrinkled. His spine was noticeably
deformed, and his legs were drawn up and locked in a
tight bend. He was definitely a male heir, though, no
question about that. His first cry was thin, weak, nothing at all like Ivan's angry, hungry bellow. Behind her, she
heard Piotr hiss with disappointment.

"Has he been getting enough nutrition?" she asked
Vaagen. It was hard to keep the accusation out of her
tone.

Vaagen shrugged helplessly. "All he would absorb."

The pediatrician and his colleague laid Miles out under
a warming light, and began their examination, Cordelia
and Aral on either side.

"This bend will straighten out on its own, Milady," the
pediatrician pointed. "But the lower spine should have
surgical correction as early as possible. You were right,
Vaagen, the treatment to optimize skull development also
fused the hip sockets. That's why the legs are locked in
that strange position, m'lord. He'll require surgery to crack
those bones loose and turn them around before he can
start to crawl or walk. I don't recommend that in the first
year, on top of the spinal work, let him gain strength and
weight first—"

The surgeon, testing the infant's arms, swore suddenly

and snatched up his diagnostic viewer. Miles mewed. Aral's hand clenched, by his trouser seam. Cordelia's stomach sank. "Hell!" said the surgeon. "His humerus just snapped. You're right, Vaagen, the bones are abnormally brittle."

"At least he has bones," sighed Vaagen. "He almost didn't, at one point."

"Be careful," said the surgeon, "especially of the head and spine. If the rest are as bad as the long bones, we're going to have to come up with some kind of reinforcement. . . ."

Piotr stamped toward the door. Aral glanced up, his lips thinning to a frown, and excused himself to follow. Cordelia was torn, but once observation assured her that the bone-setting was under way and the doctors' new caution would protect Miles from further damage today, she left their ingenious heads bent over him and followed Aral.

In the corridor, Piotr was stalking up and down. Aral stood at parade rest, unmoved and unmoving. Bothari was a silent witness in the background.

Piotr turned and saw her. "You! You've strung me along. This is what you call 'great repairs'? Gah!"

"They are great repairs. Miles is unquestionably much better than he was. Nobody promised perfection."

"You lied. Vaagen lied."

"We did not," denied Cordelia. "I tried to give you accurate summaries of Vaagen's experiments all the way along. What he's delivered is about what his reports led us to expect. Check your ears."

"I see what you're trying, and it won't work. I've just told him," he pointed at Aral, "this is where I stop. I don't want to see that mutant again. Ever. While it lives, if it lives, and it looks pretty damned sickly to me, don't bring it around my door. As God is my judge, woman, you won't make a fool of me."

"That would be redundant," snapped Cordelia.

Piotr's lips curled in a silent snarl. Cheated of a cooperative target, he turned on Aral. "And you, you spineless, skirt-smothered—if your elder brother had lived—" Piotr's mouth clamped shut abruptly, too late.

Aral's face drained to a grey hue Cordelia had seen but twice before; both times he'd been a breath and a chance away from committing murder. Piotr had joked about Aral's famous rages. Only now did Cordelia realize Piotr, though he may have witnessed his son in irritation, had never seen the real thing. Piotr seemed to realize it, too, dimly. His brows lowered; he stared, off-balanced.

Aral's hands locked to each other, behind his back. Cordelia could see them shake, white-knuckled. His chin lifted, and he spoke in a whisper.

"If my brother had lived, he would have been perfect. You thought so; I thought so; Emperor Yuri thought so, too. So ever after you've had to make do with the leftovers from that bloody banquet, the son Mad Yuri's death squad overlooked. We Vorkosigans, we can make do." His voice fell still further. "But *my* firstborn will live. I will not fail him."

The icy statement was a near-lethal cut across the belly, as fine a slash as Bothari could have delivered with Koudelka's swordstick, and very accurately placed. Truly, Piotr should not have lowered the tone of this discussion. The breath huffed from him in disbelief and pain.

Aral's expression grew inward. "I will not fail him *again*," he corrected himself lowly. "A second chance you were never given, sir." Behind his back his hands unclenched. A small jerk of his head dismissed Piotr and all Piotr might say.

Blocked twice, visibly suffering from his profound misstep, Piotr looked around for a target of opportunity upon which to vent his frustration. His eye fell on Bothari, watching blank-faced.

"And you. Your hand was in this from beginning to end. Did my son place you as a spy in my household? Where do your loyalties lie? Do you obey me, or him?"

An odd gleam flared in Bothari's eye. He tilted his head toward Cordelia. "Her."

Piotr was so taken aback, it took him several seconds to regain his speech. "Fine," he sputtered at last. "She can have you. I don't want to see your ugly face again.

Don't come back to Vorkosigan House. Esterhazy will deliver your things before nightfall."

He wheeled and marched away. His grand exit, already weak, was spoiled when he looked back over his shoulder before he rounded the corner.

Aral vented a very weary sigh.

"Do you think he means it this time?" Cordelia asked. "All that never-ever stuff?"

"Government concerns will require us to communicate. He knows that. Let him go home and listen to the silence for a bit. Then we'll see." He smiled bleakly. "While we live, we cannot disengage."

She thought of the child whose blood now bound them, her to Aral, Aral to Piotr, and Piotr to herself. "So it seems." She looked an apology to Bothari. "I'm sorry, Sergeant. I didn't know Piotr could fire an oath-armsman."

"Well, technically, he can't," Aral explained. "Bothari was just reassigned to another branch of the household. You."

"Oh." *Just what I always wanted, my very own monster. What am I supposed to do, keep him in my closet?* She rubbed the bridge of her nose, then regarded her hand. The hand that had encompassed Bothari's on the swordstick. So. And so. "Lord Miles will need a bodyguard, won't he?"

Aral tilted his head in interest. "Indeed."

Bothari looked suddenly so intently hopeful, it made Cordelia catch her breath. "A bodyguard," he said, "and backup. No raff could give him a hard time if . . . let me help, Milady."

Let me help. Rhymes with *I love you,* right? "It would be . . ." *impossible, crazy, dangerous, irresponsible,* "my pleasure, Sergeant."

His face lit like a torch. "Can I start now?"

"Why not?"

"I'll wait for you in there, then." He nodded toward Vaagen's lab. He slipped back through the door. Cordelia could just picture him, leaning watchfully against the wall—she trusted that malevolent presence wouldn't make the doctors so nervous they would drop their fragile charge.

Aral blew out his breath, and took her in his arms. "Do you Betans have any nursery tales about the witch's name-day gifts?"

"The good and bad fairies seem to all be out in force for this one, don't they?" She leaned against the scratchy fabric of his uniformed shoulder. "I don't know if Piotr meant Bothari for a blessing or a curse. But I bet he really will keep the raff off. Whatever the raff turns out to be. It's a strange list of birthday presents we've given our boychick."

They returned to the lab, to listen attentively to the rest of the doctors' lecture on Miles's special needs and vulnerabilities, arrange the first round of treatment schedules, and wrap him warmly for the trip home. He was so small, a scrap of flesh, lighter than a cat, Cordelia found when she at last took him up in her arms, skin to skin for the first time since he'd been cut from her body. She had a moment's panic. *Put him back in the vat for about eighteen years, I can't handle this. . . .* Children might or might not be a blessing, but to create them and then fail them was surely damnation. Even Piotr knew that. Aral held the door open for them.

Welcome to Barrayar, son. Here you go: have a world of wealth and poverty, wrenching change and rooted history. Have a birth; have two. Have a name. Miles means "soldier," but don't let the power of suggestion overwhelm you. Have a twisted form in a society that loathes and fears the mutations that have been its deepest agony. Have a title, wealth, power, and all the hatred and envy they will draw. Have your body ripped apart and re-arranged. Inherit an array of friends and enemies you never made. Have a grandfather from hell. Endure pain, find joy, and make your own meaning, because the universe certainly isn't going to supply it. Always be a moving target. Live. Live. Live.

EPILOGUE

VORKOSIGAN SURLEAU. FIVE YEARS LATER.

"Dammit, Vaagen," Cordelia panted under her breath.
"You never told me the little bugger was going to be
hyperactive."

She galloped down the end stairs, through the kitchen,
and out onto the terrace at the end of the rambling stone
residence. Her gaze swept the lawn, probed the trees, and
scanned the long lake sparkling in the summer sun. No
movement.

Aral, dressed in old uniform trousers and a faded print
shirt, came around the house, saw her, and opened his
hands in a no-luck gesture. "He's not out here."

"He's not inside. Down, or up, d'you think? Where's little
Elena? I bet they're together. I forbade him to go down
to the lake without an adult, but I don't know. . . ."

"Surely not the lake," said Aral. "They swam all morning. I was exhausted just watching them. In the fifteen
minutes I timed it, he climbed the dock and jumped back
in nineteen times. Multiply that by three hours."

"Up, then," decided Cordelia. They turned and trudged
together up the hill on the gravel path lined with native,

Earth-import, and exotic shrubbery and flowers. "And to think," Cordelia wheezed, "I prayed for the day he would walk."

"It's five years pent-up motion all let loose at once," Aral analyzed. "In a way, it's reassuring that all that frustration didn't turn in on itself and become despair. For a time, I was afraid it might."

"Yes. Have you noticed, since the last operation, that the endless chatter's dried up? At first I was glad, but do you suppose he's going to go mute? I didn't even know that refrigeration unit was supposed to come apart. A mute engineer."

"I think the, er, verbal and mechanical aptitudes will come into balance eventually. If he survives."

"There's all of us adults, and one of him. We ought to be able to keep up. Why do I feel like he has us outnumbered and surrounded?" She crested the hill. Piotr's stable complex lay in the shallow valley below, half a dozen red-painted wood and stone buildings, fenced paddocks, pastures planted to bright green Earth grasses. She saw horses, but no children. Bothari was ahead of them, though, just exiting one building and entering another. His bellow carried up to them, thinned by distance. "Lord Miles?"

"Oh, dear, I hope he's not bothering Piotr's horses," said Cordelia. "Do you really think this reconciliation attempt will work, this time? Just because Miles is finally walking?"

"He was civil, last night at dinner," said Aral, judiciously hopeful.

"*I* was civil, last night at dinner," Cordelia shrugged. "*He* as much as accused me of starving your son into dwarfism. Can I help it if the kid would rather play with his food than eat it? I just don't know about stepping up the growth hormone, Vaagen's so uncertain about its effect on bone friability."

A crooked smile stole over Aral's face. "I did think the dialogue with the peas marching to surround the breadroll and demand surrender was rather ingenious. You could almost picture them as little soldiers in Imperial greens."

"Yes, and you were no help, laughing instead of terrorizing him into eating like a proper Da."

"I did not laugh."

"Your eyes were laughing. He knew it, too. Twisting you round his thumb."

The warm organic scent of horses and their inevitable by-products permeated the air as they approached the buildings. Bothari re-appeared, saw them, and waved an apologetic hand. "I just saw Elena. I told her to get down out of that loft. She said Lord Miles wasn't up there, but he's around here somewhere. Sorry, Milady, when he talked about looking at the animals, I didn't realize he meant immediately. I'm sure I'll find him in just a moment."

"I was hoping Piotr would offer a tour," Cordelia sighed.

"I thought you didn't like horses," said Aral.

"I loathe them. But I thought it might get the old man talking to him, like a human being, instead of over him like a potted plant. And Miles was so excited about the stupid beasts. I don't like to linger here, though. This place is so . . . Piotr." *Archaic, dangerous, and you have to watch your step.*

Speak of the devil. Piotr himself emerged from the old stone tack storage shed, coiling a web rope. "Hah. There you are," he said neutrally. He joined them sociably enough, though. "I don't suppose you would like to see the new filly."

His tone was so flat, she couldn't tell if he wanted her to say yes, or no. But she seized the opportunity. "I'm sure Miles would."

"Mm."

She turned to Bothari. "Why don't you go get—" But Bothari was staring past her, his lips rippling in dismay. She wheeled.

One of Piotr's most enormous horses, quite naked of bridle, saddle, halter, or any other handle to grab, was trotting out of the barn. Clinging to its mane like a burr was a dark-haired, dwarfish little boy. Miles's sharp features shone with a mixture of exaltation and terror. Cordelia nearly fainted.

"My imported stallion!" yelped Piotr in horror.

In pure reflex, Bothari snatched his stunner from its holster. He then stood paralyzed with the uncertainty of what to shoot and where. If the horse went down and rolled on its little rider—

"Look, Sergeant!" Miles's thin voice called eagerly. "I'm taller than you!"

Bothari started to run toward him. The horse, spooked, wheeled away and broke into a canter.

"—and I can run faster, too!" The words were whipped away in the bounding motion of the gait. The horse shied out of sight around the stable.

The four adults pelted after. Cordelia heard no other cry, but when they turned the corner Miles was lying on the ground, and the horse had stopped further on and lowered its head to nibble at the grass. It snorted in hostility when it saw them, raised its head, danced from foot to foot, then snatched a few more bites.

Cordelia fell to her knees beside Miles, who was already sitting up and waving her away. He was pale, and his right hand clutched his left arm in an all-too-familiar signal of pain.

"You see, Sergeant?" Miles panted. "I can ride, I *can*."

Piotr, on his way toward his horse, paused and looked down.

"I didn't mean to say you weren't *able*," said the sergeant in a driven tone. "I meant you didn't have *permission*."

"Oh."

"Did you break it?" Bothari nodded to the arm.

"Yeah," the boy sighed. There were tears of pain in his eyes, but his teeth set against any quaver entering his voice.

The sergeant grumbled, and rolled up Miles's sleeve, and palpated the forearm. Miles hissed. "Yep." Bothari pulled, twisted, adjusted, took a plastic sleeve from his pocket, slipped it over the arm and wrist, and blew it up. "That'll keep it till the doctor sees it."

"Hadn't you better . . . containerize that horrendous horse?" Cordelia said to Piotr.

" 'S not h'rrendous," Miles insisted, scrambling to his feet. "It's the prettiest."

"You think so, eh?" said Piotr roughly. "How do you figure that? You like brown?"

"It moves the springiest," Miles explained earnestly, bouncing in imitation.

Piotr's attention was arrested. "And so it does," he said, sounding bemused. "It's my hottest dressage prospect. . . . You like horses?"

"They're great. They're wonderful." Miles pirouetted.

"I could never much interest your father in them." Piotr gave Aral a dirty look.

Thank God, thought Cordelia.

"On a horse, I could go as fast as anybody, I bet," said Miles.

"I doubt it," said Piotr coldly, "if that was a sample. If you're going to do it, you have to do it right."

"Teach me," said Miles instantly.

Piotr's brows shot up. He glanced at Cordelia, and smiled sourly. "If your mother gives permission." He rocked on his heels, in certain smug safety, knowing Cordelia's rooted antipathy to the beasts.

Cordelia bit her tongue on *Over my dead body,* and thought fast. Aral's intent eyes were signaling something, but she couldn't read it. Was this a new way for Piotr to try and kill Miles? Take him out and get him smashed, trampled, broken . . . tired out? Now there was a thought. . . .

Risk, or security? In the few months since Miles had at last acquired a full range of motion, she'd run on panicked overdrive, trying to save him from physical harm; he'd spent the same time near-frantically trying to escape her supervision. Much more of this struggle, and either she'd be insane, or he would.

If she could not keep him safe, perhaps the next best

thing was to teach him competence at living dangerously. He was almost undrownable already. His big grey eyes were radiating a desperate, silent plea at her, *Let me, let me, let me . . .* with enough transmission energy to burn through steel. *I would fight the world for you, but I'm damned if I can figure out how to save you from yourself. Go for it, kid.*

"Yes," she said. "If the sergeant accompanies you."

Bothari shot her a look of horrified reproach. Aral rubbed his chin, his eyes alight. Piotr looked utterly taken aback to have his bluff called.

"Good," said Miles. "Can I have my own horse? Can I have *that* one?"

"*No,* not that one," said Piotr indignantly. Then drawn in, added, "Perhaps a pony."

"Horse," said Miles, watching his face.

Cordelia recognized the Instant Re-Negotiation Mode, a spinal reflex, as far as she could tell, triggered by the faintest concession. The kid should be put to work beating out treaties with the Cetagandans. She wondered how many horses he'd finally end up with. "A pony," she put in, giving Piotr the support that he did not yet recognize how badly he was going to need. "A gentle pony. A gentle *short* pony."

Piotr pursed his lips, and gave her a challenging look. "Perhaps you can work up to a horse," he said to Miles. "Earn it, by learning well."

"Can I start now?"

"You have to get your arm set first," said Cordelia firmly.

"I don't have to wait till it *heals,* do I?"

"It will teach you not to run around breaking things!"

Piotr regarded Cordelia through half-lidded eyes. "Actually, proper dressage training starts on a lunge line. You aren't permitted to use your arms till you've developed your seat."

"Yeah?" said Miles, hanging worshipfully on his words. "What else—?"

By the time Cordelia withdrew to hunt up the personal

physician who accompanied the Lord Regent's traveling circus, ah, entourage, Piotr had recaptured his horse—rather efficiently, though Cordelia wondered if the sugar in his pockets was cheating—and was already explaining to Miles how to make a simple line into an effective halter, which side of the beast to stand on, and what direction to face while leading. The boy, barely waist-high to the old man, was taking it in like a sponge, upturned face passionately intent.

"Want to lay a side-bet, who's leading who on that lunge line by the end of the week?" Aral murmured in her ear.

"No contest. I must say, the months Miles spent immobilized in that dreadful spinal brace did teach him how to do charm. The most efficient long-term way to control those about you, and thus exert your will. I'm glad he didn't decide to perfect whining as a strategy. He's the most willful little monster I've ever encountered, but he makes you not notice."

"I don't think the Count has a chance," Aral agreed.

She smiled at the vision, then glanced at him more seriously. "When my father was home on leave one time from the Betan Astronomical Survey, we made model gliders together. Two things were required to get them to fly. First we had to give them a running start. Then we had to let them go." She sighed. "Learning just when to let go was the hardest part."

Piotr, his horse, Bothari, and Miles turned out of sight into the barn. By his gestures, Miles was asking questions at a rapid-fire rate.

Aral gripped her hand as they turned to go up the hill. "I believe he'll soar high, dear Captain."

Miles Vorkosigan/Naismith:
His Universe and Times

Chronology	Events	Chronicle
Approx. 200 years before Miles's birth	Quaddies are created by genetic engineering.	*Falling Free*
During Beta-Barrayaran War	Cordelia Naismith meets Lord Aral Vorkosigan while on opposite sides of a war. Despite difficulties, they fall in love and are married.	*Shards of Honor*
The Vordarian Pretendership	While Cordelia is pregnant, an attempt to assassinate Aral by poison gas fails, but Cordelia is affected; Miles Vorkosigan is born with bones that will always be brittle and other medical problems. His growth will be stunted.	*Barrayar*
Miles is 17	Miles fails to pass physical test to get into the Service Academy. On a trip, necessities force him to improvise the Free Dendarii Mercenaries into existence; he has	*The Warrior's Apprentice*

Chronology	Events	Chronicle
	unintended but unavoidable adventures for four months. Leaves the Dendarii in Ky Tung's competent hands and takes Elli Quinn to Beta for rebuilding of her damaged face; returns to Barrayar to thwart plot against his father. Emperor pulls strings to get Miles into the Academy.	
Miles is 20	Ensign Miles graduates and immediately has to take on one of the duties of the Barrayaran nobility and act as detective and judge in a murder case. Shortly afterwards, his first military assignment ends with his arrest. Miles has to rejoin the Dendarii to rescue the young Barrayaran emperor. Emperor accepts Dendarii as his personal secret service force.	"The Mountains of Mourning" in *Borders of Infinity* *The Vor Game*
Miles is 22	Miles and his cousin Ivan attend a Cetagandan state funeral and are caught up in Cetagandan internal politics.	*Cetaganda*

Chronology	Events	Chronicle
	Miles sends Commander Elli Quinn, who's been given a new face on Beta, on a solo mission to Kline Station.	*Ethan of Athos*
Miles is 23	Now a Barrayaran Lieutenant, Miles goes with the Dendarii to smuggle a scientist out of Jackson's Whole. Miles's fragile leg bones have been replaced by synthetics.	"Labyrinth" in *Borders of Infinity*
Miles is 24	Miles plots from within a Cetagandan prison camp on Dagoola IV to free the prisoners. The Dendarii fleet is pursued by the Cetagandans and finally reaches Earth for repairs. Miles has to juggle both his identities at once, raise money for repairs, and defeat a plot to replace him with a double. Ky Tung stays on Earth. Commander Elli Quinn is now Miles's right-hand officer. Miles and the Dendarii depart for Sector IV on a rescue mission.	"The Borders of Infinity" in *Borders of Infinity* *Brothers in Arms*

Chronology	Events	Chronicle
Miles is 25	Hospitalized after previous mission, Miles's broken arms are replaced by synthetic bones. With Simon Illyan, Miles undoes yet another plot against his father while flat on his back.	*Borders of Infinity*
Miles is 28	Miles meets his clone brother Mark again, this time on Jackson's Whole.	*Mirror Dance*
Miles is 29	Miles hits thirty; thirty hits back.	*Memory*
Miles is 30	Emperor Gregor dispatches Miles to Komarr to investigate a space accident, where he finds old politics and new technology make a deadly mix.	*Komarr*
Miles is 31	The Emperor's wedding sparks romance and intrigue on Barrayar, and Miles plunges up to his neck in both.	*A Civil Campaign*

EARTHLIGHT

Also by Lois McMaster Bujold
Shards of Honour

Cordelia Naismith is enjoying something of a baptism of
fire, as her scientific mission for the peaceful Betan
Astronomical Survey runs afoul of unexpected enemy
forces on an uncharted planet. Treachery within the
Barrayaran Imperial command leaves her and her
opponent, Captain Lord Aral Vork Vorkosigan – better
known throughout the civilized worlds as "the Butcher
of Komarr" – as prisoner and captor to make their way
across dangerous terrain.

They soon find they must rely on each others' abilities –
and honour – to survive not only the trek but its even
more perilous aftermath. Yet their separate peace is
soon challenged as the larger political situation
between their two worlds spins downward into war,
and the two are forced into deadly opposition once
more . . .

Price £6.99
ISBN 0 7434 6842 2

EARTHLIGHT

The Warrior's Apprentice
Lois McMaster Bujold

A Miles Vorkosigan novel

Young Miles Naismith Vorkosigan's first task is to conquer
himself. After that, the universe will be easy . . .

After failing to pass the physicals for the Barrayaran Military
Academy, the brittle-boned, dwarfish son of Cordelia and
Aral Vorkosigan refuses to be daunted for long. An ill-
advised impulse to rescue others, even if (or is that, *because*?)
he cannot save himself, leads Miles to a galactic adventure
that would most definitely not have been approved by his
concerned parents, if he had mentioned it to them. Miles
pushed the dictum 'It is easier to gain forgiveness than permission' to its limits as a chain of self-inflicted circumstances
leads him into a war zone. Where, to his dismay, he discov-
ers it's not a game any more . . . and the consequences of his
attempted chivalry can become a deadly threat to all he
holds dear.

'One of SF's outstanding talents'   BOOKLIST

Price £6.99
ISBN 0 7434 6840 6

EARTHLIGHT

Diplomatic Immunity
Lois McMaster Bujold

'Intelligent, well-crafted, throughly satisfying' LOCUS

A rich Komarran merchant fleet has been impounded at Graf
Station in distant Quaddiespace, after a bloody incident on the
station docks involving a security officer from the convoy's
Barrayaran military escort. Just the sort of situation that calls for the
attention of the Imperial Auditors, Barrayar's special, high-level
trouble-shooters.

As luck would have it, Lord Miles Vorkosigan, the empire's
youngest Auditor, just happens to be in the area. Of course, he and
his wife, Lady Ekaterin, have other things on their minds, such as
getting home in time to attend the long awaited births of their first
children. But when duty calls – in the voice of Barrayar's Emperor,
Gregor – Miles has no choice but to answer.

Waiting on Graf Station are diplomatic snarls, tangled loyalties, old
friends, new enemies, racial tension, lies and deceptions, mysterious
disappearances, and a lethal secret with wider consequences than
even Miles anticipates. The entire system is in danger and time is
running out. Miles Vorkosigan is uncomfortably aware that the
downside of being a trouble-shooter comes when the trouble starts
shooting back . . .

Price £6.99
ISBN 0 7434 6840 6

EARTHLIGHT

These books and other **Earthlight** titles are available from your bookshop or can be ordered direct from the publisher.

☐ 0 7434 6802 3	**Diplomatic Immunity**	Lois McMaster Bujold	£6.99
☐ 0 7434 6842 2	**Shards of Honour**	Lois McMaster Bujold	£6.99
☐ 0 7434 6841 4	**Barrayar**	Lois McMaster Bujold	£6.99
☐ 0 7434 6840 6	**The Warrior's Apprentice**	Lois McMaster Bujold	£6.99
☐ 0 7434 3065 4	**Hidden Empire**	Kevin J. Anderson	£6.99
☐ 0 7434 6121 5	**A Forest of Stars**	Kevin J. Anderson	£10.99
☐ 0 7434 2897 8	**The Praxis**	Walter Jon Williams	£6.99
☐ 0 6710 3753 6	**Desolation Road**	Ian McDonald	£5.99
☐ 0 6710 3754 4	**Ares Express**	Ian McDonald	£6.99
☐ 0 7434 6117 7	**Felaheen**	Jon Courtenay Grimwood	£12.99
☐ 0 671 77369 0	**Effendi**	Jon Courtenay Grimwood	£6.99
☐ 0 7434 2998 2	**From the Dust Returned**	Ray Bradbury	£6.99

Please send cheque or postal order for the value of the book, free postage and packing within the UK; OVERSEAS inc. Republic of Ireland £1 per book.

OR: Please debit this amount from my:

VISA/ACCESS/MASTERCARD ....

CARD NO...

EXPIRY DATE...

AMOUNT £ ....

NAME...

ADDRESS...

....

SIGNATURE...

Send orders to: SIMON & SCHUSTER CASH SALES
PO Box 29, Douglas, Isle of Man, IM99 1BQ
Tel: 01624 836000, Fax 01624 670923
www.bookpost.co.uk
Please allow 14 days for delivery. Prices and availability subject to change without notice.